WE'RE THE NORTH STAND

D1738824

ALAN GARRISON

DEDICATION

I'd like to dedicate this book to all those that were there with me. Especially Mickey Greenaway, Maggie and Mandy God rest their Souls.

ACKNOWLEDGMENTS

This novel is based on actual events at Chelsea games from 1969 to 1971. It plots the Genesis of the North Stand Firm, who became infamous in the 1980's as the Chelsea Headhunters. I've written it in novel form in order to show the personalities behind the names; to show that they weren't the mindless Neanderthals as normally portrayed in the media, but normal people with normal lives, who were just tribal and enjoyed a good fight.

When countries go to war, millions of people are killed; when the terraces go to war, it's extremely rare for anyone to be killed (unless you're a Liverpool supporter), but unlike soldiers, football supporters are vilified.

People's names and some places have been changed to protect those involved, and any resemblance to anyone living or dead is purely coincidental.

I'd like to thank Nicholas Harrison who talked me into writing this book; Maureen A. Worthen, over there in Tasmania, for proofreading the manuscript; Mark Worrall and Martin King for keeping me at it; and special thanks to Angus, Steve and "Little" John, for without these three, the North Stand would never have been what it grew into.

And last but not least, Respect is given to the supporters of other clubs, who never made anything we did, easy.

CONTENTS

PROLOGUE

"Do You Know The Way To San Jose?" sang Dionne Warwick; well, if you're English and work in California's Silicon Valley, you know it's straight down the 101 Freeway. 6.15 a.m. on a sunny April, Saturday morning in Foster City, 25 miles south of San Francisco, a white La Baron convertible drives down the on-ramp to the south-bound 101. From as far away as Sacramento, ex-pat Englishmen are driving towards their 'Mecca', a pub called The Britannia Arms, in the San Jose suburb of Cupertino.

6.50 a.m., Alan Chandler, a Londoner working in Silicon Valley, smiles as the pub comes into view. Situated in a typical one-storey row of Mediterranean style shops, complete with palm trees, it has its own parking lot. The founder of the San Francisco Chelsea Supporters' Club, slowly inches along looking for a free space to park, counting himself lucky to find the last one. Getting out of the car, he is quite happy to leave the top down as this is a safe part of town. Looking up, he sees that the sun is out early and it's already in the low 70s.

Walking across the parking lot towards the front door, he is greeted by another ex-pat, Mark Diamond, living locally in San Jose, "Well, we gonna win today?" Opening the front door, Alan replies, "Well seeing we're at home, I can't see us losing. I just hope George Weah is playing, he'll run rings round Heskey." Today it's Chelsea versus Liverpool, and it's a full house. 'The Brit' is owned by another ex-pat Englishman from Blackburn. He has done his best to bring a little piece of England to the Californian suburbs. The result is a very un-American bar with walls adorned by Union Flags, and football shirts from all major British football teams. The bar itself runs along the far wall for almost the full length of the building. The tables and chairs are occupied by ex-pats eagerly watching the giant screen TV in the corner. The room is packed.

Going through the front door, they are greeted by the rest of the San Francisco Chelsea regulars. Dave Hughes, sitting by the bar, has driven from Oakland. Spotting Alan, he hands him a Miller Genuine Draft and asks, "You went back for the away game last year didn't you?" Alan nods as he takes a deep swig of the cold "MGD" before replying, "Yes, we lost, and those Scouse bastards only started singing after they'd scored. If it hadn't been for us singing, 'In Your Liverpool Slums,' the place would have been like a fucking morgue.

"You lucky bastard," said Dave smiling. "I ain't been back to London since 1992." "So you've not had the pleasure of freezing your nuts off while getting drenched in quality English rain," Mark

6

cut in with a sarcastic smirk. "Any trouble?" asked Ian Kirkman who had driven 60 miles from Livermore. "No, I couldn't believe it, first time I'd been up to the slum since the '70s. Ian and I went into their pub, 'The Arkle', and they bought us drinks. Totally different from the old days."

LIVERPOOL AWAY

Saturday October 3rd 1970

There is a light drizzle falling on Liverpool's Lime Street Station, a wrought iron Victorian cathedral to the steam train. Like much of the British Rail infrastructure, it has started to show its age. Barring the fact that the locomotives are now diesel-powered, little had changed underneath its imposing metal arches in over one hundred years. Lime Street is a terminal with all its platforms ending at a communal barrier, each platform having its own ticket barrier. Past the barrier is a soot ridden brick edifice, with a glass-fronted café and bar which still manages to betray its Victorian origins.

An InterCity train slowly pulls into platform three. Amongst its regular payload of commuters and holidaymakers, are two hundred Chelsea supporters. The first train doors swing open even before the carriages have come to a halt, while a chorus of "LIV-ER-POOL," echoes across the damp station. The alighting passengers freeze as they glance towards the ticket barrier where over three hundred Liverpool supporters are chanting, "COME ON CHELSEA."

You didn't have to be a proverbial 'rocket scientist' to know that this is an invitation to battle. The first Chelsea supporters jump onto the platform, then stop and stare; smartly dressed in a black Crombie coat, The General, is gathering the members of the notorious Chelsea 'Shed' together. "Wait for the passengers to go through the barrier," he orders as he quickly sizes-up the situation around the ticket barrier, "Then we'll all walk together. No-one runs!"

As he is organising The Shed, another group of eight Chelsea supporters congregate separately. One of them, Jock, is closely observing the activity. The General looks over to them and commands, "You lot stay with me." "Bollocks!" Jock replies in his broken Scots accent, "We're the North Stand."

He turns to the man standing next to him and smiles. Merrill, wearing an ex WW2, SS camouflaged combat smock, is intently looking towards the barrier watching every move of the waiting Liverpool supporters, who stand out from their London counterpart as they still dress in Skinhead fashions. Then glancing back at the passengers, now standing around waiting nervously, says to the man, "Right, let's get to the barriers before these passengers are kicked to shit by those Scouse cunts."

Joined by some of the Shed eighteen men run up the platform towards the barrier. As they move, the remaining members of The Shed start chanting, "NORTH STAND, NORTH STAND, DO YOUR JOB." As the small group passes the first bunch of passengers, Big Steve points back at them and shouts, "Stay here until we move that lot out of the station." The passengers stand transfixed as they try to understand what is happening. As they near the barrier, Big Steve starts smiling before shouting at the top of his voice, "CHELSEA!"

Meanwhile, an advanced guard of the Merseyside welcoming committee has slipped through the ticket barrier onto the platform, confident in their numerical superiority. Taken aback by the unexpected attack, most of them quickly turn and start to run back through the gap. Only a few stand their ground. One of these aims a wild kick towards Jock who catches the heel of the man's shoe and lifts it skyward in a single, smooth movement, sending him crashing onto the platform. Jock then stamps on him with his right foot, generating a crack of ribs loud enough to start a panic among the remaining Liverpool group. They now start fighting amongst themselves in a 'suave qui peut' crush, back through the open barrier.

One throws a desperate punch back towards Merrill, who ducks it easily before grabbing hold of the extended wrist. He then quickly pulls the youth around, using himself as the pivot-point, sending the helpless body crashing into the gate's upright. The sound of the impact echoes through the station. Merrill releases his iron grip, allowing the body to fall face downward on the platform, blood gushing from a deep cut in the back of the skull. Spider, meanwhile, has picked up a small chalk black-board containing train schedule details; charging through the gap into the station forecourt, he swings it wildly from side to side, causing bodies to fall left and right.

Little John runs to the barrier, his long jet-black hair flowing down his back like a cloak, and charges into a Liverpool group that is trying to regain some composure. He leaps up and drop kicks one of them, who falls straight to the floor. "Come on you bastards," screams Big Steve. Those few remaining Liverpool fans that had not yet made it through the barrier, jump down onto the tracks and run as if their lives depend on it. "Come on, Merrill's through the gates," Jim shouts at Big Steve. "Let's go then," he replies. As they jog towards the barrier, Colin and Lenny are having a stand-up fight with six of the Liverpool group that had failed to get away. "Chelsea!" screams Dave Osborne (known as "Ghost") as he joins in the fight through the barrier.

Back on the platform, The General has organised the members of The Shed together into a single group. Looking towards the barrier, he leads a headlong charge along the platform towards the fight. Cue: a mad rush by the Liverpool supporters for the exits and the relative safety of the streets. However, some panic and run into the station bar with Big Steve, Little John and Colin, close on their heels. A hail of chairs greets the pair, one of which crashes through the plate-glass front window of the bar. Colin leaps the bar with a single athletic stride, while Big Steve picks up one of the chairs that has hit him and starts to wade through the terrified group, its members now prepared to risk jumping through the broken window to effect an escape.

One turns and throws a plate at Colin, who sees it at the last second and ducks, allowing it to fly past safely. Merrill enters the bar and kicks the thrower in the back, propelling him into the arms of Colin. The dull thud of knee hitting testicles, sends an agonising jolt through his body as he sinks screaming to the floor. Little John aims a kick at a Liverpool supporter as he runs past one of the Columns in the bar; there is a soft thud as his Dr Martin boot hits the column. "Fucking Hell," he screams, as the toes in his right boot smash against the steel toe cap. With the bar cleared of all potential opposition, the eighteen Chelsea supporters chant in unison: "WE'RE THE NORTH STAND, WE'RE THE NORTH STAND, WE'RE THE NORTH STAND, STAMFORD BRIDGE."

The General, who is not impressed, strides into the bar shouting, "You stupid bastards, you'll get us all nicked before the game starts." Raising his eyebrows, Merrill inquires, "You got a better way of getting out of the station?" The General is clearly annoyed as members of The Shed start to gather around him. "You're on your own now, don't ask us for help," he declares, then angrily looks back at The Shed before issuing the curt order, "Come on, we're out of here."

At that moment, the sound of police sirens scatter the massed ranks of Liverpool supporters waiting outside the station. The foot police, now assisted by mounted colleagues, move in to form a cordon around The Shed. The mounted officers promptly start to hit out indiscriminately with their three-foot batons. Undaunted, The Shed taunts the police with a favourite away song:
"IN YOUR LIVERPOOL SLUMS, IN YOUR LIVERPOOL SLUMS;
YOU LOOK IN A DUSTBIN FOR SOMETHING TO EAT,
YOU FIND A DEAD RAT AND YOU THINK IT'S A TREAT.
IN YOUR LIVERPOOL SLUMS, IN YOUR LIVERPOOL SLUMS;
YOUR MUM'S ON THE GAME AND YOUR DAD'S IN THE NICK,
YOU CAN'T GET A JOB COS YOU'RE TOO FUCKING THICK.
IN YOUR LIVERPOOL SLUMS, IN YOUR LIVERPOOL SLUMS;
YOU SHIT ON THE CARPET AND PISS IN THE BATH,
YOU FINGER YOUR GRANDMA AND THINK IT'S A LAUGH.

The police fail to notice the North Stand Firm entering the Lime Street Station.

None of the small group ever identify themselves by wearing Chelsea colours. They prefer to dress in normal, smart, street clothes, so they blend in easily with the rest of the passengers, who are now moving through the barrier into the station forecourt. "What are we going to do now?" asks Big Steve as he watches the police, who seem to know instinctively that there are still Chelsea supporters inside the station. "Split up and make for the side exit. We'll get cabs to the ground," suggested Merrill. 'Two by Two', according to Noah," laughs Little John.

Ghost and Colin are the first to make their way out of the station by the side exit into Skelhorne Street. Turning right, they walk towards a line of 'black cabs' parked in Lime Street. Unnoticed by either police or Liverpool supporters, they tell the drivers to wait. Little John, Steve, Lenny and Jim get into one of the cabs. "We'll see you outside the ground," says Ian as he clambers into the other cab. "Hold on, Merrill ain't here yet," warns Big Jim, looking around anxiously. "Here he comes! Look over there," reassures Jock, pointing towards the station from inside the cab.

Merrill finally arrives; Jock still insists that the driver continues to wait. The driver is now a worried man. He knows that having fares with Cockney accents in his cab on a match day could prove a recipe for disaster. "You lot are Cockneys. Any trouble and I'll call the bizzies over," he says as firmly as he can in the circumstances, glancing towards the police. Jock shakes his head and with a frown, pulls out his wallet, "Here's a 'fiver', just do as you're told and you just might have a cab left tonight."

The police and The Shed are now disappearing out of sight as they move past the Empire Theatre and walk off towards Anfield, home of Liverpool Football Club, but the faint strains of another Chelsea song hang in the air:

"IN THE DEEPEST, DARKEST LIVERPOOL,
WHERE THE MILE END'S NEVER BEEN;
LIES THE MUTILATED BODY OF A SCOUSE GIT,
WHERE THE NORTH STAND KICKED HIM IN.
TO HELL WITH LIVERPOOL,
TO HELL WITH MAN CITY;
WE WILL FIGHT, FIGHT, FIGHT FOR THE CHELSEA,
TILL WE WIN THE FOOTBALL LEAGUE."

Looking avariciously at the five pound note, the driver asks, "You want the ground then, or do we wait here all day?" Jock looks him in the eye and states deliberately, "We'll tell you when to go. There's still some Chelsea that haven't left the station yet." "Did you see those idiots run? I can't believe that the 'filth' have it down on us," muses Big Steve.

"They're no' bothered about their own. They can have them anytime they want. The only thing they're after is a Cockney scalp," replies Jock, pointing to two police vans as they move off to bring up the rear of the Chelsea supporters. "Well, you've got nothing to worry about then, have yer?" Little John chuckles. "Hold on! Look over there!" Big Steve is looking over towards the station entrance where a Chelsea supporter and his two boys are walking out onto the street. The younger of the children is no more than eight-years-old. "Look, that little mob sitting on the steps of St. George's Hall has seen them," Merrill says, anxiously pointing to a group of Liverpool supporters running ominously across Lime Street towards the station.

The group of about twenty, dodge cars as they eagerly traverse the wide road to the front of the station. "Cockney bastard!" one of them yells as he runs up to the father, punching him in the face. Another grabs one of the small boys' scarves, but the child clings onto it crying in fear. "Give me that, you little shit," screams another in the group, slapping the child angrily across the face. He wants a 'trophy of war' and if he cannot get one any other way, he is prepared to bully schoolchildren.

"That's it, let's go," shouts Merrill, flinging open the cab door. "Don't you move! We'll be back!" Jock shouts back to the driver. The four race across the road, with Big Jim the first to reach the Liverpool group surrounding the father who is trying his best to protect his young sons. He lets fly with a kick that knocks the first of the group he encounters, straight into the station wall. Moving through the group, Little John grabs the scarf back and hands it to the father. "Take your kids into that cab," Merrill gestures to where the taxi remains obediently parked across the road, "It's paid for," he adds as an afterthought. "Run for the cab!" shouts Ian, "We'll hold them off." Jock, grabbing one by the hair, smashes his head against a bus stop's glass partition. Merrill then aims a kick squarely into the man's groin. Big Steve pushes another against the station wall before immobilising him with a sharp knee to the side of his left leg. Ian then aims an accurate kick at his lowered head. The man's nose disintegrates with a thud as he stumbles under the blow. Lenny and Jim shepherd the father and his sons safely into the cab, then turn and jog back over to the disintegrating scuffle; disintegrating because the Liverpool group had started to run.

"After them!" shouts Lenny. "No, stay here, and keep quiet or you'll have the 'filth' back," cautions Merrill. "Where's the fucking cab gone?" exclaims Little John as he looks around and watches it drive off. "I put the kids and their dad in it," said Merrill. "How's your foot, you mad Scots Git? I was afraid his head was going to fly all the way to the ground and score our first goal!" laughs Little John. "It fucking hurts you English cunt. Anyway if you're that interested, go and ask the prat himself. He's still laying over there," barks Jock, pointing to a heap on the pavement.

"We'd better get another cab. Don't want to get caught here by a bigger mob," suggests Colin. "Had enough for one day, have we?" teases Jock. "Cut the crap, there's another cab over there. Let's get to the ground," Merrill interjects as he walks into the road with his hand up. "Can you fucking believe it? Attacking primary school kids with their dad?" says Big Steve, shaking his head in disbelief.

"Oh yes, I can believe it, and the press still reckon this vermin are the best-behaved football supporters in England," replies Merrill, angrily.

CHAPTER ONE

"Yes!" says Alan Chandler, as the final whistle goes. "Two nil, fucking sweet," replies Mark Diamond, "Yes, your 'foreign legion' are getting better," chips in Kevin Darcy, a Liverpool supporter around forty years old, with receding hair. A classic Mr. Angry type, and another regular at 'The Brit'.

"Well, you lot had five strikers on at the end," says Jock Kirkman, with a smirk, "And you still couldn't score in a brothel." "Oh I wouldn't go that far," disagrees Kev, looking up and enquiring, "You lot want a drink?" "No, that's alright. It's too early for me," Jock chips in, "It's not nine o'clock in the morning yet!" "Hey Kev, they should give Heskey an Oscar, taunts Dave Hughes, as Kev looks up from his table and looks around for the waitress. "Heskey is a class act and will represent England in Euro2000," Kev proudly replies, "And a damn sight better than your Sutton!" "Now, now Kev, don't be a bad loser," replies Jock with just a hint of sarcasm. "They should stick Sutton in the reserves until he finds his form, then we might get a return on the investment," comments Dave. "Agreed. Weah came on loan, and I bet they keep Sutton and send Weah back," says Jock, in an unhappy tone.

"Ain't it amazing," muses Alan, "Thirty years ago, we'd be kicking each others' heads in." The assembled Chelsea supporters laugh as Kev looks across with a glint in his eye. "You weren't one of those bloody hooligans were you?" Kev says, beckoning the waitress. "No," replies Mark, then looking around, "We are all normal supporters, but I think Alan may have been a wee bit naughty in those days." "If I remember right," interrupts Dave Reeves, a Chelsea supporter over in California on holiday, "Weren't you in the North Stand?"

Alan Chandler slowly turns his head and throws an angry frown at Reeves, "Might've been, but that was a long time ago." Sensing he had touched a raw nerve, Reeves changes tack, "Sorry, I must be mistaking you for someone else. It's just that I always wondered why the North Stand broke away from The Shed."

Alan puts on an act of thinking, and then slowly says, "I think it started at the night game against Arsenal in 1969, but I couldn't say for sure."

ARSENAL AT HOME

Monday April 14th. 1969, Chelsea 2 - 1 Arsenal.

Saturdays are always the busiest day of the week down the North End Road street market in West London. Shoppers throng the stalls, some buying fruit and vegetables, while those in the know search out the odd bargain on the bric-a-brac stalls. Women with pushchairs, abandoned by their husbands in the name of football, examine apples and barter over prices, but being a Monday evening, the few stallholders that have opened are busy packing up. Every now and then one of them gives an apprehensive glance as 'away' supporters walk down the North End Road from West Kensington Underground Station.

Other eyes are also watching, but these are the eyes of predators. The Cock pub, near the corner of Shorrolds Road and the Lower North End Road, is a typical Victorian pub, long and rectangular in shape. A favourite watering hole for members of the North End Road Boys, its dark wood interior gives the impression that it's smaller than it actually is. This group of locals makes up an important part of the notorious Shed End supporters of Chelsea Football Club.

Lenny Blake is standing by the doorway of The Cock, scanning the market for red and white scarves. A 5ft 5in, 25-year-old ex London Transport ticket inspector from Battersea, he now works with his father on a fruit and veg. stall in the North End Road. His black hair hangs down to the collar of his blue 'Ben Sherman' shirt. 'Mr Angry' is a long time member of the North End Road Boys; he loves a good fight and lives for Chelsea.

"Hey look!" he says in surprise, "Some twat is driving a bleeding 'Roller'". Big Steve, who is standing just inside the door, turns his head and watches as a black Rolls Royce slowly navigates past the pedestrian walking in the road. Big Steve Williams, a 5ft 10in, 19 year-old, dark haired, round faced Cockney, wearing a white 'Fred Perry' tennis shirt so beloved by the Mods, shows just the hint of a beer gut. He left school with six GCE 'A' levels and is a trainee secondary school teacher. Being both quiet and intelligent, he seems out of place on the terraces, but while careful to avoid arrest, he enjoys his double life. He's been engaged for a year and always said he would move to the stands when married.

"They used to be called 'Roycesons'," Big Steve says, as if thinking out loud." Lenny turns his head in confusion and looks at him, "What the fuck you on about?" he queries. "Rolls Royce," answers Big Steve, "They started as a partnership between Royce and a guy called Robinson. Then Rolls came along and, seeing the quality of the cars, he struck a deal to market them on condition he got his name on them." "Yeah, whatever," says an uninterested Lenny, "There's four Arsenal over there."

Lenny's remark catches the ear of Cliff Worthington, known to his friends as Spider; he brushes some ash off the sleeve of his Black Crombie coat. A 5ft 10in, 20 year-old building site manager from Fulham, and the joker of the pack. Intelligent and humorous, his fair hair just shows through his skinhead hair cut. He writes songs like they're going out of fashion, and often prints out new ones and hands them out at games so everyone can join in. His sarcasm is both provoking and funny; a born sergeant major type, he loves not having the responsibility of being number one. He's the perfect back up, as his ideas are asked for and taken up. He has two brothers, who occasionally go to games. The youngest, Barry, is 13 years old and is kept clear of any fights. The oldest, Robert, has been known to fight, but isn't a regular as he works in a West End Department Store and works most weekends. He walks over to the door and looks left up the North End Road. "Where?" he asks, scanning the street.

Lenny raises his left hand and points, "Over there, the Roller's just passing them." Spider sees the four Arsenal supporters. They are wearing bomber jackets and each has a red and white scarf tied to their right wrist. Turning his head to look back inside The Cock, "John!" he shouts, "We've got company!" John Andrews is a 5ft 5in, 19 year-old, round faced barman from Wandsworth. Known as 'Little John' to his friends, he is quiet and keeps himself to himself, but step on his toes and he'll strike back like a rattlesnake. He is quite a ladies man but he keeps them well away from the games. An individualist and ex-Mod, he is always impeccably dressed and kept his long jet-black hair, even at the height of the original skinhead craze.

"OK," he says, walking to the door, "Let's teach them they're in the North End Road." "Hold on a mo'," says Spider. He walks over to the jukebox, pauses a moment as he searches for the desired track, then dropping a shilling in the slot, he pushes C, then 3. Turning around, he walks back to the door of The Cock. As the Rolling Stones, 'Street Fighting Man', starts to blast out of the Wurlitzer, he turns to his companions and smiles. "Right let's go," he says with a smirk.

The four Chelsea supporters start to walk up the North End Road. Dressed in black Crombie coats, they mingle with the pedestrians unnoticed.

"John, Steve," says Spider, never taking his eyes off the four Arsenal supporters, "Keep on this side of the road and come in behind them." Little John nods as Spider and Lenny cross the road and walk up the opposite pavement. One of the Arsenal supporters walking past a fruit stall, stops and picks up an apple. Seeing the stall-holder bending down moving some empty boxes together, he takes a bite and walks on. The stall-holder looks up, and realising that something is not right, shouts, "Oi! I saw that!"

The Arsenal supporter looks back in arrogance and mutters, "Fuck off!" As he turns his head back, it is met by Spider's right fist, the impact sending him staggering back into the corner of the fruit stall. Before he realises what is happening, Spider kicks out with his right leg. The steel toecap of his 'Dr. Martens' boot, smashes into the supporter's right thigh, sending him crashing to the pavement.

The second Arsenal supporter, thinking Spider is on his own, turns and brings his right leg up in an attempt to kick him. But Lenny grabs the booted foot and pulls it towards him, at the same time sending a deadly kick into the supporters exposed crutch; the other two supporters, taken by surprise, turn and start to run. Little John, who is halfway across the road, runs a couple of steps and sticks out his right foot, sending one of the Arsenal supporters flat on his face. Big Steve grabs the last one around the neck and runs the heel of his boot down the calf; a cry of pain is met by an elbow crashing down on his head. "Shit!" cries Steve, the pain of the impact shooting up his arm.

Little John stands over the spread-eagled body of his prey and waits as the supporter starts to get back up on his feet. His right boot flies into the supporter's head, sending him crashing back to the pavement. "Should've stayed there cunt!" he screams, as he bends down and unties the red and white scarf from the lifeless wrist.

Spider looks around, scanning for any sign of the police. Seeing none, he shouts, "Right! Let's go to the ground." The stall-holder, standing on the pavement along with open mouth pedestrians, smiles and shouts, "Cheers Pal!" as the four members of the North End Road turn left into Vanston Place. Spider turns his head back towards The Cock, and waves to over a dozen Chelsea supporters now standing outside, "Come on, we're off to the ground." The group starts to walk across the road to join them. Spider then turns to Lenny, and with a broad grin, he says, "You can't say I don't have a positive attitude about my violent habits!"

"We've got to win this one," says Colin Davis, as he sits in the Ifield Pub. A 5ft 8in, 18 year-old barman and part-time actor. His medium length, wavy fair hair and boyish looks, helped him to become a male model, with his photo appearing in many barber shop windows across Britain. He's an extrovert and likes to be noticed, and is always in the thick of things. Although cold blooded, he has the ability to control a quick temper. He always says his ambition is to own his own chain of pubs and wants to die in a vat of beer.

"Ha! We've only won two games so far, and those six draws in a row, ain't helping," replies an indignant Jim Raven. A 5ft 6in, slim, 17 year-old shop assistant, from Fulham, an ex-Mod that still dresses the part, and another member of the North End Road Boys. Although a hard fighter, since moving in with his girlfriend, he prefers to stay in the background.

"After that loss at Leeds, and that draw against them in the League Cup last week, they've got to turn it around tonight," says Colin, as he downs the last of his pint of Bitter. The Ifield pub, sitting on the corner of the Ifield and Finborough Roads, is another favourite watering hole of the North End Road Boys. It also holds a well-kept secret, as many members of the Chelsea team can be found here having a quiet after game drink. The sound system is playing The Edwin Hawkins Singers, 'Oh Happy Day', softly in the background.

"I hear that Arsenal are bringing a big crew down tonight," comments Colin, looking at his empty beer glass. "OK hint taken," moans Jim as he takes Colin's glass. "No," exclaims Colin, looking at his watch, "It's six-thirty, we better get going." He pauses a moment, lost in thought, "I have a feeling they're going to try and take The Shed tonight." "Mm, They won't take us, or the Stockwell," Jim says, more thinking aloud than actually talking. "Yeah," replies Colin, getting up from his chair, "It's all the ones that ain't in a crew that tend to run, no matter how hard The General and his Stockwell boys, try to keep them in order."

Walking out of the Ifield, they stand on the corner of the Finborough Road, looking up towards Earls Court. "Seems quiet enough," observes Jim. "Seems too quiet if you ask me," replies Colin, "I don't like it." They start to walk south towards the Fulham Road, "Well we have Derby, West Brom, and Everton at home coming up," says Jim, changing the subject, "Should be six points there for the taking, not to mention Newcastle and Sheffield Wednesday away." Colin thinks a moment and then says, "talking about Newcastle, Merrill says he fancies going in the Leazes this year." Jim Raven stops and looks at Colin, "You got to be fucking kidding!" he exclaims, "Newcastle are the hardest in the country on their own turf." Colin, still walking, shakes his head and replies, "No, he reckons it's all to do with respect. No-one has ever taken them, so if we go in their end, even though we won't win, it'll put Chelsea top of the pile."

"So is he talking the whole Shed, or just us?" queries Jim. Colin smiles as he says, "Just us!" "Fuck that!" exclaims Jim, shaking his head, "It's alright for him, he's ex-Army." He pauses a moment in thought, then turning his head to look at Colin, continues, "He's right! Thought, it would give us the bragging rights." Colin smiles and says, "I knew you'd be up for it." "I heard Lenny talking to him last week," says Jim, as they reach the Fulham Road, "They're thinking of splitting from The Shed and going down the other end." Colin stops on the corner and looks left across the road to the Gunter Arms, a run down Victorian pub, "Mm, looks pretty quiet," he says in a low voice, as if thinking out aloud, then turning to face Jim Raven, he continues, "Sounds like more suicide brain waves if you ask me."

"Any Arsenal yet?" Colin shouts across to those gathered drinking outside the Gunter Arms. "No! Just the occasional few," comes the short reply. Colin waves back across the road as he turns right to walk along the Fulham Road, "It's too fucking quiet! I don't like it." "Maybe they ain't coming!" laughs Jim in reply. Colin looks across to the corner of Hortensia Road and watches two Arsenal supporters getting out of their Ford Consul Classic 315, "No, I reckon that's all we'll get tonight, just yer normal ordinary supporter." They continue their walk along the Fulham Road towards Stamford Bridge.

The Rising Sun Pub is situated on the corner of Fulham Road and Holmead Road, directly opposite the main gate of Chelsea Football Club. A favourite watering hole for home supporters, many of the Shed Enders gather here to talk football and drink among friends, before a game. A well-known landmark, it has been attacked by away supporters before, and tonight it attracts a token police presence. "So where's those two nutters then?" asks Spider, as he crosses the Fulham Road and walks towards the Rising Sun." "We only fight when we have to, or to protect our turf," replies Big Steve, "Those two go out of their way looking for it." "True!" cuts in Lenny, "But I'm starting to learn what they get out of it." "Oh yeah, and what would that be?" asks an astonished Little John. "Well," replies Lenny, a frown forming on his forehead as he thinks, "It starts out as safety in numbers, don't it? I mean you go to an away game on yer own and walk into a group of opo's! Well you're gonna get done ain't ya?"

He looks at the assembled silent faces, raises his eyebrows in self-confidence, and continues, "You get an away scarfer in The Shed, you have a go, don't yer? And why?" He looks around at the gathering crowd, "I'll tell ya fucking why! it's our turf, and fuck anyone that comes on to it." "OK, I take your point," interrupts Big Steve, "but you're talking basic animal instincts here ain't yer." "Yeah, as it happens I am," continues Lenny, his voice getting louder as he gets more impassioned, "And hey! It's wake-up time people, 'cos I've got news for yer, we are fucking animals! We're just a hair's breadth away from the chimpanzees, but all those airy fairy fuck heads like to pretend we're the creation of some super being," he pauses to emphasise the point, "What a load of bollocks!"

"Yeah, I get what you're saying, but it ain't just that is it?" says Little John. "Oh, so what is it then?" says a confused Big Steve. Lenny looks over smiling, and continues, "Well, take you for instance, you ain't a born fighter and if you'd never gone to a game, you would probably never had a fight in your life. Correct?" Big Steve thinks for a moment, then looks up and answers, "Well yeah, I suppose I wouldn't. I've never been into violence until I started going to games." "Exactly my point," says an excited Lenny, "It's the camaraderie, the feeling of belonging, the feeling of being able to rely on your friends and they relying on you. That's why you don't let them down. We come together for mutual protection, we're a family, we're a fucking tribe for gods sake, fighting for the common cause." "Fuck me! You should be a politician," laughs Spider. "He's right in a way. I never thought I'd be in a gang, but you do get sucked into it, don't yer?" observes Little John, as he looks across the road and catches sight of a taxi slowing down outside the main gate.

"So what about Merrill and Jock?" asks Big Steve, "They're into another level, they go out looking for it." "To them it's an adrenaline trip. They've become fucking addicted to it," says Big Steve, "I know 'cos I'm starting to enjoy it too. I call them nutters, but we're all just a step behind them." "Talk of the fucking devil, and in they walk!" says Little John, pointing to the cab that has now stopped outside the main gate. Two men get out and look around.

"How much is that then?" says Ian Wallace to the cabby. Known as Jock to his friends, he's a 20 year-old, 5ft. 9in. native Scot with fair curly hair, his oval face highlighted by prominent cheekbones. His parents moved to London when he was seven years-old, and he has lost most of his Scottish accent but still breaks into it when angry. On leaving school, he joined his fathers Hatton Garden diamond company and travels abroad a great deal on business. Hard as nails, and his habit of always being first in, quickly ensured a sharp rise to the top of the pecking order. He has a long and steady relationship with his girlfriend, Veronica but always tells his close friends that he'll never marry her. Totally loyal to the North End Road Boys, and a born leader, he has a long and strong friendship with Alan Chandler; many people have mistaken them for brothers as they are inseparable.

"Three and six pal," replies the cabby, reaching for his wallet. Jock raises his eyebrows in mock astonishment and then pulls out a handful of change. "Here, have four bob," he says, dropping the money into the cabby's hand. Looking around, he sees the gathered North End Road boys outside The Rising Sun looking over towards Chelsea's main Gate. Turning to Alan, he says, "Looks like everyone's here already." "They're not the only ones here!" says Alan, tapping Jock on the shoulder and pointing to a youth standing alone in a black Crombie. Alan Chandler is a 23 year-old 6ft. 2in. half-Scot, half-German, long faced with shoulder length, straight black hair and rugged looks; a fiercely loyal Chelsea supporter since his father took him to his first game at aged five. Born a Jew (he adopted his Mother's religion) but became a practising Pagan at the age of 11. Recently, he bought the lease of a discotheque on the Finchley Road through his links with the Maltese Mafia in Soho. Spider gave him the nickname of Merrill, after the war movie, 'Merrill's Marauders, because of his habit of wearing his father's SS camouflage combat jacket.

"Be careful of Hawkins," warns Jock, "he always carries a switch-blade." Merrill stands silently looking at the youth, a clean-shaven 20-year-old and leader of the Arsenal North Bank. Standing in the middle of the main entrance, Chelsea supporters walk around him, little knowing who he is, but aware that something is in the air. "Look at that cunt, standing there as though he's Cassius fucking Clay or something," says Merrill as he turns to Jock, and for the first time sees the North End Road Boys standing outside The Rising Sun. He also sees five policemen standing near them engaged in casual conversation; they are either unaware of the situation or for some reason, are ignoring it.

"The filth don't seem to know what's going on," Merrill says calmly to Jock. "So why is he just standing there on his own?" queries Jock, looking up the Fulham Road, past the supporters club shop towards the humped back Stamford Bridge, for any signs that Hawkins is not alone. Jock looks over to the police outside The Rising Sun and hears Thunderclap Newman's, 'Something In The Air', blasting out of the jukebox. "Fuck it," exclaims Merrill, "Let's have the bastard." "What here? queries a bewildered Jock, "What about the filth?" Merrill looks back to the police and then turns to Jock, and with a smile says, "Let's hope he's carrying his blade then." "I'll cover your back, just in case," reassures Jock.

Merrill slowly walks past Hawkins, pausing to look over to the turnstiles in front of the broad stairs that lead up to The Shed. Hawkins, instantly recognising Merrill, turns his head warily around towards the street. His hand goes to his right hand coat pocket as he sees Jock standing ten feet away with a broad smile on his face. As Hawkins turns his head back, the side of Merrill's left hand smashes into the front of his neck. Hands instinctively shoot up and hold the rapidly numbing neck. With his eyes watering, Hawkins coughs profusely in order to free his airway. People nearby, turn and look on in startled curiosity. Hawkins is helpless as a fist slams into his exposed nose; giving a cry of pain, he vainly tries to defend himself.

Merrill stands back, and seeing the police running across the Fulham Road, lets go with a kick into Hawkins' left thigh. Overwhelmed with such speed, he falls into an agonised heap on the concrete. "Watch out!" shouts Jock as the police run past him and grab Merrill by the arms. "You're nicked pal," says an excited policeman, as he tries to force Merrill to the ground. Two of the officers bend down and try and help Hawkins, who is still gasping for breath. "Hold on!" screams Merrill, "He's got a knife!" The first policeman's face turns to one of shocked disbelief, turning to look down at Hawkins. "He's got a knife, I saw him put it in his pocket," shouts Jock, running forward and grabbing the arm of one of the policemen bending over Hawkins.

A large crowd rapidly gathers around trying to see the action; Spider, and the rest of the North End Road, push their way through the gathering throng. "He had a knife, I saw it!" shouts Lenny Blake. The crowd takes up the chant and push forward towards the police, who are now starting to lose control of the situation. "Check his pockets," orders the officer, holding Merrill's arm. His colleague, kneeling over Hawkins quickly discovers the evidence, and with eyes wide op-en in amazement, holds up a closed six-inch switch-blade. "See told yer!" exclaims Merrill, as he struggles to free himself from the vice-like grip restraining him. Spider, having forced his way through the crowd, pushes into the officer holding Merrill. "Oops, sorry Pal," he mocks, as Merrill seizes his opportunity and stamps his left foot down hard on the officers foot. The sudden pain works in distracting his attention and Merrill, yanking his arm free, turns and runs into the depths of the crowd.

"Come here!" winces the officer, as he sees Merrill disappear into the milling crowd. "He ain't done nothing! What about the bastard with the knife?" queries Jock, quickly moving into the way to block any intended chase. "Damn it!" exclaims the policeman as the crowd push ever closer, stopping any chance of recovering the prisoner. Turning back towards the prostrate body of Hawkins, he looks up at the other four officers, "At least we got this one," he says, more to reassure himself and at the same time, save face.

Stamford Bridge, the home of Chelsea Football Club, is a large stadium similar to Wembley in that they both have a running track surrounding the pitch and a sloped one level terrace, but they differ in that Chelsea has stands which run along both sides of the pitch. The pride of Stamford Bridge is the West Stand, a covered single level seating area, sloping up and back till it reaches the refreshment area. In total contrast, is the East Stand, a narrow wooden stand dating back to the birth of the ground; it has a covered access passage at the rear that connects the north and south terraces.

For the away supporters, the north end of the ground is a semi-circular amphitheatre, but this one is narrow and open to the air. At the east side of the terrace, there is a small, run down rustic stand that was built in 1939 and has a café cum bar on the ground level; this is the North Stand.

At the southern end of the ground, there is another semi-circular amphitheatre, with an open walkway halfway up the terrace; scattered around at regular intervals are metal crush barriers that serve to prevent people from being pushed en masse, down the terrace. The centre section is covered by something you'd expect to see on a farm; and the home supporters affectionately call it The Shed, after the smaller similar looking covered area at the team's training ground at the Welsh Harp. The main gate area serves as the main access, with a wide and high open staircase leading on to the right-hand side of The Shed. Another smaller entrance is located on the left-hand side of the terrace.

"Did you see the filth bottle it!" exclaims a joyful Lenny as he climbs the wide stairs to The Shed. "They did seem rather nervous, didn't they," laughs Spider, "Don't think they were expecting the knife though!" "I think that's the only reason Merrill was able to get away," observes Big Steve, who is the first to reach the terrace. Looking across the pitch, he sees that the North Stand Terrace is half-empty, which for a night-time London Derby game, is rather strange. Turning left, they start to walk along the central walkway towards the normal position of the North End Road Boys, behind the goal on the lower terrace in front of The Shed.

Jock turns and looks up into The Shed, and seeing it packed to the gills, he looks for familiar faces. "Well the Stockwell and Southfields are here," he says, as he starts to walk down the terrace to his normal place. "Arsenal's gonna try and take us, I can just feel it in the air," says Lenny. Little John shakes his head as he looks around, "No way, they won't take The Shed, there are too many of us." A head turns in the crowd and says, "Numbers are nothing if they ain't organised." "Oh you made it then!" says Jock, as he sees Merrill leaning against their normal crush barrier vantage point. "Do you think Arsenal will take The Shed tonight?" asks Ghost, who has been in the ground ten minutes. "Bollocks!" snaps Spider, "Not with us and the Stockwell, they won't." "He's right though," Jock cuts in. "Apart from us and the Stockwell, there are too many hangers on, and you've seen it at away games; as soon as the going gets a bit tough, they fucking run, then panic sets in and the rest run. If it weren't for us, the Stockwell and the Southfields boys standing firm, The Shed would be shit."

"There's also the Pimlico Boys, they stand firm," says Big Steve. "The West Hampstead/Kilburn boys too," cuts in Little John.

Don't forget the Battersea Boys also,"adds Ghost. "My point exactly! The General controls the Stockwell like an army, but he can't control the masses, and they're the weak link," answers Merrill. "Well if you ask me, we should move to the North Stand," says Lenny defiantly. "Are you fucking mad?" queries Big Steve, "We'd get our fucking heads kicked in." "Wrong," says Jock looking across the pitch to the North Stand. "A small organised crew could wreak havoc down there." "And the filth are so unorganised, they couldn't control it," adds Merrill, "We'd be our own masters, with no hangers' on to spoil the party."

Spider, looking around The Shed and seeing so many people, ponders the idea. Then looking back, he defiantly says, "There's no way Arsenal can take The Shed." "Have it your way, but if the hangers' on run and leave us to carry the can one more time, I'm with Lenny," says Jim, leaning back on the crush barrier. "Bloody hell!" cries Spider, as he catches sight of Merrill's shoes, "Fucking Hush Puppies, are you having a laugh?" Everyone's eyes look down and open wide in surprise at Merrill's shoes. "Been down Carnaby Street ducky," Spider laughs. Merrill stands straight face and lifts up his right leg, "Feel the toe caps, and tell me if these are Hush Puppies?"

The laughter stops as Spider reaches out and feels the toecap. He then slowly looks up at Merrill and says, "Shit, what the fuck are they?" "Industrial shoes. The steel toe caps are guaranteed to a weight of twenty tons," says Merrill, as he watches the astonished faces of the North End Road boys. "Fuck me!" exclaims Little John, "Where'd ya get 'em?" Merrill starts to smile, "Well if you plonkers thought they were Hush Puppies, then the filth will too. If you want a pair go to Rawhide Belting on the corner opposite Great Portland Street Station. They only cost a tenner." "I like it," says an astonished Lenny, "So when the filth take the shoelaces from our Dr Marten's you can walk through unchecked."

As the evening light fades, the floodlights start to cast wispy shadows across the terraces. The atmosphere is building as the last strains of Harry J. & the All Stars, 'The Liquidator', fades from the loud speakers and The Shed shouts a final "Chelsea!" to the chorus. Now rival sets of fans sing their songs and chant insults at each other.
"I WAS BORN UNDER THE STAMFORD BRIDGE,
KNIVES WERE MADE FOR STABBING,
GUNS WERE MADE TO SHOOT;
IF YOU COME DOWN TO STAMFORD BRIDGE,
WE'LL ALL STICK IN THE BOOT."

Chelsea supporters, their voices amplified by The Shed roof, raise their scarves in unison. Viewed from all sides of the ground, in the twilight they resemble the waves of a blue and white sea.
"YOU COME IN ON YOUR FEET,

YOU GO OUT ON YOUR HEAD,
YOU AIN'T SEEN NOTHIN' LIKE THE MIGHTY SHED."

From the far end of the ground, the chants of "Arsenal! Arsenal!" are soon drowned out as different parts of The Shed sing their own songs.

"WE ALL COME FROM STOCKWELL,
DO-DAH, DOH DAH;
WE ALL COME FROM STOCKWELL,
DO-DAH, DO-DAH, DAY."

Not to be outdone in the friendly banter stakes, the boys from Battersea take up their satirical reply.

WE ALL COME FROM BATTERSEA
WOOF WOOF
WOOF WOOF
WE ALL COME FROM BATTERSEA
WOOF WOOF WOOF WOOF WOOF

Then unison is joined again as the combined choir of the Chelsea Shed sings their anthem...

"FUCK 'EM ALL, FUCK 'EM ALL,
UNITED, WEST HAM, LIVERPOOL;
'CAUSE WE ARE THE CHELSEA AND WE ARE THE BEST,
WE ARE THE CHELSEA, SO FUCK ALL THE REST."

Boos from the Arsenal supporters on the North Stand are drowned out as The Shed, now jumping up and down in human waves, burst in too.

"BERTIE MEE SAID TO BILL SHANKLY,
HAVE YOU HEARD OF THE NORTH BANK HIGHBURY?
BILL SAID 'NO, I DON'T THINK SO,
BUT I'VE HEARD OF THE CHELSEA AGGRO."

Then from the middle of The Shed, Mickey Greenaway starts up his famous chant.

"ZIGGA ZAGGA, ZIGGA ZAGGA"

And The Shed choir to a man answer back,

"OI, OI, OI"

Mickey again chants,

"ZIGGA ZAGGA, ZIGGA ZAGGA,"

The Shed again answers,

"OI, OI, OI"

Then Mickey slows it down with a long and single,

"ZIGGA,"

The Shed answer with a long,

"OI,"

Again Mickey slowly cries out another long,

"ZIGGA,"

Answered with another long,

25

"OI,"
Then Mickey speeds it up again,
"ZIGGA, ZAGGA,"
And the massed choir of The Shed, reply,
"OI, OI, OI,
OH WHEN THE BLUES,
GO MARCHING IN,
OH, WHEN THE BLUES GO MARCHING;
I WANT TO BE IN THAT NUMBER,
WHEN THE BLUES GO MARCHING IN."

Suddenly, the evening air is cut by an eerie silence; Gary Montgomery's eyes scan the crowd. A fair-haired 5ft 8in, 20 year old Chelsea supporter and second hand car dealer from Stockwell, he is the leader of the Stockwell Boys. Due to his leadership skills, he now leads The Shed on away games. Built around a nucleus of his own "Stockwell Crew", The Southfields Crew, The Battersea Boys, and the North End Road Boys, The General has turned The Shed into one of the most feared groups of supporters in England. However, there were still some weak links; while the Stockwell and North End Road were solid, others had displayed an unnerving ability to run away in the heat of battle.

Heads in The Shed turn to their left as a silent movement of bodies pour out of the left-hand side entrance. Gaps appear in the tightly pack crowd, then the silence is broken by joyous shouts of "Arsenal! Arsenal!" As three hundred Arsenal supporters charge into the space created by the rapidly growing panic, The General turns to the Stockwell boys and screams, "Charge!" Throwing caution to the wind, he runs forward and throws himself headlong into the advancing Arsenal. Seeing their leader throwing punches left and right, the Stockwell move in to support him closely followed by the Battersea Boys, but the majority of The Shed turn and flee in panic, creating more gaps in which the Arsenal supporters advance.

Thrown back by the speed of the advance, the Stockwell are slowly pushed back to the right hand side of The Shed. Spider looks around to the North End Road boys and shouts, "Come on!" and starts to run up the terrace. "NO! Wait!" screams Merrill, "Wait 'till they pass us and take them in the rear." "Fuck that!" shouts Little John, "They're going to take The Shed." Jock holds his ground, and quickly scanning the terrace shouts, "No, stay here or we'll be lost in the momentum." Spider stops before he gets to the walkway and turning back to shout, "But they're pushing us back." "Wait until they're past or they'll end up taking us," shouts Merrill, as fleeing Chelsea supporters push past him. Jock and Lenny start to lash out at the panicking Chelsea supporters, "Don't run, fight you cunt!" screams Lenny as he turns and shouts, "See what I mean about the

26

fucking masses?" Spider, against his instincts, stands his ground as the top half of The Shed are slowly pushed back. The Stockwell are fighting a valiant rear guard action supported by the Pimlico & West Hampstead/Kilburn boys, but the Arsenal supporters, now sensing victory, flood into the walkway and run forward in an attempt to encircle The Shed.

Waiting until the last of the Arsenal run past, Merrill now looks back to the North End Road and screams, "Charge!" Thirty youths stream forward in one wave and strike into the rear of the Arsenal. Taken totally by surprise, they hardly have time to think as the fists and boots of the North End Road cut them down. "Bastard!" screams Lenny, grabbing one by the hair and swinging him around into one of the crush barriers; then kneeing him in the crotch, he throws a punch at the head as the youth falls to the concrete. "Alan, look at her over there," shouts Jock. Merrill turns and sees Jock pointing over to the middle of The Shed where a girl is having a stand up fight with three Arsenal supporters. "Over there," he screams, as he too points to the middle of The Shed. "Bloody hell! Who the fuck is that?" queries Big Steve as he runs toward the girl. "Fuck knows," says Spider, running at his side, "But I'm glad she's on our side."

With their backs now against the rear wall of The Shed, the Stockwell rally as The General leads a counter attack that starts to push the Arsenal down the terraces, but they are met by the first wave of police running in to break up the fighting. Coming from the main staircase, the police move along the walkway into the middle of The Shed and then start to move up the terrace to separate the battling mobs. Lenny, running past the girl, hits out at the nearest Arsenal supporter, while Jim jumps on the back of another, both falling to the stepped terrace. Rolling off him, Jim jumps up, only to see the girl kick the supporter in the head.

"Hey hold on girl!" Jim shouts, "Don't kick 'em when they're down." "Fuck 'em!" screams the girl, landing another kick into the prostrate body. Jock runs up to one of the crush barriers and grabs the shirt of an Arsenal supporter, pulling him back against the barrier; he swings his right arm around his neck as Merrill calmly walks over and rains a series of punches into his face. "Shit, look over there!" shouts Ghost, pointing to a small boy at the front of the Chelsea, kicking Arsenal supporters as they run past him. "Fuck Me" gasps Lenny, "He must be only nine or ten!" Little John and Steve join the fray just as the Arsenal start to run back up the terrace to the back of The Shed. Little John, turning around, sees the advancing police line and sensing that they will be cut off, he shouts a warning. Spider, grabbing the girl by the arm, shouts, "Come with us, or you'll get nicked."

Seeing the police, Lenny shouts, "Fall back, the filth's coming!" Merrill and Jock move down the terrace towards the walkway and join the others. "Who's the bird?" says Merrill. "I ain't a bird!" she snaps indignantly, "I'm Mandy White." "Well Mandy," cuts in Jock, "Come with us if you don't want to get nicked." Having calmed Mandy down, he turns and walks down the terrace and joins the rest of the North End Road as they look back up the terrace. Merrill looks in disbelief at the 5ft 3in, 22 year-old counter assistant with National Provincial Bank. A born tomboy, with no fear, wearing skin tight shrunk jeans and Dr Marten's boots, she is still coming to terms with the fact that she was adopted, and is filled with bitterness at what she sees as a betrayal by her parents.

The police, now having arrived in force, form a human U shaped barrier between the Chelsea and Arsenal supporters in the upper Shed terrace. Long lines of arrested supporters are led by the police towards the main staircase. Sensing victory, the Arsenal supporters start to sing:

"WE TOOK THE SHED, WE TOOK THE SHED,
E I ADDIE OH, WE TOOK THE SHED."

A human wave of Chelsea supporters surges forward but are held by the police line. "Look at that shit!" screams Lenny, "I fucking told yer those cunts would fucking run." "Let's move 'round the back of them and steam in," says Jim, as he starts to walk forward. Merrill, grabbing his arm says, "No! Leave it, there's too many filth up there now." "Well that settles it! I'm down the North Stand from now on," says an indignant Lenny. Merrill looks at Jock and nods, "Yeah, I think we'll join yer." "I'm with yer too," adds Jim. "You're fucking mad," says a disbelieving Spider, shaking his head," If you four don't get kicked to shit first, the filth will nick yer." "So what would you prefer," says Jock, "A small well organised group, or this fucking rabble?"

Spider turns and looks up at The Shed, soaking up the reality of what has happened, "I've always been a 'Shed Boy' and always will be," he says with pride. Jock, slowly turning back, looks at Little John and Steve, and then casually says, "What about you?" Little John looks at Steve who nods at him with a knowing smile, "No mate, we'll stay with Spider and The Shed. Jim Raven walks over to Jock and Merrill, "What's going on then?" he queries. "Lenny says he's had enough of The Shed and is going to go down to the North Stand from now on," then looking at Jock, he continues, "Me and Jock are joining him." Jim laughs out loud then looks at Merrill, "You mean you three are going down the North Stand from now on, and taking on all comers?" Jock shrugs his shoulders, then answers, "Yeah, so what's wrong with that?"

Jim shakes his head, and then turning to Merrill, he laughs and says, "OK, the North Stand it is!"

CHAPTER TWO

Ian smiles as he moves off to collect some of the empty coffee cups and ease the workload on Maureen, who has worked part-time as a waitress at "The Brit" for two years whilst attending Stanford University. She walks over with a smile and takes out her note pad, "Hi guys, what'll it be?"

Kev orders MGD's, and a coffee for Mark. He then looks over at Alan, tilts his head to one side, and frowns, "So were you one of those bastards that nearly ruined our game and made our name dirt in Europe?" he asks.

"No, I was more late 60s, early 70s," Alan replies, a surprised look on his face, "I retired when the inmates of the asylum jumped on the band wagon in the '80s and ruined it all."

"You clearly still get a buzz out of reliving it," says Kev, clearly annoyed.

"Not really. I enjoyed what I did, but like I said, that was years ago. But I make no apologies to self-righteous air heads like you," replies Alan, looking Kev in the eyes.

"Ah, but I'm one of the few people who's ever stood up to you and refused to worship at the altar of your hooligan "greatness," and it drives you fucking nuts," says Kev, as he sits back smugly and looks around at the assembled faces.

Alan starts to laugh, and then says, "I don't know what planet you're living on, but it ain't planet Earth, either that or you've been living out here too long."

Dave, still trying to keep from laughing, looks across at Alan, "Looks like we've got a live one here, "Merrill"."

Kev, clearly upset that he isn't making any headway, bangs his fist on the table as he recognises the name, and shouts, "You're so used to people kissing your arse and calling you "the legendary "Merrill"," and for what? Kicking people's heads in! Wow, what a thing to be proud of."

NEWCASTLE AWAY

Saturday October 25th, 1969, Newcastle 1 - 0 Chelsea

"The state of this fucking carriage!" exclaims Lenny, sitting in the buffet car of the 'Football Special' taking Chelsea supporters to Newcastle. Built in the '30s and affectionately called 'Rhubarb and Custard' after the red and yellow colour scheme that is still barely clinging to the outside surfaces of the coach, the carriages have seen their best days and are no longer fit for front line passenger service. "You sit down in the seat and it seems like a bomb has gone off," answers Jim, sitting opposite. "Yeah, I know what you mean pal," Lenny says as he hits the back of the seat and watches the cloud of dust explode into the air.

Jock walks back from the bar carrying four cans of lager, "Oh, do behave you lot," he says, putting the cans on the table and waving the cloud of dust away. "They've got a point though, seven carriages and all over-loaded," says Merrill. "You been down to the guards van then?" asks Lenny. "No, why?" replies Jock. "Go and have a look. You know where the parcel cage is?" Big Steve asks Jock. "Well there's standing room only and with gezza's looking out of the cracks in the wood, it looks like the last fucking train to Auschwitz."

Realising what he has just said, he looks over to Merrill, "Sorry, no offence." "None taken," replies Merrill, "But I know what you mean." Big Steve, a 6ft 3in., mousy haired 18 year-old civil servant, from Guildford, is sitting in a seat on the opposite side of the buffet car; a pleasant chap who loves the group feel but nevertheless, a fierce fighter. Renamed Big Steve by Spider because of his height, he too was a member of the North End Road firm and has just started going down the North Stand. He looks over to Merrill and says, "Ghost wants a word." Merrill puts his can of lager down, looks across at Ghost, and says, "Yeah, fire away."

Ghost gets up out of his seat and walks towards the end of the carriage. "Hello," says Lenny, "What's his problem then?" "Mind your own business and deal the cards," says Jock. Leaning against the carriage door, Ghost looks at three of The Shed talking at the opposite door, "Oi! You lot," he shouts. Looking over, one of them casually says, "What?" "Fuck off down the train," Ghost commands. The Shed boys look at each other, but Merrill walks into the doorway and says, "You heard him, fuck off." Realising they are no match for two of the North Stand, they begrudgingly walk off down the train.

"So you're a Jew, ain't yer?" queries Ghost. "No mate, I'm what's called a lapsed Jew," replies Merrill, slightly taken aback by the comment, "And the worst kind of lapsed Jew seeing I'm now an idol worshipping Pagan." Ghost frowns as he tries to understand what he has just heard, "But I thought!" "It ain't a problem! I lapsed when I was ten so I don't really count when it comes to being Jewish. I never liked all the rules and the hypocrisy that went with it, so never had a Bar Mitzvah," answers Merrill, lighting a cigarette. Taking it out of his mouth, he blows a smoke ring in the air, then looks at Ghost and asks, "So what's your problem? you anti-Semitic?" Ghost pauses a moment, then says, "No, it's just I had a bad experience and sort of blame them all." "Well?" says Merrill, as he pulls up the carriage door window. "I used to go out with this Jewish bird," starts Ghost, "We went out for about a year. I really fell for her." "What d'you mean, you fell in love?" queries Merrill. "Well, I didn't think so at the time, but now," Ghost pauses as his eyes search for somewhere to look, "Well you don't realise what you've got 'till you lose it. Do yer?"

"True, but what's all this got to do with me?" asks Merrill. "We went to her parents' house for dinner one night. They were orthodox, but Deanne didn't give a shit," says Ghost. "Deanne being your girlfriend?" asks Merrill. "Yeah, so anyway, there we are eating this salad, they had some sort of multi-layer plate thing in the middle of the table that you could turn it round and help yourself to. So I takes this vegetable salad and really liked it, then I asked her mother what it was." "And she said, "What's a nice Jewish boy like you not knowing that," smiles Merrill."Yeah, how the fuck d'you know that?" says a surprised Ghost. Merrill smiles, "Let's just say I've been there." "So I looks at her mother and says, "But I'm not Jewish." Well, she hits the fucking roof, shouting crap like, what are you doing bringing a gentile into our house!" Ghost's lips tighten as he casts his mind back.

"Well her parents tell me to leave. Deanne says she's going with me, but her old man grabs hold of her to stop her. So I tells her I'd see her tomorrow, and left." "So what happened, you move in with each other?" asks Merrill. "No, she worked in her parents' newsagent's shop, so when I phoned it, her old man tells me she's moved to family in Brighton. Well, I goes and sees her best mate Carmen, and she tells me that her parents forced Deanne to have an abortion. Those fucking bastards murdered my kid." "I'm sorry pal, but what's all this got to do with me?" asks Merrill. "Well, it's just my way of saying that anything I say about Jews ain't aimed at you. Just her fucking parents," replies Ghost. Merrill nods his head and says,

"Not a problem. If that had happened to me, I'd feel the same. Besides, I fucking hate those right wing bastards as well." He throws his cigarette on the floor and steps on it. Ghost looks at him in puzzlement. "Don't worry about it," Merrill smiles, as a thought enters his head, "Tell yer what, how about we go in the Leazes!" "You having a laugh?" replies Ghost, "They're the hardest in the country on their own turf. Not even Glasgow Rangers took them." "Well a dozen of us can't take a whole end, but at least they'd know the North Stand means business." Ghost shakes his head as he thinks it over, then looks up and smiles, "You're on!"

"Hold on!" says Merrill, holding his right hand up. He turns his head and listens to the sound of breaking glass. "That toilet over there!" says Big Steve, as he walks across the carriage connector to the toilet door at the end of the next carriage. A Shed boy standing out side, looks at them as they walk towards him, "What do you want then?" he says with an attitude. Big Steve throws a straight right and knocks him to the floor as Merrill kicks opens the toilet door. A surprised head turns as the door swings open, "What's you're fucking problem?" says the youth. "You are!" shouts Merrill, as he sees that the glass cabinet door has been smashed. "So what's the fucking problem with smashing up the bleeding train them?" says a second youth standing behind him, kicking the water cistern.

Merrill takes a step back and kicks out with his right leg, catching the first youth in the chest. Falling back under the impact, he crashes into the second youth, sending them against the toilet window. Merrill rains a series of blows on the youth's head, sending him to the floor. The second youth throws up his hands, screaming, "Don't hit me! We're just having a bit of fun!" Big Steve pulls Merrill back out of the toilet as a crowd gathers, attracted by the noise. "What's going on here?" demands The General, pushing his way through the growing crowd. "Just a couple of idiots trying to smash up the train," says Big Steve. "So you've become coppers have you?" answers an indignant The General. "Well lets put it this way," says Jock, as he forces his way through the crowd, "The filth in Newcastle see a smashed up train, how the fuck we going to get back to the smoke after they take it out of service?"

The General looks at Jock as he thinks for a moment, "OK, you have a point, but the North Stand don't fuck with The Shed." "So, we just stand back and let them smash up the train, do we?" says Merrill. "No, you come to me, and I'll sort them out," answers an angry The General. Colin Davis, sensing the growing tension between the North Stand and The Shed, pushes his way through the crowd. Standing in front of The General and looking around at the crown, he says, "Let's just all calm down shall we." The General looks at Colin who has just started to go with the North Stand, "I run

The Shed and they're answerable to me, so just stay away, got it!" says a stern The General. "No problem. Next time, we'll come to you," replies Colin, trying his hardest to be the diplomat and stop a civil war. "Yeah, we'll just let them smash the fucking train up and wait for you to pick up the pieces," says Merrill. "No problem General," shouts Lenny, as he grabs Merrill's arm and pulls him away. "No point in falling out over this," says Jock, "We're all Chelsea after all." The General stands his ground as he watches the North Stand walk back into the buffet car. Looking at the two youths as they leave the toilet, he punches the second in the head, "Stupid cunts!" he shouts, "No-one smashes up my train, you hear! No one!" He emphasises the point by sending a kick into the leg of the youth.

An hour later, tempers have calmed down and carriage door windows are lowered. Heads start to stick out into the open air as the football special pulls into Newcastle's Central Station. Chants of "United" echo around the low, rustic station roof, from the crowd gathering outside. "Here look," says Lenny, pulling his head in and looking back into the carriage, "Newcastle have a reception committee." "Well, let's get at 'em then," exclaims an excited Colin. "Hold on," shouts Jock, pushing his way forward and looking out of the window. Turning back towards Merrill, he smiles and then says, "Looks like The Shed have a fight on their hands." "Fuck 'em," snaps Merrill, "We have an appointment with some United in the city centre, remember?" Big Steve looks around in bewilderment, "You don't mean you're going to leave them to it, do yer?" Merrill walks over to Big Steve and puts his right hand on his shoulder. Lenny looks down the platform and up to the street, "That's the Leazes, out there," he says. "I know," replies Merrill, "We're going up the other end of the platform, up the slope and over the fence, and take them in the rear." "What, all eight of us?" Colin says in amazement. Jock looks around and waves his hand towards the opposite end of the platform.

Jim and Lenny start to walk east along the platform towards the embankment. Jock is just about to follow when he sees Spider get out of the train. "Spider!" he shouts, waving his arm. "What's up?" says an anxious Spider, as he watches The Shed start to pass through the station building towards the waiting Newcastle supporters. "Come with us, we're going to take them from the rear." Jock says. Spider looks at the last of The Shed as they disappear into the station booking hall. "OK, just this once, but I'm Shed remember?" demands Spider. "Whatever, but lets get going," interrupts Merrill. They turn and run along the platform and climb the grass embankment to the white wooden fence. Colin jumps the low fence and looks down the hill towards the front of the station. He sees the Newcastle charge The Shed, and looking around, he sees a group of around twenty other youths running towards them from the West Gate cross roads, "Oh fuck, we're trapped," he yells, looking and pointing to the advancing mob. Jock jumps the fence, looks up the road, and starts to laugh, "They're Chelsea, Pal." Colin looks at the front of the mob and starts to recognise faces. "That's that little northern crew that go to away games," says Lenny. "Yeah," says Jock, "That's what's their name's crew." "Tommy & Martin from Wigan!" says Merrill. "Yup, but Martin's from London, his family moved up here last year," adds Ghost.

Jock runs into the middle of the road with his arms in the air and stops the charge. "Tommy ain't it?" he says to the youth at the front. "Yeah, you're Jock, so why ain't yer mucking in with The Shed then?" asks Tommy, a 23 year-old butcher's shop assistant, who travels down to every home game and has his own firm in Bradford. They go to away matches in the Midlands and some in the North. A born fighter lurks beneath a jovial and warm-hearted exterior. Jock turns and looks towards Martin, "Good to see you again, how's life in Manchester?" "Good, but I miss the Smoke!" Martin replies, an eighteen year old from Battersea. He is five foot ten and well built, and studies Law at Manchester University. Merrill looks down the hill, where The Shed are outnumbered and having a bad time. He looks at the mob of youths, then back to Jock and Lenny, "Well, the North Stand could use a 'Foreign Legion'," he smiles. Turning to Tommy, he says, "Well fancy joining the North Stand then?" Tommy looks back to his firm, and then looks back to Merrill and Jock. "You're on Pal." "Wonderful!" says Colin, "So let's get it on then.

The newly expanded North Stand, turns and charges into the rear of the Newcastle fans. Racing into the mass of bodies fighting outside the station, Lenny jumps up and drop kicks a Geordie; he falls to the floor, then looks up in astonishment only to see Big Steve's Dr. Marten boot smash into his face. Merrill grabs another Geordie by the shoulder and swings him into the station wall; the body bounces off and meets Jock's fist. Spider, screaming 'Chelsea!' runs into the back of the Newcastle swinging a post ripped out of the station fence.

Taken completely by surprise, the rear elements of the Newcastle break and run; members of The Shed trapped in the booking hall, now charge out and join in the fray. Now outnumbered, the remaining Geordies turn and join their rear elements. "Well, that's the first time I've seen Newcastle on the run up here," says an exhilarated Tommy, as he walks along Mosley Street towards the city centre. "Where's Spider?" says Colin, looking around. "Over there, with The General," answers Lenny, pointing back to the station. "That's alright," says Jock, "He's a Shed boy."

Lenny, walking over to Tommy says, "So thinking of joining up with us then, or you going with Spider and The Shed?" Tommy looks around and nods to Dave, a 22 year old from Salford who works for a firm of accountants. A 5ft. 8in., mousy haired youth, whose rugged looks portray his Viking ancestors of Northumbria, like other Northern Chelsea supporters, he has taken to London fashions and sports the current fashionable 'uniform' of Black Crombie coat, white button down collared shirt, blue jeans that have no turn ups, and Dr. Martens boots. Like Tommy, he travels down to home games, and leads his own firm in Salford; they too go to away games in the north, and the larger ones in the Midlands. Intelligent and articulate, he lives for the weekends. "Yeah, I've see you nutters steaming in down the North Stand," says Dave, "I reckon it could be fun." "Don't under estimate them," says Merrill, walking over to a telephone box, "We were lucky to take them by surprise." Tommy watches Merrill as he pulls out a notebook and writes the phone number down. "What the fuck's he doing?" asks a puzzled Tommy. "He collects phone box numbers from every place we go," answers Jock, "You never know when you may need them."

Dave, who is walking near Jock, overhears the conversation and queries, "I'm not with you, how would you need them?" "He's ex-army and reckons that if we get split up, he can still communicate by using the phone boxes," replies Jock. Tommy and Dave look at each other in amazement, and smile. "How can anyone in their right mind live in a dump like this?" asks Big Steve, looking at the soot-covered brickwork of the buildings. "Look, they even have to have metal cages over their shop fronts," points out Lenny. "And this fucking street ain't been swept in a month of Sundays too," joins in Jim. "Christ this whole shithole is one giant fucking slum," laughs Lenny. "If you listen long enough, you can hear the screams of the roof jumpers," laughs Merrill.

Turning into Grey Street, Colin walks up to Big Steve and points to two youths walking on the other side of the road, "Look at that," he sneers, "You can tell those northern bastards anywhere." Big Steve, turning his head, laughs softly, "Jeans with turn-ups, rainbow braces over white T-shirts. God, these sad wankers are so out of date." Colin notices Tommy looking at them, "So what do you think of these northern slags, old son?" Big Steve, seeing Tommy's indignant look, chuckles to himself as he puts his arm on Tommy's shoulder, "Don't take offence pal. You ain't a northerner, you're a Chelsea supporter." Tommy looks at Big Steve, thinks a moment and squints his eyes. "Hey! He's just pulling your plonker," says Colin, seeing the tension rising, "Besides with that Crombie coat, you look like a southern softie." "Hey you lot break it up!" snaps Merrill, pointing down High Bridge, "I just saw a Paddy Wagon sitting down there." "In the city centre?" says Lenny, "They must be on their tea break." "If it was just patrolling, it would have been moving, not just sitting there waiting," replies Merrill. "He's right!" snaps Jock, "Tommy, take your boys across the road." Looking at Dave he says, "Take your boys and drop back, if the filth do come just carry on like nothing's happening." "If we get stopped, keep walking. No point in everyone getting nicked," says Merrill. "We'll meet up by the Haymarket bus station. I've got the phone box number there."

As Tommy crosses the road and starts walking along the pavement, two large Austin police vans turn the corner from Market Street and head south towards the North Stand firm. Jock, seeing them, looks back as a third screeches around the corner of High Bridge with its bells ringing. He looks over to Tommy and nods his head to tell him to carry on. The first of the two vans turns and brakes as it mounts the pavement, blocking it. The one on the road stops level with the North Stand firm; the rear doors burst open, and out jump six policemen. Big Steve turns, but stops as the third van skids to a halt behind them.

"No!" shouts Tommy to one of his boys, "We go to the ground." The youth looks at him in disbelief, "Do as you're told! They're stopping us getting nicked as well," Tommy snaps as he carries on walking. They watch helplessly as eight officers disembark from each van and surround the eight Londoners. He looks over to Dave who seems to be going through the same dilemma. "Look!" shouts Tommy, as he sees Merrill look over to them and motion with his head to carry on walking. Turning back to Dave, he waves him over. Merrill watches Dave as he walks his firm across Grey Street, then turns to Jock, "Looks like we're in for a beating." "Bollocks, let's have the fuckers," says Big Steve, turning to face the rear van. "No!" replies Merrill, "They can't arrest us, we've done nothing but walk down the road." The police stand watching the eight, waiting for the first hostile move, when a sergeant moves through the line and looks at Jock.

"OK gentlemen, if you wouldn't mind getting in the vans." "What's going on here?" asks Jock, "We being arrested? And, if so, what for?" "Just be good boys and get in the vans," replies the sergeant as he motions with his arm. "Ah this is bollocks," says Jim, "If I ain't under arrest, then I'm walking." "Jim!" shouts Merrill, as two policemen grab his arms and start to walk him towards one of the vans, "That's what they want yer to do. Take it and don't resist." Jim looks at Merrill and Jock as they are frog marched into a van. He looks around at Lenny, who is being frog marched into another van, "You gotta be fucking kidding!" he says, as he realises for the first time just what is happening.

Merrill and Jock are thrown onto the floor of the police van; looking up, Merrill sees the first of four police grabbing the rear door handle and climbing up into the rear of the cage like van. Sitting on one of the iron benches that run along each side of the van, he looks down at the two Chelsea supporters sprawled on the floor. Jock starts to get up as the last officer slams the rear door, throwing the interior into near darkness. He doesn't see the boot that slams into his stomach, but the impact forces him back the metal floor.

"Right you cockney bastards," screams the sergeant, "You come up here for trouble, we're going to give you some." With that, all four police start kicking and punching the two bodies as they roll up into balls to afford them some protection from the blows raining down on them. Merrill's eye catches sight of Jock, and he shakes his head in warning as another punch smashes into his liver. The van door bursts open and two bodies are thrown onto the cobble stoned road; the police gather in the door and laugh at the two prostate bodies now laying motionless in the road. "Now fuck off back to London," shouts the sergeant, "We don't want your sort up here."

Watching the police vans as they drive off, Big Steve staggers to his feet, "So where the fuck are we?" "Fucking bastards!" shouts Lenny at the disappearing vans. Merrill stands up and lifts his blue Ben Sherman shirt, and looks down at the growing bruises on his stomach, then looking around for a street sign, he says, "Beamish Street." "Oh great, so where the fuck is Beamish Street?" says Big Steve. "Err, Newcastle?" chuckles Jock. "Hold on I've got a map," says Merrill, reaching to his back pocket. "Well that was fun weren't it!" snaps Colin, pulling up his 'Tonic' mohair trousers, "Look at these fucking bruises," he shouts in disgust. "Those cunts can't do that, they're the filth!" screams Lenny. "So what d'you want then? For them to nick us and miss the game?" says Jock, as he puts his hand on Lenny's shoulder. Lenny shrugs Jock off and starts to walk off, "I'd rather take the ten quid fine, thank you very much." "Oh what, and get a police record for the rest of your life," says Colin, "I'd rather take the beating, thank you very much."

"This church is St. Ann's," says Merrill, studying the map. We turn left and it will take us to City Road. We should be able to get cabs there." "No, but that was fucking out of order," Big Steve says to Jock. "We were just unlucky," cuts in Lenny, as he looks at Merrill, "So we still going in the Leazes even if Martin and the others ain't there," says Jock in defiant mood. "Too fucking true pal," replies Big Steve, "After that beating, I need to get me own back on some cunt before leaving this fucking dump." "Well then, let's get to the Leazes then!" snaps Big Steve.

The home of Newcastle United, sits just south of Saint James' Park from which it gets it name. The home end is a large covered terrace, which is probably the biggest end in England and gets its name from the access road of Leazes Terrace. There are small standing terraces that run down both sides of the pitch in front of the seated stands. At the south end of the ground, there is another large but open terrace; due to lack of away supporters at a lot of games, this is the end where the local Dockers gather.

"United! United!" roar the crowded Leazes end of Newcastle United, the feared home that has never been taken. The large stand is packed and few people notice the eight people moving slowly through the crowd near the front of the terrace. "Tommy must have got fed up waiting," says Big Steve, as he moves through the mass of Newcastle supporters. "Either that, or the filth moved them down the other end," replies Colin. Lenny looks down to the other end and smiles as The Shed sing,

"IN DUBLIN'S FAIR CITY,
WHERE THE GIRLS ARE SO PRETTY;
I FIRST SET MY EYES ON SWEET MOLLY MALONE,
AS SHE WHEELED HER WHEELBARROW;
THROUGH THE STREETS BROAD AND NARROW SINGING,
clap clap
clap clap clap
clap clap clap clap
CHELSEA!"

One of the Newcastle supporters looks at him with suspicion, not believing that any Chelsea would dare to walk into the hallowed ground of the Leazes. "I think we've been sussed," Jock says softly to Merrill, as he looks at the faces staring at them from the crowd. "They've noticed the clothes," replies Merrill. Overhearing them, Big Steve shouts "CHELSEA!" as he turns and punches out at the nearest Newcastle supporter. Lenny walks over to the Geordie who was watching him and head-butts him. A gap opens up around the North Stand firm as Newcastle supporters, taken by surprise, move back; the mass of Newcastle supporters further up the Leazes, see what is going on and start to move down towards the fighting. People start to fall against crush barriers and police standing near the corner flag, start to move along the side of the pitch towards the goal. Merrill, seeing a youth in a leather 'Rocker' jacket, ducks as the Geordie swings a wild punch; moving forward,
Merrill throws a punch that hits the 'Rocker' between the eyes, sending him to the floor. Jock side steps a number of kicks, then charges into the mass of bodies behind the goal. Lenny and Colin are forced by the weight of numbers, towards the small barrier that separates the terrace from the pitch. Jim, seeing that they are getting separated, shouts to Merrill, "Get back! We're going to get cut off!" Jock hears him and turns around to see that the masses of the Leazes

are bearing down on them from behind, "Down to the pitch!" he shouts to Merrill. Turning around, Merrill gets kicked in the leg but stays standing; seeing that things are hopeless, he nods at Jock and they move to the fence.

The police are waiting for them, and while being helped over the barrier, Jock shouts, "What you nicking us for, we didn't know this was the Leazes!" "Yeah, there's only eight of us for Christ sake!" exclaims Big Steve. "OK, OK," says the first policeman, we'll take you down to Chelsea end. Lenny looks disbelievingly at Colin, and smiles. "Bit stupid of you to get into this end wasn't it," the policeman says to Lenny, "This lot would have torn you to pieces." "Yes, thank you officer, we won't make that mistake again," says Big Steve, in a sarcastic voice. As they near the Chelsea end, a huge cheer goes up, and The Shed start to sing,
"WE TOOK THE LEAZES, WE TOOK THE LEAZES."

"Hark at theses fucking wankers," shouts Merrill, "They ain't even got the guts to go in there but take the credit anyway; besides going in an end ain't taking it, if you ain't got the numbers to stay in there." "Fuck 'em," snarls Lenny, pointing to the top of the steep away terrace, "Let's get up there." Climbing over the barrier into the terrace, they start to make their way up until they are near the scoreboard at the top.

"Fuck me!" exclaims Jim, "It's all fucking Dockers up here." "Not a problem," answers Jock, "They're OK." As they stand with their backs to the Dockers, Merrill rubs his right fist. "What's the problem?" asks Jock. "I hit some idiot between the eyes, and this fucking ring nearly broke me finger," replies Merrill. "I don't know why you wear that fucking thing at football," continues Jock, "You get that bloody skull and crossbones caught in someone's clothes, it'll rip your bleeding finger off." "Hello, there's Tommy, Dave, and Martin over there," says Lenny, pointing down the terrace. "Tommy!" shouts Big Steve, at the top of his voice. "Fuck Tommy," says Lenny, "Look at the Leazes!" Big Steve looks across the pitch to see a line of over one hundred Newcastle supporters moving out of the Leazes and along the side terrace. "They're coming for us," smiles Merrill. Turning to where Tommy and Dave are standing, he waves for them to move up the terrace to join them.

As Tommy and Dave's group rejoin the North Stand firm, Dave looks at the line of Newcastle supporters who are now moving past the halfway line. "Sorry for not waiting outside," says Tommy, as he reaches Jock and Merrill, "The police sussed we were Chelsea and marched us down here." "Not a problem," replies Jock. "Jesus! You look like you took a right beating over there," gasps Dave, looking at Big Steve and Colin. "That lot didn't happen on the Leazes," replies Big Steve, "That was the fucking filth." "What in those vans?" says an astonished Dave, "I thought they were just nicking you for the fight at the station." "No," says Merrill, turning to look at Dave, "Get your boys behind us, the Leazes are almost here." Dave waves to his group and moves behind, in among the Dockers. Tommy also moves in with Dave, and as he walks past Merrill, Jock turns and says to him, "Don't do anything 'till we do."

"Here look," laughs Lenny, pointing down the terrace, "The Shed are getting nervous." A silence descends on the away end as the line of over one hundred Geordies move along the walkway, halfway up the terrace. Then a Geordie in a leather 'Rocker' jacket stops and looks up to the top of the terrace. Turning his head and saying something to those behind him, he starts to walk up the terrace towards the North Stand firm. Jock looks at Merrill and smiles as he recognises the youth. As the youth stops in front of Merrill, he recognises him straight away as he has a red wield of a skull and crossbones reddening between his eyes. Merrill stares at him as he raises his right hand and starts to scratch his nose. The youth sees the skull and crossbones ring and looks Merrill in the eyes. Everyone on the terrace watches in silence as the two stand nose to nose. Then the silence is broken as the Geordie turns, and says, "It's not him!"

As the group from the Leazes start their trek back, one of the Dockers taps Jock on the shoulder. "You should have had that little 'Gob Shite'. We'd have helped yer." Jock looks around in astonishment, "You're fucking kidding ain't yer?" he replies. "Nay lad, we hate the little buggers," answers the Docker. "Bloody hell," gasps Merrill, "Now yer tell us." "Never mind," says Lenny with a broad smile, "You know what this means?" pointing to the departing Leazes. Merrill thinks for a moment, and then says, "No, tell me, what does it mean?" "Well!" exclaims Lenny, "We did the Leazes." "What you on about, laughs Martin, "They beat you black and blue." "True, but at least we went in there; plus that's the hardest end in England, they're like Millwall, only there's ten times as many of the buggers," exclaims Ghost, "But now they know that Southerners are all softies!"

CHAPTER THREE

"I couldn't give a fuck what people think; I don't live for the past like you. I'm far too busy making money out here to be bothered by all that crap. Besides, I wasn't around when the weapons were being used; they were the people that came after me," replies Alan, shaking his head in disbelief. "Above all, what really gets to me about your past is how utterly un-remorseful you are about it," says Kev, as he leans back in his seat watching Maureen walk over to the window and draw back the blinds that keep the early morning California sun from shining on the TV screen.//Walking back to the bar, she looks over and smiles. Kev turns back to the table, raising his eyebrows, "So you'd say that you were saints in those days, and it was the people that copied you that did the damage?" Kev replies, with a stern look on his face, "Don't you have any guilt?"

Alan thinks a moment, and then looks across to Kev, "So you would condemn anyone who in his or her youth went nicking apples, for instance, and hold it against them for the rest of their lives?" "Fair enough, if Merrill is a reformed person today, that's well and dandy," replies Kev, clearly annoyed that no remorse is forthcoming, "You'd have thought a person with your criminal record would want to steer clear of further brushes with the law."   "In my day, the attendance figures were higher than they are today," says Alan, "As for getting England banned, well that was the fault of the media. They're the ones that blew the whole thing up in the first place. They alight on a sub-culture just to sell more newspapers, then all the idiots that think that they're being big boys, come and jump on the bandwagon. One little punch-up is magnified a million times, splashed across the front pages and becomes the main item on the TV news." "What the fuck do you expect?" says Steve Diamond, "There's more trouble in Holland, Turkey and Germany right now than there ever was in England, but we still get the blame. Meanwhile other countries hypocritically point their fingers at us while washing their hands of their own problems."

Dave looks up as Maureen walks from behind the bar, carrying a tray full of drinks, "So now you're saying that anyone that went to Chelsea games in the seventies is a criminal?" Alan, sticking his hand up and looking at Dave says, "Hold on, this is directed at me." He waits for Maureen to hand out the drinks and walk back to the bar, *"Like I said I'm not ashamed of what I did, they were some of the greatest days of my life pal!"*

"But you clearly still get a buzz out of reliving it," snaps an increasingly agitated Kev.

THE IFIELD

Wednesday January 13th. 1970

The Carnaby Market is on Beak Street, opposite its more famous namesake, Carnaby Street. It is in fact a mini Carnaby Street under one roof, for its two floors are full of fashion, jewellery, and shoe shops, as well as a couple of record stalls. Veronica Casey, Jock's girlfriend, looks back and waves goodnight to her manageress, then walks up the circular staircase to the street level. Keeping an eye on the large window that overlooks Beak Street, she stops at the fashion boutique by the double front doors to look at the latest spring fashions. A quiet 5' 3" ash blonde, 20 year-old shop assistant, from Potters Bar, wearing a white mini dress with an open long collarless blue jacket, is a naturally shy girl and keeps herself to herself. As a result, she watches Chelsea's home games from the stands; whilst being friends with Debbie, she finds her intimidating, and avoids her at games.

As she stops to look at a rack full of the new long floral print skirts, a large green American car catches her eye, through the large windows as it pulls up outside. Taking a look at the price tag of one of the dresses, she thinks about buying it, but pressing her lips together in thought, she decides to leave it for another day. Walking towards the double doors, she glances back for a last look at the dress, and then walks out onto the pavement and smiles as she sees Jock sitting in the passenger seat of the waiting car. Looking more like a boat, the long green 1960 Chevrolet Impala convertible, is equipped with something that British cars have yet to discover; an air conditioning unit as standard, for the white canvas roof does little to keep out the cold of a London winter.

Veronica stops by the front of the car, and shakes her head at the over the top chrome and four headlights; looking up she sees Jock getting out of the far side front and walk around the back past the oversized butterfly wings of the boot. Stopping by the rear passenger door, he opens it and looks at Veronica with a decidedly lustful glare. "Good day at the office?" he jokes as she parks her well-rounded bottom on the plush leather rear seat. Looking up, Veronica sees that Jock's eyes are totally fixed on her exposed thighs as she lifts them up to swing them into the interior of the Impala.

42

"I've seen a really nice skirt for the spring!" she smiles, as she shimmies across the back seat. As she does, she notices that Merrill is watching her every move in the driver's rear view mirror. "Had a good look then, have we?" she snaps, as she realises that he has just witnessed a flash of her white knickers. "Hey take it easy!" laughs Jock, as he climbs into the back seat, "It's the first time he's ever seen that far up a girls skirt." "So what's the skirt like then?" enquires Merrill, as he puts the automatic gearbox into drive. Veronica throws an annoyed look at him, and says, "It's one of those long floral print numbers." "Ha ha," laughs Jock, "That'll stop all those Saxon perverts from looking up girls skirts." "Bloody hell!" mocks Merrill, "So it's back to looking up your bleeding trouser leg then."

Veronica glances around the interior of the Impala, then looking at Merrill, asks, "So what happened to the mini-van then? Did you sell it?" "Oh I forgot you haven't seen this one before have yer?" replies Merrill, "No, I use that for going to games when not using the train, and for shopping, I've had this a few years, but I'm thinking of trading it in for a Mustang. "Glancing into the rear view mirror, Merrill sees Veronica shaking her head in disgust, then turning into Regents Street, he continues, "So you two want dropping of at your favourite hotel, after the pub?" Jock throws a hopeful glance at Veronica, who smiles as she nods her head. "Turn the bloody radio on then!" says Jock, as he snuggles up to Veronica and slides his arm around her. Merrill leans forward and turns on the radio, then glancing in the rear view mirror, smiles to himself as he sees Jock's hand slide from Veronica's shoulder onto her right breast. "Oh, I love this one," exclaims Veronica, as the Archies "Sugar, Sugar," blasts out of the car's radio. "How can you like this bubblegum rubbish," teases Jock, "It ain't even a proper group." "Wrong!" shouts Merrill, as he drives into Piccadilly Circus, "It may be a cartoon, but it's a studio group, with some of the best session singers out of the Brill Building." Raising his eyebrows in surprise, Jock shouts back, "Alright smart arse, fucking name them, then!" as he smugly gives Veronica's right breast a gentle squeeze. "Right then," replies Merrill, as a broad grin creeps across his face, "The lead singer is Ron Dante, who is also The Cuff Links, then there's Ellie Greenwich, Toni Wine, Andy Kim, and Tony Passalacqua." "Bollocks!" laughs Jock, "Tony bleeding what? Never heard of any of them." "He was the lead singer of the Fascinators, who sang "Oh Rose Marie, in the early sixties," retorted Merrill. "I've heard of Ellie Greenwich," says Veronica triumphantly, "She was one of Phil Spector's songwriters." "Smart Arse," says Jock realising his wind up isn't working, "Right James, take us to the Ifield."

"Your friends in Soho still giving back handers to the filth in West End Central?" he asks softly." as they drive down Regent

Street, "You pay the police?" inquires Veronica, who has been keeping both ears open. Merrill turns back and glances at her, then turning forward again, he reassures her, "Yeah nothing wrong with that. Those I work with keep the streets quiet so they can run the gambling and sex shops, that way the filth don't disturb them and everyone's happy. They just sweeten the pie with a pay off, nothing wrong with that, it's just good business sense."   Veronica shakes her head in disbelief "They can't afford not to my dear, or we'll fucking grass the bastards up for being on the take," Merrill glances back at Jock, and they both laugh out loud at the top of their voices.

Jock smiles to himself, looks at Veronica, then leans forward and says, "Tell her about your mate." Merrill frowns in thought, then looks into the rear view mirror, and says, "Who's that then?" Jock looks out of the side window and watches Harrods go by, then says, "The nutter, what's his name?" he asks. Merrill smiles as he realises just who Jock is on about, "Oh Pat O'Shea?" "Yeah that's the one," Jock replies, then turning to Veronica he says, "Listen to this, it's a killer!" Veronica then looks at Merrill in wonderment, "Go on then, I'm all ears," she says nonchalantly.

Merrill stops at a set of traffic lights and turns around to look at Jock with raised eyebrows. Then turning back and seeing the lights go green, he lets off the footbrake and glides forward. "Well, Pat is a copper at West End Central, and one day he was in Wimpole Street, with a new bobbie, when they see some bird on the roof of one of the buildings, so he sends the Bobbie up to talk her down, while he clears the street. So after half an hour, he's getting fed up, as they are at the end of their shift, so he goes up onto the roof." "So who was looking after the crowd?" asks Veronica. "I don't know. By that time I suppose more coppers had arrived," he replies, annoyed at the interruption, "So Pat gets to the roof and walks over to the girl, who is standing on the ledge holding on to a metal railing, "I', he says to her, we finished our shift ten minutes ago, and I'm going out tonight, so make your fucking mind up. Either get of the ledge, or stop wasting our bloody time and jump."   "You're kidding," says Veronica, who looks at Jock, only to be greeted by a nodding head, "So what happened?" "Well this bird just looks at Pat with a glare, then turns and jumps," replies Merrill. Veronica throws her hands up to her mouth, in shock, "Oh my God!"

Jock throws his head back, laughing out loud, and Veronica turns and slaps him on the arm. "Then there was the time that he was watching a drug dealer," continues Merrill, "He was waiting outside the guy's house in Mayfair, but hadn't seen him for two weeks. Then on the last day, before they gave up on him, the geezer turns up, so Pat, and a number of detectives, rush into the house and nick him."

"So what's so funny about that?" queries a blank looking Veronica. Jock smiles and says, "Hold on girl, he ain't finished yet." "Well," continues Merrill, "they search the house and come up empty handed, so Pat says strip search him." "Are they aloud to do that?" asks Veronica looking worried. "Fuck knows," replies Merrill, "but they stripped him naked and stood him up against the wall of his front room. But they still come up empty handed, then Pat sees a piece of thread hanging down out of his arse." Veronica screws her face up in disgust. Merrill glances into the rear view mirror and smiles when he sees her face, "So Pat shouts out, 'There, he's got them up his arse', and runs forward grabbing the thread and yanks it out." Veronica winches at the thought, and huddles into Jock closer. "Well the geezer lets out a horrific scream, and starts to climb the wall, with blood streaming out of his arse." Merrill glances again into the mirror, and laughs seeing Veronica snuggling into Jock in horror, "Well it turns out the geezer wasn't smuggling drugs, he'd been in hospital having a piles operation, and the thread was his stitches."

The Ifield Pub is on the corner of Finborough Road and Ifield Road, just off the Fulham Road, near Stamford Bridge. The Saloon Bar door is in Ifield Road and leads you into a long and plush cosy bar, often used by a number of the Chelsea team after home games. Tables and chairs sit beside a deep pile carpet, leading all the way up to a slightly raised area, which has deep padded sofas lining the wall. It is on one of these sofas that a number of Chelsea supporters are sitting, enjoying an after work drink.

"Ha, that reminds me of that all time classic," laughs Spider. "Oh, here we go again," sighs Big Steve, picking up his drink. "Why is the word 'lisp' used?" asks Spider, with a broad grin, "When those that have it can't fucking say it?" Sandy White is the only one that laughs, as the others have heard it a million times before. She stops short and looks around, "Well I thought it was funny!" "So why is it that when you scream in a library," says Big Steve in a silly mood, "Do people stare at you?" Then looking around to make sure he's got everyone's attention, he continues, "But when you scream in a plane the same people all join in?" "Ha, ha," laughs Spider, "Talking about planes, you have an airport building full of scared people, and you call it a terminal?" "Gawd, you two are pathetic," says a smiling Sandy, shaking her head in mock disgust. "Yeah," continues Big Steve, looking at Sandy, "It's like Americans throw rice at weddings, so why don't the Chinese throw burgers?" "Is a slug an evicted snail?" cuts in Little John, who then hides his head in his pint.

Everyone stops and looks at Little John, whose eyes are flashing back and forth, over the top of his beer glass. Putting it back on the table, he smiles and says, "So why don't those with photographic memories, have negative thoughts?" The front door opens, and all heads at the table look up and see Colin, Jim and Ghost walk in and stroll over to the bar. Colin sees the group at the far table and waves a welcome, "Usual?" he shouts. A big cheer goes up from the table, "Hello," exclaims Big Steve, "Jim must have done another office." Sandy looks at him with a blank expression, "What'd mean?" "You mean you haven't heard about the Ghost?" says Little John, in surprise.

Sandy looks across to the bar where Colin is buying a round, "No, I hardly know him." "Well if you're sitting comfortably," mocks Little John, "He walks into office blocks, and dips all the coats, and has been known to get into any desk, even locked ones." Sandy not taking her eyes of Jim sighs, "You're fucking kidding, he's a bleeding tea leaf?" "Yeah, and never been caught, that's why we call him the Ghost," replies Little John, "Anyway, here he comes so keep quiet."Colin puts the tray he's carrying on the table and starts to hand out drinks, as Jim looks at the empty table next to them and pulls it over, then turns to get a couple of spare chairs. "So where you been?" queries Big Steve, as he raises his glass in thanks.

Ghost sits down and casually says, "Oh we've just been having a look around the Chelsea Drug Store." "Oh!" says an angry Steve, "And I suppose you walked past the 'Six Bells', looking for queers again." "Fucking perverts!" sneers Jim, as he picks up his drink. Big Steve flashes him a look of disgust, "So what the fuck have they ever done to you?" "They'll never get the fucking chance, pal!" says Ghost as he puts his glass down. "So what the fuck you defending that slime for anyway, thinking of becoming one?" Ghost sits back in his chair with a broad grin. Little John leans forward, putting his hand in the air to stop Big Steve, "You're fucking sick in the head pal," he sneers, "I wouldn't do what they do to each other to a woman, but that don't mean I have to have it down on them." Ghost, starting to get defensive, looks around the table, then to Colin for support. "Don't bring me into it pal!" Colin snaps. "Well it ain't fucking normal, is it!" Ghost pleads. "No, you're the one that ain't normal," says Big Steve looking around the table, "They do say that those that shout loudest against queers, are scared stiff that they might turn into one." "Ha, ha," laughs Spider, as he leans back in his chair, "Going to be a shit shoveller then, are we?" "Bollocks!" snaps Ghost, "I'm going to the bog."

"Right, who's got a sixpenny bit?" says Sandy, changing the subject, before it gets out of hand. Steve reaches for an empty glass as he watches Jim walk towards the toilet. "Pass a tissue then," he asks Colin. Colin picks up one of the tissues from the holder on his table and hands it to Steve, who after running his finger around the top of the glass to take away any excess beer, spreads the tissue across the top. "Ten bob a shot then?" queries Spider, pulling a ten-shilling note from his wallet. "Sounds good to me," replies Big Steve.

The Chevrolet Impala glides up the Finborough Road and turns left at the Ifield Road. "Far Out!" exclaims Merrill, as he sees ample space to park. "How long are we going to be staying here for then?" asks Veronica, looking at the Ifield. "Thinking of that hotel room are we?" taunts Merrill, turning his head to reverse park. Veronica doesn't qualify the remark with an answer. "Now, now you two behave yourself," mocks Jock with a smile. Merrill pulls on the handbrake, and opens the driver's door, "It depends on whether you want to stay and get a lift when we've finish, or leave early and get a cab." "We'll get a cab, thank you very much," snaps Veronica, as she gets out of the car. Jock walks around to the pavement, looks at Merrill and shrugs his shoulders. Merrill gives a knowing smile, and they walk to the front door of the Ifield. "I hear you're going out with Linda!" says Veronica walking through the door, "Taking a risk there aren't you?" "Why? Want to make it a threesome?" jokes Merrill. "No thanks! I'm happy with what I got," she replies looking at Jock. "I wouldn't say no pal," jokes Jock with a sarcastic grim. "No you bloody well don't," snaps an angry Veronica. Merrill and Jock look at each other and burst out laughing. "Linda's OK, as long as you know how to handle her," says Merrill, as he walks to the bar.

"Oh really," replies Veronica, "And you're an expert on handling women are you?" Merrill leans on the bar and turns his head to look at Veronica, "Put it this way," he says slowly and deliberately, "The woman is a control freak, who, if she doesn't get her own way, (she) throws a tantrum. You just have to let her think that she's getting her own way." "Oh I see," replies Veronica, "So what you're saying is that you manipulate women to get your own way?" Merrill turns to Jock, and they both raise their eyebrows. "Linda takes cocaine, and that makes here very paranoiac. She has to be in control, or she throws a wobbly," says Merrill, "I hate drugs and everything to do with them. They change people's personalities, and it's always the weak who can't face the realities of life that run away and hide in drugs." "So you admit that you're just using her then! Wow that makes you a really big person then doesn't it."

Merrill orders the drinks and watches the barman pour a bottle of Newcastle Brown into a glass; turning back to Veronica, he says, "No, I try and help people like that face up to the reality of what they're doing to themselves." He takes the glass of Newcastle Brown from the barman and hands it to Jock. "I see, so now you're just a Good Samaritan?" Veronica says sarcastically. "No, she's just bloody good shag!" exclaims Merrill, with a knowing wink to Jock. You disgust me," says Veronica as she turns away. "So tell me!" says Merrill, "Do you take drugs?" Veronica steps back in mock shock,

"Do I look like someone who can't handle the reality of life?" "No, I think that you have a very strong personality and don't need to hide away in drugs, but some people feel that they're weak and need too," says Merrill who turns to the barman as he hands him a vodka and tonic.

Taking the drink from Merrill, Veronica takes a sip then says, "I'm surprised that someone like you would even think about someone else's welfare." "I like the woman, as a friend, but that's as far as it goes," says Merrill, as he takes his glass of Pepsi, "I don't think she has the personality to face up to herself and is in a downward spiral, into a sad and lonely life." "This is boring, let's go and join the others," says Jock, as he starts to walk towards the rear of the pub. "So what do you think will happen to her then?" says Veronica, giving Jock a dirty look, but nevertheless turning and following him. "I don't know," replies Merrill, "But woe betides anyone that doesn't understand her head and just tries to use her for quick shag." Veronica turns her head back to Merrill, and asks, "Isn't she the one that has gone through half the team?" Merrill smiles and shrugs his shoulders, "I wouldn't know, I don't go around talking about things like that, someone's sex life is their affair and fuck all to do with anyone else." "Hmm, maybe there's hope for you yet," says Veronica with smile.

Sandy takes a draw of her cigarette, and holding it with her right hand, gently blows on the tip until all the dead ash has fallen off. Then slowly, she brings it down onto the tissue covering the beer glass; at the first sign of a red glow on the tissue, she pulls it back. "Shit!" exclaims Jim, as he looks at the sixpence slowly swinging on the three thin strings of tissue stretched across the top of the glass. "Your go Big Steve," she says with beaming smile, thankful that the sixpence didn't drop to the bottom of the beer glass. "Fuck sake you jammy cow!" smiles Big Steve as he blows the tip of his cigarette. Leaning over the glass, he carefully studies the thin threads of tissue, looking for somewhere to burn without the sixpence falling, then having made his decision he slowly brings his cigarette tip to the edge of one of the threads, "Shit!" he screams, as the sixpence drops to the bottom of the glass, with a ting. "Ten bob pal," says a triumphant Big Steve, leaning back and laughing his head off. Jim raises his eyebrows in resignation of his defeat and pulls out two ten shilling notes, throwing one to Big Steve, and the other one to Sandy.

"Hello, where's the camouflage jacket then?" says Sandy looking up and seeing Merrill walking towards her, in a long black leather coat. "I only wear that for games," he replies, "don't want to get me decent schmutter ruined do I?" "Flash cunt," laughs Spider, as he puts another tissue over the beer glass. Merrill takes his coat off, and pulls an empty chair over and lays it on the seat, and then pulling over another he sits down. Sandy looks at the black tennis shirt, and asks, "What's the pirate badge?" Merrill looks down at the emblem on his chest, and replies, "That's the Oakland Raiders, the American Football team I go over to watch." "You fly all the way to America to watch a bunch of fucking Septics play football?" says an astonished Sandy "Yeah, but it's not football as you know it," replies Merrill, "It's more like rugby with a forward pass." "And the pussies wear padding," cuts in Big Steve. "They also wear helmets," continues Merrill, "but it's more like battle chess, than rugby, as you can block anyone, whether he's got the ball or not." "So what's happening Saturday?" cuts in Little John, "You phoned that prat, Archer yet?"

"Jock, pass me coat," says Merrill, pointing to the chair where his coat lies. "Archer? He's that Arsenal wanker ain't it?" inquires Sandy. "Yeah," says Jock, as he stretches over and picks up Merrill's coat. Sandy looks at Merrill, not understanding the need to call an Arsenal supporter, "So what you phoning him for Alan?" Merrill takes his coat from Jock and turns to Sandy as he takes a small black book out of his coat pocket, "To arrange the off on Saturday." "You mean you're going to arrange a fight?" says Sandy still looking puzzled, "So what happened to just turning up and taking the North Bank? What needs arranging about that?"

Merrill gets up, and putting his coat back on the chair, he turns to Little John, Explain to her how we work. I'm going into the public bar to use the phone." Little John nods and turns to Sandy. Taking a cigarette out, he puts it between his lips and lights it. Blowing the smoke out, he looks at Sandy, and says, "This ain't about having them at Highbury, this is to arrange at ruk, at Kings Cross, before the game." Sandy sits there fascinated; this is the first time she has become aware of any pre-arranged fights. "So how do you get the numbers of other crews then?" Little John smiles to himself, then continues, "We meet crews from all over when we go to England away games." "Shit!" exclaims Sandy, "I suppose you lot are going to Mexico for the World Cup then?" "Merrill and Jock are. The rest of us ain't got that sort of money, but there'll be loads going from clubs all over the country," replies Little John.

"But don't you get trouble with other crews at England games?" Sandy asks. "Asking a lot of questions ain't yer!" interrupts Big Steve. Sandy raises her eyebrows and turns to Big Steve with raised eyebrows, "What's your problem then? "My problem little girl, is that we've had problems with the filth at away games," replies Big Steve forcibly. "Meaning what?" demands Sandy.

"Oi! Cut it out you two!" shouts Merrill, as he walks back to the tables. "I don't like people that get too nosy," replies Big Steve in his defence. "Nosy about what?" Merrill asks as he puts the black book back into his coat pocket. "Relax," says Jock, who has been sitting listening, "This is the first time she's been with us for a drink, besides she's just a nosy cow by nature." He laughs trying to defuse then tension. "OK, OK," replies Big Steve, "But you can never be too careful." Sandy throws him a look and says, "Well thanks pal, nice to know I'm trusted." Yeah right!" snaps Big Steve, who picks up his beer and starts drinking. "So what's happening then?" asks Colin.

Merrill sits down, picks up his Pepsi and drinks, while watching the eager faces of those around him. He slowly puts the glass down, enjoying his moment of suspension, "One o'clock at Kings Cross, he reckons they'll have around fifty," says Merrill at long last. "Far out!" exclaims Big Steve.

"So are Tommy and Dave coming down for this one?" enquires Jim, who has been keeping a low profile. Merrill raising his eyebrows, turns to Jock. "Well?" Jock nods as he looks at Jim, "Yeah, they're bringing their full crews with them." "Too much!" exclaims Colin, "Should be a good day out." Veronica, who has been sitting in the corner and getting progressively more bored by the minute, looks at her watch, and turns to Jock, "Can we go now?" "Hello," says Spider with a laugh, "I think someone's feeling randy." Everyone at the table starts laughing, and Veronica stands up and puts her coat on, demonstrating that she is not happy. "Hmm, looks like I'm on a promise," says beaming Jock. "Go for it my son!" says Big Steve giving a knowing wink. Veronica and Jock walk down the saloon bar of the Ifield, watched by the two tables at the back, when Little John starts singing "WE KNOW WHAT YOU'RE DOING."

Spider starts laughing as Veronica turns her head back with a look that could kill. Seeing this, Little John joins in the song. //Jock then turns his head to look back, but Veronica, seeing the beaming smile, elbows him in the ribs. At this everyone stands up and joins in the song. As they go through the door, Sandy sits down and looking at the laughing faces, she says, "You lot are bloody wicked." "What'd yeah mean?" mocks Colin, picking up his drink. "Well she's got the right hump now," she replies, shaking her head. Spider looks at Little John and winks, then turns to Sandy, and says, "No darling, the humping comes later." Before Sandy can reply, the rest of them fall about laughing.

"Oh no, not a fucking Zulu!" exclaims Ghost, looking at the street door. Sandy looks up and sees a black man walk over to the bar, "That's out of order mate;" he snaps. Ghost flashes a glare at Sandy, and says, "Trust you to defend them." "So tell me?" asks Merrill, "Is there anyone you like?" "Yeah leave it out pal, you know nothing about him," adds Little John. "Oh right! We just sit back and let all the foreigners overrun us then?" says Colin, who turns and smiles at Ghost. "Oh for fuck sake grow up!" shouts Steve, who is starting to get annoyed. "The National Front will sort them out," snaps Ghost, grinning at Colin. "Bollocks!" exclaims Merrill, "The National Front are there for their own power trip and couldn't give a fuck about the likes of you."Ghost stops grinning and looks at Merrill, "What you on about?" he says with a puzzled look. "Well any political party that only has one policy, is a total waste of time," replies Merrill.

"The National Front are going to keep this country white pal, and they have more than one policy;" says Colin lighting up a cigarette. "OK, name one!" says Merrill glaring at Colin. Colin sits and thinks a moment, and then looking to Ghost for support, he sees that Jim is also drawing a blank to that question. He then turns to Merrill and shrugs his shoulders. "The National Front will never get any credibility in this country, 'cos their only policy is unworkable," says Merrill slowly. Jim looks at him a moment, then asks, "So how do you work that one out?" "Merrill smiles to himself, then leaning forward to enforce his point slowly says, "Well let's take this one thousand pound repatriation deal." Jim nods as he draws on his cigarette. "Well OK, here you are at Dover, with all the Blacks neatly lined up waiting to get on a boat out of the country," says Merrill, "And there you are sitting at the table, with thousand pound bundles in front of you." "Fuck that!" laughs Spider, "Ghost would fucking nick the money." Everyone including Ghost laughs.

Merrill waits for the laughter to die down, then continues, "Say the first one hundred quietly take the money and get on the boat. Then the next guy walks up to the table, but he says he ain't taking the money, 'cos he ain't going," Merrill looks at Jim in the eyes, "So what are you going to do? And remember you have a thousand Blacks standing in line behind him, all waiting to see what you're going to do." He leans back in his chair, and then slowly says, "So tell me what are you going to do to make this geezer get on the boat, for if he doesn't, then you fail."Ghost sits in thought, and then dogs his cigarette in the ashtray to disguise the fact that he's having trouble finding an answer.   Merrill, seeing that Ghost is lost for words, leans forward himself, then says, "There is only one answer to that question, so why are you having so much trouble in saying it." Sandy, looking around the table, and feeling uneasy at the tension, says, "I think this is starting to get out of hand. Can we change the subject!"

Merrill raises his right hand to stop any reply to Sandy, then still looking at Jim says, "I'll tell you the only answer," he then looks around the table at the silent faces, "You fucking kill him, otherwise the rest of them won't go." Then leaning back in his chair he says, "And that's why the National Front is a load of bollocks, you can't do that anymore, the Austrian Corporal showed that." Little John smiles and says, "You say you only want whites in this country, so you don't mind if a million French come over here, and demand that we change to a French culture then?"

Big Steve who has kept out of the conversation so far then says, "That's why I don't like all these foreigners coming over here. It ain't the colour, is it? It's the fact that they will all want their own fucking culture." Colin looks at Big Steve and nods, "Yeah put that way, I agree. No one forces anyone to come here, but if they do then they have to respect our culture." "Why?" asks Jim. "Oh fuck off pal," snaps Big Steve, if they liked their culture so much, why the fuck are they coming here?" "That's not the point," replies Ghost. "Yes it is," says Little John, "I don't mind people coming here, but they have to respect our culture and our way of life." Steve gives Little John a surprised look, and then looks over to Merrill for support.

"Sorry pal," says Merrill in reply, "As far as I'm concerned, anyone can come here as long as they come here with the intention of obeying our laws and customs, integrating and and contributing to the welfare of society, on one proviso!" "Yeah what's that then?" snaps Jim. "That we actually needed them here. At the moment over one hundred million people with British subject passports can turn up in Dover, and we can't do anything about it. We should have a government that says to the Commonwealth, you fought against us for independence, well now you have it, so we're voiding all British subject passports."

"Oh! So you wouldn't kill them, because they shouldn't have been here in the first place!" exclaims Jim, "So what would you do if they didn't?" "I'd legally deport them," replies Merrill, "You know Israel has the best answer to immigration." "It does?" says a shocked Big Steve. Merrill looks at him and smiles, remembering their talk about Jews, "They have settlement camps that all incoming immigrants have to live in until they learn to read and write Hebrew, and learn Israeli culture." Ghost looks at him with a puzzled look, "I never knew that!" Then, thinking a moment, he continues, "That would be a great idea, but I can't see the left wing or Liberals over here agreeing to that."

"Ah!" exclaims Colin, "I thought you were a lefty?" Steve smiles and shakes his head, "No mate, I'm just someone that doesn't like people picking on others for no good fucking reason." Merrill laughs, and says, "I'll remind you of that next time we play Tottenham." "Bollocks," Steve grins, "That's different, that's tribal." "Don't forget what's going on in Uganda right now, we could have thousands of fucking Pakis flooding in here." Say Jim. "What the fuck you on about?" says a surprised Sandy. "There are stories in the papers that Uganda wants to throw out all the Pakis, and as they are all UK subjects," reminds Jim, "That means they will all come here demanding houses and jobs."

"We need a strong right wing government," says Merrill, "One that don't take shit from no-one, but one that does it within the law of the land." Meaning what?" asks Little John. "Well for a start, there are three things that are the corner stone of every country.. First is security, that means a strong Army & Police force. Second a strong Health Service. And Third, a strong Education system, that trains people for Medical, Science, and Industry, making sure that our youth leaves school with full command of written and spoken English, and strong in Maths. A proper Education, not the sham we have at the moment. That way we won't need to import so many people to fill jobs that our own people are uneducated to do. I'd reintroduce National Service. Most of the foreign scum will fuck off straight way with that." "But that means we'd be called up," says Little John. "So what, you like a good fight, that will teach you how to do it proper" cuts in Big Steve. "Then," continues Merrill, "We pull out of the United Nations, and NATO, stop trying to get into the Common Market, and become a neutral country. One that is Independent, so will Scotland, Wales and Ulster" have their independence, but under a Federal Britain, who's Parliament will be in London, but the English Parliament will be at the seat of the original Saxon Parliament at Winchester."

He looks at the surprised faces, and then continues, "Then re-introduce the death penalty for illegal entry into the country, and also for murder and first degree rape." Hold on a minute Pal," screams Jim, "That's going a bit too far." Merrill turns to him and says slowly, "I'm not talking about date rape, where a slag gets a guilty conscience the next day, I'm talking about when if you ever have a daughter, and she's walking home, and some animal she's never seen, drags her into a back ally and rapes her. Those sick cunts have no right to life." "Too fucking true," agrees Sandy. "That's rich, coming from someone that spends half her life lying on here back with her legs in the air," taunts Jim. "You're just jealous that you can't get any," snaps Sandy.

"I'm starting to like this idea. So who else we going to hang then?" says Colin. "Anyone that kills while driving drunk," replies Merrill. "Now hold on, that's going too fucking far!" snaps Little John. Ignoring him, Merrell continues, "I'd also top any and all IRA gunmen, I'd also take off the kid gloves the army are wearing over there - the fucking IRA wants a war, then give them one." "Yeah, like shoot all known gunmen, by turning up at their front door at midnight, and then throwing their slag families across the border into the Free State." says Jim. "I'd also build a Berlin Wall along the border. I mean those Free State Pope arse lickers wanted out, so let's keep them out." agrees Colin. "So you have a military state then?" say a surprised Big Steve. "Only 'till we got our own house in order and put the welfare of our own people first," replies Merrill, "Then things would return to normal. "Talking about normal, what time we meeting for the Arse game?" asks Big Steve.

CHAPTER FOUR

"Guilt!" exclaims Alan, as he sits back in his seat, looks at Kev, then after a short pause asks, "You ever been in the army?" "Yes, I was in the Falklands," replied Kevin Darcy, with a puzzled look on his face, "But what has that got to do with football hooligans?"

Alan leans forward and starts to smile, "So tell me, how many people did you kill?"

"WHAT?" shouts Kev, as he frowns in disbelief, "You have the audacity to accuse me?" he grits his teeth in anger, "That was a War! I fought for my country, and I'm proud of it."

Alan takes a sip of his Miller, and then fixing a stare on Kev, he says. "That's my point. You sit there in your arrogance, with blood on your hands, and accuse me. When your world goes to war, millions are killed, when my world goes to war no-one gets killed. Chelsea is our tribe, our world, just as England was for you. You think nothing of blowing someone's brains out, then sit there and tell me I'm the fucking monster!"

"Oh yes, you're so innocent, 'no people were killed' by what you did. What about Heysel then, don't tell me that Chelsea weren't there?" Kev says, as he sits back with the smile on his face, of a man who's just laid down a 'full house'.

"What happened at Heysel wasn't by design. It was a tragic accident, brought about largely by letting supporters of both teams into the Natural zone, where supporters from other teams were, and by incompetent policing. No-one set out to kill anybody there. Anyway, all we got in my day were a few bruises, and maybe the odd broken bone," retorts Alan.

"That was then, this is now," points out Jock, "And if you don't have the intelligence to understand the difference, that's your problem." Kev throws an angry look across to the Chelsea supporters, "Oh, I suppose that makes all the difference! Excuse me, for being so bloody dim, you created mayhem and just blow it off as meaningless."

ARSENAL AWAY

Saturday January 17th, 1970, Arsenal 3 - 0 Chelsea

"I reckon this is gonna be our year," says Jim, looking up from the Evening News Racing edition. "Oh, so we beat the Brummies and you reckon we're gonna win the Cup?" chuckles Lenny, as he stands holding the hanging tube strap. "What if we meet Carlisle again?" queries Colin. "We only lost one-nil away," Jim reassures himself. "Far out man!" exclaims Big Steve, "So winning three-nil, means we can beat fucking Leeds then?" "This is gonna be our year, just you mark my words," says Jim confidently. "But Leeds have done the double over us already!" interrupts Colin. "You're forgetting something pal!" continues Jim. Colin looks across the tube compartment at Jim, slowly squints, and asks, "So what's that then?" "We fucking beat Leeds in the League Cup before we lost to Carlisle," replies Jim. "And we've never lost to Leeds in any Cup game Ever!"

"Fuck me!" exclaims an astonished Jim, as he looks through the race card of the Evening News. "What's up? Lost a pound and won a penny!" laughs Colin. Jim turns and mocks a glare at Colin, "No, here look, there's a horse call Big Dick, running today." Jim holds the paper up so that everyone can see the horse's name, when Big Steve shouts out, "Put everything you've got on it." Jim frowns in puzzlement as he looks over to Big Steve, and queries, "Why?" Big Steve looks at Jim and laughs, "Because it'll win by a length."

"We're coming into Edgware Road, keep an eye out for the others," warns Colin as he walks towards the tube doors. "And if they ain't here yet?" asks Jim. "Then you'll have to give up your seat, old son!" snaps Big Steve. Jim folds up his Evening News and cranes his neck to look towards the platform of Edgware Road station. "Looks like the Wimbledon train has just pulled in," says Big Steve, as he sees that the train sitting on the other side of the platform has just opened its doors. Being the terminal for the Wimbledon line, the six-carriage train disgorges its entire content of passengers. "There they are!" shouts Lenny Blake, pointing to the rear carriage of the Wimbledon train. All eyes strain to catch a familiar face, as the Circle Line train slows to a stop.

"Got them!" cries Colin, "Big Steve jump out and call them." Big Steve turning to Colin, and says with raised eyebrows, "Don't mind if I wait for the train to stop, do you?" As the doors open, Big Steve steps out and looks down the platform, trying to see through the bodies of the passengers that are now getting off and those boarding the Circle Line train. "Lenny!" shouts Jim, "Put your foot in the door." Lenny walks towards the double door of the carriage and looks back, "Would you like breakfast in bed while you're sitting there?" "There they are!" shouts Lenny from the doorway. Big Steve catches sight of Merrill and Jock looking into the carriages of the Circle line train, as they walk along the curved platform. "Merrill!" shouts Big Steve, waving his arm to make himself noticed. Jock looks up the platform, seeing him he nudges Merrill, and then turns to Little John and Big Steve, behind him. "Big Steve! The doors are shutting," warns Lenny. Big Steve looks back at the closing double doors of his carriage, "So put you're fucking foot in the way!" he commands. As the doors close on Lenny right foot, he looks down in nervous apprehension and is relieved as the doors bounce on his Dr. Martens, then open again. "Come on!" shouts Big Steve, as he moves to the doors and leans against one of them to hold them open. "Cheers Pal!" sighs Jock, as he jumps into the carriage, closely followed by the others.

"I'm sorry," says Little John, as he bumps into a male passenger standing just inside the doors. He looks at Little John and gives a nervous smile. "So what's the plan?" asks Lenny, as he moves into the middle section of the carriage. "Well, I've phoned St. Pancras, Tommy and Dave are already there with their firms," says Merrill, leaning backwards against the end of one of the seats, "Tommy has been down into the Kings Cross tube booking hall, and there are already around thirty Arse wankers, milling around waiting for us.

"Did they suss Tommy?" asks Big Steve. "No, he's waiting in St. Pancras station. They'll hear us when we start, then steam down the tunnel from St. Pancras into Kings Cross booking Hall," replies Merrill. "Sorted!" says Big Steve, as a smile winds its way across his face. The passenger by the door turns and walks further down the carriage. "You know something," Steve says, thinking out aloud, "If they ever privatise the Post Office, they ought to give you shares, the number off fucking calls you make."

"The fuck they will," laughs Jock, then says to Merrill, "You should use those radio things you brought back from the States."What are those?" asks Little John. Merrill turns to look at Little John, "Oh I never told you about them did I." "Nor me, sounds interesting," adds Big Steve. "Well they're nothing much, just a few short-range hand held radios," replies Merrill. "You on about CB?" queries Colin, "I've read about them." "Yeah, but they don't work underground, so they ain't no use today," replies Merrill. "Besides, they are illegal, and you can get ten years just for being caught with one," warns Jock. "You're fucking joking ain't yer?" laughs Big Steve, "You get fined a tenner for kicking some cunts head in, but can do ten years for having a bleeding radio?"

"Hello!" exclaims Jim, as he looks out of the tube window, "Next stop, Kings Cross!" The Circle Line train slows to a halt in Euston Square station, and the double doors open. "Right!" shouts Merrill, "Everyone out!" "What!" says a surprised Lenny, as he starts to follow Jock and Merrill out of the carriage. "We walk up the stairs from the Metropolitan platform into the corridor to the other booking hall, and we'll get swamped," says Jock, walking along the platform, "So we're going in via Kings Cross Main Line station." Big Steve slaps Jock on the back as he says, "You're a fucking genius old son." "No!" snaps Merrill, "Just shrewd," he says turning to Big Steve, smiling.

Merrill shows his return ticket at the barrier and starts to walk up the stairs to Euston road. "There they are," says Tommy, leaning against the wall at the front of St. Pancras station. "Let's go and say hello then," says Dave, as he starts to walk down the slope to the street. "No!" shouts Tommy, "Too many people will attract the peelers." Dave stops and watches a Scammel three-wheel arctic tractor drive up the slope, "Hey someone's nicked his trailer," he says looking to Tommy. "Bloody Cockney's will nick anything that ain't tied down," Tommy laughs, as he looks to down on Euston Road, watching the North Stand walk past St. Pancras Town Hall. "They look like a bloody fashion show, compared to the lads back home," says Dave as he joins Tommy at the wall.

"What'd do expect. They're all ex-Mods," says Dave with a smile. "Oh shit! The peelers!" says Tommy, as he hears the bells of a police car ringing out its approach. "Oh I like it," laughs Dave, looking down at the Euston Road, "Look at the North Stand. Some go up the side of the Town Hall, while others cross the road and the rest keep walking. Smart arsed bastards." A broad grin snakes it's way across Tommy's lips as he watches the Humber Super Snipe police car drive past the North Stand and head for the Pentonville Road. He gives a quick thumbs up as Jock and Merrill look up to the wall. "Right! Let's get this into the station and wait for all hell to break loose," says Tommy, as he turns to see twenty-five youths standing under the station arches waiting for them.

Kings Cross main line station was built between 1851-52 and named after a monument to King George IV that stood at a nearby crossroads. The Metropolitan station that followed, serving both Kings Cross and St. Pancras station, was built between 1868-72. As the Underground expanded, a larger separate booking hall was built to serve the new Northern and Piccadilly lines. These had escalators leading up from the platforms to a separate larger circular booking hall. The hall itself had entrances from Kings Cross and St. Pancras, plus a short corridor to the original Metro booking hall, with numerous exits to the street on the far walls.

Gathered in the newer booking hall, were around seventy Arsenal supporters; those who couldn't get in were standing around impatiently in the corridors and at the head of the Metro booking hall stairs. Their mood was expectant as they were here by arrangement to attack the North Stand. Numerous phone calls between opposite leaders had pre-arranged this meeting, which had taken the police by surprise. The four officers in the booking hall were being reinforced in an effort to clear the hall for normal use. Ten police had moved down the stairs from Kings Cross station and were linking arms, and starting to herd the mass of Arsenal supporters towards the exits on Euston Road.

There was an air of joviality among the Arsenal supporters who started walking towards the exits, taking time out to joke with the police. The police seeing no resistance was being offered, were taking things in a relaxed mood; none of them saw the North Stand boys as the walked down the Kings Cross stairs behind them. Had they turned around, they would have seen nearly two dozen smartly dressed youths who, unlike their Arsenal counterparts, wore no scarves or identifying badges, or colours.

Merrill, reaching the bottom stair, holds both arms up to stop those following, in their tracks. Jock walks forward to join him and they stand for a moment watching the police moving the Arsenal supporters out of the booking hall. "We need to charge over there," says Merrill, pointing towards the ticket barrier, "We have to keep the tunnel to St. Pancras clear, as an escape route." "But that's where Tommy and Dave are coming down," replies Jock.

Big Steve walks up, and says, "The filth will want those Arse wankers out as fast as possible," pointing towards the corridor to the Metro booking hall, "That's where they'll push them. We have to get at 'em before the filth throw them out." Merrill, turning to Little John, waves him forward, "As we charge, take half a dozen and go round the side, and charge them from by that exit, towards the ticket barrier. That way we've got them in a pincer and they'll think there are more of us than there are. Little John looks back to Steve, waving him forward, "Right, we still going for the St. Pancras corridor?" "Yes," says Jock, "Do it now." Little John and Steve, with Lenny and Jim, walk along the side wall towards the exits and are seen by two of the police, who start to walk towards them. "Come on you lot out of the station," says a policeman. Lenny stops, looking at the policeman; he turns his head towards the Kings Cross entrance and starts to laugh. The nearest policeman frowns in disbelief at this laughing, and then starts to turn his head as he hears the cry, 'charge' behind him.

Merrill and Jock lead the charge into the back of the police line; Big Steve kicks out sending a policeman sprawling forward into the Arsenal supporters. Jock grabs another policeman from the back by both ears, swinging him around he lets him go; his momentum hurls him against the wooden barrier by the ticket booth. Jock runs up and punches him in the face, knocking him over the barrier. A gap opens up in the police line, and Merrill, Big Steve Ghost and Colin charge through' The Arsenal supporters taken totally by surprise, start to run towards the Metro corridor.

Some of the Arsenal standing around near the Metro corridor, see what is going on and charge through their own supporters to get at the North Stand. Big Steve sees them and grabs Colin by the arm, "Over here!" he shouts, as he runs headlong into the Arsenal. Ducking a punch, he throws a right upper cut that hits the Arse supporter under the chin with such force he almost takes off. Colin grabs a scarf hanging around the neck of another Arse supporter; tightening his grip he puts a strangle hold on the supporter. Laughing as he sees the eyes start to bulge, he swings the youth around and lets him go. Then running forward he is kicked from behind and falls to the ground; another Arse supporter kicks him in the stomach as he tries to get up. Big Steve sees him, and jumping the gate of the ticket barrier, he runs into the mass of the Arsenal supports, hitting out right and left, until he gets to Colin. Grabbing him by the left shoulder, he drags him up.

Little John punches the policeman in the ear, knocking his helmet off, then grabbing his own right hand, he screams, "Fuck it". "What's up?" asks Steve, as he kicks the policeman to the floor. "I hit his skull, I think I've broken me fucking knuckles," answers Little John. Lenny runs towards the barrier screaming, "Chelsea!" followed by Jim, hitting out at anyone who got in their way. Seeing that a path is being created, Little John and Steve follow. As they run, a policeman grabs Little John around the chest with both arms. Steve just catches sight of him, then turns and starts to rein kicks into the right leg of the policeman, sending him crashing to the stone floor. Little John is pinned under the policeman and is kicked by an Arse supporter. Steve jumping over the bodies, punches the Arse supporter, sending him to the floor as Little John climbs out from under the policeman.

Meanwhile Tommy and Dave lead their group into St. Pancras station, and turning right they walk down the staircase that leads to the corridor linking the two stations. "It should kick off any minute, so keep you're ears open," says Tommy, looking back as he reaches the bottom of the stairs. "And remember!" warns Dave, "We're gonna be outnumbered, so just go in hard and fast." As they walk slowly and cautiously along the corridor, Dave draws level with Tommy, "You still thinking of moving down here then?" Tommy stops halfway along the corridor and puts his hand up to halt everybody, then with one ear on the end of the passage, he turns to Dave, "Yeah, Jock has fixed me up with a flat in Wandsworth. You should move down as well." "It's a big step to take, but I'm still thinking about it," he pauses a moment, his ears pricked.

The first sounds of battle echo their way along the corridor; anxious glances are exchanged, as the tension before battle grips everyone. Tommy turns to the group of youths, raises his arm and then drops it shouting "CHARGE!" Two dozen of the North Stand's 'Foreign Legion' rush headlong towards Kings Cross underground station. Tommy and Dave are the first to break out into the booking hall and immediately charge into the Arsenal supporters milling around the corridor entrance. Taken completely by surprise at the force of the attack, they panic and start to run towards the Metro link corridor, but the pressure of numbers means that they are forced to stop and are immediately picked off.

Now attacked on three sides and not realising that they still outnumber their attackers, both the Arsenal supporters and the police run for the exits. Merrill, seeing Tommy and Dave charge out and scatter the Arse on the far side of the booking hall, grabs a fire extinguisher from the wall; he runs forward swinging at anything that gets in his way. Then suddenly, stopping in his tracks, Merrill listens intently; just above the noise of battle he can just make out the sound of multiple bells.

"It's the filth!" he warns at the top of his voice, "Down the Piccadilly line." Jock, hearing the warning stops and listens to the ever increasing sound of police bells as reinforcements rush to the station. "Move!" he yells pointing to the top of the escalators. The North Stand charge through the ticket barrier and start to run down the escalators to the Piccadilly line; Merrill, Jock and Big Steve stand at the top of the stairs and look back as six Arsenal supporters charge at them through the barrier. Merrill smashes the fire extinguisher against the side of the escalator, and grabs the hose as white foam gushes out towards the advancing Arsenal.

"Come on! Let's get down," shouts Jock, as he runs with Big Steve down the moving stairs. //As the foam suddenly runs out, Merrill turns and jumps onto the moving side panel of the escalator and slides down to the bottom. Dave runs out from the platform shouting, Come on, there's a train in." As Jock and Big Steve reach the bottom of the escalator, they run past Merrill, who kicks the large red button. at the bottom of the escalator. The moving staircase instantly stops dead in its track, sending the Arse supporters, headlong down it. Merrill sees one of the Arsenal supporters sliding down the side of the escalator and stands waiting. As the supporter slides towards Merrill, he raises the empty extinguisher and swings it into the face of the Arse supporter, knocking him into a backward somersault. Turning and running for the waiting train, he sees Little John, whose right foot is holding open the door of the last carriage, shouting, "Come on!"

"What the fuck have you lot been up to now?" comes a familiar voice as the doors of the carriage shut and the train starts to pick up speed. Heads turn in surprise as Spider stands in the carriage holding on to one of the overhead straps. "Jesus!" says Colin, shaking with excitement, "You should have fucking seen it, we have the Arse and the filth on the run." Big Steve pushes through the crowd laughing his head off, "Man, that was fucking far out." "So you bloody nutters gonna tell us what the fuck happened then?" says a voice from behind Spider. "It's Parkhead!" shouts Little John, with a broad smile on his face. Parkhead, is a 5ft 5in, 21 year-old Scot, with short wiry hair. James Stirling got his nickname from Spider for his habit of wearing the green-hooped Celtic shirt; another Anglophile, who came to England at the age of 10. Although quiet, he has a vicious temper and he is a born fighter; another long-time member of the North End Road Boys.

"So is someone gonna tell us what you Saxon nutters have been doing?" asks Parkhead again. Jock, starts laughing and breaks into song,
"HAIL, HAIL,
THE CELTS ARE HERE!"
"WHAT THE HELL DO WE CARE,
WHAT THE HELL DO WE CARE."

"Shut the fuck up!" screams Big Steve, "Fuck me it's the Sweaty Sock chorus!" Everyone starts laughing as Little John starts to tell the tale of Kings Cross. "Fuck it!" exclaims Parkhead, "I miss all the fun these days." "So come with us down the North Stand then. It'll be like the old days again." "Oh yeah, I remember when you got nicked at the 'Park Lane Massacre'," laughs Big Steve. Parkhead smiles as he remembers the first game Chelsea played at Tottenham after the 1967 Cup Final. "Yeah, I loved it when that old biddy saw your photo in the Evening News and wrote in, telling them of you hitting the Yids over the head with a mallet," says Lenny, collapsing with laughter. "Bollocks that cost me fucking three months," shouts Parkhead.

"So you gonna came down the North Stand then?" asks Merrill. Parkhead thinks a moment, then smiling, looks up and says, "Why the fuck not, you Saxon Bastards need a good bodyguard."

Merrill then looks at Spider with raised eyebrows, "I suppose you're still a Shed Boy then?" "Yeah, but I'll tag along today," says Spider, "Don't wanna miss out on all the fun." Big Steve looks over to Spider, and pointing to Parkhead, says, "You can get Robert the Bruce to be your bodyguard." "Oi! Watch it, you bloody Hun," smiles Parkhead, "The Bruce was a Scottish hero." "Wrong!" exclaims Steve, standing by the door, "Robert the Bruce was a fucking French speaking Norman Lord, with more land in Kent than in the Norman held lowlands of Scotland." Bollocks!" shouts Parkhead, "that's blasphemy." "No, it's true actually," says Steve, "His real name was Robert Sire de Breaux. His forefathers came over with William the Bastard, in 1066. The only reason he fought was for more land in Norman controlled Scotland.

"And that other hero of yours wasn't a sweaty either!" joins in Little John. "Who's that then?" asks Parkhead. "William Wallace of course," cuts in Merrill, "He was descended from Welsh Celts in Strathclyde. His name was 'Willelmus Wallensis', that means Welsh William." "How can you say that," queries Jock, "You're half Scots yourself." "Ah!" smiles Merrill, "But my better half is pure Saxon. And I fucking hate those Norman French fucks of the Plantagenet's. It was them that conquered Ireland, Wales and Scotland, and we got the fucking blame for it." "Yeah," cuts in Steve, "The Anglo-Saxons had no say in the matter, as they were the first to be conquered. And don't forget, it was a Norman French army with more Welsh and Scots than English that beat the Scots, not Saxon." "This is all bollocks, I don't believe a word of it," says Parkhead, rapidly getting annoyed. "No!" says a wary Jock, "Edward 'Longshanks' only spoke French, the same as their own 'Good King Richard the Lion Heart.'" Parkhead starts to laugh at this revelation, "Oh I love it! Your own kings couldn't speak fucking English." "Shut the fuck up you lot!" screams Big Steve, "We're here!" All eyes turn to the carriage windows as the train starts slowing down in Arsenal station.

"All joking apart thou," says Merrill, "You know those fucking idiots in the National Front, not only do they worship a Jew in Jesus, but these anti-Catholic wankers carry a papist banner." "How d'you work that one out?" asks Spider, as they walk towards the carriage doors. "The English flag of St. George was the Papal banner, given to William the Bastard, for his invasion of England in 1066." As they leave the train and start to walk along the platform, Merrill puts his arm on Parkhead's shoulder, and asks, "So you gonna join the North Stand then?"

Parkhead starts to smile as he says, "Well, you're gonna need some help getting over the thought that you Saxon bastards were ruled by the fucking Frogs." They both laugh as they start to climb the stairs that lead off from the platform. "Only one thing," says Merrill, "They were bleeding Vikings." Walking out of the station and into Gillespie Road, they are met with a human wall of supporters, some of whom are just milling around, while others are walking into the small alleyway that leads to the right hand side of the North Bank turnstiles. There are so many people in the street that the North Stand emerges unnoticed.

"Right, split up and make your way to the North Bank," says Jock, looking around to make sure they have not been spotted by police or Arsenal supporters." "So what's the game plan then?" queries Spider. "Once you're in, make your way to the right side of the covered area, and stay quiet," says Merrill, who seeing a familiar face, walks off towards the vast brick edifice that is Highbury. "Where the fuck's he going then?" asks a puzzled Little John. Jock, watching him walk towards a smartly dressed young woman says, "Oh no! I don't believe it!" "Well you going to let us all in on the secret? begs Little John.

"He's going with the human trampoline," answers Jock, shaking his head, "She's the team groupie and a walking time bomb."You mean she's trouble?" says Dave, who hasn't taken his eyes off her since the second her first saw her. "Yeah, she'll chew you up and spit you out in pieces," says Jock, turning to Dave and shaking his head when he notices his interest, "She's an arrogant control freak, prone to temper tantrums, and is fucking trouble." Walking over, Jock puts his hand on Dave's shoulder, "Put your eyes back in their sockets pal, and forget it."

They start to walk off towards the North Bank alleyway, but as they do, Dave turns his head for a last glance. Linda Tout is a 26 year-old, 5ft. 10in. blonde, dressed in skin-tight black slacks, which flare out from the knees into flapping bell-bottoms. She wears a white cheesecloth blouse, which is see-through enough to let everyone know that she isn't wearing a bra; it hangs down over her slacks and is completed by a loose hanging black belt. She is topped off with oversized tinted fashion glasses. This is a full on 'Sex Machine' and looks the part; arrogant as hell, she likes to get her own way. While she doesn't like the fighting, and always sits in the stands, she had a nasty temper when not being worshipped. "Well I'd fuck it" smiles Dave.

"So you still on for tomorrow night then?" asks Linda, as Merrill walks up to her and puts his right arm around her waist. "Yeah, I thought we'd go to the San Marino Bar on the Charing Cross Road," says Merrill, sliding his hand slowly down onto her bottom. "Oh, I bought the car, by the way," Linda boasts with a radiant smile. "What that Capri?" queries Merrill. "Oh yes," says Linda pouting her lips with pride, "First one on the block with Fords super new sports car." Merrill makes an effort to raise his eyebrows to show that he is impressed; Linda seeming to believe she is yet again the cat's whiskers, thrust out her ample chest. "So how much did you get knocked off the list price then," asks Merrill, as his eyes start to lower their gaze. Linda, in her excitement grabs Merrill's right arm as she jubilantly says, "Eight hundred and forty pounds," she gives a quick glance around to make sure she is being overheard, "I got a fifty pound discount for cash." Merrill smiles, and says, "Sure it wasn't for shagging the salesman?" as he pinches her bottom. Linda's eyes open wide as she tilts her head to one side, "Well a girl's got to live you know."

Highbury Stadium, home of Arsenal Football Club, is a massive brick building that stretches along Avenell Road; the shear size of the place is the first thing that hits anyone turning the corner after coming out of the tube station. At the north end of the pitch, there is a large standing terrace that is partly covered from the middle to the left-hand side of the goal. This is the 'North Bank' and the home end for Arsenal supporters. The south end of the ground is not only half the size, but is not covered and is called the 'Clock End' after the large white clock that stands at the rear of the terrace; this is where the away supporters stand. Arsenal versus Chelsea is always a grudge match, and after the North Bank took the Shed at Chelsea, revenge is on the mind of every Chelsea supporter.

As Jock, Big Steve and Colin, walk towards the North Bank turnstiles, they notice a familiar face walk towards them. Jock looking with surprise at Big Steve puts his hand out to stop the plainly frightened youth. "Hey!" says Jock, "What's up?" "Where have you lot been?" comes the reply, the youth's head nervously looking all around him. "Calm down," says Big Steve, "What's happened?" The youth calms down enough to regain his senses, and says, "The Shed went into the North Bank," he looks around again to reassure himself, and then continues, "We got just under the covered part, when they came around the back of us."

"What about The General?" asks an anxious Jock. "He and the Stockwell led us in, but when the Arse got behind us, most of the Shed ran, leaving only The General and the Stockwell in there." "Cunts, have done it again," screams Colin, "So what happened then?" "Most ran down to the Clock End. I got surrounded, so came round this way." "So how's The General?" "He got out OK. I saw the Stockwell fighting outside the ground as I got out," says the youth, who looking around again, walks off. "You know something?" says Colin, "The Shed would be nothing without The General and the Stockwell." "Yeah, but he's starting to get the rest of them under control. Look at Wolves and Forest!" says Big Steve. Jock nods, and says, "True, but he still can't rely on then yet, as today shows." "So let's get in there then," replies Big Steve, "And show these wankers the North Stand's, here!"

Ten minutes later, Jock, Big Steve and Colin, are standing just to the right of the covered area; looking around they see, Little John and Steve moving through the Arsenal crowd towards them. They are soon joined by Tommy and Dave's boys, and Carlos's crew also move towards them. Soon all of the North Stand, bar Merrill, have gathered into a loose group.

They look towards the Clock End, where the Shed has regrouped and have found their voices again. Choruses of 'Chelsea! Chelsea!' float across the pitch, when there is a sudden movement near the left-hand corner. All eyes in the North Bank watch as a gap opens up, signalling the advance of a group of Arsenal supporters charging into the mass ranks of Chelsea supporters.

The North Bank erupts into a chorus of,
"A-G,
A-G-R,
A-G-R-O,
AGRO."

Jock looks over to the covered area to make sure that the silent group around him has not been sussed. Turning again to the 'Clock End', Jock sees the Stockwell counter attack. Sensing a victory, half of the 'Clock End' turns to their right and charge into the Arsenal. A full-scale battle now ensues; some of the Arsenal fall back and spill out onto the pitch, and then those left on the terrace turn and run for the exits. The West Hampstead/Swiss Cottage/Kilburn boys who have just arrived, join in the charge and reach the turnstiles in the corner, then after a few minutes the 'Clock End' is cleared of Arsenal and a clam descends on the ground.

The North Bank falls silent as they witness the Chelsea victory, then from under the covered section, a chant starts that is soon taken up by the entire end:
WE HATE CHELSEA! WE HATE CHELSEA!"
Heads start to turn towards the silent section at the back of the open part of the North Bank. "Have I missed anything then?" smiles Merrill, as he moves next to Jock. "Where the fuck have you been then?" queries an annoyed Jock. Merrill gives a knowing smile and taps his right index finger on his nose, "Right," he says, "We gonna stand here all day, or we gonna have these fuckers?" Little John turns his head and looks at Merrill, "So say the word then!" Merrill looks at the vast expanse of the covered area, and starts to sing:
"WE'RE THE NORTH STAND,"
Then the silent section bursts into song as they join in.
"WE'RE THE NORTH STAND,
WE'RE THE NORTH STAND,

STAMFORD BRIDGE."

Turning as one, Jock and Merrill charge into the covered section of the North Bank with such force that they open up a wedge shaped gap. Big Steve, Colin, Little John, and Steve run into the gap, while the rest of the North Stand charge down the terrace to a crush barrier, then turning to the left, they fight their way through those that are trying to get away. Those members of the North Bank that were expelled from the South Bank, hear the noise coming from their end and start to run along Avenel Road towards their end. Jock and Merrill have forced their way deep into the covered section of the North Bank and become surrounded; Big Steve and Little John fight their way into the open circular area that has now opened around Jock and Merrill as they take on all comers. Merrill turns to punch out at the newcomers, but catching sight of Little John, holds his punch. "Fuck me!" exclaims Little John, as he holds up his arms.

"Stay together!" shouts Big Steve, as he wades into the Arsenal supporters attacking Jock and Merrill. Colin rushes forward across the open area to join Big Steve as Big Steve stands besides Jock and sees blood coming from his nose, "You OK?" he quickly inquires. "Yeah!" beams Jock, as he hits another Arse supporter, "I'm having the time of my fucking life!" he turns to Steve, laughing as he says, "I love this shit!" Tommy, hearing the manic laughter looks up the terrace to see the open area rapidly closing around the Chelsea supporters fighting there; turning to Dave and the others, he shouts, "Quick up there, they're in trouble!" Lenny, pulling an Arsenal supporter over a crush barrier, head butts him then looks up the terrace, "Come on let's get up there!"

Parkhead, hearing the order, looks over and sees an Arse supporter about to hit Lenny from behind, jumps on him and they both fall to the ground. Spider runs over and pulls Parkhead up while he kicks the prostrate body of the Arse supporter. "Here's the filth," shouts Jim, as he starts to run up the terrace hitting out as he goes.

The others form up and follow, as the police finally reach the small wall at the side of the pitch and start climbing over into the terrace. Merrill advances towards the wall of Arsenal supporters, who slowly back off, but one of them runs forward and kicks out at Merrill, who catches the right foot with both hands, and pulls it towards him. The supporter falls to the concrete steps of the terrace and Merrill stamps on the left thigh.

Big Steve reaches the wall at the back of the North Bank, and followed by Colin they turn as one, "Come on, you fuckers!" screams Big Steve, as the excitement of the moment takes him over. "Gawd! This is better than sex," screams Colin. Big Steve stops to look at him, "You've been fucking the wrong women Pal," he laughs.

As the police advance up the North Bank, the Arsenal supporters open up to let them through, then stand and watch, the fight having gone out of most of them. The North Stand firm are now all together forming a wedge at the top of the North Bank. Then as the police reach the open area around them, they form a cordon to keep the Arsenal supporters back.

Jock looks around and says to Merrill, "That's it, they ain't nicking anyone." Little John turns to him shaking with excitement, "We've fucking took the bastards!" Spider walks over to Jock laughing, "You lot are fucking mad!" he says, shaking his head. Jock smiles, and says, "So you're enjoying your Beano with the North Stand then?

Oh yeah! But!" replies Spider, and Jock laughs as they both say, "I'm still a Shed boy."

Merrill stands alone at the front of the group and looks over to the left hand side of the North Bank; he watches as those Arsenal supporters returning from the battle of the South Bank, are stopped by another police cordon near the exit gate. Realising that the last threat to their victory has been cancelled out, he turns to Little John and starts singing,

"WE'RE THE NORTH STAND,"

Little John smiles and holding his arms up in victory, he and the rest join in,

"WE'RE THE NORTH STAND,
WE'RE THE NORTH STAND;
STAMFORD BRIDGE."

Jock walks over and stands next to Merrill as the teams come out for the game, "Well, we did it," he says with pride.

Merrill smiles, and says softly, "Yes, revenge is sweet, and best served cold."

CHAPTER FIVE

Alan chuckles to himself, then continues, "Like I said, it's idiots like you that created the situation. You blew it up out of all proportion and encouraged outsiders to jump on the bandwagon; when I was at it no-one used weapons and it was localised."

"You people make me sick! You sit there and tell me it's OK to kick people's heads in as long as you don't use weapons!" screams Kev, the veins in his necks starting to stick out as his blood pressure rises, "What utter rubbish!"

"Listen you Scouse get," shouts Dave, "We only went for those that were up for it."

Ian, looking a bit embarrassed by this outburst, tries to calm the situation, "Hold on a moment Kev, there's no need to act like one of the people you're criticising."

"No, let him rant on," interrupts Alan, who looks over to Dave and shakes his head, "I'm enjoying this."

"This is beyond reprehensible and shows me you're totally incapable of appreciating the seriousness of your actions, or taking responsibility for them," retorts Kev.

"So who's acting like a hooligan now?" questions Alan.

"Aw, what's-a-matter, baby dropped his rattle? Upset 'cos someone stands up to you," says Kev in a childish voice, shaking his hand in the air, "Ha ha! I see that's really rattled you!"

Everyone on the Chelsea table looks at each other and then bursts into laughter.

"People are scared to go to games because of vermin like you," Kev says smugly, noticing that he is attracting an audience. Three Americans sitting at the bar, who have been listening with interest, walk over to the table next to Kev.

"Hi! They call me 'Big Al'. I hope you don't mind me interrupting." A 6 foot plus, bearded American, who with two others had moved from the bar to a table next to the Chelsea supporters, "I overheard you guys talking about the English soccer hooligans."

"Yes, we've seen it on the TV news," added Mike Gilmartin, a 32 year-old, 5 foot 6 inch native Californian, "You guys are maniacs, how can you do that."

Laughter erupts from the Chelsea supporters, "It's a hobby we have. Anyway it's better than walking into a school and blowing away a few dozen kids." laughs Dave Hughes.

· "Hold on guys, we didn't come here for an argument," said Big Al, "It's just that we've never met any hooligans before."

Alan Chandler sits back in his chair, takes a mouthful of Pepsi, slowly puts the glass down on the table, and looks at Mike Gilmartin, "You're having a laugh ain't yer?" he says "There ain't no hooligans in here pal, we're having a quiet talk about the 60s and 70s. The hooligans were in the '80's when they started using weapons."

Big Al looking thoughtful says, "So in the World Cup over here in '94, I suppose that riot by English Supporters up in Burlingame wasn't by hooligans?"

"Excuse me for being a bit slow here," Ian Kirkman says, leaning forward with a frown, "But what bloody riot in Burlingame? There was no riot."

Alan laughs as he realises just what the Americans are on about, "This is exactly what we are talking about." He looks at Big Al, "You're referring to that headline in the local paper?"

"Yes, that's right," Mike replied, "I suppose you're going to tell us there wasn't one!"

"OK," says Alan, "I'll tell you exactly what happened, then you can make your own mind up."

MANCHESTER UNITED
AT HOME

Saturday March 21st. 1970, Chelsea 2 - 1 Manchester United

Lenny Blake is standing in the main concourse of the nearly refurbished Euston station, waiting for three new recruits to the North Stand. "This is going to be a nice station when they finish it," he says, thinking aloud. Parkhead, who is standing next to him, looks back, and shrugging his shoulders, says, "Who gives a fuck, just another excuse to jack up the fares."   Lenny shakes his head and then looks around at then main concourse of Euston Station. Built at Euston Grove and originally designed in the classical Greco-Roman style by Phillip and P.C. Hardwick, the station was finished in 1838. Its most notable feature was the huge Doric Arch entrance and, for many years, it was the only northbound railway from London. Now rebuilt in typical '60s style, the main building resembles a corn flakes box with windows; the main feature of the huge concourse is the giant train indicator. As he looks towards the glass entrance, he sees Big Steve walking towards him.

"Ah! Just made it, "Big Steve says, as he approaches the two Chelsea supporters, "Bloody train got into St. Pancras late." "No problem," replies Parkhead, "We're still waiting for the Inter-City from Manchester."   Big Steve walks over to Lenny; noticing that something is wrong, says, "What's up?" Lenny shrugs his shoulders and says thoughtfully, "Nothing really, it's just this place reminds me of those bastards in London Transport." Big Steve flashes a puzzled look at Parkhead, then turns to Lenny, "You used to work for them didn't yer?" "Yeah, but I got stabbed in the back to save their corporate face," says an indignant Lenny. "Sounds interesting! What happened?" asks Parkhead, as he leans against an advertising board.

Lenny looks at both of them, pauses a moment in thought, then says, "Well I was checking a number 12 bus at Piccadilly Circus with another inspector, I did downstairs while he did upstairs. Anyway I'd finished and was standing on the platform by the stairs, when these three black kids come running down the stairs, but couldn't get off as we were still moving." "Shit! You were a fucking ticket inspector?" gasps a shocked Big Steve. Lenny glares at him and says; "I started driving a bus at 18, then last year I became a Revenue Inspector, So yeah, you got a problem with that?" Big Steve, surprised at the reaction, smiles and answers, "No, I just can't see you in a uniform, that's all!" "So what happened then?" says Parkhead.

"Well John Brown, the other inspector comes running down the stairs," Lenny continues, "And grabs a pass out off the hands of one of the kids, 'You've altered this,' he shouts at the kid, 'And it looks like you dipped a spear in some ink to do it with.'" "You've got to be fucking kidding," gasped Parkhead. "So what did the spade do then?" queried Big Steve. "Well," Lenny continues, "The kid says, 'You can't talk to me like that, you're an inspector,' so John just looks at him and says, 'So where do ya live?' 'None of your business,' says the kid, 'Come on pal, where's your fucking mud hut then?'" "Oh bollocks! You're fucking making all this up!" says an astonished Big Steve. Lenny shakes his head as Parkhead says, "So what did you do?"

After a sarcastic chuckle, Lenny continues, "Me, I couldn't believe what I was seeing, so I just stood at the edge of the platform holding on the bar in the middle. Then the kid whose ticket it was snatched it out of Brown's hand, turned to get off the bus, saw me standing in the way, so kicked out trying to kick me off the bus. If I hadn't have been holding onto the bar, I would have been too. The other two jump off, but I grab the kid's arm as he swings a punch and push him into where the conductor stands. He tries to punch me again, so I give him a couple around his right eye." "Fucking ace man!" says Big Steve. "So what happened to this Brown twat?" queries Parkhead. "Oh, that cunt jumps off the bus as I grapple the kid down onto the platform. The bus comes to a stop and the conductor gets everyone off, then the police arrive and I say I want the kid arrested for assault. Brown comes back and, as he was in charge, he says 'No'." "I suppose he didn't want any repercussions after what he said," laughs Big Steve. "Right!" says Lenny, "So the police let the kid go and we get another bus." "Hold up!" shouts Parkhead, "Here come the 'Foreign Legion'."

Heads turn and watch as passengers off the Manchester train walk up the slope towards them. Tommy stopping to buy cigarettes, waves over to the reception committee. "You know it's fucking typical!" says Dave from Salford, as he walks over from the ramp. "What's that?" queries Big Steve. "We walked the length of the train, and guess what? The only football supporters on it are Chelsea." Tommy walks over having bought a packet of Number 6, "Hey guess what?" he announces with a big grin. "The only supporters on the train were

Chelsea," comes the answer in four-part harmony. Tommy looks at Dave and laughs, "Oh, you told them then!" "Come on," says Parkhead, "Let's get the tube, it's getting late." "Better off getting a cab mate," cuts in Lenny. Big Steve starts to walk over to the staircase leading down the cab rank and looking back he shouts, "Come on then!" The five Chelsea supporters walk across the Euston forecourt and disappear down the staircase.

Gloucester Road Underground Station was opened on October 1st, 1868 as part of the then "new" District Line. 'New', in more ways than one, as it was only the second underground railway line to open in the world. It was constructed by the 'cut-and-shut' method, which entailed digging a deep trench in the middle of a road, then laying the tracks before covering it up again with a newly laid road generally supported by brick walls. The straight-walled tunnels are wide enough to carry two tracks. The eastbound passes through Victoria Station, where it crosses the Victoria line from Euston British Rail Station. The westbound goes to Earls Court, where one branch veers south to pass through Fulham Broadway, the nearest station to Chelsea Football Club.

Merrill and Jock walk down the stairs of Gloucester Road station and saunter out onto the platform. Taking a lengthy look around the station, they note that it appears normal for a mid-day Saturday afternoon. The few passengers on the opposite platform ignore them as they amble along. There are only two people on their side of the station; a middle aged man reading the 'Daily Mail,' and a young girl in a long floral skirt. "Looks OK to me," says Jock, looking back towards the stairs, "You know I still can't get over Martin Peters going to the Yids for Two Hundred Fucking Thousand Pounds." Say Merrill, as he looks intently though the carriage windows as a train enters the station. Quickly glancing at the train's passengers as it pulls up in front of them. The doors open with a hiss and the man and girl step on board.

"Well there's no 'United' on that one," Jock observes, "I hope the others get here before their train does. I'd hate to have to let those Northern Bastards go through untouched." As the train pulls away, they notice that all half-dozen waiting passengers had boarded, leaving the platform deserted. The sound of another approaching train makes the pair turn their heads to the tunnel mouth. "We've built up a nice small mob of around forty," Merrill raises his voice as another train emerges from the tunnel and slows down alongside the opposite platform, "And that's the way I want to keep it. Each one is a proven fighter, so we keep it mean and lean. "Yeah replies Jock "The problem with the Shed is there are far too many small firms, all doing their own thing." As the train leaves Gloucester Road Station, Jock and Merrill notice that three people are walking along the platform. Their eyes follow them as they start to ascend the stairs at the end of the platform. They slowly cross the bridge before descending onto their platform.

Slowly, Spider, Colin and Ghost walk towards them, stopping about twelve feet away. "Spider, I thought you were a Shed boy?" says Merrill as he greets him. "True, but I like a bit of action and you lot are certainly having fun lately," Spider replies, as he looks around the station checking for escape routes, "Seems like a good place for an ambush." "Yes, and if the 'Old Bill' turn up, we can leg it up the other stairs and down the other side and jump a train or make a go for a taxi," suggests Colin. "This is going to be good! The 'Manure' trapped in the train! We can pick our carriage and be off before anyone knows what's happening," observes Jim, with glee. "I hope none of them have rabies" says Ghost. "That outbreak at Newmarket is totally under control" answers Colin. "Yeah but look on the bright! At lest 18 year olds can vote at last." Says Spider. "And they voted in Tom King for the Tory's at Bridgewater on Thursday, so they know what they're doing" replies a jubilant Colin. Four people start the walk down the stairs to the platform. Five pairs of eyes turn their way and follow them down; Little John and Big Steve are engaged in an animated conversation. Behind them, sharing a joke, come two girls; Mandy White waves as she sees the assembled group on the platform. All eyes look back at the stranger walking with Mandy.

As they approach the main group, Merrill looks at Mandy, dressed in skin-tight jeans and white shirt. Looking at the undone top four buttons, he slowly says, "Who's your friend?" "Oh this is Maggie, we've been friends for years," answers Mandy, with a smile. Feeling the air of suspicion, her smile drips off her face, then looking at Merrill she pleads, "She's OK, and she ain't scared when it comes to a ruk either." Merrill looks at Margaret Hills, a 5' 6", 19 year-old P.A. stockbroker's assistant. His eyes scan her black leather coat, black leather mini skirt and black knee length leather boots. Her shoulder length blonde hair hangs loose over her white cheesecloth blouse collar, which does little to hide a figure other girls would die for. A lifelong friend of Mandy, she has only recently been sucked into the fighting. The daughter of a wealthy business family, a quiet girl who prefers the company of her friends; to the socialite sect of her parents. While believing in free love, she's a million miles away from being a tart. Looking back to Mandy, he says sternly, "You're responsible for her, then pausing a moment, he lowers his tone, "Until she proves herself." Mandy smiles, as she throws out a mock Nazi salute; and says, "Sieg Heil."

Merrill turns and starts surveying the station for anything out of the ordinary. Aside from the recently assembled North Stand group, he could only see a young mother with her two children on the other platform. "Spread out and wait for the word," he whispered. "Do you girls know what to do?" asks Jock. "Yes," replies Mandy, "If no one gets out of the carriage, we're to push the button at the end to shut the doors." "What happens if someone does get out?" inquires Maggie, her shoulder length blonde hair hanging loose over her collar. Spider approaches her with a reassuring smile, "If they're passengers, just wait 'till they're clear before shutting the door. If they're 'Manure', shut the doors and kick their fucking heads in." "Manure?" queries Maggie. "Yes Manure," smiles Spider, "As in Manchester United, Man U, Manure, get it?" Maggie raises her eyebrows and mockingly says, "Sorry for being so dumb, it goes with the hair colour." Little John feels the breeze in his hair, heralding the next train, "Hold up," he says, "Here's a train."

As the train rumbles to a halt, Colin shouts, "It's 'United!' Let's go!" "NO!" exclaims Merrill, looking up and down the length of the train, "They're normal supporters, let 'em go. Don't move until I say the word." "Shit, this is nerve-wracking," mumbles Maggie to Mandy, as she folds her arms and shuffles her feet. "The waiting is always the worst part," Jock empathises, "Just make sure you get it right. Shut the doors before a shit load of 'Manure' get off and take us in the rear." "Relax," shouts Mandy angrily, "We know what we're doing," her last words echoed across the station as the train disappeared into the tunnel. "So where are Lenny and the others then?" says Spider, as he looks at his watch. "He and Big Steve are picking up Tommy and Dave, from Euston. They'll be here," says Jock, as he looks towards the empty stairs.

The black cab drives past the theatres of Shaftsbury Avenue and turns right into the neon wonderland of Piccadilly Circus. Over the cabby's radio can be heard The Contours, 'Just A Little Misunderstanding.' "Hello! Recognise this place Lenny?" says Big Steve with a smile. "Yes, this is where the bus stopped," Lenny replies, pointing to the bus stop in the Haymarket. "Err, what we talking about here?" says a puzzled Tommy. Lenny looks out of the back window as the cab turns right into Morris Street; he then turns back to face Tommy who is sitting in the left hand drop down seat, "Oh I had a fight on a number twelve bus, and London Transport fitted me up and sacked me." "Oh I remember you telling me a few weeks ago about that," says Dave, who is sitting in the right hand drop down seat, "You were waiting for the appeal, so what happened?"

"Yeah, how did the union handle the case?" queries Parkhead. "Ha, don't make me fucking laugh," says Lenny in with an angry tone "Those bastards were more interested in their own promotion prospects than handling a case like mine." "You mean they bottled having a pop at upper management in case it stopped them climbing the ladder? says Tommy, "Fucking typical!" "Well, listen to this," said Lenny, as he leaned forward, "LT never gave my defence their case notes, so I couldn't form a proper defence and as I didn't know what evidence they had, it left them free to invent it." "But isn't that Illegal?" asks an astonished Dave. "Yup, of course it is, and when I asked for it, LT refused and my union rep. told me off for asking." Big Steve shakes his head in disbelief, "But they're supposed to give the defence any witness statements and a report of all the evidence." Lenny laughs, then his face turns to stone, "It was a kangaroo court from start to finish. First I was charged with stopping the kid from getting off the bus, but at the first hearing I asked him if at any time I stopped him getting of the bus and he says, no, he could of got off anytime. Then they said I made racist statements, so I asked the kid again, and he said he made the only racist remark when he called me a 'white pagan bastard.' So they then found me guilty of hitting a passenger."

"Fuck me, talk about a stitch up," exclaims Big Steve. "So at the appeal, I proved I used minimum force in self defence. So you know what the fuck pigs came up with next?" shouts Lenny, who by now is near boiling point. Four faces stare back in silence. "They said that I hit a passenger when I was a driver, so that proves I was too violent to be an inspector, and that I was fired." "How can you hit a passenger," queried Big Steve, "You're shut away in the driving cab." "Four cunts held up my conductor at knife point and robbed his takings at Golders Green. I heard the scuffle, so got out of the cab and ran back, when this prick flashes a switchblade, so I decked him and got the knife and money off him, and gave it to the police." "And they found you guilty of that, and not the number 12?" says an amazed Tommy.

Lenny nods his head in angry silence as he looks out of the cab window and sees the Natural History Museum, "Right get your money ready, we're nearly there." Dave pulls out a pound note, and handing it to Lenny asks, "Knowing you, you must have got your own back?"

Lenny counts the cash as the cab turns left into Gloucester Road and pulls up at the Tube Station. Getting out he talks to the cab driver, then turns round and says, "Twelve shillings change."

"Keep it for the first round," says Tommy, as he walks into the station, "I just hope we ain't too late." Five men walk through the barrier and start to walk down the stairs as Dave repeats his question, "So come on, how d'you get your own back?" As Lenny walks down the stairs, he sees the others lined up along the platform; smiling to himself, he half turns and looks Dave in the eye, "One night, I went back to a bus garage in South London with a can of petrol and set fire to a dozen buses."   Lenny, with a smug smile on his face, pauses a moment as he steps onto the platform, "He who laughs last, laughs longest."

"Here come the others," says Little John, as he looks towards the stairs. "Yes, the gang's all here," laughs Spider. Lenny and Parkhead lead Big Steve, Tommy from Bolton, and Dave from Salford, as they walk briskly along the platform. "Ain't missed anything then?" inquired Lenny, looking around. "No, hopefully, they'll be along any minute. If we stay here much longer someone's going to smell a rat," says a worried Steve. They spread out along the platform.

\   "Here's a train now," Spider said, with anticipation in his voice. "Everyone ready?" asked Little John, as he checks over his shoulder to make sure, "Wait for the word." The train moves slowly along the platform and finally comes to a stop, allowing them to clearly see who was inside each carriage as it passed. Everyone sees that the middle coaches are obviously filled to the brim with aggressive Manchester United supporters. Merrill points to the carriage he has selected as he shouts, "This is it, we'll take this one." The twelve men rush forward, while the two girls run to the opposite ends of the carriage as the two sets of double doors open. The girls' arms go up in unison; their hands cover the buttons on the outside of the carriages. Nimble fingers gently push the button; a hiss of compressed air is heard as the barely open doors start to shut, trapping those inside. They run in opposite directions and repeat the action on the adjacent carriages.

Merrill, Jock and Spider, lead Big Steve and Parkhead into the carriage. Merrill hits a Man United supporter holding onto the overhead bar in the doorway as Parkhead screams,
"CHELSEA!"   The man collapses in a heap. Jock jumps up, catches the bar with both hands and swings feet-first like a trapeze artist into the mass of people standing in the door area. Taken totally by surprise; the red-scarfed standing passengers back away to avoid the battle. They shout in panic to each other in accents that are more Greater London than Greater Manchester, as Big Steve and Spider fight their way into the seating area. "Look none of these cunts comes from Manchester," laughs Spider aloud. "Look out, Merrill!" warns Parkhead, as he shoulder checks a United supporter who was about to punch him on the back of the head. The United supporter falls to the floor under the force of the impact. Parkhead steps on the body and advances into the carriage

At the other door, Lenny and Jim are throwing punches left and right as they lead the charge into the carriage. When a United supporter falls over in the crush, as he starts to get up Little John carefully aims a kick at his lowered head. There follows a muffled crack as Little John's steel toecap smashes into the man's cheekbone.

"Should've stayed down Dickhead." He screams. A United supporter tries to imitate Jock's trapeze swing, but fails to hold onto the overhead rail. As he falls to the ground, Colin knees him in the side, twisting his body over so that he falls onto his back. The panicking United supporters don't notice him as they run straight over his body.

Tommy head butts, a supporter wearing a red jacket, bringing his knee up into the man's groin, he screams, "Ever been to Manchester, cunt?" Dave runs up behind Tommy, "I'm the only fucker in here that comes from Manchester!" Seeing a seated supporter wearing a Manure scarf, he raises his right leg and kicks him in the face; the head bounces off the window behind him. A Manchester supporter, recovering faster than most from the initial shock, aims a kick at Little John that hits him in the right thigh muscle; Steve, seeing Little John limping towards the door, swings his left arm into the man's throat, sending him falling onto seated passengers; bringing his right foot up he kicks out, hitting him in the chest. Lenny swings his right arm around the neck of one of the Manchester supporters, and bringing his left arm up, grabs his own right wrist to apply a tight head lock; he then shouts Jim, "This is their leader, he comes from Twickenham!"

Jim turns his head and sees the man's face; his eyes are already looking like they are about to pop out of his head. In a flash, he smashes his left elbow down onto the nose, following up with a right cross to the left cheek. Lenny lets go his grip and watches as the body falls to the ground, "Wanker!" he shouts as an afterthought. "The doors are closing!" warns Maggie. Jock moves towards where Maggie stands with one foot against the door to prevent it closing, punching a United supporter as he tries to get out of the train. "No you fucking don't, cunt!" Maggie screams at the man. He stops in shock only to receive Big Steve's elbow in his face. As he falls, Mandy kicks him squarely in the stomach. "Leave him be!" Merrill shouts as he fights his way out of the carriage. "Quick, everyone out NOW!" exclaimed Jock despite the blood coming from his nose. The doors shut as the last of the North Stand Firm jump clear. Realising that the doors were now closed, the Manchester United supporters in the carriage suddenly discover a new bravado, shouting muffled curses of revenge. "Wankers!" shouted Lenny back at them. "Fuck 'em. Let's get out of here," commands Merrill, as he rearranges his attire. "Meet up at The Weatherby?" yelled Spider. "No, it's too late, better make for The Wheatsheaf," replied Jock

The Wheatsheaf is a medium sized pub on the corner of Kings Road and Wandon Road. Wandon Road leads to Stamford Bridge, home of Chelsea Football Club on Fulham Road. It has two bars. One, the Public bar, is small and sparse with few chairs, but it has the obligatory dartboard. The bar itself is in the left-hand corner and runs through the wall into the right-hand side of the Saloon Bar. Here you'll find sofas and padded chairs, and a colour TV. Both bars are full of Chelsea supporters, drinking and talking about the imminent match with Manchester United. In the Public Bar, the North End Road Boys cluster around the closed dartboard near to a window that looks out onto the Kings Road. From Fulham Broadway Underground Station to The Wheatsheaf, is a ten-minute walk up Fulham Road, past Stamford Bridge, as far as The Rising Sun Pub, on the corner of the Fulham Road end of Wandon Road.

The Public Bar door of The Wheatsheaf swings open and in walks Merrill, Jock, Spider, and Lenny. The General watches them walk in, then turns away. Although remaining friendly with the growing "North Stand Firm", The General regards them as potentially dangerous mavericks that he can't control. "Hello, I see the girls beat us back," observes Jock, as he looks around the bar. "And that old lecher, Ghost, is crawling all over Maggie," adds Lenny. Andy Grey, a stocky, 5ft 6in, balding 28-year-old British Railways ticket clerk, from Hither Green, is well know for trying his luck with 'fresh meat', but Maggie backs away from his advances. The jukebox is playing The Vibrations classic original version of 'My Girl Sloopy'. "Why can't they play the fucking original," says Spider looking over to the jukebox. "Err this is the original!" corrects Merrill. "No it ain't, the McCoys were the originals," says Jock, as if to back Spider. Merrill looks at them and shakes his head, "It was written and produced by Bert Berns, and was a huge R&B hit, but not a big pop hit. So when Berns started his own label a year later, he took an unknown white group and re-recorded it as a pop song. That was the McCoys version." "Well I prefer the McCoys," replies an annoyed Lenny.

CHAPTER SIX

"Hi! They call me 'Big Al'. I hope you don't mind me interrupting." A 6 foot plus, bearded American, who with two others had moved from the bar to a table next to the Chelsea supporters, "I overheard you guys talking about the English soccer hooligans." "Yes, we've seen it on the TV news," added Mike Gilmartin, a 32 year-old, 5 foot 6 inch native Californian, "You guys are maniacs, how can you do that."

Laughter erupts from the Chelsea supporters, "It's a hobby we have. Anyway it's better than walking into a school and blowing away a few dozen kids." laughs Dave Hughes. "Hold on guys, we didn't come here for an argument," said Big Al, "It's just that we've never met any hooligans before."

Alan Chandler sits back in his chair, takes a mouthful of Pepsi, slowly puts the glass down on the table, and looks at Mike Gilmartin, "You're having a laugh ain't yer?" he says "There ain't no hooligans in here pal, we're having a quiet talk about the 60s and 70s. The hooligans were in the '80's when they started using weapons." Big Al looking thoughtful says, "So in the World Cup over here in '94, I suppose that riot by English Supporters up in Burlingame wasn't by hooligans?"

"Excuse me for being a bit slow here," Ian Kirkman says, leaning forward with a frown, "But what bloody riot in Burlingame? There was no riot." Alan laughs as he realises just what the Americans are on about, "This is exactly what we are talking about." He looks at Big Al, "You're referring to that headline in the local paper?" "Yes, that's right," Mike replied, "I suppose you're going to tell us there wasn't one!" "OK," says Alan, "I'll tell you exactly what happened, then you can make your own mind up."

Alan takes another swig of Pepsi and sits back in his chair; looking around to Kevin Darcy, he shrugs his shoulders and smiles, "Well about one hundred of us, English and Irish, and yes sorry to disappoint you," he pauses to emphasise the point, "But we all get along over here with no animosity, another fallacy that the press would like you to believe. Well we all caught the Cal Train to Stanford to watch the Russian game."

"You see," points out Dave Hughes, "The Russian goal keeper is our local club keeper in London. Ever heard of Chelsea?" Mike Gilmartin nods.

"So anyway," Alan continues, "There we are on the terraces with a big Union Flag with Chelsea written on it, when these Americans come over and ask, 'You're English, why are you supporting Russia?' So we tell them about Kharine, the goal keeper and one of them, looking puzzled, asks why we have the name of the president's daughter on our flag."

Even Kev laughs at this, then looks at the Americans and stops in embarrassment.

"Anyway," Alan continues, "The game finishes and we all go and catch the Cal Train back to Burlingame. There's a lot of singing and chanting on the train, but we get the locals to join in, and even they had a great time." He pauses to light an Imported John Player Special cigarette; he blows out the smoke and continues, "So the train stops at Burlingame and we all get off, The English chanting, 'ENGLAND! ENGLAND!' Then we notice that the station is encircled by police cars. We start to walk out and cross the road to walk up to the Irish Bar we use as a local. The main road is lined by cops all holding batons, so we put the Union Flag at the front and walk up the road, chanting "ENGLAND!"

"Didn't the cops do anything?" asks Big Al.

No, they just stood there looking very nervous," points out Dave, "All the locals came out of the shops, but realising there was no trouble, started clapping. Anyway, to cut a long story short, we all turn the corner and go into the bar."

"Yes, and no windows were smashed, no people were hit or beaten up," says Alan. "And," continues Dave, "The local rag runs the headline, "ENGLISH SOCCER HOOLIGANS BRING TERROR TO BURLINGAME."

"So, you see gentlemen," Alan says, taking another pull on his cigarette, "What we have here is what we're talking about. Another case of sensationalist misrepresenting of the truth in order to sell more papers. And what's worst, people like you, that weren't there, believe it."

THE WEATHERBY PUB

Friday September 18th. 1970

It is a dark and damp night in Wandsworth, for what seems like the hundredth time, Jock looks up along Warple Way in search of the elusive green mini van. Stamping his feet impatiently, he reaches into his damp, coat pocket and takes out a packet of Embassy Regal. Pulling out a cigarette and putting it to his lips, he thinks, "Sod's Law says it'll come round the corner as soon as I light it." Striking a match, his face is illuminated by the yellow glow. He draws in the smoke and slowly blows it out; he glances up along the road again, just as a pair of headlights come round the corner. Squinting his eyes, he peers through the smoke; as the lights get closer he sees that it is in fact the same green mini van he has been waiting for. "Thank God for that," he thinks, "At fucking last."

The Mini van stops on the white zigzag lines by the Zebra Crossing. Jock walks over irately, "About fucking time," he shouts' "Bollocks you old woman. I'm eight minutes late. You drive from bleeding Hampstead in better time," Merrill says, as he leans over the passenger seat to open the door. As he does, he notices for the first time a set of new markings at the crossing, "What are these white lines for then?" "Fuck knows," replies Jock, "They weren't here yesterday. He pauses as he looks at the strange zigzag lines; shrugging his shoulders he gets into the mini van, slamming the door with satisfied yank, then turns and looks at Merrill, "So you've got the map of Coventry then?"

Merrill pulls away looking around for a street sign that might explain the zigzags, and drives to the traffic lights at York Road. "Hold on!" he shouts, as he swings the steering wheel around and pulls up the hand brake momentarily. The mini van slides through one hundred and eighty degrees, and back along Warple Way heading back towards the River Thames and the Kings Road, "Yes I've got it!" he says, smiling to himself. "Jesus, you fucking idiot!" shouts Jock, as he rearranges himself after being thrown against the door, "You drive like a fucking mad man." "I don't like new road markings," says Merrill thinking out loud, "You keep

81

thinking the 'filth' are about to jump out and nick you for some new law you've never heard of before."

"Is Little John still going with Linda?" inquires Jock, as he throws his cigarette butt out of the window. "Depends how you define going out, I don't think they're an 'item'. She don't own him you know," Merrill replies, as he slows down to turn onto Wandsworth Bridge. "She thinks she does! Had a right go at me on Tuesday. She wanted to know what the fuck he was playing at," added Jock. Merrill throws a quick glance at Jock and with a surprised look, says, "Bleeding cheek! Jock laughs, then continues, "We all know she's the team groupie. You can't blame a man for finding out how good a human trampoline she is." Merrill throws a lightning glare that cuts short Jock's remark. Suddenly he remembers, "Oh, sorry I forgot you went out with her once." "How'd you know that?" asked Merrill with surprise. "She told me," Jock says with a smile. "Not a problem," answers Merrill, as he nods his head, "But she's not the 'full shilling', she can turn nasty that one. I just hope he knows how to handle her," he adds as an afterthought. "Ah this weeks number one." Says Merrill, as "Tears Of A Clown" comes on the radio. Then as the mini crosses the Wandsworth Bridge, the drizzle, at last, stops. "What I do with any woman is no-one's concern but mine, and she's out of order talking about it," Merrill states turning to Jock to emphasise the point.

"Hey look at the arse on that!" said Jock, happy to change the subject as he caught sight of a young girl in tight jeans standing by a set of traffic lights, "I saw you looking at Maggie's arse on Saturday. You're not thinking of moving in on her are you?" Merrill smiles to himself, "Now that would be telling, wouldn't it," he replied, "As I said, my sex life is my business, you nosy Scots Git." Jock laughs out loud, then turning to look at Merrill, says, "You fucking Scorpio's, you love your little secrets. "Hey! Do I ask you for all the details on Veronica then?"

Jock shakes his head, knowing that he is likewise hesitant of talking about his girlfriend, "Yeah, know what you mean." "Hey this is gonna be a number one record, it's brilliant and written and produced by Holland, Dozier and Holland!" Interrupts Merrill, as Freda Payne's "Band Of Gold" comes on the radio. "Holland Who?" queries Jock. "Only the best writing team at Motown, that's who!" exclaims Merrill.

The Mini continues up the Wandsworth Bridge Road and past South Park, when Merrill, changing the subject says," I read a good book last week, about Atlantis." Jock frowns in surprise, "What the lost continent? That's all a fucking myth." "I'm not so sure. It's called 'Maps of the Ancient World' and has a load of maps drawn up in the 1500s that show the Antarctic continent next to South America."

"And you believe all that bollocks then? How can you have a map of Antarctica when first it's covered with ice, and second it wasn't even discovered in the fifteen hundreds?" Jock replies with a smug grin. "Well this Hapgood, the geezer that wrote the book, says that there was an advanced civilisation that lived over ten thousand years ago and that they could be the only ones to have known about it to map it." "Sounds a bit fishy to me. Why don't we know about them then?" retorts Jock. "He thinks the earth tilted, that's why the magnetic poles moved. I mean these maps showed mountains and rivers, and he says that the ancient Egyptians knew about it, and that's where the people that drew the maps got the knowledge from. The only trouble is, that they've found the remains of a Minoan city under the water on the Island of Santorini, and Santorini is a volcano that blew up in 1265BC. So if you want my take on it, Atlantis was capital of the Minoan Empire and was an island inside an island, just like Homer wrote." "What the fuck is an island inside an island?" queries Jock.

"Look down on a volcano and what do you see?" asks Merrill, but before Jock can reply, he continues, "You see the rim and a small hill called a caldera., in the middle. Now picture that in water, and you have an island inside an island, and that's what you have today. By the way the Egyptians wrote about Atlantis and placed it north of Crete. "Jock's eyes light up, "Oh, so that's why you read it, you're into all that Egyptian stuff ain't yeah." Merrill nods, as he turns right into the Kings Road, "I'll let you read it if you want." "Eh, I don't know. You look at that von Daniken book where he reckons that most of the unexplained ancient artefacts are down to visiting spacemen," says Jock, with a smirk. "If you ask me, the only spaceman to visit Earth was that idiot!" laughs Merrill.

"Yeah, OK then, I'll give it a shot," says Jock, as Merrill parks the Mini outside the Weatherby. Jock gets out of the mini and notices that the Cockles and Mussels stall outside the World's End Pub is open, "Hold on, I'm going to get some mussels." Looking back at Merrill he continues, "So why do you read all these history books then?" "If you can't learn by the mistakes of history, then there's no hope. Take, for instance, bullet proof glass in banks!" says Merrill, as they run across the road to avoid a number thirty one bus. "What the fuck you on about now," sighs a confused Jock, as he walks up to the stall, "A shilling's worth of mussels please." "Simple question. What is the only thing to penetrate bullet proof glass?" Jock takes the bag of mussels and putting one in his mouth, thinks a moment, "I ain't got a fucking clue." "A steel tipped Bodkin arrowhead from a long bow," smiles Merrill. Jock stops in his tracks, puts another mussel in his mouth and looks at Merrill, "Very interesting, but who the fuck is going to walk into a bank carrying a shagging long bow. Get real man?" A broad grin cuts across Merrill's face, "Oh yes, but if you take the Bodkin arrow head and put in on the end of a hand held crossbow bolt!"

Lenny looks out of the window of the number fourteen bus, and sees the Chelsea Hospital, "Hello we're here!" Walking to the rear of the upper deck, Lenny starts down the staircase, when he meets a ticket inspector walking up. "Tickets please!" Lenny stops on the stairs looking at the inspector, then says, "We're getting off." "I still need to see your tickets," replies the inspector. "Wrong!" shouts Lenny, if you don't know your job, don't take it out on me." The inspector nervously grabbing the handrail says, "I need to see everyone's ticket, whether you're getting off or not." "Bollocks! After a directive issued two years ago, you are not to stop anyone getting off a bus. Furthermore, you are not to check the tickets of anyone getting off a bus as that will be construed as stopping a passenger from getting off." Lenny moves down one step and looking the inspector in the eyes, "If you don't know your job, I do, so go and have a chat with Inspector Del Trigger, who now works in the legal department." The inspector looks at Lenny in bewildered silence, and then quickly glances down to the conductor. Not sure how to handle the situation, he then turns and walks down the stairs, and moves to the inside of the bus. Lenny and Jim walk onto the platform as the bus slows down for the Gunter Grove stop. Jim looks at the smiling conductor, then at the inspector, "You can check upstairs now." "No!" exclaims Lenny, looking at the inspector, "there's no one up there, so just write correct on your docket and get the conductor to sign it." "I can't do that," replies the nervous inspector.

Lenny walks into the lower passenger deck and stands in front of the inspector, "Oh yes you can, now do it," he snarls. The inspector glances at Jim standing on the platform, then shakily pulls out a clipboard and scribbles something on it. "Good, now get the conductor to sign it, and get off the bus," orders Lenny. After a second's pause, the inspector walks to the platform and hands the clipboard to the conductor, who looks at Lenny then signs the clipboard. Jim moves forward, putting out his hand, he steadies the clipboard and checks it, "Wonderful," he sighs, "Now fuck off." The inspector steps off the bus, just as Jim rings it off, "You won't get away with this you know," he shouts from the pavement, "I'm going to phone the police!" Jim shakes a loose fist shouting, "Wanker!"

Lenny walks onto the platform and looks at the conductor, "Don't worry pal," he reassures him, "he won't report it, it will make the bastard look incompetent." The bewildered conductor nods his head as Lenny and Jim jump off the bus at the traffic lights. "Parasitic cunts like that get right up my nose," snaps Lenny. "Yeah, I sort of noticed," smiles Jim. Lenny shaking his head continues,

"Those conductors are the only source of revenue collecting that London Transport have, and these tossers, instead of helping them and keeping their moral up in a very stressful job, just hound them." "I forgot you used to be a conductor, and an inspector didn't you?" says Jim. "Yeah, and those fucking inspectors have this thing called a dot, where they can book the conductor just for having his ticket machine straps twisted. Then at the end of the day, they get together and boast about who has the most dots," rants Lenny, as they walk down Gunter Grove, "One of the reasons they kicked me out, was because I used to help the conductor, unless I found him stealing the ticket money." He pauses a moment, "I hate those back stabbing bastards."

The Weatherby is an old corner pub, the public bar of which consists of a large drab room. The paint peeling from the walls tells the story of a rundown working class bar. Around the dartboard, Big Steve watches Spider throwing for a double top to finish the game. Sitting around the middle table, are Little John, and Colin, talking amongst themselves. Parkhead, standing by the bar, orders a drink for himself. At the large table in the corner, sits Maggie, Debbie and Veronica. Two locals are sitting at the table near the bar. One is reading a copy of the Evening News, that has the headline that Jimi Hendrix has been found dad from a suspected Drug overdose.

"Yes!" yells Spider, as he walks forward to pull out his winning darts. "Jammy Git," moans Big Steve, as he turns and walks to the bar. "Loser buys the drinks," laughs Spider. "Mine's a Brown Ale, shouts Jock, as he walks in. "Shit! You can tell he's a Jock! He always turns up when it's my round," Big Steve chirps. "Still got that bloody camouflage jacket on; No wonder Spider named you after that "Merrill's Marauders" movie," he says to Merrill, with a smile. "Hey don't knock it, this is my trademark." Merrill laughs. "Here they are, you can ask him now," Debbie says, turning around to give Maggie a knowing look. "What's the point, he's not going to tell me is he," replies Maggie, "I'll just wait and see what happens.

"Jock says he thinks you're going with Ghost, and that's enough to turn anyone off." Veronica laughs. Maggie squints her eyes as she throws a deep look at Veronica, "I've told yer, I ain't going with Ghost. I wouldn't touch him if he was the last man on earth," she snarls. Colin looks up, "Ah, good you're here at last, got that map of Coventry then?" he asks Merrill. "Yeah, let's get a drink," replies Merrill, and looking around, he adds, "Pull the tables together and we'll get started."   "Come on girls, pull your table over," says Parkhead. Little John and Steve drag an empty table from the corner. Steve turning his head sees four chairs along the wall, "Grab those chairs lads," he shouts to Spider and Big Steve. Russell, the barman, a 50 year-old ex-boxer, hands Merrill a pint of lager,

"Another meeting of the War Cabinet?" he laughs; Merrill nods and walks over to the group of tables, and sits down next to Maggie.

Spider sits down and looks round the table, "So, who we sending to Coventry this time?" he laughs. "You!" says Little John, "If there's any more of those bad jokes." They both laugh. "I reckon we stand by the right hand corner flag of their end, by the little café then, when the time's right, we steam in," Maggie says. "If we steam in from there, it will give their mob time to act," Lenny points out. "You're right," Jock replies. He thinks for a moment then adds, "What if we meet at the corner, then slowly move into their end. That way they won't know we're there till it's too late." "Good idea," says Merrill, taking the map out and spreading it across the table. "And don't forget now we've won the cup, every mob in the country is up for having a go," says Little John, pulling his chair in. "Yeah, I remember Leeds throwing those pennies as we charged into their terrace," smiles Colin.

"You know, I don't know why all those idiots take drugs," muses Big Steve, "This is the best turn on in the world." "Err, we lost 1-0, pal," says Parkhead. "Fuck the score, we won the fight!" laughs Little John.   "Hold on," shouts Jock, "Let's get Coventry organised." "I've got a friend in Coventry," Big Steve says gleefully. But before he finishes, Debbie interjects, "You got a friend in Coventry. Wow! You'll be telling us you've got a big dick next." Big Steve's reply is drowned out by the laughter, "You mean you haven't found out yet Debbie?" Spider laughs. "Oi you lot! Shut it!" shouts Jock, "We need to arrange what we do on the way to the ground."

"Yes we don't want to get ambushed like last year," says Parkhead, "They nearly did us." "Yeah, that precinct is like a bloody rabbit warren," Big Steve adds, "They know all the rat runs." "So leave the Precinct to the Shed, while we detour and go along Corporation Street, then hit them from behind by the bus station," says Merrill. "Sounds good. So how do we do it?" answers Spider. "When we come out of the station, we turn left and go down by the Irish Club and under the Fly-Over, into Corporation Street," says Merrill; pointing to the map. "That way we can get away from the Shed," adds Jock. "Not many regulars in here tonight," says Big Steve looking around, "Yes they all caught the clap off Debbie," Parkhead laughs. "No chance of you catching it then, is there, cunt?" snarls Debbie. "Yeah," laughs Maggie, "The only female he's had in his bedroom is an inflatable one." Everybody laughs, "Bollocks!" snaps Parkhead..

"Cut the crap you lot," shouts Merrill. "So what do we do if the filth follow us to the bus station?" asks Little John, "They'll be too busy following the Shed to worry about us, especially if we break off in small groups," answers Jock. Little John leans forward, thinking, and then asks, "So what do we do on the way back then?" "Just before the Precinct," says Merrill, pointing at the map, "Turn right here and walk along Hertford Street. Follow it all the way down and it becomes Warwick Road, and you'll see the fly-over. Walk to the left, by the roundabout, and wait in this small park, by this bridge," his finger moves along the map, "And into the park." "Sounds easy enough," Spider nods, "What if they get there first?" "They won't," says Jock, "'cos the mobs will have it off in the precinct, while we go straight for the park." "Fair enough, looks straight forward enough to me," says Little John.

The bar door opens and Lenny and Jim walk in, looking over at the group huddled around the table, "Missed much?" queries Jim. Merrill looks up and shouts, "Sit down and I'll bring you up to date." "Well, if that's it I'm going to the loo," Debbie says, as she gets up from the table. As she opens the toilet door, Little John says to Jim, "You still going out with Debbie?" "No," Jim replies, "we're just good friends. Why?" Little John, looking relieved, thinks for a moment and asks, "OK if I go out with her then?" "I thought you were with Linda?" Jim queried. "Na," Little John replied, "She's too fucking freaky, I like normal women." "Ha! Fancy giving Debbie a good porking then?" laughs Jim. "You lot make me laugh, says an angry Veronica, "You think we're just a piece of fucking meat." "Calm down girls," says Spider, "They're just have a laugh!" Veronica looks Lenny in the eyes and snarls, "You're like those fucking builders, whenever a girl walks by showing a bit of leg, you whistle and shout "cor", then end up with nothing and wonder why."

Debbie walks back to her chair and, sensing she's missed out on something, looks around the table and says, "I missed something then?" "No," says Colin, "Just Jim acting the cunt again." "Your problem Lenny," Merrill says calmly, "Is you don't realise that women like sex just as much as you do, but it's OK for you to screw around as much as you like, but when a girl does the same, you brand her a slag." He finishes his drink and puts it down, "If a bird is good enough to go to bed with you, you should respect that, not mouth it to everyone." He pauses to make his point, "I'm grateful for what I get, and don't go and ruin it by bragging about it to everyone."

"Yeah, I'm already visualising the duck tape over your mouth," laughs Veronica. "What the fuck am I? Flypaper for freaks?" asks Jim, (he) stands standing up and walking over to the bar. Maggie looks at Merrill and says, "So you respect your women then do you?" "Well, put it this way," he says, "When a girl is leered at by those builders, she covers up and that spoils it for everybody. A bird likes to know that she turns men on, but prefers it when a guy just looks and smiles. That way they show a bit more." He turns to

Maggie and smiles; she leans forward slowly and picks up her drink, knowingly showing her cleavage in her low cut top.

"Want a drink Alan?" Jock asks Merrill, as he gets up from the table. "Yeah, I'll have a Pepsi, I'm driving," replies Merrill. "Ever   the goody, goody," laughs Spider. "Ever the Shed Boy," replies Merrill, "The last thing I want on my conscience is running some kid over 'cos I was drunk. No mate, I couldn't live with that." He looks up at Jock, and starting to laugh, he adds, "Make it a double." Spider and Little John get up and walk over to the bar, "We're off, see yer tomorrow at Euston," says Spider. "Yeah see yer tomorrow," replies Jock, looking worried. "Right, see yer tomorrow," says Little John, as he turns and follows Spider out of the door. Merrill looks over to Jock, "You want a lift home?" "No it's OK," Jock replies, looking at Veronica, "Me and Veronica are getting a cab." Little John walks over to the table where Debbie and Maggie are sitting, "You getting the tube?" he asks Debbie. She looks at Maggie, who smiles, "No, it's alright," says Maggie, "You go I'll catch a cab." Merrill walks back over to the table carrying his Pepsi, "I'll give you a lift if you like," he says to Maggie. "Yeah," she smiles, "That'll be nice." She gets up, puts her leather coat on, looks at Merrill, and says, "Home James."

He puts his arm around her back, his hand resting on the side of her waist. He feels the curve of her small waist, and smiles to himself. "See you two tomorrow, and don't sleep in," laughs Jim. The green mini van drives slowly down Trinity Road, approaching Tooting Bec. "Take the next left and park at the junction," says Maggie, "I live in that one on the corner." The mini van pulls up next to the gate. Merrill looks Maggie in the eye and says, "Don't be late tomorrow." He leans over to kiss her on the cheek, she turns her head and their lips meet. He feels her moist lips and puts his arm around her waist, gently squeezing it. Their lips part, Maggie opens her eyes and says, "Why don't you come in for a coffee?" "Better not," whispers Merrill, "Don't want to disturb your parents." "It's OK," replies Maggie, "They're away on holiday. They don't get back 'till Monday." She smiles, "Come on, we've got the house to ourselves."

Maggie turns the key and opens the front door; walking in, Merrill follows her. They walk into the large front room, the lights come on and he sees a regency style setting. Maggie pulls the wall length heavy drapes together. She points to the plush three-seat settee, "Make yourself at home, I'll make the coffee. "Oh, the TV's in that box." He looks over to the corner and sees a polished walnut cabinet; walking over he opens the door to reveal a 21-inch television. Turning it on, he looks around and sees four large copies of old masters' paintings. He sits down on the settee, and looking up at the crystal chandelier, he hears the whistle of a kettle.

Following the sound he walks through an open door into the kitchen. Maggie is standing with her back to him, unplugging the kettle. The fitted pine kitchen, is spotlessly clean; he walks over to Maggie and puts his hands on her waist, "Some gaff you have here," he says. "Daddy works in the stock Market. It's not my style, too old fashioned for me." she replies. He kisses the back of her head, and she doesn't resist, "Do you want the coffee now," she whispers, "Or later on." He starts to kiss the side of her neck and gently pushes his groin into her bottom. "Would later be alright, I've something on my mind right now," he answers, and moving his hands slowly up the side of her ribs, he stops when he feels her soft, but firm breasts. "No prizes for guessing what that could be," she says with a smile, as she puts the coffee pot down and places her hands on his. Moving them up 'till they cup her breasts and gently squeezes; his thumbs, finding her erect nipples, slowly caresses them. She turns around to face him; their lips meet and tongues dance with each other. He moves his hands down her back and slowly fondles her bottom. She opens her eyes and whispers, "Let's go into the bed room, it's more comfy."

Maggie walks out through the door and climbs the stairs; Merrill follows her, watching her bottom wiggle its way up the stairs. She leads him into a large bedroom; they embrace again and he nibbles her neck and along her collarbone. He moves his hands up her bottom and under her top. Feeling the warmth of her skin, he moves his left hand up till it finds her bra strap. With fore finger and thumb, he unclips her bra. Moving his head, he starts to nibble her left ear as he gently pulls her top up. She looks him in the eye, and whispers, "Do you want to stay the night?" He nods, she stands back and says, "Good, sit down." She smiles as she pulls her top and bra off. He sits on the bed, watching her throw them to the floor. She starts undoing the top button of her jeans; putting her thumbs into both sides, she slowly pulls them down, stopping only to put her thumbs into her panties. She then pulls them down together and, bending over, she steps out of them. He looks at her feet and then slowly moves his eyes up her body, 'till their eyes meet. He smiles and says, "Nice bush."

CHAPTER SEVEN

"So you put all the hooliganism down to the press. Isn't that copping out of the responsibility you share for being part of it?" Says Kevin angrily.

"No," replies Alan looking over to the yanks, "I don't put it all down to the press, they just took it to a new level. They opened the floodgates for the Neanderthals with weapons. Times change, that was then, this is now. People that can't change with the times are doomed."

He scratches his nose, lost for a moment in deep thought, then looks up and continues, "You can't do those things today, and football is better for it, even if the atmosphere is getting Yuppified and sterile. It's good to see women and kids at grounds these days. I make no apologies for what happened, I for one enjoyed it. It was a buzz, but like I said that was then, this is now."

"Oh very interesting," says Kevin Darcy sarcastically; "What about the innocents that you put the fear of God into."

"The North Stand were the heavy mob, let me remind you," David Hughes says, pointing his finger at Kevin to get his point across. "The Shed loved the North Stand most of Chelsea loved the North Stand. They were the cavalry, the heroes and we were their willing audience. When matters got seriously out of hand between the committed; people got hurt. So what! Make no mistake there were very few "innocents" at Chelsea in those days."

Big Al pulls his chair nearer the table and looking at Kev he says, "It's refreshing to hear straight facts about 'the way things were'. It's also refreshing, to get the facts in an undiluted form from a person that was there, and who doesn't feel the need to kneel, bow, wring his hands and beg the pardon of an entire nation for his past sins."

COVENTRY AWAY

Saturday September 19th. 1970, Coventry 1 - 0 Chelsea

Big Steve looks out of the Inter-City carriage window, then turns to Parkhead, "We're slowing down, we must be coming into Coventry!" Parkhead quickly looks out of the window and then sweeps up the playing cards from the table that is between their seats, "Must be," he says, raising his eyebrows. Little John, overhearing them from the seat in front, stands up and turns around. Leaning on the top of the seat, he says, "No, this is just Rugby, Coventry is the next stop; should be there in around ten minutes."

Ghost looking at the Daily Mail, says "I see the PFLP have hijacked a BOAC VC 10!" "yeah I saw that, we'll have to send a Gunboat!" mocks Parkhead. "you seen "Tora, Tora, Tora yet?" say Ghost. "Yeah" replies Parkhead, "Some great battle scenes in it." "You bought the new Melanie album yet?" asks Big Steve "What? Leftover Wine?" queries Little John, turning back to Big Steve, who is sitting opposite him, "Yeah, bought it Monday. I like 'Peace Will Come', but it ain't another 'Candles In The Rain'. "I loved her version of 'Mr. Tambourine Man', she really added something to that," says Alan Merrill, sitting by the window.

"Yeah, but Dylan's version was the best sing-a-long version," says Jock Wallace, sitting opposite Merrill. "Ah! But 'It takes a lot to laugh, It takes a train to cry', is the best sing-along," says Big Steve, who starts to tap out a rhythm on the table top, then starts to sign, "DON'T THE MOON LOOK GOOD, MAMA," Little John, Jock and Merrill join in, "SHININ' THROUGH THE TREES?" Big Steve solo's, "DON'T THE BRAKEMAN LOOK GOOD, MAMA," The others, augmented by Parkhead, who pulls out a harmonica, from nowhere, again join in. "FLAGGING DOWN THE "DOUBLE E" Big Steve solo's again, "DON'T THE SUN LOOK GOOD," Now joined by Mandy, and Maggie, They all sing, "GOIN' DOWN OVER THE SEA?" Then they all stand up and sing the final verse at the top of their voices; "DON'T MY GAL LOOK FINE,

WHEN SHE'S COMIN' AFTER ME?" Jim, still sitting down across the aisle, looks over and laughingly says, "You lot are fuckin' nutters!" Colin sitting next to him, then starts to sing "WE'RE NOT MENTAL IN THE HEAD." And then even Jim stands up and joins in, "WE'RE THE NORTH STAND, NOT THE SHED; LA LA LA LA - LA LA LA - LA LA - OH!"

Walking out of Coventry Station, Jock and Merrill lead a group of thirty Chelsea supporters down the slope., and turn left towards the pedestrian walkway, that takes them around the corner towards the Tax Office, but instead of walking down to the Irish Club as planned, Merrill turns around as shouts, "Right this way!"

"What's going on? I thought we were going down to the flyover!" says a confused Little John. "Change of plan," says Jock, as he turns around to make sure everyone is following. Then calling Mandy and Maggie over, he says, "Right you girls, go under the flyover and walk down Corporation Road, and see if the filth are there. There's a phone box on the corner by the old pub, ring this number and let us know." Mandy looks confused, but takes the paper and walks off with Maggie. "So where are we going then?" asks Spider. "To the 'Hen and Chicks', says Merrill, with a smile. Colin walks up and says, "What the fuck is the Hen and Chicks?" Jock turns and points along the straight road, "See that pub at the bottom of the slope?" He looks at the gathered group, then smiles and continues, "Well that's where we are meeting Tommy and Dave."

"I don't want any trouble in here, or I'll call the police!" says a nervous landlord to Merrill and Jock, as they lead thirty members of the North Stand into the Hen and Chicks pub. The Hen and Chicks is a thriving 'lunch time' pub, serving the nearby polytechnic and growing numbers of office workers. At night though, it turns into a 'biker' pub and can get rather rough. The large kitchen serves a comprehensive menu; of not just pub lunches, but also sit down meals. Tudor beams can still be seen on the walls, and one must be careful not to strike your head on the large overhead beams as you walk through its seating area, with its mock Tudor table and chairs and large, padded leather sofas. The off-colour paint on the walls though, looks as old as the beams and, in some places, is peeling off the wall, but this just adds to the atmosphere. At the far end is a sunken area where a snooker table is surrounded by long bench type sofas that hug the walls.

"Don't worry," Merrill reassures him, "We're not here for trouble just a quiet drink." "But, I've already got a group of football supporters in here," the landlord says, as he points to the 'L' shaped part of the pub where Tommy, Dave and the 'Foreign Legion' are crowded around the pool table. Jock laughs as he looks over to the pool area, "That's OK pal, they're with us." The landlord stands silent for a moment as he tries to comprehend the fact that his pub is now full of Chelsea supporters, "But," he says in his confusion, "But, they're not Cockneys." "No, they're from Lancashire actually. Now are we going to get a drink?" says Little John.

Lenny is the first to walk into the snooker area and is greeted like a hero, "See!" says Big Steve, "We're all friends, and there is no trouble." The landlord walks behind the bar, still a bit confused, "OK lads what will it be?" "I'll have a Pepsi," says Merrill, who looks at the end of the bar and sees the lunch counter, "You doing food today?" "Yes, we are actually," says the landlord's wife, who has just walked through a door behind the bar. "Any trouble at the station?" says Tommy. "No we're too early for the Coventry, or the filth," smiles Big Steve. Dave walks over and shakes hands with Colin, "Where's Mandy?" "Oh don't panic, she's on walk-about, checking to see if the way is clear," Dave smiles and turns to take his shot.

"Mm, lust rears its rampant head," smiles Colin, as he turns to walk to the food counter. The phone rings as the landlord is pulling pints; he leans over to the small payphone on the counter, "Hen and Chicks!" "That'll be the girls with any luck," says Jock, as he picks up a pint of Brown Ale. "Is there an Alan Merrill in here?" says the landlord. "Yeah, that's me," says Merrill, who takes the phone. The landlord shakes his head in amazement that, not only have both Northerners and Cockney's peacefully invaded his pub, but also now they're getting phone calls. "Right OK, we'll see you by the soup stand," says Merrill, who then hangs up.

Highfield Road, the home of Coventry FC, isn't a big ground; the home end, behind one of the goals is a modern, but narrow terrace, with a low roof that amplifies the cheers of the crowd. To the side of the right hand corner flag, is an open section of terrace, with a hot soup and coffee stand. A group of around twenty supporters are standing there, with an eye on the home terrace. Heads turn as another group of supporters start to move into the area, "It's OK, it's only the North Stand," says Spider "Hello," says Jock, in mock surprise; "So what's the Shed doing here?" "Learning from the masters," says Spider with a sarcastic grin. Merrill laughs as they shake hands.

"Right, split up into small groups and slowly make your way up to the rear," says Jock, motioning to the home end. Merrill is looking at the massed Coventry supports who are still unaware of the gathering Chelsea supporters; thinking, he turns to Jock, "We all go together, and they'll suss, we're Chelsea." "He's got a good point there," says Spider. "OK, split into groups of threes and fours. Tommy, Dave take your boys and do the talking," Then turning to the others, he continues, "Jock you lead us in, that way they won't hear a London accent."

"Little John, Big Steve, you're with us," says Jock, as he starts to slowly move into the corner of the Coventry home end. Lenny motions to Colin, Spider, and Jim, "Come on, and take it easy." Big Steve turns to the girls and says, "OK girls, you're with me and Parkhead. Ghost walks over and grabs Maggie by the arm, "You're coming with me," he commands. "Fuck off you pervert!" snarls Maggie, "Or I'll kick you in the nuts." They wait till the other groups are well onto the terrace and then move off. Big Steve looks back to Ghost, "You bring those," pointing to a small group of Shed boys. Ghost nods and looks around at those that are left, "But I always bring up the rear," he says indignantly. "That's so you can watch and learn from the experts," laughs Big Steve. Ghost looks at Big Steve, snarls his lips and turns to survey those that are left.

"Excuse me," Jock says, as he moves through the crowd; the locals move to let them through, and the four move forward and up to the back of the terrace. The Coventry supporters are starting to find their voices, chanting, "COVENTRY! COVENTRY!" at the assembled mass of Chelsea supporters behind the opposite goal. Tommy and Dave are in position at the rear of the terrace and when the song changes to, "CHELSEA WHERE ARE YOU?" they join in with just, "CHELSEA!"

A few heads have followed the groups on their way in, but have little idea that they are watching the Chelsea North Stand Firm moving into position. During a brief lull in the chanting, the Coventry supporters hear a chant coming from the opposite end. "NORTH STAND WHERE ARE YOU? NORTH STAND WHERE ARE YOU?" The Coventry supporters, as a sarcastic re-frame, take up the chant. Merrill nods to Jock as he puts his fingers to his mouth and lets go with a single shrill whistle, and the group of Chelsea supporters start to sing, "WE'RE THE NORTH STAND, WE'RE THE NORTH STAND, WE'RE THE NORTH STAND STANFORD BRIDGE."

The whole of the Coventry terrace goes silent for a moment; the Coventry supporters nearest the North Stand move back, half in surprise, half in fear. A gap of around five yards opens up around them, and then the silence is broken as Mandy runs forward screaming "CHELSEA!" She punches the first person she comes to; he falls back into the crowd. The surprise is total, and panic sets in as Coventry supporters start to move down the terrace towards the pitch. Merrill looks around at the panic and sees what he's been waiting for. A group of over a hundred Coventry supporters are standing their ground to the right of them.

"That's them over there," he says pointing over to them, "CHARGE!" Merrill and Jock are the first to reach the group. Merrill swings a right, and a man of 30, falls to the ground. Jock jumps on the back of a Coventry supporter that starts to run; they both fall to the terrace. Jock turns him over and punches him in the face; Spider grabs the back of his shirt and pulls Jock back as a Dr. Martens boot swings inches past his head. Big Steve catches the boot in mid-flight and kicks the owner in the crotch; he falls to the terrace screaming in agony. Lenny runs over to a man twice his size, half turns, then swings his elbow and smashes the man in the mouth. He falls to the ground. "Shit!" shouts Lenny as he looks at the teeth marks through his ripped shirtsleeve. Little John grabs a supporter from behind, locking his arms around him, "Colin, " he shouts, "He's one of their leaders." Colin runs over and swings a karate chop into the man's neck; he falls to the floor. "Leave him, he's had enough," shouts Lenny. Colin looks down at the body, smiles and moves on.

"Oi! Cunt!" screams Mandy, at a Coventry supporter who just punched Merrill in the back. The man, taken by surprise, turns around only to be met by Mandy's forehead smashing into his nose. Parkhead turns after kicking a running Coventry supporter and starts to laugh as he sees Mandy's forehead. "What's up with you?" Mandy says, as she stands still a moment with a puzzled look on her face. "You look like a Paki woman," Parkhead replies.   "Eh, what the fuck you on about you sweaty bastard?" says Mandy still puzzled. "You've got a spot of blood between your eyes," he smiles, "All you need now is a bleeding sari." Mandy puts her right hand to her forehead and looks at the blood on her fingers. "Don't worry," says Parkhead, as he hits a Coventry supporter that gets too near. It's not yours." "Fuck off!" Laughs Mandy, as she runs after the retreating Coventry mob.

"The filth's coming," shouts Carlos. Jock, hearing him, looks over and sees three policemen moving through the crowd towards them. The Coventry mob starts to run down the terrace to join those already on the pitch. Merrill looks over, sees there are only three police, and shouts, "Have 'em." Big Steve, Colin, and Spider run over to the packed side of the terrace, just as the police move onto the empty space left by the fighting. Big Steve swings a right hook, but the policeman ducks and comes up with his truncheon, and hits Big Steve on the back. Colin kicks the policeman in the side of his leg, and he falls to the ground. Lenny races over and lands a kick square in the face, just as the policeman was getting back up; he falls back on to the terrace.

Colin stands at the edge of the crowd, soaking up the atmosphere, when Jim comes up to him, grabbing his arm and turning him around, "You OK?" he asks, with concern. Colin looks at him and smiles, "Yeah man," he says, "Just soaking up the buzz. God this is better than any shit those idiots can shoot up their arms." "Well, don't soak it up too much or you'll either get kicked to shit, or nicked," says Jim. Carlos looks about at the half empty terrace and sees a long line of police moving through the crowd standing at the side of the terrace, Quick let's finish off those two filth over there, and get down the other end." They run over to behind the two policemen hitting out with their truncheons; Carlos grabs the raised arm of one policeman and pulls it towards him. As he does, Jim kicks out and hits him in the right calf muscle, sending him crashing to the terrace.

Merrill grabs the hand of another policeman as he raises it to hit Jock with his truncheon; he puts his foot behind the policeman's leg and pushes him to the ground. He looks down and stamps on his right leg. "Come on, let's get out of here," shouts Jock, holding his shoulder. "You OK?" says Merrill, as he sees Jock is in pain. "Yeah, yeah, I just got a whack, it's nothing," he says, as he turns and sees the first of the police line start to run towards them across the open terrace, "Come on, let's get the fuck out of here!" The North Stand moves into the crowd and disappears.

"Five minutes to go, and another two points in the bag," says Spider, looking around the terrace of the Chelsea end. Big Steve nods, "I think it's time we got going." He turns and walks towards Colin, and then notices that the police have started to walk along the front of the terrace. "I don't like this," says Lenny, "Time we weren't here." Jock moves through the mass of Chelsea supporters and reaches Tommy, "Pass the word, we meet outside, start moving." Colin sees Jock and nods, then turning to Spider and Jim, he commands, "This is it, let's get out of here." They join the small number of supporters that always leave a game early, edging their way towards the exit. Ghost is standing in the middle of the terrace, leading the victory singsong. "JINGLE BELLS, JINGLE BELLS, JINGLE ALL THE WAY. OH WHAT FUN IT IS TO SEE, CHELSEA WIN AWAY." Seeing movement on the terrace, he continues to sing, but his eyes are following the supporters making their way to the exit. Then he sees Maggie and Merrill moving together, and sensing something is up, he starts to move towards them.

As he nears them, he shouts, "Maggie!" They either didn't hear him, or they are ignoring him. Getting annoyed, he shouts again, "Oi! Maggie!" "Shut your mouth," says Parkhead, as he passes, "You'll get us noticed." "But I want to know where Maggie's going!" he says. "Ghost," says Jim angrily, "Shut it!" Ghost, not giving up, shouts one last time, "Maggie!" Little John has seen what's going on and pushes through the crowd. As he gets to Ghost, he grabs him by his jacket collar and tightens his grip, "Shut your fucking mouth, you big cunt. You'll have the filth all over us." "Get off me!" Ghost says, as he struggles to get loose. Parkhead moves closer, "Look Ghost, keep it quiet, and don't follow us, right!" Ghost, realising the odds are against him, pleads, "I just want to talk to Maggie." Lenny slaps Ghost around the face, "Well it looks like she don't wanna talk to you, so tell that to your fucking newspapers. Now, go back to your little Shed boys, you're not wanted here." "The filth have seen us, let's go," says Parkhead, "Now look what you've done. Fuck off, Ghost." Ghost looks around and sees the police looking up and pointing at him, "Fuck you!" he snarls, turns and walks away.

After the game, the North Stand hold back outside the ground, allowing the Shed to walk off down Catherine Street on their way to the precinct. As the Shed reach the precinct, the Coventry mob ambush them at the main square. The General takes control as the Stockwell boys charge through the narrow shop lined streets. Spider sees a group of Coventry supporters standing on the upper pedestrian deck of a row of shops, "Look out they've got bottles," he shouts, as the first of over a dozen missiles crash around them. "Come on, let's get them!" he shouts, as he storms up a flight of stairs, followed by over twenty of the Shed.

The Coventry supporters run to the end of the walkway and start to rush a revolving door, that is the main entrance of a club. This leads to a backlog as they can't all cram their way through. As Spider reaches the door, those left outside realise they are now outnumbered and run in panic, but due to the crush, the revolving door has jammed, and those trapped in the section facing the street are beaten savagely. The General leads the rest of the Shed through the rabbit warren of streets and comes to a square with a statue in the middle. As the Shed walk through, they are again ambushed on two sides. The fringe elements of the Shed, again run in panic, but the hard core of Stockwell and Battersea, now joined by a growing number of the Swiss Cottage/West Hampstead/Kilburn, hold firm. Spider leads his group down the stairs; and turning the corner, he sees the battle, and screaming, "Charge!" he leads his group into the back of one of the Coventry mobs. Taken by surprise, they turn and run.

Meanwhile the North Stand are nearing the station. "Oh, by the way Al," Lenny says, as they start to walk along a road that is lined by shops on one side and a narrow park along the other, "Ghost was looking mighty upset that you were with Maggie, seems he thinks she's still his." Merrill looks around and laughs, "Well, she never was and never will be, and that's from her. She's a free agent and goes with who she wants. to." "We're too bunched up," says Jock, "Some of you move over to the other side, the filth come down here they'll suss us in a second." "Shit!" laughs Little John, "Just when we're going to find out about the birds and bees, as well."

"If yer don't know now," says Jock, "You never will." Little John, still laughing, looks at him and says, "OK, OK, looks like I'll have to ask Uncle Ghost." They all laugh as they split up into small groups.

Leaning on the railings at the edge of the small park and start of the pedestrian underpass that leads into a circular ghost, Little John looks around at the path and sees a boy walking with his mother, wearing a Manchester United scarf. "Why do most of the kids in Manchester support Manure?" he asks with a smile. "I don't know," replies Big Steve, "Why do most of the kids in Manchester support Manure? Because all the mothers tell their kids, not to go near the 'Main Road'." "God they get worse," laughs Lenny.

The bell starts ringing in the red telephone box on the corner and Merrill, who is standing outside, walks in and picks up the receiver. All heads turn and watch as he puts down the phone and walks across to the railings. "How many fucking telephone box numbers does he have for Christ's sake," says Colin shaking his head in disbelief. "Everywhere we go, he notes down numbers. One thing he learnt in the army is, preparation plus good intelligence wins wars," replies Jock. "That was Maggie, the Shed has been ambushed in the precinct and they're on their way now, so get ready," warns Merrill. "So let's go then!" shouts Parkhead. "No! We stay here," says Jock. Merrill points his right arm and says, "Look, if the Coventry come up from that flyover, then the Shed ain't going to make it to the station." "So we stay here, then we can take over so the Shed can make the station," says Jock. "Fair enough," says Colin, "It's just that it goes against the grain to stand by while there's a fight going on."

"No, Jock and Merrill are right," cuts in Little John, "If we were with the Shed, we couldn't stop the ambush, but from here we can take them by surprise in the flank." "Here I don't want to be funny," says Big Steve, a little hesitantly, "But ain't that a pigsty behind us?" Everyone turns around to look at the large building set in it's own grounds. "Yes," says Merrill, "That's the Coventry Police HQ." "Ah fuck 'em," shouts Parkhead, as he spits toward the building, "They're all out on the streets." Jim points over towards the flyover, "Here come the girls." They all watch as the girls walk across the roundabout under the flyover and past the Martyrs Memorial. "That's where those bastards ambushed us a couple of years ago," says Big Steve watching the girls.

Merrill points to a pedestrian bridge spanning the main road, "No-one crosses that bridge until their mob is in the circle, then we cross and have them coming out of the walkways." "Hold up," shouts Jock, "Here's the Shed." All eyes turn to New Union Street, where the first of the Shed are running towards the underpass. "Perfect," says Merrill, "Look, there's the Coventry." He points to where the girls have just walked past the Tax Office. The first of over three hundred Coventry supporters are running towards the pedestrian walkways that lead to the circular green. "Wicked!" laughs Little John, "The perfect fucking trap, I like it." "When?" asks Big Steve. "Whenever you fancy it, lead away," answers Merrill.

Big Steve looks down to the circle where the first of the Coventry are starting to fight with the Shed, some of whom panic and run. Then he looks over to Ringway as the main Coventry mob is charging to cut the Shed off from the station. "Look! Only The General and his crew are standing firm," shouts Colin. Big Steve walks towards the bridge, turns and commands, "No shouting 'till we're down there." "Well say the fucking word then!" says Big Steve, as everyone is bursting to get going.

"Oh, we small band, we happy few," romances Big Steve, at the top of his voice, "Cry Havoc and let rip the North Stand." "Spider will be proud of you," laughs Jock. Walking out of the underpass, The General, seeing Big Steve leading the charge, turns and shouts, "Don't run, we have 'em." Some members of the Shed hearing him, stop and turn; seeing the North Stand charging into the Circle, they run back and join in the fight. Police sirens start to echo around the Circle; the Coventry start to run into the walkways, "North Stand to the rescue" laughs Spider. "Fuck off," replies The General, "Where were they in the city then?" "Waiting to save your necks, here" says Spider, "Why?" The General looks him in the eyes, "If we'd all stuck together, they wouldn't have nearly run as in the precinct." The North Stand run through the small circular garden and into one of the tunnels under the ring road, straight into the main Coventry mob. Finally realising what is going on, The General leads the Shed up towards the station, and looking back he sees the Coventry mob running back towards the flyover, followed by the North Stand. He stops and turns to those still making their way to the station, "Come on, the Specials are already in."

Police sirens ring out from all directions as the battle rages under the flyover. As the first of the police panda cars skid to a stop, two officers, get out. with truncheons drawn. "Quick, let's get the fuck out of here," shouts Big Steve, as he sees a Black Maria pull up next to the police car. Jock looks around and sees that three more Black Maria are blocking the road to the station, "Right follow me!" he screams, as he runs towards the Maria's. Two green police coaches pull up under the flyover; police start to pour out and run towards them. The North Stand start to run, following Jock towards the Maria's. /Lenny jumps in the air, sticking his arm out and clothes lining one of the policemen, and drags him to the ground. Big Steve runs up behind him and kicks the policeman in the head. "Whatcha doing?" shouts Big Steve, as he sees Mandy standing at the back of one of the Maria's. "Got a match then?" she says as he runs over. Seeing the hankie in the petrol cap, he pulls his Zippo lighter and sets fire to the hankie. "RUN!" they shout, as the hankie bursts into flames. "Oh fuck that!" gasps Little John, as he sees the flames.

Lenny and Merrill have opened the door of a parked Hillman Super Snipe. Merrill lets off the hand brake as Lenny pushes from behind, jumping out as it gathers speed down the hill. Merrill stands and watches the Hillman as a group of police from the coaches jump out of the way, just as the Hillman hits the burning Black Maria. The flash of flame is followed by a hollow boom; panic sets in amongst the police, who are now too busy trying to put the fire out to go chasing Cockneys. "Fucking hell!" gasps Tommy, "You lot are fucking mad." "But don't yer just love it!" shouts Dave, as he runs past. Tommy starts to laugh as he sees the police are not following, "I do, when we get away with it." "Why ain't the filth following?" asks Maggie, as she walks over to Merrill. "I don't know, maybe trying to put the fire out and clear the road?" Maggie turns and walks with Merrill up the station walkway, "Looks like the Shed's special has gone already." "Alan, I'll phone yer," shouts Tommy, as he walks into the station, "We're on the other platform, train to Brum is in, in three minutes," he says, looking at his watch. "Fuck that, we'll come with yer to Birmingham," shouts Jim, as he starts to run into the station.

The bar on Coventry Station is on the southbound platform; the walls of which are plate glass, allowing a view out onto the start of the pedestrian walkway. Running along the only brick wall, is a long bar, split into two sections; the first is for food, and the second is the bar. The tables and chairs are were of the typical minimal metal BR type. "They don't have any lager, Al," Maggie shouts across the bar to Merrill, who is sitting at a table with Jock, saving places for Maggie and Mandy. "Make it a Pepsi then," he replies, and as he turns his head, he looks through the glass window and sees over twenty police walking into the station. "Well, we'll see if we can blag this one out," smiles Jock. "Just as well the others made that Birmingham train," smiles Merrill.

Seeing the station is nearly deserted, a sergeant walks into the bar. Taking a long look around at the empty tables, he walks over to where Merrill and Jock are sitting, then stops and says, "Up here for the game then lads?" Maggie and Mandy stand in silence at the bar. "No, we've been to the cathedral and museum with the girlfriends," says Merrill, "Mind you, that's the last time we come up here on a match day." The sergeant stands looking at the pair sitting at the table; studying their clothes, and seeing that they are dressed in smart jackets and trousers, he looks at the shoes. Clearly annoyed, he turns and walks out of the bar and starts talking to the police on the platform. After a moment, they walk down the slope and disappear.

"Jesus! We dodged the bullet there," sighs Jock. "Yeah, that was just a bit too close," says a relieved Merrill as they both collapse in laughter. Mandy walks over to the table and puts the drinks down. As she does, she notices Ghost walking up to the station, "Oh shit! Look what the cat dragged in!" Ghost walks into the bar, and seeing Maggie getting served, he walks over to her and says, "Get me a beer then love!" Maggie turns and looks him in the face, "I ain't your love, so get your own," she replies. "That's no way for a girlfriend to behave," putting his arm around her shoulder, "Get me a beer," he orders. "Listen here, you idiot. For the last time," Maggie says angrily, "I am not your girlfriend, and I never have been, so piss off, get in the queue and act like a human being for once in your fucking life."

"There ain't no queue, it's just you and me," he says, as he puts his other arm on her shoulder. "Don't fuck me about, just get me a beer," Ghost snaps. "Oi!" says Jock, "Who the fuck do you think you're talking to?" Ghost turns, and for the first time, notices Jock, Merrill and Mandy sitting at the table. His temper now boiling over, he looks at Jock, "Shut it, this has nothing to do with you, you Scots Git." He turns to Maggie, his face getting flushed, "Well?" Maggie holding a tray with crisps and a Danish Pastry on it, starts to walk past Ghost, "Get lost Ghost." With this, Ghost loses his top, turns and slaps Maggie across the face. Taken by shock, she half stumbles as she tries to save the tray and its contents, from falling to the floor.

"You cunt," screams Jock, as he gets up from the table and charges towards the counter; Ghost sees him coming and lands a punch full in the face. Jock half falls back, but manages to kick Ghost on his inside right thigh. Merrill runs over to the bar; looking at Maggie and checking her face, he says, "Go and sit down." Then he turns to Ghost, who is bending over rubbing his leg; a kick lands with a bull thud in Ghost's stomach. As he falls to the floor, Merrill grabs him and picks him up bodily, then throws him across a table. Ghost lands with a crash on a second table, sending it and the chairs flying to the floor. Jock runs over to Ghost, who is sprawled out on the floor, and kicks him in his side, "You fucking cunt" he screams.

"Leave him," commands Merrill, "He ain't fucking worth it." He turns to Maggie, puts his hand up to her face and looks at the red weld that is getting brighter. "I'm alright, that pig couldn't hurt me if he tried," she says, in anger, "I can't believe he did that." There is total silence in the bar as everyone looks at the still body of Ghost lying on the floor. "Hey the train's coming," shouts Lenny from the door. "What do we do with Ghost?" queries Mandy "Leave him here," commands Merrill.

"Where the fuck did you lot come from?" says Jock, in surprise. Little John looks at Big Steve, and then says, "We went on the other platform, with Tommy and Dave's boys, then hid in the waiting room when we saw the filth." Merrill shakes his head and laughs, "I wondered where you lot had got to." "So you missed us then, did yer?" smiles Colin. "Yeah right, let's get the train before it goes." Running for the train, Jim holds the door open as everyone jumps aboard. The carriage is empty and everyone sprawls out on a seat each. "Hey you seen "Two Mules For Sister Sara "asks Big Steve looking across the small table at Little John. "Yeah" replies Little John, "A bit slow, but another great soundtrack from Morricone," Comes the reply. "You should go and see "Blood On Satan's Claw" cuts in Colin. "Linda Hayden's in it, and she gets her kit off," "Nice Bush?" queries Jim. Maggie looks at Merrell, and burst out laughing.

CHAPTER EIGHT

Jim Doyle sits back, and drumming his fingers on the table, he looks up and says, "What seems to rub most people up the wrong way is that Merrill is not interested in justifying to them what he did. He doesn't feel the need, and that seems to piss people off. It's apparently not enough to say,
'It was wrong.' It's not enough to say, 'Times have changed.' It seems a bit of grovelling is called for."

"The North Stand never attacked normal supporters, and in fact, on a number of occasions, we steamed in against the Shed, who were," commented Merrill, and looking at the Americans, says, "The North Stand protected Chelsea Supporters at away games and we also stopped away supporters at home games from getting out of control."

David nods his head, "I don't condone violence and I don't resort to it, but neither do I condemn people, categorically, for having done so. None of us are saints, so why the fuck should we expect people to come before us and grovel?" Looking over at Kevin, he continues, "I guarantee, that if you were to be attacked by opposition supporters at a game, you and your ilk, would be the first ones with your hands up begging for help from people like the North Stand Firm. I know I would, and I would be grateful for such help."

A NIGHT IN DURRELL ROAD

Wednesday September 23rd. 1970

Durrell Road is a one hundred-yard row of Georgian houses, off the Fulham Road, about a mile south of Fulham Broadway. In the ground floor kitchen of number five, Merrill is keeping an eye on a saucepan of mince, while chopping up green and red peppers. Maggie, who arrived an hour before, is stirring a pan of spaghetti. That was a good win last night," says Merrill. Maggie looks up and smiles, "Yeah, but it was only Sheffield Wednesday." "Don't matter, two, one is a result," he replies. "Thank Gawd they didn't bring a mob down," Maggie says as, she turns the gas down. Merrill chuckles to himself, and says, "Well, what do you expect on a Tuesday night?" Gathering up the chopped peppers, he drops them into the pan with the mince, then pours in a can of tomatoes, "So, you're having second thoughts about fighting then?"

Maggie looks at him a moment, then says, "I was never really into it. I just back Mandy up." Merrill frowns, "You mean without Mandy, you wouldn't fight?" Maggie thinks a moment, then replies, "No, to tell you the truth, it scares me, but it turns me on as well." "You don't have to do it just because of Mandy you know. I mean she's one in a million," replies Merrill. "Yeah, but she expects me to," says Maggie, a little sheepishly. "Oh, don't give me that bollocks! She loves it, but if you think like that, then fuck what people think, you just take it easy." He looks over to her, "No-one expects you to fight, least of all Mandy, so start standing with Veronica."

"You know, last week when Ghost slapped me?" she says, casually changing the subject, "You looked like you'd seen a ghost." Merrill looks over to her, "No, you're imagining things. I just couldn't believe he hit yer, that's all." Maggie walks over to the side door that leads into the garden, "God it's hot in here with that cooker on." Opening it, she looks back, "It was more than that," she adds, "I think it affected you more than it did me." "No it was nothing," he says looking guilty. He turns to the sink and drains the water out of the pan. "Want to talk about it?" says Maggie softly. "No!" he replies, forcefully. "What time are the others getting here?" she asks. "In about twenty minutes, we can keep this lot warm in the oven if we have to."

"I wondered why you had it on," she says, as she moves to the sink to drain her pan, "Look I know we ain't been together long, but if you want to get it off your chest, it won't go any further." He stops and looks at her, his mind ticking over, then he answers, "It's nothing, just something that happened once and I've never really got over it, besides we hardly know each other." "That's the point, isn't it," she says. "How'd yer mean?" he answers, bending over to open the oven door. "Let's put the grub in the oven and talk. You'll feel better," she says. "You're not going to let this go, are you?" he retorts. "I'm not trying to box you in, you're a free agent and I'm just a ship passing in the night," she adds.

Merrill covers the saucepan, turns around, and looks long and hard at Maggie, "OK, but you don't put down any anchors, right?" She smiles, "I'm just a friend, and if I read you right, that's all I ever will be. But friends should be there for each other and you need to unload." Merrill puts the saucepan into the oven, then takes the spaghetti and pours some water into the pan, and puts that in the oven too. Checking that everything in the kitchen is OK, he bends down to make sure that the oven is on low. Then he turns and walks through the door, and along the hallway into the living room. Maggie walks in and sees him sitting on the sofa, deep in thought, staring out off the bay windows into the garden. She sits down in the armchair and lights up a cigarette.

After a few moments, he looks over and says, "I married this bird from Glasgow three years ago. Still not sure why, but if the truth were known, I was properly infatuated by her blonde hair, wonderful cheek bones, and hourglass figure." He leans over to the small coffee table and takes out a JPS; after lighting it he blows out a smoke ring, "We went out a few times, then started sleeping together. That's when she told me she was pregnant, by a Canadian called Pete." He looks for a reaction from Maggie, but she just sits there listening, "When he found out, he fucked off back to Canada, and like a Prat I said I'd marry her." Maggie puts the cigarette in the ashtray, and then looking up she asks, "You regret marring her?" Merrill thinks for a moment and then continues, "Not at the time. We got on quite well, then in the January she had a miscarriage."

He pauses in thought a moment, then continues, "This changed her completely. At first, I thought it was because of the miscarriage, but a friend of mine, who knew her, told me that she had been sleeping around quite a lot, even when we were married." He leans forward and drops some ash into the ashtray, then looking at the cigarette packet laying on the table, he leans over and picks it up and looks at it, then continues, "It was a packet of fags just like this that started it. We were in the tube going to a party, and she asked for a fag. I got my packet out and playfully tossed it up in the air, so it would land on her lap. When it did she went mental, screaming and shouting, so when we got to Finchley Road Station, she just got up and walked out of the carriage without waiting."

Pausing a moment, he puts the packet back on the coffee table, then looking over to Maggie, he continues, "Well, I let her walk ahead, and to give her a chance to calm down, I popped into this Italian café. I had a quick cup of coffee and then went to the party in Goldhurst Terrace. When I walked into the front room, she was dancing slowly, up close with some guy who was feeling up her arse, so I went up and asked if I could have a dance. The geezer said, "Fuck off". "So what did you do?" Maggie asks "I told him she was my wife, he said sorry and walked off, looking guilty." Merrill sat in silence then leaning forward, stubbed out the cigarette. "Didn't you mind?" asked Maggie. "No," he replied, "I was half expecting something like that. Anyway she went ballistic, screaming and shouting at me, then she punched me in the face."

He stops, and looking up at the ceiling, continues, "I slapped her around the face, not hard, more like a reflex action. Anyway, she looked at me, then fell to the floor, making out she was knocked out." "You knocked her out with a slap?" queries Maggie. "No, No," he says, more reassuring himself than anything else, "She was putting it on for all the people at the party. I think they knew that as no-one said a word, so I just walked out. "So what happened?" says Maggie softly. He looks over to her, smiles a guilty smile and continues, "She divorced me for cruelty. I never contested it, but I've felt guilty about it ever since. I should never have done that, I still can't believe that I slapped her."

"And when Ghost slapped you, it all came flooding back," says Maggie, in a concerned voice, as she sits back and looks at Merrill; leaning forward and picking up the cigarette, she blows out the smoke and watches as a smoke circle floats up to the ceiling, "You've had that on your conscience ever since, haven't you?" she says, sitting back in the chair and crossing her legs. Yup," he said sadly, "It still haunts me." "Would you ever do it again?" she asks. He flashes a look at her, then says, "No that taught me a lesson. A man should never hit a woman, no matter what the situation." "Well

I'm glad to hear that!" Maggie said, light-heartedly, in an effort to break the tension. Merrill smiles, "No, you're quite safe, anyway I feel better just getting it off me chest," he adds, "Lets get the food done before the others get here."

He gets up and walks towards the door. Maggie watches him and then follows. "Anyway, she says, "You'd didn't hit her, you just slapped her face to stop her having a tantrum. There's a world of difference between the two." "True, but it don't matter, I slapped, and it don't matter that it was a light slap, I slapped her," he says as he walks into the kitchen, "Anyhow, as we're playing the truth game, what really got you into fighting?" he turns and looks at her. "You serious?" she queried. "Yup, I've always wondered just what makes a woman fight, and what you said earlier was just the tip of the iceberg, wasn't it." "Where's the cheese," she says, as if wondering out loud. He points to a cupboard, "In there, so come on then." She takes the cheese out of the cupboard and takes the grater off the wall, "I was bullied at school, 'cos I was the first one to blossom so to speak." He stops, turns and looks puzzled, "In what way?"

"Well you know, me tits started to show, and the other girls couldn't hack it, so I got bullied. They picked on my blonde hair and said I was a rich bitch tramp. They were jealous. It was so stupid, but it scared me shitless, then they started to beat me up." She stopped grating the cheese; a tear slowly ran down her cheek, "I used to go to the games and when I saw you lot, it was as if I could get my own back."

Merrill looked up as he takes the spaghetti pan out of the oven and drains the water off into the sink; pouring the spaghetti into a bowl, he looks up and says, "You're kidding! You use football as a way of getting back at the girls in your old school?" Maggie looked at him and half smiled as if to hide her guilt, "I was at an Arsenal game and I saw Susan Carolhassen standing there with an Arsenal scarf around her neck." Pausing as if to picture the scene, she continues, "She was the worst one. A fight started, and I just ran up to her and started hitting her. It was the first time I'd ever hit anyone." She looks over to Merrill and smiles, "It felt so good. Then she went down and I felt like I was in a different world. Then some bloke came over, I don't know who he was, but I just started punching him."

The sound of the doorbell punctuates the silence. "Oh shit, look at me," she cries in panic. "Go in the bathroom and tidy up, I'll get the door," Merrill says, as he walks into the hall towards the front door. Maggie disappears into the bathroom as the door swings open. Jock holds up a bottle of wine, and laughing, says, "Here you go you old English cunt." Merrill laughs, "Fuck me, a Sweaty Sock, spending money, that's a first!" "He borrowed the money of

Veronica," laughs Little John, standing behind Veronica, Big Steve. They walk in, followed by Dave and Mandy who, looking around, says, "Where's Maggie, ain't she here yet?" Merrill shuts the door, turns and answers, "Yeah, she's been helping me with the dinner, she's in the bathroom." "What! Been having a quick one then?" chirps Little John. "I should be so lucky," Merrill replies, "Dump your coats in the bedroom and go into the dining room, I'll get the grub."

Dave takes his jacket off and throws it to Little John. Merrill," he says, "Any plans for the Yids?." "I'll tell yer in a minute, just take a seat," he shouts from the kitchen. After dinner, everyone watches Jock as he licks his plate clean. "Shit that wasn't half bad," he says, with a surprised look on his face, after having finished seconds. "Cheeky Scot's Git," smiles Maggie, as she gets up from the table and leans over to collect the dirty plates. Little John looks at her low cut top, then says, "Looks like Alan's getting two hard boiled eggs for afters." Dave breaks the laughter, "So what's the score with the Yids?" Merrill picks up the bottle of wine and starts pouring a glass. Veronica gets up and looks at Mandy, "Come on, we'll help Maggie out in the kitchen, before this lot bore us with tactics." Veronica picks up the pasta and cheese bowls, and the two girls walk to the kitchen.

"Right," Merrill says, as they disappear, "I've arranged with the General that he'll start to move the Shed into the East Stand tunnel when he here's us sign "Chelsea Where Are You." What!" exclaims Little John. "Why the fuck are we gonna sign that?" "Because we'll be wearing Yid scarves and when we sign that, we'll get them to attack the Shed, by going into the East Stand tunnel" replies Merrill. "What and have us come up behind them and trap them in the tunnel says Dave thoughtfully, Nice plan if it'll work."

Maggie walks back in, and says, "Right you lot, we've done coffee so move your arses into the front room." "Yeah, but Merrill's front room is at the back," observes Jock, with a smile. "Bollocks!" snaps Maggie, looking at the faces making no effort to move, and then she continues, "Move your arses into the sitting room," as she walks back out. They all get up and walk down the hall towards the sitting room. "Bloody hell!" exclaims Big Steve, as he walks through the door into the spacious sitting room, dominated by the large French windows that look onto a long well kept garden. Over a dozen wooden Schweppes soft drinks crates, are stacked up by the windows, filled with forty-fives. Along the left hand wall is a series of shelves full of albums. Big Steve walks over to the albums, and his wide-open eyes flash back and forth along the rows. "My God," smiles Jock, "He's like a kid in a toy shop." "Well, let's have some background music then," comments Little John, as he flops into one of the armchairs, "How about some Dylan?" "Nah, you've got to sit and listen to Dylan, not talk over him. Answers Big Steve.

"OK put a live recording on, how about the new tones album Get Yer Ya-Ya's Out" says Little John. "Symphony For The Devil & Street Fighting Man, are better on that album than the studio versions. says Jock. "There's always the best live album ever!" Little John says thinking out loud, "The Who Live At Leeds." "Ah buts that's with modern day recording equipment says Big Steve. "The best all time Live album is James Brown at the Apollo." "Great choice and a classic, but what about the Motown Revue Record Live at the Apollo, says Merrill. "Talking about Motown, says Jock, you got the new Motown Chartbusters yet?" "Yeah it's over there on the shelf" Merrill replies.

Put something instrumental on," says Dave, sitting down on a beanbag. Big Steve, pulling out one of the albums, turns and says, "How about this one then?" holding up Booker T. & the MG's Soul Dressing. "Yeah, that'll do," replies Merrill, taking the album and walking over to the turntable. Big Steve walks over and sits on a beanbag, then looks over to Jock sitting on the sofa, "I was reading a book a couple of weeks ago that said your namesake was Welsh." "Ah?" questions Jock, in total confusion. Big Steve smiles and continues, "William Wallace, the Scots geezer that took on the Normans." Jock half laughs shaking his head, "Yes you've said that before." "I haven't heard it though," says Maggie, as she walks in carrying a plate full of biscuits, "Carry on then, it sounds interesting." Jock throws her a look, not wanting to be reminded by the English of an ancestor, "I wouldn't say I was related, but you never know my luck, besides it was the English army." "Wrong, there were hardly any Saxons in it, as Henry I still had them under the thumb and didn't really trust them, and there were more Scots in the Norman army than in the Scots one," retorts Big Steve.

"Oh, don't give me that bollocks pal," says Jock, in disbelief. "No, seriously, but I had to laugh when it said that Wallace was really called Wallensis, the Gaelic Celt for Welsh, so his name was William Welsh." "It's all English bollocks, written by someone that had the arsehole because you once had a Scottish Royal family." Big Steve smiles as he reaches over to a Schweppes box and flicks through the forty fives. Without looking at Jock, he continues, "It also said that Charles I was just as big an oppressor of the Scots as Henry I. It was him that outlawed the Celtic tongue in Scotland and almost taxed them out of existence.

Veronica walks in with a tray full of coffee cups, and sensing the growing wind up, she looks at Jock and asks, "So how did you fall in with this lot of rouges in the first place then?" "Yeah, I've always wondered how you lot got together," said Maggie as she walks in behind Veronica, carrying a plate of custard cream biscuits, and puts the coffee-pot on the coffee table. "You're kidding, you don't really want to know all that rubbish do yer?" asks a surprised Jock. "Yeah why not? Should be interesting," adds Mandy.

Jock laughs and looks at Merrill, then sits back in his chair; putting his hands together, he starts tapping his fingertips, "Well, If I remember right, the first time I met this Anglo-Saxon bastard was at Leicester in 1965." He looks over at Merrill, who smiles as he nods, "I'm walking back from the ground with the Shed, and the Leicester mob come steaming round the corner, and all hell breaks loose." "In that park was it?" asks Little John, reaching for a coffee. "No, we'd passed that," continued Jock, "This was near the station. Anyway the Shed breaks and runs, and all of a sudden I'm on my own, with around one hundred of these fucking Northern Neanderthals, baying for me blood." He pauses a moment as Maggie hands him a coffee, "I thought I was a gonna."

"Should've left you to 'em, you old Scots cunt," laughs Merrill, as he lights a John Player Special. "Leicester is in the Midlands," says Big Steve still looking through the record collection, but with one ear on the conversation. "Norf of fucking Watford, init?" says Dave in a mock East End accent. Jock reaches over to the cigarette packet Merrill just tossed on the coffee table; taking one out, he sits back and lights it, "So there I was thinking, I'm a gonna, when this great ugly Git bursts through and asks if I'm OK," Jock chuckles, "I'm about to die, and he asks if I'm alright!" Mandy laughs and nearly chokes on her coffee. "So he says, 'let's have 'em,'" Jock continues, "We were outside a Wimpy Bar and there was this crate of empty milk bottles by the door, he says grab one and gives it to me," Jock takes a drag, then continues, "Mind you, he makes sure he has two. So there I am holding this fucking milk bottle, shouting, 'Come on yer bastards,' thinking to myself 'I'm gonna die', when this prick shouts, "First one forward gets it."

"So what happened then?" says Dave, leaning forward and looking fascinated. "Well, there's always one ain't there?" continued Jock, looking around, "This fucking idiot steps forward and starts to say something, but before he gets one word out, smash! These two bottles disintegrate into his face. Another one steps forward, so I land him one on the head with my bottle." "So you were both having a smashing time them?" Little John laughs. Ignoring him, Jock continues, "I grabbed one of them by the arm as he went to punch me." Leaning forward he sips his coffee, then carries on, "Merrill sees it, and grabs the other arm and shouts, 'The window'. So we both throw this cunt into the window. Of course, I expected him to bounce right off." "Ha, when was the last time you saw someone bounce off a window?" Merrill says, with a big grim. "So what happened?" asks

110

Maggie. "Well, he goes straight through the fucking thing, lands on a table and slowly slides off, blood spurting fucking everywhere. The Leicester see this and do a runner. I'm standing there still wondering what the fuck had just happened when this idiot just looks over and says. "I hope we ain't missed the train."

"Oh my Gawd, I'd loved to have seen that!" Little John says above the laughter. Dave stops laughing, gets up and walks to the window, looking out he says, "OK, Johnny why did you start fighting?" Little John looks surprised, but leans forward and pours another coffee, and then leaning back, he looks up at the ceiling as if in search of lost memories, "Well I used to go to games with a friend from school, we got set on a couple of times at away games. You know how it is, walking to Anfield from the station and some Scouse cunt comes up and asks you for the time. He hears your Cockney accent, and ten of the slags kick you to shit. Brave fuckers those northern bastards," he adds with spit, "Anyway, I got pissed off with that, thought there was safety in numbers, so started going with the Shed, then fell in with the North End Road Boys."

Dave smiles to himself, and says, "The best crew in the Shed, and the genesis of the North Stand." Maggie looks over to Big Steve, who is still looking out of the French windows, "Your turn." Big Steve turns around. then looks back at her, "It's the passion of the game init, Chelsea is my tribe, and when some barbarian northern Neanderthal gets in my face and slags Chelsea off," his lips tighten, "Well you know, you gotta ain't yer. I love kicking the fuck out of those cunts." He pauses, a smile slowly creeps across his face, sorry Dave." Then he looks at Merrill, "OK Merrill, how about you?"

Merrill looks around and raises his eyebrows, "Well," he said slowly, "It's the camaraderie, the excitement, the never knowing if you're going to get through it. Never really caring if you get through it, but just getting the other geezer, that's all that matters. Showing him whose turf he's on, and what the cost of being there is. Of taking his turf, at away games, showing him not to fuck with Chelsea." He pauses a moment, looking over to the wall, "I mean it's like when I was in the army, all they do is teach you how to kill, then when you get a head wound, and they kick you out, they expect you to be all nice and normal." He looks around at the assembled faces, "Well yer can't just fucking switch off, not like that. Fear is a drug, and the will to control that fear is better than any shit you can sniff up your nose. You move onto another plane, everything is so clear, so tranquil, so precise." Maggie looks down at Merrill's tightly clenched fists, and gently puts her left hand on it.

"There's no such thing as a coward," continues Merrill, "If you can't find that switch to turn on the adrenaline." He pauses, sweat running down his forehead, "The thing that gets you the most, is why you."

He slowly wipes a bead of sweat off, "Why, when your mates, better blokes than you, get killed all around you. And you live." He pauses again, "WHY?" Getting up out of the chair, and without saying a word, he walks out of the room.

CHAPTER NINE

"But you never get organised violence at American games," says 50 year-old Irish American and Jimmy Rogers look-a-like, Jim Doyle, proudly. "That's because your psyche won't let you," answers Mark Diamond, with a wry smile. Jim looked puzzled at this reply, "Sorry, I'm not with you, what are you getting at?" Dave takes a mouthful of beer, looks at the Americans, and then continues, "No disrespect here, but you people are so egotistic and gun-ho, you think you're the greatest thing on the planet, yet in reality you're very divided," he pauses a moment for the customary rebuff, but is pleased to see that it doesn't come, "White Americans look down on the Mexicans and Blacks, and as long as you do that you'll never unite as a nation, let alone to come together to fight at football games."

Big Al sits up straight in his chair, "I find that very offensive, we didn't come here for an argument." Alan Chandler looks over at Big Al and, putting his hand up, says, "No, no-one is trying to be offensive, we're just having a discussion, so let's keep it on that level." Alan looks at Big Al, but seeing that now he's controlling his anger continues, "But that's part of what Mark just said, you're too quick to jump to conclusions. You never take the time to think a thing through." "Exactly!" exclaims Mark, "A group of English soccer supporters that go to Raider games have been getting the Blacks and Mexicans together, now they've succeeded in getting White Americans to join together with them. That's why, when the Raiders went to San Diego, there was organised fighting on the terraces for the first time." "That was you guys?" roared Big Al in shocked disapproval. "No of course not, but we hear things," Dave said reassuringly.

The Americans look at each other but are interrupted by Alan, "Let's give you an example of not thinking things through. Take the events that led to the Pan Am Airliner bomb over Lockerbie in

112

Scotland. There's a theory that it all started in the Prussian Gulf because a US warship captain was too gun-ho." "Oh please," sighed Jim Boyle, "Now you're just being ridiculous." "No, not at all," says Alan, "Look at the facts of the case. You were a neutral nation, patrolling the Gulf to protect International shipping right?" Big Al nods and says, "Well yes that is my understanding," Jim with a puzzled look on his face asks, "But what are you getting at?" "Well," continues Alan, "The Iranians use small gun boats called Bog-hammers to attack shipping going to and from the Iraqi oilfields. You had a Missile Cruiser called the Vincennes on station, when a loud explosion was reported. The Vincennes sent a 'chopper to investigate, it found some Bog-hammers, in Iranian not International waters, but no shipping under attack." Mike Gilmartin looking intrigued cut in, "Err, excuse me for asking, but how do you know all this?" Dave leans back in his chair and looks up to the ceiling, "There was a British TV crew on board the Vincennes, at the time, and their footage has been show on TV back home." Jim looks at the other Americans in surprise and asks, "But what has this to do with the Pan Am flight?" asked Jim.

"Well," continued Alan, "The Bog-hammers fire a warning shot for the 'chopper to keep away, so it flies back to the Vincennes, where upon the Captain crosses into Iranian waters and opens fire with his cannon at the Bog-hammers," "This in it's self is an act of war." Mark Diamond points out. The Americans look at each other and sit and listen in puzzled silence. "Then a plane is sighted on radar flying in Iranian airspace, they wrongly assume that it's an Iranian F14, and Captain Rogers orders it shot down. Now if he wasn't trigger happy, wouldn't he have listened for the IFF on both the military and civil bands, to find its true identity?" Jim Doyle looks puzzled, "What's an IFF signal? He asks. "That's a signal all aircraft put out, it's identifies friend and foe," adds Alan. "Why do you say he was Gung-ho?" queries Big Al. "Well you could see and hear them on the bridge; they appeared to be acting like a bunch of school kids squashing their first beetle." Adds Mark.

TOTTENHAM AT HOME

Saturday November 14th. 1970

The Wheatsheaf Pub was throbbing with anticipation and filling up fast. Tottenham is always the biggest game of the year; ever since defeat at the 1967 FA Cup Final, the first game following that defeat has gone down in Chelsea folk law as the "The Park Lane Massacre". The General was standing by the pub door with the Stockwell and the Southfield boys, some of whom were milling around outside; grouped around the dartboard were some of the Battersea Boys, while over by the bar were members of the North End Road and North Stand.

"So no more Ten Bob Notes from next week." Says Merrill as he and Jock walk along the Kings Road, towards the pub, "I don't get it" Jock replies, Things still cost Ten Schillings, it just means more bloody Shrapnel in yer pocket." As they walk nearer to the Pub, Jock stops and looks at the traffic waiting at the lights. "That's the new Cortina," he says with surprise. "That's the first one I've seen." "I like the Coke Bottle curve over the back wheel." Replies Merrill, "Very Chevrolet!" "A great new design, look at the new Austin Maxi, they just revamp that ugly pile of shit!" says Jock. "When British Leyland should have done what Ford has done, and restyled it completely." "Yeah but the problem with British Leyland, is the fucking left wing unions, who object to everything if it don't lead to more tea breaks, and a pay rise;" laughs Merrill, Then just as they are about to walk through the door, they bump into Linda, who is looking very annoyed.

"Why don't you look where you're going?" snaps the 26 year-old, 5 foot 10 brunette; her oversized fashion glasses and short mini skirt making everyone's head turn. "Oh sorry!" replies Jock, sarcastically. Merrill looks at her, tilts his head and softly says, "What's the matter?" It's obvious that Linda is fuming and she replies,

114

angrily, "Why don't you ask your mate Dave, he thinks it's funny to have a one night stand, then tell the world about it." Jock sniggers then looks away. At this, Linda storms off without another word. "Looks like Dave's opened a can of worms there," says Merrill, as they walk into the bar. "Well, what the fuck does she expect?" laughs Jock.   Merrill, walking to the front door of the Wheatsheaf, turns as he replies, "A can of worms like that, we can do without. The bitch is trouble, and I told him what she's like." "He says he's actually moving down to London," says Jock, as he pushes the door open. "That's to be with Mandy," observes Merrill, "I think they're going to shack up."

Stepping into the Wheatsheaf, Merrill heads for the bar. Jock looking around, sees The General and walks over to him. "Hello mate, we sticking to the same plan?" greets Jock. "Yes," answers The General, his head turning to follow Merrill, "But keep that maniac under control, we don't want him wading in before we're ready and spoiling everything." Jock frowns, "Oh come on, I know you two don't get along but we ain't about to spoil your show," he answers, reassuringly.

"Alright mate, what yer drinking?" asks Dave "Lowenbrau," replies Merrill, as he nears the bar, "And what the fuck have you been doing to Linda?" he adds angrily. Dave smiles and turns to order the beers. "What's your problem?" Dave shouts over the noise of the bar, "I did ask if it was alright to go out with her." Merrill looks around the bar and sees that everyone is there; Spider and Carlo standing by the bar, nod hello. "So what the fuck have I done wrong then?" Dave asks, as he turns back from the bar with two pints of larger. Merrill takes one and puts it to his mouth, and taking a refreshing first drink, he brings the glass down half empty and looks at Dave, "I told yer to be careful with her, and what do ya do, bang her then drop her." Dave looks puzzled, "I don't see what the problem is," he says, "She's a bike, so she should be used to it, besides, she reckons she had half the team."

"It's all that shit she snorts up her fucking nose that makes so mental," says Carlo through torte lips. "Yeah that slapper is so fucking arrogant, she struts around like the big cheese and expects everyone to fucking worship her," replies Dave. "Yeah I don't like junkies," says Spider, "They make out they're your best friend then turn on you at the drop of a hat. Paranoid bastards, that's what they are!" "There's a thing called style," Merrill says, glancing up to the ceiling in disgust, "If you don't treat a woman with respect, it gets around and they'll all be pulling up the draw bridge."

He pauses to drink some more larger, "So what if she sleeps around, don't you?" "Yeah, buts that's different, besides you gave her one," Dave replies, angrily. Merrill shakes his head, "No, we're just friends, and it ain't different, and do you see her complaining about me?" Dave shakes his head, and Merrill continues, "You going around shouting about it is dumb. I've told you, appreciate what you get and treat them with respect, and you'll get more. Treat them like shit, and you end up wondering why everyone else is getting it and you ain't." Merrill finishes the last of the lager, looks at Dave and adds, "Besides she can turn nasty and has to be treated with kid gloves. Play up to her ego and part on good terms."

Dave, beginning to realise where he's gone wrong, finishes his drink, then and holding out a packet of cigarettes says, "OK so I got this one wrong, I'll do it different next time." "You should take Mandy to the movies "Kelly's Heroes" is on in Leicester Square," says Merrill. "Funny you should say that, she's already said she wants to see Solider Blue;" replies Dave. "Mind you!" adds Merrill, "El Condor, Lee Van Cleef's new film has a well fit Blonde bird getting her kit off and goes full frontal." "Oh what I'm supposed to take her to that in order to get her in the mood?" laughs Dave.

Before Merrill could reply, Jock walks over and interrupts, "Well that's all arranged," he says with a smile, "We better get going if we're to sneak in without the Yids knowing we're there." Jock notices the new barman give an angry glance in their direction, "It's OK," he reassures, --"It's their nick name the same as ours is the Blues and West Ham is the Hammers." The barman shakes his head in disbelief, "OK, so tell me, how did they get that name in particular?" "Well," says Merrill, leaning against the bar, "You know where Stanford Hill is, right?" The barman nods. "Most of the Ultra Orthodox Jews live in Stanford Hill and support Tottenham as that's their local club, yes?" queries Merrill. The barman gives a disbelieving look to this question,

"But the non-Orthodox Jews don't like them, 'cos they're the ones," Merrill pauses to make sure the barman is following his logic, "That don't accept the state of Israel, they still want an Orthodox state, The Orthodox are seen as the troublemakers. Ordinary Jews just want to live in peace and have a quiet normal life." Merrill pauses to take a drag, "So some of Arsenals normal Jews started the chant Yiddo at the Orthodox, and that's how the name came about. Now everybody calls them it. It's not the big racist thing you're trying to make out is. In reality, there are probably more Jews at Chelsea!" "Yeah!" Jock says, with a smile, "And he should know, he's one of them." The Barman's jaw drops open as he looks in amazement at Merrill who laughs and replies, "Well I was, but I'm Wicken now."

The barman looks even more puzzled at this remark, "But I thought the Jews were a race. How can you just drop out and become whatever it was?" "You'd call it Pagan," Merrill replies, "But I won't go into that. The Jews are not a race, I mean is Mosha Dyan the same race as Sammy Davis Jr.?" The barman shakes his head. "Most people think that the Jews are a race because they started in the Middle East. The City of Ur to be exact. But after the Romans pushed them out of Israel, they moved to the four-corners of Europe. The Ultra Orthodox are in fact a Polish Sect. That's why they wear the black. Anyway, I ain't got all day to give you a history lesson, we're off."

Spider laughs, then burst into song. " IF YOU'RE TIRED AND WEARY, AND YOU'VE GOT A JEW BOY'S NOSE." The rest of the pub joins in, "YOU'LL GET YOU'RE FUCKING HEAD KICKED IN, IF YOU WALK DOWN THE FULHAM ROAD. AND AS YOU PASS THE RISING SUN, YOU'LL HEAR A MIGHTY NOISE. FUCK OF YOU TOTTENHAM BASTARDS, WE ARE THE NORTH STAND BOYS. NOW BIG TIM IS THEIR LEADER, HE'S GOT A HEART OF GOLD. AND HE HASN'T HAD A FORESKIN, SINCE HE WAS ONE DAY OLD. AS HE WALKS IN THE PARK LANE END, THE YIDS BEGIN TO WAIL. BIG TIM IS OUR LEADER, THE KING OF ISRAEL." There is a short pause followed by a chorus of WE HATE TOTTENHAM, WE HATE TOTTENHAM." "We best get going, the North Stand should be filling up nicely by now," says Merrill, as he walks over to Jock..

2.50p.m, The North Stand is packed with visiting Tottenham supporters who are busy in a vocal battle with the Shed. OH WHEN THE SPURS GO MARCHING IN, OH WHEN THE SPURS GO MARCHING IN, I WANT TO BE IN THAT NUMBER, WHEN THE SPURS GO MARCHING IN TOTTENHAM, TOTTENHAM. Unseen by the visiting supporters, a group of over a hundred supporters are slowly gathering on the west side of the North Stand. Big Tim, the 5 foot 8inch leader of Tottenham's main mob, who got his nickname from his large girth, is slowly scanning faces on the North Stand. He knows the leaders of the North Stand by sight, and this is their hunting ground. Like wise Lenny Sykes, the 5foot 10inch West Indian leader of the Tottenham Shelf Mob, is likewise looking around, expecting trouble at any moment.

From the Shed end, the vocal battle continues. "TAKE THE LAST TRAIN TO CHELSEA, AND I'LL MEET YOU AT THE STATION. YOU'D BETTER HAVE YOUR BOOTS ON, 'COS THERE'LL BE SOME AGGRAVATION." The Tottenham retort with a simple, "WE HATE CHELSEA, WE HATE CHELSEA." "Pass the word," says Jock in a low voice, "Join in with their songs." Alan Merrill smiles and turns his head towards the main Tottenham mob, "There's Big Tim, he's looking for us, keep low." Carlo looks over and ducks down, "I hate this hiding shit, why can't The General start moving?" "Give him time," Spider chirps in, "He's got to warm them up first." Lenny looks over to Spider, smiles, and says, "Oi! What the fuck you doing here, I thought you were a 'Shed' Boy?" "I am, but someone has to keep you lot in order and make sure you don't jump the gun," Spider laughs.

Merrill, looking towards the Shed, then, as if by cue, the whole of the Shed start singing. "OH, THE YIDS, YOU SHOULD OF SEEN THEN RUNNING. RUNNING OUT THE PARK LANE END, BECAUSE THE SHED WAS COMING. BIG TIM, LENNY SYKES, YOU SHOULD HAVE SEEN THEIR FACES. RUNNING OUT THE WHITE HART LANE, ALL DRESSED IN BOOTS AND BRACES. CHELSEA, CHELSEA." From the North Stand, five thousand Tottenham supporters retort with, "TOTTENHAM, TOTTENHAM." Again the Shed reply with yet another of their Tottenham anthems, "HE'S ONLY A POOR LITTLE YIDDO, WHO STANDS AT THE BACK OF THE SHELF. HE GOES TO THE BAR, TO BUY A LAGER; AND ONLY BUYS ONE FOR HIM SELF. HE'S ONLY A POOR LITTLE YIDDO, YIDDO, YIDDO."

The atmosphere is electric, then during a momentary pause in the battle of the vocal chords. Then a lone voice can be heard, wafting across Stanford Bridge. ZIGGER ZAGGER, ZIGGER ZAGGER. Fifteen thousand voices from the Shed end answer as one, "OI!OI! OI!" It was Mickey Greenaway in full flow with the song that made him a legend. A chorus of Boo's ring out from the massed ranks of Tottenham. From the public address speakers, Edwin Starr starts to sing his current hit 'War'. Then silence falls and you could hear a pin drop as the Tottenham supporters watch in amazement. First they see a small movement in the Shed as a group of Chelsea supporters turn to their right and move towards the East Stand. "Chelsea's coming!" shouts a lone Tottenham voice. All eyes are on the Shed. Carlo shouts at the top of his voice, "Come On Chelsea!" and waves both arms towards himself in an effort to make out he's Tottenham. Heads turn, and then Merrill shouts, "Come on, let's get them!"

Merrill and Jock, start to push to their left and shout to the Tottenham supporters who look at them, "Come on, let's have the Shed." Slowly, the Tottenham start to move towards the East Stand. More of the Shed turn and start moving to the right. "Yes, let's get them," shouts a Tottenham supporter, as the North Stand en mass, start moving towards the East Stand. "Move down the terrace," shouts Merrill, "Let's get them on the move." The North Stand Firm spread out in a line down the terrace and start to move right, towards the East Stand. Two thirds of the Shed are now on the move; the front elements are running towards the covered passage of the East Stand.

"Come on! Let's get them," cries a voice from the far side of the North Stand. Merrill looks over and sees it is Big Tim, who is now waving his arm, for the Tottenham to follow him. "This is working out like a treat," smiles Jock. As he takes off his Tottenham scarf and drops on it on the concrete terrace The first elements of the Shed, led by The General, enter the covered passage under the East Stand and start to run towards the North Stand. Big Tim and Lenny Sykes, leave the North Stand and turn the corner by the end of the East Stand and enter the passage. "Charge!" cries Lenny, at the top of his voice. Over five thousand Tottenham supporters run towards the passage. The rear elements of Tottenham reach the corner, closely followed by the line of the North Stand Firm. Merrill looks back across the now empty terrace, and shouts "Now!" One hundred members of the North Stand now take off the Tottenham scarves they are wearing and sing in unison, "CHELSEA, CHELSEA."

The rear of the Tottenham turn in horror as they now realise that they have fallen into a trap; they start to run in terror as the line of the North Stand hits them. "Leave 'em, this lot don't want to know," shouts Carlo. "Forward!" screams Jock, who runs with Merrill through the massed ranks of Spurs supporters, punching as they go. Closely followed by Spider and Carlo , Mandy running past the North Stand bar, smashes a punch into the face of a Spurs supporter, who gets caught off balance and goes down. Two other Spurs supporters see her, one shouts, "What the fuck d'you think you're doing." "This!" bellows Maggie, as she runs to him and punches him on the back of his neck as he turns to avoid her. "Shit!" he screams, and turning, he throws a punch, but seeing a girl, he stops. "Fool" she shouts, as she kicks him in the groin, and as he bends over under the force of the blow, Mandy kicks him in the right leg; with this he collapses in a heap.

The General charges into the front section of the Tottenham; the noise is deafening, amplified by the low tunnel effect of the East Stand. The Tottenham charge falters under the momentum of the Shed. The General is decking Spurs supporters left and right, then out of the corner of his eye he see Big Tim. Running over he catches him by surprise; a right hook to the chin, is the first Big Tim knows of The General's presence. A stand up fight between the two leaders ensues but is unnoticed, by the eager rush of the Shed. The General throws his umpteenth punch; Big Tim goes down and is trampled by the rush of oncoming Shedites.

The North Stand have now made it into the passage. Colin smashes an elbow into the face of one of the fleeing Tottenham, who are now in full flight back to the North Stand. Jim and Lenny, corner four Tottenham by the players' entrance, and kicks them to the ground. Little John jumps on the back of another and they both fall to the floor; Little John rolls over and jumps to his feet, but as the Spurs supporter gets up, Parkhead sends a wild kick into head. "Teamwork!" he says, turning to Little John, "Ain't it fucking wonderful!"

There are now only five hundred Tottenham left in the passage; the rest have fled in panic, only to be greeted by the North Stand Firm, "Over there!" Merrill shouts to Jock, seeing Lenny Sykes fighting a rearguard action. "Let's have the cunt," screams Jock. They both run over to Sykes, and Jock swings a punch but misses as Lenny ducks just in time. Merrill comes up behind him, "Lenny!" he shouts, and Lenny turns to be met by a chop in the throat. He staggers back, hands grasping his neck, "Leave him," Merrill warns, as Jock goes to kick his feet away; "He's mine." Sykes runs at Merrill, who standing on his left leg, and throws a high sidekick with his right leg. It catches Lenny in the middle of his chest and he falls back. Merrill runs forward and lands a punch on the side of his skull. "Fuck it!" he yells, as he bruises two of his knuckles. Sykes falls to the ground and is trodden under foot by the Shed as they charge forward in a wild frenzy.

"How the fuck is that?" exclaims Lenny, looking over towards the railway. Colin looks, but fails to see just what has interested Lenny so much, "What you on about?" "There that big black geezer!" shouts Lenny, pointing to a six foot plus Chelsea supporter locked in combat with four Tottenham. Lenny is so fascinated by the fight, that he casually leans against an East Stand support column, "Jesus, that cunt can fight," he gasps, as the figure floors the Tottenham supporters, then cuts a swathe through the mass of bodies and disappears into the crowd. "Now, that's someone we need in the North Stand," says Colin, as he prods Lenny on the arm, "You on fucking strike then?" Lenny turns to Colin, laughing, "That my old son was a fucking Watusi, he had to be six-foot fucking six, he's name is Bo, and his dad is the Ambassador for Kenya."

Merrill, looking around at the fleeing Tottenham, sees four young boys aged between eight and ten, warring Spurs scarves come out of one of the stand doors, "Get them back inside," he shouts to Big Steve and Jim. Six members of the Shed see them too and, in a victorious blood lust, start to kick and punch the young lads. Jim runs over and throwing a punch, he knocks the first Shedite clean out. Big Steve runs over and drop kicks another; they both fall to the floor. Steve, jumping up, sees Jock herding the boys' back through the door. Merrill grabs another Shedite by the collar with both hands and head butts him in the face.

The General, who has now reached the end of the passage, shouts "Hey, what's going on?" "Just teaching some idiots not to pick on little kids," answers Jock, "Well their my Boys, and I'll deal with them not your Bloody North Stand," shouts The General, clearly annoyed and pointing to the fleeing youths. "North Stand over here," shouts Merrill, in an attempt to re-form, but few hear him over the noise of battle. Maggie and Mandy come running over bubbling with excitement, "Fuck! This is brilliant," beams a jubilant Mandy, holding a bruised right arm. "To the North Stand," bellows Jock, as they turn and run towards the North Stand, but they are greeted by a line of police with truncheons drawn. "Get back up to the other end!" barks a sergeant. "Bollocks!" shouts Mandy, looking across the North Stand, seeing more police move through the Tottenham and pushing them out of the way, to get to the front line and form a cordon.

"Hello, here come the fucking Mounties," observes Carlo, pointing to the half dozen mounted police trotting down the running track. There are so many Chelsea supporters in the tunnel that they tail back onto the Shed itself, but in one voice they chant, "CHELSEA, CHELSEA." Carlo, not to be outdone, starts to sing, "WE'RE THE NORTH STAND," and is immediately joined by the rest of the North Stand, "WE'RE THE NORTH STAND STAMFORD BRIDGE."

The police form a four deep cordon across the North Stand, starting at the edge of the bar. "OK form up here, at least we can get to the bar," laughs Spider. Carlo , still eager shouts, "God I love this!" "We're going back to the Shed," says The General. "Right, we're gonna stay here," replies Merrill, "We can get them in another pincer at the end of the game as they walk down the slope onto the Fulham Road." Turning, The General raises his arm, "Back to the Shed," he commands to the massed ranks of Chelsea supporters. The Shed move off, leaving the North Stand Firm in the corner by the bar who, now in victory, taunt the Tottenham by chanting, "THE FAMOUS TOTTENHAM HOTSPUR WENT TO ROME TO SEE THE POPE,
THE FAMOUS TOTTENHAM HOTSPUR WENT TO ROME TO SEE THE POPE,
THE FAMOUS TOTTENHAM HOTSPUR WENT TO ROME TO SEE THE POPE, AND THIS IS WHAT HE SAID. FUCK OFF! WHO'S THAT TEAM THEY CALL THE CHELSEA? WHO'S THAT TEAM WE ALL ADORE? THEY'RE THE BOYS IN BLUE AND WHITE, AND WE'LL FIGHT WITH ALL OUR MIGHT, AND WE'RE GOING TO SHOW THE WORLD THE WAY TO SCORE. BRING ON TOTTENHAM AND THE ARSENAL, BRING ON SPANARDS BY THE SCORE. BARCELONA, REAL MADRID TOTTENHAM ARE A LOAD OF YIDS,
YIDDO YIDDO YIDDO."

The police line starts to move towards the North Stand Firm who move down the terrace and stand at the side of the East Stand.

Content that there is now a large enough buffer zone, the police line stops advancing and stands watching the North Stand firm. "Don't they remind you of a line of penguins waiting to be feed at London Zoo," quips Carlo. "Shit! you alright!" Bellows an astonished Mandy, as she sees Dave move through the crowd towards her, sporting a growing bruise under the left eye. "Hello, looks like Dave's in for some TLC," smiles Carlo. "Ah! Come here Jim, love!" taunts Lenny, with a broad smile. "Fuck off you idiot!" screams Jim, as he realises Lenny is winding him up.

"Everyone here?" shouts Jock. "Apart from a few bruises," shouts Little John, leaning against the wooden wall of the East Stand. Jim walks to the front of the group, staring across no-mans land, at the police and the massed ranks of Tottenham behind, and starts to shout. "WE'RE THE NORTH STAND," One hundred voices join in. WE'RE THE NORTH STAND, WE'RE THE NORTH STAND STAMFORD BRIDGE." Then with a final burst of venom. "WE HATE TOTTENHAM, WE HATE TOTTENHAM."

The Shed stream down the massive stairs at the side of the Shed end, in a vile mood, having just seen their team lose to the most hated enemy, two-nil. Tempers are near boiling point as a police line outside the Rising Sun, blocks their way to the Kings Road, but this day no-one has any intentions of marching to the Kings Road. As a single body, The Shed, with The General at its head, turn right and march the short distance down Fulham Road to the gate behind the West Stand. "Stand here!" commands The General, as he comes to a stop outside the Britannia pub, looking across through the gate and up the slope that leads to the North Stand. Three thousand Chelsea supporters now totally block the Fulham Road and police, now realising what is going on, start to clash with the rear elements still pouring out of the Shed.

"We've got a clear run at them," says an excited Lenny, looking at the rear of the Tottenham departing the North Stand. "No, we wait till they're near the gate, move in behind them, but do nothing 'til The General gives the signal," commands Merrill, as he starts to walk across the empty steps of the North Stand. Jock, looking around, turns back as he sees the last of the police run around the corner of the East Stand, "Nice of the filth to fuck off and leave us a clear run." "They're going to stop the Shed," says a smiling Little John. "Here they come," says a fuming Spider, standing next to The General. "No wait till they get to the gate," The General warns. The Tottenham march in a jubilant body towards the gate singing,; "TWO NIL TO THE TOTTENHAM, TWO NIL TO THE TOTTENHAM." "Look!" shouts one of the Stockwell, "There's the North Stand!" "Brilliant! We've got the bastards trapped," says The General, an evil smile breaking across his stern face.

The first elements of the Tottenham reach the gate and, seeing the milling throngs of the Shed, their joy turns to instant fear. They turn to run back into the ground, only to be met by the mass flow of their fellow fans blocking their way. A few fall over and are trampled by their unsuspecting colleagues as they march in triumph towards the narrow gate. Six police horses race out of Britannia Road and charge the Shed, who caught off guard, start to back off from the gate. "Don't run!" screams The General, "Have the fucking horses." He runs across to the first police horse, and jumping up, he swings his arm around the neck of the rider. Gravity pulls The General back to the road, but he hangs on and the policeman is torn from his saddle. Spider runs up, and kicking the policeman in the head, grabs The General, pulling him to his feet. A long truncheon falls on Spider's back from another mounted policeman. He falls forward but managing to stay on his feet, he turns and runs to the pavement, out of range of the truncheon.

Taking advantage of this moment of confusion, the lead elements of the Tottenham move through the gate and run down Fulham Road towards Fulham Broadway station. "Charge!" screams Merrill, as he runs forward kicking out at the rear elements of the Tottenham. The North Stand stream down the slope and into the back, of the now panicking away supporters. All hell breaks loose as the Tottenham are attacked on two fronts; those that stand are cut down, while most rush for the gate and are met by the waiting Shed. Police vans now screech to a halt on the Fulham Road, and police with truncheons drawn, race into the mass of Chelsea supporters, cutting a clearing large enough for the Tottenham to break out on to the Fulham Road. "This way!" shouts The General, as he turns and runs up Britannia Road. Large numbers of the Shed follow, instantly knowing that they are going on a D-tour to Fulham Broadway.

Spider stops on the corner of Park Road, "Turn right!" he shouts to the running mass. Seeing the Shed turn the corner, he runs after The General. Reaching the Fulham Road, Little John ducks a truncheon and runs across the road to the Britannia, "Fucking hell man," he shouts to Big Steve, "This is fucking brilliant." "Too many filth though," answers Big Steve , looking at the cordon protecting the Tottenham supporters, as they stream towards Fulham Broadway. "Over here!" shouts Little John, as he sees Jock and Merrill. Running across, Jock looks down the road at the mayhem, "The Shed will cut them off at the station." He pauses, looking up at the now clear Britannia Road, "Up the back streets and pick off the stragglers."

"Mandy, take Maggie out of this," orders Merrill, looking at the cut on her forehead. Mandy walks over and looks at the cut, "It's only a small scratch!" she exclaims. "Take her out of here!" bellows Merrill. "OK, OK, keep you're fucking hair on," she replies and, looking around, she leads Maggie towards the Rising Sun. "I'll go with them," says Dave, "To make sure their alright," he adds, turning back to the others in an attempt to hide his real reason. "Yeah, we know Dave!" laughs Tommy, as he waves sarcastically. They start to walk up Park Road, when Jock, looking around to make sure that everyone is there, stops in his tracks.

"What's up?" asks Merrill. "Anyone seen Parkhead?" he replies. Walking past them, Big Steve says nonchalantly, "He got nicked." "What?" exclaims Jock, "When?" "Under the tunnel. Some big black geezer, was getting nicked, and Parkhead ran up and dragged him free, but he got overwhelmed," says Big Steve, still walking. "What! And you did nothing?" bellows Colin. "Oh fuck off," Big Steve roars, pulling up his blue Ben Sherman shirt to reveal a large red weld on his right ribs, "I got this from a filth truncheon trying to rescue him. I can't beat ten coppers pal, I ain't fucking superman!" "Hold on!" shouts Merrill, "You did your best! What about this black bloke?" "He ran off and joined in another fight," answers Big Steve, "He didn't even know Parkhead had got nicked." "Hey! Shit happens," says Colin, "Let's cut the crap and get some Yids."

"And here comes one now!" shouts Lenny, pointing to a Ford Consul Classic with a Tottenham Scarf tied to the drivers door handle. The Consul speeds up as it approaches the group of Chelsea supporters walking in the road. "Look out!" warns Little John, jumping in between two parked cars. As the Consul drives by, Jock and Merrill manage to land kicks on the side doors. "Cunt!" shouts Lenny, running into a garden; picking up a few stones, he runs back into the road and throws them after the car. "Fucking mad bastard," says Colin, "He fucking meant to kill us." "Let's get him," bellows Big Steve. "Oh yeah! I can just see you catching up a fucking car," laughs Colin, "Besides, you'll run straight into the filth." "Forget it! He's got a few dents to remind him of us, let's get to the Broadway," says Merrill.

Crossing Britannia Road, Jock looks down towards the Fulham road, "Shit look at all the filth." "Well, let's hope they stay that side of the Yids, it'll give us a free hand clearing up those that run from the Shed." Hearing a screech of tyres, Jim swings his head around to see the Consul speeding north down Britannia Road, towards them, "Here's that fucking nutter again." "Fuck him!" screams Big Steve, as he runs into a garden and grabs a dustbin. Seeing the North Stand run onto the pavement, the Consul swerves and mounts the curb. "Jesus H Christ, this cunts fucking possessed," shouts Colin, as he jumps over a garden wall. Merrill and Jock aim a hail of stones from behind another garden wall as Big Steve raises the dustbin above his head and throws it at the windscreen. The

Consul swerves back into the road as the driver throws himself across the passenger seat, just as the car smashes into the brick wall of a garden on the opposite side of the road. "Fucking Hell!" exclaims Lenny, as he stands looking at the damage.

"Get the cunt!" screams Merrill, as he runs across the road to the car. Big Steve runs after Merrill and, grabbing the driver's door handle, yanks it open, "Fucking Hell!" he cries, as he sees the unconscious driver has been thrown against the dashboard cutting his forehead open. The passenger is slumped against the buckled passenger door, his white Fred Perry tennis shirt rapidly turning red from blood gushing from his head where a piece of the smashed windscreen is sticking out. "Look out, it's the filth!" shouts Little John. Merrill looks around to see around a dozen police rushing towards them from Fulham Road, "Leg it!" he commands. "Everyone split up, meet up back at the Weatherby," shouts Jock, turning from the car with a massive grin of satisfaction on his face.

CHAPTER TEN

"So after 27 attempts to launch a missile," continues Alan, "They finally get one off and bring down Iran Air flight 655. Can you blame the Iranians for hitting back? Would not America have hit back in the same circumstances?" "But there is another theory!" cuts in Big Al. "Oh, you're on about the Libyans, ain't yer cha," says Jock. Big al nods, "Yeah, there are those who say it was them in revenge for the bombing attacks." Jock nods in agreement, "Well, it looks like we'll never know for sure."

"Excuse me, but what has this to do with soccer riots in England?" queries a shocked and puzzled Kevin Darcy. Alan looks him in the eye and replies, "You go somewhere and get attacked, you fight back, yes?" He looks at Kev and then continues, "In our case, we had The Shed. Its strengths were the Stockwell, Southfields, and North End Road firms, together with the leadership of "The General". He would organise, plan and then do it." "Hold on a minute!" exclaims Kev. "So, the North Stand split from The Shed and became a separate gang?" Alan smiles, "I fancy a fag," he says, looking looks at the shocked Americans, "By the way, a fag in England is a cigarette." The Americans look surprised and laugh. "Well, let's sit outside," suggests Dave. Getting up and walking outside into the California sunshine, they pull three tables together and then sit down. Big Al Realises that they have fallen into a trap, looks back to the English with a frown, "OK, but remember Vietnam is a touchy subject, treat it with respect." Alan looks at the faces of the American's knowing that it could turn ugly at any moment. He nods, and raises his arm in the direction of their empty chairs, "Sit back down, there's no need for all that, we're not looking for trouble?" The Americans reluctantly walk back to their chairs and sit down, but it is clear they are very annoyed.

Alan sensing his fish have bitten knows all he has to do now is reel them in, "In Vietnam, you made the mistake of underestimating your enemy, you fought a tactical war, not a strategic one." "I'm not with you, how do you mean a tactical war?" queries Mike Gilmartin tapping his fingers on the table. "Well, you thought the Vietnamese would cave in to your superiority in weapons," interjected Mark Diamond. "That's Right," cuts in Alan, "you fought the war as a series of local actions, you had no strategy. You should have invaded North Vietnam, but you were scared of China." "Aw that's hog wash!" exclaimed Big Al, "If we'd done that we'd have started World War III! He leans back in his chair, shakes his head and says, "Now I know you're trying to yank my chain, I'm out of here Alan looks him in the eye, and half smiles. "Hold on pal;

if you start a war without the will to win, then you shouldn't start it in the first place. That's the whole thing about war, it's win at all costs."

"You can't say that, what about civilian casualties? Mike says in an astonished tone. "Like Alan said, you don't start a war, unless you have the will to win," cuts in Ian. "And if that means civilian's get killed, if that means your own side takes a heavy 'body count' as you call it; tough! You fight on regardless, and you do all you can to support your army."

Jim Boyle looks over to the Maureen, and calls her over, orders a round of drinks, then looks back to the English. "I suppose you're so cleaver then that you never make mistakes?" he says with a certain arrogance. "Oh yes we make mistakes," answers Dave, "But we learn from them, that's why we lost Bunker Hill over here, and Isandlwana, in South Africa. We had arrogant upper class generals who bought their commissions, and thought they knew everything. That's why we stopped the buying of rank, and started to train our officers properly." Ah, but we kicked your English buts in the War of Independence, didn't we?" says Big Al with a sarcastic smile. "Well no," answers Dave, "In 1776 there were no Americans. There were only English settlers; and it was those English settlers who proclaimed a state of independence because of the corrupt system under King George; A system they had come over here to escape from, but it had followed them over." "So in order to rid themselves of King George, for once and for all." Alan pauses to make sure the Americans are taking it all in, "The English settlers fought the Crown and finally won in 1782, so the first American wasn't born until at lest nine months after that." Then sitting back in his chair with a broad smile and continues. "So I'm afraid that you don't win the War of Independence, as there were no Americans at that time. Just generations, of English settlers."

Ian Kirkman laughs out loud, "So the English won the war for yeah, well don't you say thank you then?" Mile Gilmartin smiles as he sees the joke, and begrudgingly says; "Hey you guys know your onions." "Thank you," says Alan, "You see, the great influx of foreign immigrants, didn't start until the 1849 Gold Rush at Sutter's Creek." The Americans are still clearly upset that their manhood has been attacked, but they never the less take it on the chin.

NOTTINGHAM FOREST AWAY

Saturday December 12th. 1970, Nottingham Forest 1 - 1 Chelsea

Built in the 1850s on the New Road, but now renamed Euston Road, St. Pancras Station is an architectural wonder. A large hotel with a myriad of towers, fronts the single arch station structure. Wide ornate arches take you from the front drive way onto the wide forecourt of the station proper. A bar and café are built into the main wall, while over to the left, through a small archway, is the original wooden booking office. Access from the Underground is from a small stairwell, bringing you up onto the forecourt. Steam engines have been silent for five years; new one hundred and twenty five-mile an hour diesels now transport passengers to destinations throughout the Midlands.

Colin and Jim walk up the stairs from the tube; reaching the top, they turn towards the bar. Seeing an almost deserted station, apart from about twenty policemen, "Mm, looks like the Chelsea special has gone." says Colin. "Jesus! The filth are out in strength today," Jim replies. "Right, I'll get the eats, you get the drinks in," Colin says, looking over to the train indicator board. Four policemen walk over to them, "Where do you think you're going then?" the first policeman demands. Colin gives a puzzled look and asks, "Excuse me, what's the problem?" "You're Chelsea aren't you?" demands the second policeman, looking at their smart trousers and black Crombie Jackets. "No I'm Colin" comes the quick reply. Pushing Colin against the railings at the top of the staircase, "Watch it!" exclaims Colin, as he pulls his Jacket together.

The first policeman looks at Colin, then walks up to him and stares him in the eye, "Shut your mouth, or you're nicked," he shouts. Colin stares back with a sarcastic smile. The third policeman grabs Jim by the collar, "So what's someone like you doing here?" Jim plants his feet and stands stock still, then looking the policeman in the eye, says "You referring to the fact that I'm Jewish? Cunt," he pauses a moment, "Stubble. 'Cos if you are, I'll report yer. Where's your Sergeant?" The policeman, annoyed that he is forced to stop, snaps, "Shut it, you scum, and empty your pockets." Spider and with his 13-year-old brother, together with Little John and Big Steve, are walking up the stairs when they hear the raised voices. "That's Colin," says Little John. "Come on then!" shouts Big Steve. They start to run up the remaining stairs, then turn to see the four policemen crowding around Colin and Jim. "Oi! What you lot playing at," shouts Little John. A fourth policeman walks over to them, "Up against the wall," he demands. "No, not unless you tell us

128

why," snaps Big Steve. "You Chelsea supporters have missed the special, so we're turning you back," the policeman replies. Jock carries on walking, but looks back and says sarcastically, "Well, if you had half a brain, you'd ask us if we had tickets for the Inter-City."

The policeman stops and looks over to the indicator board, and sees that there is an Inter-City train to Nottingham in 25 minuets, "Don't give me that, you lot aren't on the Inter-City, or you'd have gone from Kings Cross" he replies. Little John, who is still against the wall, shouts over, "Oh yes we are, this one is faster, and we have First Class reserved seats as well." An Inspector standing by the ticket booth, seeing the commotion at the top of the stairs, walks over, "What's going on here?" he demands. The first policeman looks around nervously and answers, "This lot have missed the special and won't leave the station Sir." Little John looks over to the Inspector and shouts, "Is this the way the Metropolitan Police treat First Class passengers? I'm going to see my MP." The Inspector looks at the policemen and asks, "Have any of you asked to see their tickets?" "No, they haven't," chirps Big Steve, "But you seem a nice chap, can we show you?" The Inspector motions to the policemen to let the Chelsea supporters go, then gives Big Steve a dirty look, "Show me your tickets then." The five supporters get their First Class tickets out and line up by the Inspector who, looking at them very carefully, says, "Right your train is on platform three, you will board it now." "Yes Sir!" Big Steve says in a sarcastic voice, "Thank you Sir, thank you very much Sir."

Merrill sits by the window, facing towards the buffet carriage; Maggie is sat beside him, "If the others don't get here soon, they'll missed the bleeding train," he says as if thinking out aloud. "They've never missed yet, so why do you think they'll start now?" says Jock knowingly, as he walks from the door to the small table, looking back at Veronica and winking. Mandy is slouched on the single seat on the other side of the carriage, with her legs stretched across the table, looking out of the window, "Here they come now." "I hope they stop at the Buffet before sitting down," says Ghost, who is sitting in the seats in front of Merrill. "Yeah," adds Lenny, who with Parkhead, is sitting opposite him, "I could do with some room service." "Aye up," Merrill exclaims as he looks down the carriage, "Here come the others." Big Steve is first into the carriage and on seeing the others, breaks into song. "HERE WE ARE AGAIN, HAPPY AS CAN BE." The others join in the welcome, "ALL GOOD FRIENDS, AND JOLLY GOOD COMPANY."

Five minutes latter Big Steve walks into the carriage with his arms full of beer cans, while Colin walks behind him carrying packets of crisps. "Here we go boys and girls," laughs

Big Steve, putting the cans down on the middle table. There is a wild scramble for the cans, and Veronica slides a can across the table to Jock, who is busy reading the Evening Standard. "I see they've started studying the rocks that Luna 16 brought back from the moon." "The Yanks must have geed them up bringing back some from their manned trip, says Jock; " nothing like someone beating you too it, to gee the Yanks into action." "We should send John Pertwee up there in his TARDIS, that'd show 'em." Says Big Steve. "Yeah, but the Yanks would send Captain Kirk at Warp speed and beat him to it." Laughs Big Steve. Christ! You lot are like the bloody Goodies!" exclaims Veronica. "More like "Monty Python's Flying Circus," laughs Mandy. "Well we drive there, petrol's gone up to seven bloody pence a gallon.

Dave, walks into the carriage with Tommy, and picks up a beer. Maggie, looking up, nudges Merrill and says, "Here's that new geezer." Merrill looks over and sees Bo walk into the carriage, "Hi, sit next to Mandy." "He can fuck off, I want me leg room. Besides, I'm keeping it warm for Dave." she snaps. "More like room for someone to get between your legs," Big Steve chirps. "No problem, I'll take the next one up," replies Bo. "Wellingborough? Where the fucks that?" asks Parkhead, as he sees the train slow down to stop at the station. "Relax, we got a long way to go yet," answers Merrill, walking back from the buffet car. As Maggie approaches the end of the carriage, Merrill asks, "Hey, you've heard of the 'Mile High Club', "Oh Yes!" A broad grin sweeps across her face, " but this ain't a plane, is it!" she queries. Merrill laughs, "Not to worry," he opens the toilet door, "Welcome to the 'Inter-City Club'." Little John shakes his head and walks back to his seat, as Merrill and Maggie shut the toilet door behind them.

As the train pulls into Nottingham station, a number of passengers dismount and walk along the platform. Two policemen ignore them as there are no groups of more then four people, and they are waiting for the Football Special, which is not expected for another fifteen minutes. Exiting the station, most passengers head for the town centre, but four separate groups walk under the overhanging canopy, supported by brick arches. They pass three green police coaches, parked by the canopy; the police inside for the most part, ignore them, barring those whose eyes follow the three girls. "Look at those thick idiots," comments Jock, "They think that if you dress smart and don't have boots or a scarf, then you have nothing to do with football." Big Steve laughs, "But I thought that was the main qualification for a copper." "What's that?" Jock asks, "Being thick!" Big Steve answers. "OK girls, time for your D-Tour," says Merrill. "I'll go with them, I've still got the map," says Parkhead. Merrill thinks for a moment, then nods. The four carry on walking, while everyone else cross the road and walk towards the Trent Bridge. Passing a church graveyard, Big Steve looks up the side street, "Mm, looks clear from here," he thinks out aloud. "Well, we'll know soon enough," answers Jock. They continue towards the Trent Bridge, the annual location for Nottingham Forest's crew to ambush the Chelsea Shed with a shower of bricks.

"Good Lord!" exclaims Colin Davis, "We've beaten then to the punch." "Wicked," laughs Lenny Blake. "Very little filth about, no wonder their crew can do what they like," says Little John. "Didn't you know?" says Big Steve, "They're all waiting at the station, for The Shed." They walk across the Trent Bridge, looking around for any signs of the Nottingham crew. "OK!" commands Merrill, pointing up across the grass towards the ground, "Up the slope and wait," and looking around at Jock and Big Steve, "You're with me." "Where're we going?" replies a curious Big Steve "Walk about," Merrill answers. replies. Spider looks back to his younger brother, "Come on then." They carry on walking, while the others stroll up the slight grass incline to the ground. They pass another green police coach, but this one is empty, "I bet that's for all the filth in the ground," says Colin. "Wouldn't it be nice just to roll it down into the Trent," laughs Big Steve. "Burn the bastard thing more like it," Colin replies. Lenny thinks for a moment, then and says, "No, it would take too long. Better just to give it a helping hand into the water."

Merrill, Jock, Spider and his younger brother walk past the ground and take the first left. "Looks pretty quiet," he comments, as they walk along the road that. brings them to the short side street that takes you to the away supporters' end. As they reach the corner, Jock looks along the main road, as they reach the corner; "Shit! That's the Trent End Crew." he warns. The four of them stand and look. At least two hundred Nottingham supporters are walking towards them, and as they spread across the road, they bring all traffic to a stand still. "Oh shit!" exclaims Spider. "What's the matter with you?" asks Jock. "What about me brother?" he looks around to his thirteen year-old brother. "Hang on a mo," says Jock, "They may not recognise us." "Some hopes of that happening," says Merrill, "Look!" The front elements of the Trent End crew, start pointing in their direction; it becomes obvious to all that they have indeed, been recognised.

Then about a dozen of those at the front start shouting, "It's Chelsea!" and begin to run forward. "Merrill turns to Spider, "Take your brother and run!" "Fuck Off I ain't running" Spider replies. "How old's your brother?" demands Merrill "Thirteen!" exclaims Spider. "Exactly!" interjects Jock, "they target him as he's an easy target, and kick him to shit, now get the fuck out of here." Grabbing his brother's arm, they start to run back down the street. The lead elements of the Forest crew are about a hundred yards away, when the main body joins in the charge, "This is suicide!" exclaims Jock. Merrill looks at him and asks with a smile, "Do you want to live forever?"

They both laugh as they run forward and cross the side street that leads to the ground. As they get to the opposite pavement, the first of the bricks loop through the air and land in front of them.

"Fuck It!" screams Merrill, as he looks down, and seeing that one of the bricks has hit him in the side pocket of his SS camouflage smock, causing a fountain of beer to gush into the air from the beer can hidden inside. Jock looks to the side and sees another brick hit the Smock, and another plum of beer erupt from the other side. They both laugh like mad men and rush forward; the front-runners, seeing that they continue to advance, stop dead in their tracks. This causes a number of the following Forest supporters to turn and run. Another brick comes flying over and just misses Jock. He looks back as it hits the road, and in doing so, he sees the hardware shop on the far corner. "See what I see," he shouts at Merrill, pointing back at the dustbin sitting outside the shop with shiny new shovels sticking out of the top.

"Yes!" exclaims Merrill. They run back to the shop and, seeing this, the Forest start to run forward again. Merrill and Jock pull out a pickaxe handle each and start to run towards the advancing mob, "Chelsea!" they scream, as they make contact with the front-runners. A long wooden handle smashes into the first Forest supporter, who falls like a brick to the ground. Jock stops and laughs; Merrill has run into the middle of the front runners, swinging left and right, and the Forest now start to run, colliding with those behind them.

Jock is the first to see the police running towards them from the ground, "Drop 'Em!" he shouts. Merrill looks over and sees the police. Dropping his pickaxe handle, he punches the nearest Forest supporter in the face, but a hand, grabbing his shoulder from behind, stops him from hitting another. Turning, he sees the face of a policeman, "What you nicking us for, there's only two of us?" he shouts. "Shut up" the policeman yells back, grabbing Merrill's arm. Jock looks over and seeing the police running towards him, he stands still and shouts, "Oh, that's rich! There's two hundred of them and you nick us two." As more police reach them, a sergeant says, "Relax, we saw everything, you're not under arrest." "So what the fucks going on then?" queries Merrill, as the two of them are frog marched towards the ground. "We're giving you a police escort into the ground, for the safety of our own supporters;" says the Sergeant, with a smile. Merrill looks over at Jock, laughing and says, "Fuck me! That's a first."

As they reach the turnstiles, the rest of the North Stand, led by Little John, turn the corner. They stop and watch as Merrill and Jock are led into the ground, and led to the terrace beside the player's tunnel, on the halfway line. The North Stand, arriving in the ground, see them and slowly walk over to them. "Fucking hell, what have you two been up to now?" enquires Ghost, "You should have seen them fucking wankers run!" says Jock, still pumping with adrenaline. "How come the filth didn't nick you?" asks Little John. "That sergeant said they enjoyed watching the Trent End get a kicking," replied Merrill.

"Shit! You were fucking lucky," says Lenny. "How the hell do you know what's happened?" asks a puzzled Merrill. "Spider came running over and told us," replies Little John, "So we came as fast as we could, but arrived only in time to see you two getting an escort into the ground." As the sergeant stands looking out across the pitch, a number of Nottingham Forest Supporters, realising that this new group on the terrace are in fact Chelsea, start to shout abuse, and two of them climb over the fence by the players tunnel.

One looks back and, waving his right arm in encouragement for the rest to join them, cries, "Come on then Chelsea!" Jock, turning to the sergeant, points to two Forest supporters and says, in a sarcastic voice, "See those two?" The sergeant looks back over to the supporters, "Well what about them?" the sergeant replies. "Well, they look like they're going to start as soon as you walk off, so can we have a one on one fight with them?" asks Jock, more as a joke than really believing that the police would actually countenance a stand up fight. The sergeant looks the two supporters up and down, and screws his face up in thought, then looking at the gathering North Stand, he looks back to Jock and says, "Just you two against those two, and no one else joins in? "Merrill turns to the North stand and shouts, "No-one joins in, no matter what happens!" The sergeant turns to look at the North Stand boys, then looks back to Jock and says, "OK, as long as it's one on one, and no one else is involved."

At this, Jock and Merrill rush forward; caught by surprise, the two Forest supporters freeze. Merrill is first to reach them smashing a right hook into the jaw of the first Forest supporter, who falls backwards; just managing to keep his feet, he turns to run back to the fence. Realising that he can't make it without being caught, he leaps the three-foot brick wall at the side of the players' tunnel and disappears from sight. Merrill reaches the wall and looks over to see the supporter laying on the floor fifteen feet below, screaming in agony. As he looks closer he sees a bone sticking through the right trouser leg, blood flowing from the wound. Luckily Two St. John's Ambulance men, are standing at the entrance, and rush over to the supporter. Merrill looks back and sees Jock land a punch in the chest of the bigger Forest supporter; it stops him in his tracks, winding him. He bends forward; Jock waits a moment and then swings a left uppercut, but the Forest supporter sees it coming and just dodges out of the way.

The North Stand rush forward to join in, but Merrill screams, "No, let them fight one to one." The Forest supporter looks over to Merrill, who nods back. Not believing his luck at not being swamped, he kicks out at Jock. The Forest supporters at the fence shout encouragement, but do not climb over. The police sergeant, seeing what's happening, waves over a dozen constables. As they walk over to the terrace, the players who are on the pitch warming up, and walk over to watch the fight; some recognising Jock, shout encouragement. As the North Stand gather around in a school-yard circle and cheer Jock on, he throws a punch that knocks the Forest supporter off his feet. Jock steps back to let him get up and in doing so, the Forest supporter lunges forward. Catching Jock off balance, they both fall to the ground; rolling over, the Forest supporter ends up on the top and smashes Jock in the face with a mighty left. Jock stunned, brings both legs up in a double knee kick, throwing the Forest supporter forward; off balance, he hits the ground head first.

Getting up, the Forest supporter looks wildly at Jock and, wiping the back of his right hand across his face, he looks at the blood smeared on his hand; his face screws up in rage as he leaps forward. Throwing both arms around Jock, he lifts him off the ground in a bear hug; squeezing him with all his might, Jock's face turns white as the blood drains from his head, his eyes almost popping out of their sockets under the pressure of the vice-like grip. Turning his head in desperation, Jock looks at Merrill's smiling face; seeing his plight, Merrill points to the ear next to Jock's mouth and simulates a biting action. Jock looks horrified at the thought, but is beginning to lose consciousness; in a last gasp action, he opens his mouth and his teeth come down on the Forest supporter's right ear. Jock falls to the ground as the Forest supporter lets out a mighty roar, grabbing what is left of his bloody ear with both hands.

The police arrive and push their way through the crowd. The sergeant, seeing Jock standing over the kneeling body, waiting for him to get up, walks over and says, "When I said a fair fight I didn't mean GBH!" Other supporters and the players shout that it was a fair fight and that the two Forest supporters started it. The police pick up the Forest supporter and march him out of the terrace as Jock stands there with a cheeky, but bloody grin spreading across his face. "This must be you're lucky day pal," says Little John. "Yeah, that's twice now you both got away with fucking murder," beams a jubilant Big Steve.

As the final whistle goes, and the Forest supporters start to cheer, the ones on the other side of the player's tunnel, start shouting, "You're a load of rubbish!" "Shit, fucking shit," screams Little John, in a temper, "How can we fucking lose to these bastards?" "Well, you know what they say," says Big Steve, casually. "Oh Yeah, and what the fuck is that then?" Little John retorts. Big Steve looks over and, tilting his head and raising his eyebrows, sarcastically says, "Shit Happens." "OK, keep it for outside," shouts Jock. "And stay by the wall when we get there. Let's wait and see what The Shed are going to do first," says Merrill, looking back to the others. They slowly make their way out of the ground and line up along side wall of the ground, looking down the grass slope to the Trent Bridge.

The Trent End Mob are already lining up across the bridge to block their way back to the station. To the left The General is organising The Shed. "Right you lot, all walk together," he shouts at them, "Wait for the word, but stay together." Jock is looking across at them as The Shed gets organised. "He's slowly turning them into an army," he says with pride, to Merrill. "Good," he replies, "It's about time they listened to him. I think the hangers on are beginning to realise that they have a General at last." Big Steve walks over to them, "The General's doing a good job of wiping them into shape." "Let's wait for the charge," Merrill says and, looking over to the right, he adds,

"Wait here, there may be more Forest coming round the corner and if there are, they'll take The Shed in the flank." Jock looks back to Colin and Big Steve, "That's when we strike." The others nod and pass the word. As two thousand members of The Shed walk as one towards the Trent Bridge, two hundred yards away, the General turns around to make sure that they are staying in a tight unit. "Get in at the side," he shouts to a group walking wide. One hundred yards members of the Stockwell urge him to make the order to charge, but still he looks about checking and making sure that no Forest supporters are about to take them in the flank. He sees the North Stand standing watching from the wall of the ground and waves for them to join him. "No!" screams Merrill, "Stay here."

As The Shed march to within fifty yards of the bridge, some of the Forest supporters at the rear of the bridge start to get nervous and begin to run, whilst those at the front pick up stones and start to throw them towards the ever-advancing Shed. The General looks back, lifts his arm and screams, "Charge!" The Shed start to run towards the bridge through a hail of stones, many picking up the cry, "Charge!" The Shed hit the front line of Forest supporters, a right jab decks a stone thrower, as the Stockwell & North End Road boys joins the battle. The initial weight of The Shed carries them well into the Forest ranks and a free for all breaks out. "Now?" queries Ghost.

"No!" shouts Merrill and, looking back to the members of the North Stand, notices that the girls have joined them from their seats in the stand. Then Little John sees a movement to his right, and turning he sees the reason they wait. From around the corner of the ground comes a mob of around one hundred Forest supporters, charging towards the rear elements of The Shed, "Hold it, hold it," Merrill screams, as the first of the Forest run past them.

"Now!" he cries, as one the North Stand charge into the flank of the Forest supporters. Little John smashes a right-hander into the side of the head of one of them; he falls like a stone. Jock runs into another, and using both arms to push him over, he rolls under the feet of his following supporters. Bo grabs another from behind locking him in a vice-like grip, whilst Colin pummels punches into his face and body; letting him go, Bo stands and watches as he drops like a rag doll to the grass. Merrill sends a high side kick with his right leg into the chest of a Forest supporter, sending him flying to the ground; turning around, he sees Maggie fall and a Forest supporter standing over her. He runs over and takes a flying leap, the right arm connecting with the neck of the Forest supporter; they hit the ground together. Turning him over, Merrill punches him once in the neck; getting up, he looks down to see the supporter's hands grabbing at his neck in agony. Merrill then runs over to Maggie and pulls her up, whilst Mandy runs past and kicks a supporter to the ground, "Come on," she screams with glee, "Come on make War not Love; We've got them on the run."

"Have I missed the good stuff?" enquires a beaming Parkhead, who has run over from the bridge, on seeing the North Stand. "No pal," beams Jock, "Join the party." Looking about he sees that most of the North Stand are chasing the Forest towards the corner of the ground, "Come back!" he commands. Colin and Big Steve hear him, stop and call the others back. Jock looks at the police coach still standing empty, "The coach," he shouts as he points to it, "Push it into the river." Running forward, he opens the side door and jumps in. Releasing the hand brake, he sticks his head out of the window and shouts, "Push!" The coach lurches forward as everyone pushes; as it picks up speed, they stop and watch as Jock jumps out of the door, and rolls over, just as the coach hits the water with a splash. "Look out it's the police!" screams Bo. The others look around and see ten policemen running towards them with truncheons drawn. "Run to The Shed," shouts Merrill, "And mingle." Spider looks back and shouts, "Fuck it, let's have them." Jock looking over yells, "No, you look after your brother," then looking around, he shouts, "We're too exposed." They start running towards the bridge, but just before they reach it, The Shed break through the lines of

Forest supporters and start to mach along the road towards the station.

CHAPTER ELEVEN

Alan pulls out his JPS and lights one. Looking up to the cloudless sky, he smiles, knowing this will be another 90 'weekend'. "At first, The Shed didn't like it as they saw it as a break away, but as we worked with 'The General' and The Shed, The North Stand became the fire brigade behind enemy lines, so to speak, while The Shed was the main army." "So you thought things through and organised, and became stronger?" observed Big Al. "Yes," agreed Alan, "We worked together. At first 'The General' looked on us as a threat to his leadership, but then when he realised it wasn't, we worked together and got stronger."

Ian Kirkman looks around for Maureen; and seeing her, he calls her over, looks over to Big Al, and says, "You don't get organised violence over here because, like we said, you're too gun-ho and never to stop and to think things through." The Americans look surprised at Ian's choice of words, and Dave Hughes, chuckling to himself says, "It must be a cultural thing." "But we have the best army in the god-dammed world," snaps Big Al, with pride. "Wrong!" exclaims Alan, "You have the best equipped army in the world. You also have the best logistics, but you do have the wrong training, and you tend not to learn from your mistakes. Look at Vietnam," Alan looks at the Americans, expecting an explosion of wrath.

"Now look here! That's going too damn far, buddy!" shouts Big Al, as he bangs his fist down on the table. "See, you're doing it now!" chuckles Ian, looking at the Americans as they start to get up out of their chairs. "We're not staying here to be insulted! Good Day Gentlemen!" says an angry Mike Gilmartin. "Sit down! For Gods sake, we're not having a go at yer, we're having a discussion. You don't have to walk away in a 'Gun Ho' fashion," says Mark Diamond, in a raised but friendly voice, "You walk off now, and all you're doing is proving we're right!"

WOLVES AWAY

Saturday February 13th. 1971, Wolverhampton Wanderers 1 - 0 Chelsea

A Class 47 Diesel locomotive, pulling ten carriages of pre-war stock, which makes up the Chelsea Football Special, slowly pulls into the platform at Wolverhampton station.. In the 19th century, Wolverhampton was a major industrial town. Sitting to the west of Birmingham, it is now in the middle of a huge rebuilding and modernisation program. A recently finished ring road surrounds the town centre and links the station with the football ground. Walking out of the main entrance of the station, the first of the six hundred supporters; look down Railway Drive for any signs of the Queen Street firm. Those at the front become a bit bolder when they see that there is no reception committee awaiting them, and burst into song, "WE HATE NOTTINGHAM FOREST, WE HATE LIVERPOOL TOO; WE HATE TOTTENHAM HOTSPURS, YIDDO, YIDDO, YIDDO, BUT CHELSEA WE LOVE YOU."

Looking up at the overcast sky, Mickey Greenaway turns to The General, "Looks like it could rain." "Fuck the rain," replies 'The General', "It's Wolves we got to watch out for." 'The General' walks down Railway Drive to the Ring Road St. David's and stops; turning his head left and right, surveying the scene. Noticing only one police van parked a hundred yards to the right, near the cross roads, he turns his head back to the station, "Right you lot!" he shouts to the gathering crowd, "Stay together, and no singing!" 'The General' walks at the head of The Shed as they start their march along the Ring Road to Molineux, the home of Wolverhampton Wanderers.

The VW was parked in Stafford Street overlooking the side street that leads to the Molineux Pub, a favourite watering hole of the Queen Street Firm. Deciding to break the silence, Big Steve turns his head to the rear of the minibus and, looking at Maggie sitting next to Merrill, says, "Missing Sandy then?" Maggie looks up and nods, " Yeah kind of strange her not being here." "Well with Dave out on bail, someone has to keep him occupied on match days," smiles Little John. Jock looks over to Maggie and, with a smirk, says, "Don't worry she's probably shagging his balls off as we speak." Veronica flashes an angry look at Jock, then slaps his shoulder, "That's not a very nice thing to say."

Big Steve laughingly cuts in, "Now, now girls and boys behave yourselves." He pauses a moment in thought, then continues, "Any rolls left?" Little John, thinking that everyone has had their fill, reluctantly pulls the last one out of the cardboard box, which sits on the metal floor. He looks at it and then passes it to Big Steve saying, "Here you are you greedy Git."

"Ha, ha, beat yer to it Johnny Boy," Big Steve says sarcastically, sensing his good timing. (with a sarcastic sense of good timing.) 'Twist And Shout' comes on the radio, and Little John sits up in his seat and says, "Hey wasn't this the original version?" "Yes," says Jock, "The Isley Brothers did it before the Beatles." Merrill, looking out of the window, smiles and says, "No, it was the original hit version, but the original was done by a group called the Top Notes. It was one of the few things Phil Spector ever fucked up, so the writer, Bert Burns, who produced the Drifters, got the Isley's to do his version at the end of one of their seasons." He pauses a moment then continues, "Listen to that drummer! By the gods, I bet he was on fucking drugs! That is an amazing bloody record."

Big Steve looks at the pre-packed cheese roll bought at the Watford Gap service station on the M1 Motorway, then starting to unwrap it, a sudden thought comes to mind. "Baguettes!" he says wondering out aloud, "Ain't they fucking French?" "Yup," says Big Steve, from the back of the minibus. "Jesus those fucking Normans get everywhere!" he says, with disgust. "Only problem with that, Big Steve," says Merrill, who is sitting by the rear door next to Jock, "The Normans weren't French, they were Danish Vikings." "Oh bollocks!" sighs Little John, "Here we go again." Merrill looks out of the rear window and seeing nothing moving, looks at Jock, shakes his head, and chuckles. He then turns back towards Big Steve', "Well let's see," he pauses in thought, "In around 890AD, Danish Vikings that had been raiding the French coast for nearly one hundred years, started to make winter camp around the River Seine. The area had long been a favourite raiding place, The King of the Germanic tribe, the Franks, had carved out an empire in Gaul, what you know as France. Well, he thought that if he gave them the coastal area, he would use them to stop other Viking raids," Merrill smiles, and says, "Confused yet?"

"Yeah, fucking right," replies Big Steve, "So the Frogs are really Germans? Well that's a first." "No, no! In the same way as the Normans ain't English, the Franks aren't French. They gave their name to the land, and became the ruling class and the Royal family of the indigenous population, just as in England, the Normans became the Upper Class and Royal family." Big Steve, still looking puzzled, raises his eyebrows and says, "Yeah, of course any fool knows that." "OK," Merrill continues, "The Norman leader was called Rollo." Big Steve turns around with a grin, and says, "I bet he liked chocolate!" Merrill shakes his head, and then continues, "The King made him the Duke of Normandy, then over the next one hundred years, the Vikings assimilated with the local Gaul's, adopting their language and most of their ways of warfare, including replacing their battle-axe for heavy cavalry."

Big Steve thinks a moment, then says in a mocking tone, "I got it pal! I ain't thick! The Vikings came to France and became French, like I said." He looks into the rear view mirror smiling at Merrill, "So what about William the Conqueror?" "He was a descendent of Rollo and was called William the Bastard. He was a cousin of the English Saxon, King Harold, by marriage. The Vikings under Knot had gained the Crown of England, but lost it to the Saxon, Edward the Confessor. When he died, King Harold, together with King Harold of Norway and William the Bastard, all laid claim to the English throne." "Hey!" says Big Steve, as suddenly it all suddenly becomes clear, "That was the Battle of Stamford Bridge, wasn't it?" "What was?" queries Merrill "The Norwegian King invading England. King Harold defeated him at the Battle of Stanford Bridge," Big Steve proudly states.

"So the Septics have invaded Laos" observes Maggie, as she reads the Daily Mail. "Instead of sending Apollo 14 to the Moon, they should have fitted it with a warhead and targeted Hanoi." Says Little John. "No the Yanks should have the guts to invade North Vietnam, but they're too scared of China!" replies Jock. "Fuck America, we're being decimalised on Monday, which means everything is gonna go up in price!" says Merrill. "And with Rolls Royce going bankrupt, they'll sell it off to some foreign company, and it'll no longer be British." replies Big Steve. "I'm still thinking and praying for those poor souls that lost their lives at Biro." Says Veronica. "Oh my God, that puts everything into perspective that was the most horrible start to a New Year;" replies Maggie. "And those Cunts at Celtic were making up songs to laugh at the dead."

"How can anyone be so vile, as to do that, those were innocent people at a football match, it could easily have happened at Celtic, those people have no respect or shame. Says Veronica, "You went up there didn't you Alan?" she asks. "Yeah," replies Merrill, My ex wife lives in sight of Ibrox, and to see it first hand brings it all home, so many families lost loved ones."

"Sorry to interrupt," says Little John, looking out of the front window, and pointing towards the crossroads, "Here comes the Queen Street Mob." All eyes turn to the front of the minibus as around sixty people cross the ring road after walking up the southern part of Stafford Street, from the town centre. Turning the corner, they walk towards Molineux Street on their way to the pub. "So we going to have them?" queries Big Steve. "No, not yet. Let them get into the pub first, we don't want them knowing these are our motors, they'll smash 'em before we get back after the game," answers Jock. Big

Steve looks out of the windscreen of the minibus, like an eagle scanning for his next meal, and then suddenly gasps, "I don't believe it!" and turning around he turns round to face his suddenly attentive audience, says, "No sooner do the Queen Street Mob disappear around the corner, than The Shed pass along the ring road."

Big Steve sits bolt upright in an effort to see down to the crossroads, "Hey look! Mickey's walking this way." "How many with him?" asks Jock. Err," he pauses while he counts them, "There's four of them, and Ghost is with him" replies Big Steve. Seeing Ghost, Little John, says, "That prat went to Venice once and got sea sick crossing the street." Little John laughs, and replies, "Well, at least with all that fat, he'd float and then he'd sell the story to the Daily Mirror." "Leave him alone," snaps Veronica, he ain't that bad. "You're just jealous that you ain't worshipped by The Shed boys, like he is," says Maggie. Merrill looks at Maggie, "You've changed your mind all of a sudden?" Maggie, shaking her head, says,

"No way! He may be a bit of a creepy, but he's OK at games." "Just as long as he don't try it on with you again," says Merrill, as he opens the rear door and gets out. Then looking up to the other two minibuses, he waves for everybody to disembark. Jock turns to Veronica, and putting his arm around her, he says, "Here's some money, make your way to the ground." Giving her a gentle kiss on the cheek, he continues, "If you see Tommy and his boys, tell him we'll meet him in their end, but to stay quiet, 'till we get there." He turns his head to Maggie and warns, "And don't you go in with Tommy either, you're in the stands!"

Parkhead walks over to Merrill, a smile beaming on his face, "So what's the crack then?" "We're going to pay a little visit to their pub, then it's off to the ground," he replies. Big Steve, now standing on the pavement, locks the door of the minibus, then as he pulls the key out, he accidentally drops the remains of his roll, "Fucking French!" he curses. Colin, walking down from the second minibus, turns with a puzzled look on his face and asks, "What's the fucking French got to do with dropping a cheese roll?" Parkhead looks over to Merrill, then with a beaming smile, says to Colin, "Well my old son, when the Vikings invaded France." Everybody from the first minibus collapse in fits of laughter, leaving Colin with a bemused frown on his face, "You lot are off your fucking trolley."

Turning the corner, the North Stand Firm walk towards the sand coloured brick wall that surrounds the Molineux pub, looking through the wide front gate they see about forty people standing around inside the large forecourt. Busily drinking and talking, they fail to notice the North Stand casually walking across the forecourt in two's and three's towards the double front door of the pub.

"Hello, there's Mickey," says Big Steve, nodding towards the front door. Mickey is in the middle of what looks like a heated argument, with a Wolves supporter, standing with his back to the double front doors. "Jesus H Christ," gasps Jock, "That cunt is going to give the game away." "But he don't know we're here though!" says Parkhead. "Well, bang goes the idea of mingling with the wolf pack to get in their end," mumbles Big Steve. Merrill walks slowly up to the supporter and, with out warning, throws a right upper cut that knocks him off his feet, and sending him flying backwards through the double doors.

Panic breaks out as supporters start to push their way out of the trouble spot. Then out of nowhere, two plain-clothes cops rush over and grab Mickey. "You're nicked," screams the larger of the two, forcing Mickey's arm up his back and pinning him against the brick wall. Mickey turns his head and screams in astonishment, "It wasn't me!" Seeing this, Merrill turns and signals to the others to get out fast. They join the rush of supporters across the forecourt, pushing their way through the entrance gate to Molineux Street.

The home end at Wolverhampton is of average size, the low wooden roof giving it quite a dark appearance, even in the daylight. The Queen Street Firm, stand behind the goal, half-way up the terrace, as the view from the rear is obscured slightly by narrow support pillars. Few away crews venture into the home end, except for local derby matches with teams from Birmingham. The Shed is massing on the away terrace behind the far goal and underneath, The Stockwell and Southfields boys are milling around the small bar. The barman looking at all the "Cockneys" milling around says nervously, "Who's next?"

Barry known as Beck's for his love of the German beer is a top face in The Shed, is standing near the bar. A six-footer from Kentish Town, his ice-cold temperament, and fearless nature. Making him a living legend, among the "Shedites'. Losing his left hand in a car accident, adds to his mystique. The barman swallows and stays silent as he looks at 'Beck's'; Beck's gives the barman a long, silent stare, then says, "My friends would like a drink." "Yes sir;" says the barman, noticeably shaking as he picks up a pint sized paper cup. After serving over twenty pints, the barman, finally plucks up courage and says; "Hold on, I'll have to count this up." Beck's passes the last cup to a passing Shed Boy and then looks back to the barman, "Who said anything about paying?" he snaps, then turns and walks towards the stairs that lead up to the terrace. The barman stands there in disbelief for a moment, then starts to shout in panic, "Hey! You can't do that! Oi! Come back!"

At the other end of the ground, the Queen Street Firm have little idea that nearly forty members of the North Stand Firm are

142

quietly infiltrating their territory. Tommy is already standing at the rear of the stand with twenty of his crew; they slowly mingle with a dozen from Salford. To their left are a dozen of the Derby contingent; today is a big match and the North Stand's, 'Foreign Legion' from the North and Midlands are out in force. The Wolves supporters are warming up with a full recital of their songs, and the pre-match atmosphere is becoming electric. In a short break between songs, choruses of 'CHELSEA' drift across the pitch from the far end. The Queen Street Firm start chanting, "WE HATE CHELSEA, WE HATE CHELSEA."

Heads turn at the rear of the stand as the North Stand Firm finally start to ease their way through the crowd, towards the middle rear of the stand. Merrill walks over to Tommy, and shaking hands, he asks, "All quiet on the Western Front?" "Yeah, things are just beginning to warm up," he replies, relieved to see that the Londoners have at last arrived. In front of them, the Wolves supporters are working themselves up into frenzy, chanting, "WANDERERS, WANDERERS," so loud that it's nearly raising the roof. Supporters are jumping up and down, and a few of them, in their excitement, stumble and fall into those in front of them, causing human waves to flow into the many metal crush barriers. Then from the far end come chants of, "NORTH STAND, NORTH STAND, DO YOUR.JOB, NORTH STAND, DO YOUR JOB." The Wolves supporters take up their own version of the chant, mocking the Chelsea supporters in the far end," NORTH STAND, WHERE ARE YOU? NORTH STAND, WHERE ARE YOU?" "Fuck this for a laugh," says Colin, standing behind Merrill, "Let's get stuck in." All eyes at the rear of the stand turn to Merrill and Jock, who look at each other and smile, Jock raises his right hand, and shouts, "WE'RE THE NORTH STAND," then others join in, in unison, "WE'RE THE NORTH STAND, WE'RE THE NORTH STAND STAMFORD BRIDGE."

Silence descends across the terrace as shocked heads turn to look up at the rear. of the terrace. "Charge!" screams Little John, as he Jock and Merrill rush forward, hitting anyone in their way, closely followed by the North Stand and it's 'Foreign Legion'. Within seconds, a large gap opens up in the middle of the terrace as one hundred Chelsea supporters rush forward. The Queen Street Firm is the first of the Wolves supporters to recover from the shock charge and, turning to face the invaders, they are soon engulfed by the momentum. One of them pulls an iron bar from his back pocket, raising it above his head; he starts to bring it down on the Chelsea supporter who has rushed up to him. At the last moment Merrill stops and grabs the Wolves supporter's wrist, bending it back, and twisting his arm. Merrill's right leg then comes up and lands squarely in the stomach of the supporter, who winded, loosens his grip on the bar.

Merrill takes it as Little John punches the supporter in the face, sending him falling to the floor. Merrill nods at Jock as he puts the bar through his belt and into his jeans right pocket.

A wide gap has now opened up on the terrace as people rush to get out of the way, then the first of the police run along the touchline and climb into the terrace. Little John pulls a Wolves supporter by his left arm and swings him around into one of the support pillars; letting go, he smashes his right elbow into his face, then noticing the police arriving in numbers, he looks across to Merrill, "The filth!" he shouts in warning. Merrill looks around and sees that plain-clothes officers are arresting people behind him. "Down the other end!" he shouts. Jock, unaware of the warning, sees Parkhead being led away, by the plain-clothes police; shouting to Big Steve, as he runs over and kicks one of them in the back. Big Steve knees the other one in the right leg, sending him down to the terrace steps, then quickly looking around, he turns back and kicks the policeman in the head, "Cunt!" he screams. "Grabbing hold of Big Steve's arm, Merrill shouts, "Down the other end!" Jock, climbing over the low wall, which separates the terrace from the pitch, looks up and smiles as he sees the rest of the North Stand also climbing over the wall. The police form a barrier to stop them getting onto the playing area and point to the corner flag. One hundred Chelsea supporters start their march around the edge of the pitch, towards the cheering Shed, behind the far goal.

A thundering cheer goes up around Molineux as Wolves score a goal. Merrill, annoyed that Chelsea are now losing with only fifteen minutes to go, he turns to Jock, and says, "That's it! I'm going back up the other end!" "What about the plain cloths filth?" Jock retorts. Merrill looks back at Jock, his anger rising by the second, "Fuck 'em!" he shouts, "They get in the way, we have 'em!" Merrill turns and starts to make his way through the crowded terrace to the staircase that leads to a large tarmac ked area underneath the terrace. "Where's he going?" asks a puzzled Spider'. "Back to the other end," answers Jock. "Good! About fucking time," replies Spider'.

Merrill turns to the North Stand, and raising his arm shouts, "Let's go!" The North Stand starts to move towards the stairs that lead down to the ground. Some of The Shed, sensing the coming battle, start to chant, "NORTH STAND! NORTH STAND! DO YOUR JOB! NORTH STAND! DO YOUR JOB!"

Veronica, sitting in the stand near the halfway line, notices the gap starting to appear on the away terrace; nudging Maggie and pointing over, says, "Hey look! They're on the move." "Shit! I'm going," Maggie says, as she stands up. Veronica looks up in surprise, but catches Maggie's arm before she can leave the seat and pulls her back down, "Don't be a fool! I promised Alan I'd keep you here." "I fucking hate sitting up here when it's going off," snaps Maggie. Veronica turns to look at Maggie in horror, "Isn't it about time you and Sandy grew up and realised that you are women." "Oh! Fuck me! Hark at Miss Prim and Proper!" replies a fuming Maggie, "You wouldn't know a good time if it smacked you in the face!"

Merrill stands underneath the away terrace, looking up at the massive scaffold structure that supports it. As he turns and looks up at the wooden staircase, he sees over two hundred Chelsea supports making their way towards him. Walking out of the gate that leads onto the road around Molineux, he and Jock walk in front of the North Stand as they march along the pavement to the large gates that leads into the home end. "You think this is a wise move?" queries Jock, as they neared the gate, "It's crawling with plain-clothes filth, and I'm sure I saw a couple of slags from Fulham Road nick." Merrill turns his head for a momentary glance at Jock, "You know life's a funny old game." Jock frowns as he looks back at those following. He's never seen Merrill act like this before and doesn't like it. "What the fuck you on about?" Without looking back, Merrill just says, "Do you want to live forever?"

As they reach the gate, Merrill stops for a moment and momentarily looks at the mob marching towards him; he raises his arm and points to the terrace. Walking through the double gates, Merrill and Jock start to move through the excited crowd. Annoyed at the happy and cheerful faces, they start to push their way through the tightly packed mass of people. Heads turn in disgust at being pushed in such a manner, but on seeing the expression on the two responsible, they turn back to face the pitch to avoid trouble. "JINGLE BELLS, JINGLE BELLS, JINGLE ALL THE WAY; OH WHAT FUN, IT IS TO SEE, CHELSEA LOOSE AWAY. WANDERERS, WANDERERS."

The crowded home terrace is whipping itself into a frenzy of euphoric excitement. The Queen Street Firm in the centre of the terrace, are totally unaware of the impending danger. Jumping up and down, those at the edge fail to notice being pushed, until one looks back and says, "Oi!, What's your fucking game?" "Chelsea!" comes the reply, followed by blinding pain as a fist smashes into his nose of the Wolves supporter. Jock lashes out as bodies collide in the panic that now sets in. Merrill opens up a gap, as the Queen Street Firm, taken completely by surprise, move back in total disarray. Side by side hitting anyone within reach, Merrill and Jock, joined by Spider advance as the terrace opens before them. One of the Queen Street Firm is the first to realise that they are under attack by only three people; he turns and stands his ground. Jock only just sidesteps the booted foot; grabbing it, he pulls, sending the youth tumbling down the open terrace.

"Fucking hell!" cries Little John, in astonishment, "Look! They're taking the whole fucking terrace by themselves!" The North Stand pauses to watch as three people open up a twenty-yard gap in the terrace. Big Steve forces his way to the edge of the crowd to join Little John, sizing up the situation in an instant. He steps forward onto the empty terrace, and turning back, he screams, "You fucking idiots! Don't just stand there! Once they realise there's only three of them, they'll kill 'em." At this Big Steve runs alone across the open terrace and joins Merrill, Jock and Spider. Merrill ducks a fist and for the first time, he notices the empty terrace behind him. Looking back, he sees Big Steve running towards them and realises that he Jock and Spider are the only ones fighting. A boot crashes into his right thigh; turning back he sees that those at the side have also realised that they are under attack by just three people and start to encircle them. Merrill looks over at Jock, "We're on our own, Get back! They're coming 'round the sides." Jock looks around and sees the encirclement starting. Realising that they stand no chance, he starts to back off.

The Queen Street Firm now start to advance aiming kicks and punches on the three as they back away across the open terrace. Merrill backs into a metal crush barrier and, losing his balance, he falls to the concrete steps. Jock and Spider move over to help him, but are unable to reach him before one of the advancing Wolves supporters aims a deadly kick that hits him square on the left cheek. He falls unconscious by the barrier; Jock and Spider fight their way around the barrier and stand over the lifeless body, aiming punches at anyone that gets close. Big Steve is the first to reach them, and they stand back to back over the body, as kicks and punches rain down on them, The Queen Street Firm, sensing blood, move in for the kill.

"CHELSEA!" screams Little John, as he leads the charging North Stand into the mass of Wolves supporters. The battle is vicious with no holds barred on either side, but slowly the North Stand push the mass of Wolves supporters back. The General, seeing the North Stand charge across the empty terrace, hears the final whistle. He turns to The Shed and commands; "Across the pitch!" He runs down the terrace and leaps over the low wall and onto the pitch. Police run from their position near the corner flag towards him. Turning to look back onto the terrace, he sees that the Stockwell and Southfields Firms are climbing across the wall, and running on to the pitch. "Come on you bastards!" he yells to the massed ranks of the stationary Shed, The Pimlico, and the Swiss Cottage/West Hampstead/Kilburn boys are also flooding onto the pitch; but there are so many trying to get onto the pitch, that those higher up, have no chance.

Then, as one The Shed start to move down the terrace and climb the wall to join those already charging across the pitch, The General leads over 2,000 in a mass charge across the pitch. The police, unable to deal with the numbers, give up trying to stop the pitch invasion and concentrate on picking on stragglers. Those Wolves supporters near the pitch, realising that they are being charged by over 2,000 of The Shed, start to panic and run. The North Stand fan out in a wide arc, and although out numbered, they start to slowly push the Queen Street back across the terrace. Watching the battle from the other side of the ground, members of The Shed that can't get on the pitch, turn to the side and flood into the street. Wolves supporters not involved in the fighting, seeing that The Shed may be coming along the street as well, move towards the double doors in an effort to leave the ground before they arrive. Outside the ground, panic sets in as Beck's leads the first elements of The Shed, charging through the same gates and start to attacking anyone in their way.

The police, being caught off balance, start to move in, pushing people out of the way in order to get to the focal point of the battle. Seeing the police, the Queen Street Firm finally back off and run across the terrace to join the mass of Wolves supporters standing at the far end of the terrace. The General leads the elements of The Shed still on the pitch, over the low wall and into the terrace. The police start to form up from the top of the terrace and in a double line that stretches to the bottom, move towards the Wolves supporters backed up in the far end. of the terrace.

The General, seeing the battle in the middle of the terrace is over, turns the Stockwell and attacks the rear of the Wolves supporters attempting to exit Molineux. As the crowd in the middle of the terrace moves apart, Maggie, for the first time, sees what she fears most; a motionless body laying on the terrace, surrounded by helpless onlookers. "NO!" she screams in anguish, "No!" Then, before Veronica can stop her, she starts to push her way along the row of seats and then runs down the stairs to the low wall bordering the pitch; jumping over it she runs towards the fast emptying home terrace.

"Leave him," screams Jock, as Spider kneels down over Merrill's body, "He may have broken something." "Fucking Hell!" gasps Big Steve, as he sees for the first time the swelling on Merrill's face, then looks helplessly up at Jock, "What the fuck do we do?" Jock looks over to Colin and, pointing over to the St John's Ambulance Brigade Sign by the corner of the main stand, and yells "Go get help, FAST!" "I've never seen anything like it," says Big Steve to Jock, "You three have a fucking death wish. Why didn't you wait for us?" "You three cleared half the fucking terrace on your own, too fucking much man!" gasps the Ghost. "Oh! That's so fucking wonderful, ain't it," says a seething Jock, "We'd have cleared the whole fucking terrace if you lot hadn't stopped to watch." "You lot," Spider says, turning to those still standing around the body, "You fucking never stand and watch."

"Well, to be fair, you three just rushed ahead, we didn't have a chance of catching you," says an apologetic Lenny. Jock looks around and sees the concern on everyone's face, "OK, OK, sorry! We can't fight amongst ourselves. As Merrill said, Shit happen. You can't fight the fates." "So where's the fucking first aid then?" shouts Big Steve, turning to the police line. "No! No!" screams Maggie, pushing her way through to Merrill, "Not!" She falls down beside the motionless body, tears streaming down her face. Jock bends down and tries to pull her up, "Don't touch him, he may have broken something." Tommy moves over to Maggie and puts putting his arm around her shoulder to comfort her, "He'll be alright, he just knocked out." "Don't touch me!" she shouts, trembling with fear as she sees the swelling growing larger and larger. Tommy throws a shocked look to Jock who raises both hands and shakes his head, "She'll be alright, she's in shock," he reassures Tommy.

"Move, out of the way!" shouts an unfamiliar voice. Turning to see who it is, Big Steve shouts, "Move! It's the First Aid." "Come on, move back," shouts Colin, as he pushes his way through. "I think it would be better if you all moved away," says Inspector Ryan of the Wolverhampton Police, as a silence falls over Molineux. Jock looks up and notices, for the first time, that the game has finished. "You can't nick him, there were just three of us, and we were the ones that got attacked," lies Jock, in an attempt to avoid arrest. Inspector Ryan, turning to Jock and with a sarcastic smile, says, "Just be thankful my men have their hands full or I'd arrest the lot of you."

The St. John's Ambulance men pick up the stretcher with Merrill's still unconscious -body strapped to it, and start to carry it down the terrace. "I'll go with him," Big Steve shouts, as he starts to walk after the stretcher. "No you won't," says a newly arrived policeman in plain-clothes, "I want to talk to you," he says, looking straight at Big Steve. Inspector Ryan points to Jock saying, "You can go with your friend," then looking around the rest of the North Stand, he continues, "And the rest of you can leave the ground quietly. I think you've done enough damage for one day." "You can't let them go!" pleads the plain-clothes man, in astonishment. "Here!" gasps Spider, as he recognises the man, "You're out of Fulham Road Nick!" Inspector Ryan throws a sharp look of anger to the plain-clothes man, then turning to the gathering number of uniformed police says, "Escort these people to the railway station, and arrest anyone that makes any sign of trouble." "I want to go with Alan," sobs Maggie, as she stands looking at the stretcher. "Tommy looks over to the Inspector and, realising they are getting off lightly, and says, "She'll be alright, we'll look after her."

All of a sudden the air is pierced by the clanging sound of metal bouncing down concrete steps. All eyes turn and follow the iron bar that has worked its way loose from Merrill's pocket and just fallen from the stretcher. Jock looks up at the staring faces, "Who throw that?" he says as quick as a flash. "That fell of the stretcher!" shouts the plain-clothes man.

"Rubbish!" replies a laughing Spider, pointing to the last remnants of the Queen Street Firm in the corner, "One of that lot threw it." The plain-clothes man flashes an angry look at Spider, who looks back with arms outstretched and, with raised eyebrows, he mocks, "Honest Guv!" Inspector Ryan turns to follow the stretcher as his police start to move the North Stand towards the large double gates. The plain-clothes man, clearly annoyed, walks down the terrace, bends over and picks up the iron bar. Casting an angry look at the departing North Stand, he grits his teeth and follows the stretcher down the terrace.

"You OK?" asks a subdued Tommy, as he walks along the Ring Road, towards Wolverhampton Station. Maggie, walking beside him with her head bent, says nothing as a tear falls from her cheek. "Jesus! His face came up like a fucking football!" says Big Steve, in disbelief. "Can't blame Jock for blowing his top," cut in Little John, "But, I've never seen three people clear a fucking terrace before." "We should have been with them!" chirped in Lenny." Yeah, but by the time I got there, they'd already started, the crazy bastards," answered Little John

Turning the corner of Wednesfield Road, they walk up to the station, still surrounded by police. "Do yer think he'll be alright?" says Maggie, looking for some sort of reassurance. "Well, at least the ugly bastard's still alive!" laughs Spider. Little John looks over to Maggie and Tommy, and then turning to Spider, "Cut it out Spider, he could have been killed." "Not with me and Jock over his body pal!" Spider proudly retorts.

CHAPTER TWELVE

Kev being the sort of person that never misses out on a freebee says, "Are they on you then?" Alan turns to Kevin and nods "OK, yes, I'll have some." Kevin replies. She makes a note, gives a worried glance to Kev, smiles and walks off. "We were playing Burnley, as far as I can remember, but then it might have been Liverpool,"

Alan continues, as he looks at Kev, who clearly doesn't like the Liverpool reference, "We were all singing and then the Burnley supporters, who were all standing next to us, started pushing, so we pushed back, next thing you know, all hell breaks out. All the Burnley were blokes of about 30 to 40 years old, and we were all teenagers, so it came as no surprise that we lost."

"You're kidding!" says Mark. "So what happened after that?" asks an interested Big Al. "Well, a few of us all lived around the ground and we got together and planned our revenge," Alan pauses in thought, and then continues, "Yes I remember now, it was Burnley, 'cos when we went up there, we ran them down along that long stand of theirs." "And that was the first fighting at Chelsea?" queried Dave, "I always wondered what started it all off."

SUNDAY LUNCH

Sunday March 21st. 1971

The phone rings in the ground floor flat of 5 Durrell Road; a hand sleepily reaches from under a blanket, stretching over to the bedside table it picks up the black receiver, "Hello; who's that?" says a surprised voice. There is a short pause, the voice answers, "That depends on what number you want!" comes the reply. "Oh, I've got the right number my dear, so just put Alan on," demands the voice on the other end. An elbow nudges Merrill in the side, "Wake up, it's for you." A body stirs from under the blankets, "What?" "It's for you," repeats the soft female voice. Merrill's eyes open, he looks at the naked body laying next to him holding the phone, he takes the receiver and says "Hello?" The voice at the other end is confused, and asks, "That didn't sound like Maggie, who the fuck you got there?" Merrill now fully awake, the naked female body emerges from the bed, and walks across to the door, "Merrill's eyes stare at as the shadows dance across the flesh. "That was Linda, she stayed the night. What's up?" Linda turns towards the bed and asks "That's Jock isn't it?" Merrill nods, and Linda replies, "I'm going to have a shower." She turns and walks out of the bedroom; he's eyes follow the well-rounded bottom, as it gently bounces with each step. "Hello you still there?" Jock asks. "Yes." replies Merrill as he sits up in bed. Jock waits a moment as he thinks, then says, "Get rid of her, I'll meet you in the Weatherby at twelve thirty."

The phone goes dead, leaving Merrill sitting with a surprised look on his face, looking down at his watch again; he sees it is only nine thirty. Merrill listens out for the sound of the shower, then as he hears the water running, he smiles to himself and getting out of bed, he walks naked down the passage to the bathroom. Stopping in the doorway, he watches the silhouette of Linda behind the curtain, enjoying her shower. Walking over he places his hand on the shower curtain and slowly pulls it back. Linda turns her head, looks at him while slowly running her hands up her wet body and says, "Come in and join me" Merrill smiles, and steps into the shower.

The front door of the Weatherby opens, and Jock walks in; looking around he sees Merrill sitting alone at a table in the corner. Walking over to the bar, the licensee Freddy Byrne, an over weight, balding fifty year-old from Dublin, who is rumoured to have connections with the nastier side of gangland; smiles and reaches below the bar for a clean glass. "Hello Freddy," says Jock,. "Usual?" Freddy asks, putting his hand on the Brown Ale tap. "Yes please."

Jock replies. Freddy pulls back the tap and starts to pour a pint., then hands Jock the pint of Brown Ale, and says, Alan's already paid for it". Jock takes a mouthful of beer and walks over to Merrill, pulls out a chair, and sits down without saying a word. "Oh thanks for the drink." Merrill says sarcastically.

Jock picks up his drink and takes another mouthful, putting it down; he looks at Merrill's face and says, "Well the swellings going down well, it hardly notices now." Merrill brings up his right hand and gently feels his cheekbone; "Yeah the hospital says they can't put fractured cheek bones in plaster, so I just have to be careful." "Means you can't fight at Bruges then!" laughs Jock. "Does it fuck!" snaps Merrill. Changing the subject Jock says "So? What's going on, I thought you and Linda were finished."

Merrill smirks and says, "Hey she gives the best head this side of the Mojave Desert." Not knowing Californian slang Jock shakes his head.; and picks up the glass, "Oh by the way did you see that black Mustang outside?" Merrill laughs out loud, "Sure did you old tart, it's mine." Jock stops dead mouth dropping open; "You gotta be fucking kidding?" "No, it's my latest toy, a Shelby Mustang GT 350 fast back, and a snip at Two Grand." Jock shakes his head, "Bastard, if I'd know that I'd have kicked it on the way in." Merrill laughs and walks to the front door, looking back he says, "Put the glasses down, and I'll give you a quick spin." They walk out of the Weatherby, and over to the shinny black Mustang, "You'll never guess how I got it?" Merrill says as he pulls out the car keys from his pocket.

Jock walks over and runs his right hand over the newly waxed bodywork, "Shit! It's in fucking good nick, so come on then; how the fuck did yeah get it?" Merrill smiles as he opens the drivers door and sits in the racing bucket seat, "Well I know this guy who works for a record importing company, and one day he gives me a lift in it." Jock sits in the passenger seat intrigued, "And?" "Well he can see I'm as impressed as you are, so he boasts that if I like it, to bring a grand into his office on the Monday, and it's mine," says Merrill, looking at Jock with a cocky smile. "Knowing he's only bragging to show off, I thought I'd call his bluff."

"So you turned up with the Two Grand?" asks Jock. Merrill smiles as he turns the ignition key, and the engine fires up with a deep throaty raw, "exactamundo old son; I throws the Two Grand down on his desk, and his mouth drops as fast as Linda's knickers." Jock frowns and is then thrown back into his seat as the Mustang is thrown around the corner into the Kings Road; "And he just folded?" queries Jock. "Well not exactly, he says he uses it to race caravans, and he needs the race engine, but he'll put the original Shelby one back in it. I says what the heck, I'll take it any way. And here it is."

Laughs Merrill, as he guns it passed the Chelsea Drug Store towards Sloane Square. "Caravans?" Exclaims Jock, "They race caravans?" Merrill smiles as he shrugs his shoulders, "Apparently so!"

Big Steve, and Little John, walk into the Weatherby, looking around and seeing no familiar faces, they walk over to the bar. "Hello Freddy, Merrill and Jock, not here yet?" asks Little John. Freddy washing beer glasses looks over to the corner table and says, "Err, they was sitting over there, when I went into the Saloon bar to serve a minute ago." Replies Freddy as he points over to the corner table; "but it looks like Alan's left his fags and lighter, so they'll have just popped out." "Usual pal," says Big Steve, looking back to the bar, "then we'll help ourselves to a fag." "Ha, you never change." answers Freddy. Big Steve smiles as he says, " One has to take advantage of opportunities." Walking over to the corner table Big Steve picks up the packet of JPS and helps himself to one, as he sits down he uses the Zippo to light it; and slowly blows out a column of smoke. Then taking out his match ticket he looks at it and smiles.

Little John puts two pint glass of Watney's Red Barrel on the table, and taking his jacket off, hangs it over the back of the chair. Sitting down he takes a mouthful of beer, wiping his mouth he looks at Big Steve and says, "I can't wait to get over to Bruges, for the game." "I wonder where these 120 Franc tickets are in the ground?" Big Steve says as if thinking out loud. Little John looks over at the tickets, and says, "They've got to be better than those 80 Franc ones, all the Shed Boys are buying. "We better not be stuck up in some fart arsed stand," replies Big Steve, taking another drag from his newly acquired JPS.

"Shit I never thought of that!" exclaims Little John; "We'd never live it down if we can't get down to where it kicks off, the fucking Shed would have all the glory, why'll we just look down on it, helpless." Big Steve raises his eyebrows in surprise; "Don't forget you were a Shed Boy once." "Yeah and we all used to stand on the half way line once, before they built the West Stand, don't mean I'm still a Half Way Line boy, does it?" replies Little John.

"Anyway we'd better be careful over there," says Big Steve thoughtfully; "you know what the Chelsea programme said about their police!" Little John laughs as he raises his hands in the air, "What all that bollocks about police dogs? That's just the club trying to stop any trouble kicking off; they don't want to be the first club chucked out of Europe for crowd trouble." "I still reckon we should take it easy over there," says a concerned Big Steve; "They have the reputation for being the hardest set of supporters in Europe." "Yeah right, till we get there!" comes the proud retort from Little John; "you getting soft in your old age then?" Big Steve looks annoyed at that remark, and snaps back, "Oh do fuck off pal!

Like I said I don't want the club banned from Europe, don't mean I ain't going to get stuck it if they kick it off!" Calming down he continues, "Remember that they ran on the pitch and gave Jeff Astle a kicking at the end of the Sheffield game a couple of years ago." "Well there yeah go then," says Little John; "It's fucking pay back time then." Big Steve's reply is cut short before he can make it, as his head turns around when he hears the sound of the bar door opening.

Jock lets the door go with a bang, and walks over to the bar all smiles, "Ah there you are," says Big Steve, as he turns round to see who's coming through the door, "Get 'em in then." Jock looks over and flashes a mean look, knowing that he's been caught. "We've just been for a spin in Alan's new Mustang!" "Jammy Bastard! Ain't that old Mini-Van good enough anymore." barks Big Steve. "I've still got the Mini-Van, just fancied a new toy," says Merrill coming through the door. Little John gets up from his seat, and walks to the door, "Let's have a look then?" "Latter," says Merrill as he sits down at the table. Undeterred Little John walks out of the door to inspect the Mustang. "Hey nice fags these JPS," laughs Big Steve, Merrill reaches for his jacket pocket, realising he left them behind, looks over to Big Steve and sighs.

"Wonderful." Jock walks over to the table carrying a tray full of beer, and crisps, "Make room, make room." He shouts, as he puts the tray on the table. "So everything ready for Tuesday?" says Big Steve picking up his drink and smiling sarcastically at Jock. "Yeah, the coaches leave the Russell Square at 10 o'clock, so if we get their at around half eight, we can grab some grub in the greasy spoon by the station," observers Jock. "You paying then?" laughs Little John, as he walks back into the Weatherby.

Jock looks around at Little John, and sticks two fingers up. "Oi, do you mind?" snaps Maggie as she follows Little John through the door. "So where's Mandy?" asks Jock, as he takes his fingers down, with a smile. Maggie pulls over a chair and sits next to Merrill, then looking at Merrill says, "So where's me drink then?" Jock leans forward as he raises his voice, "So where's Mandy then?" Maggie frowns as she looks at Jock, and replies; "She's up in Salford for the weekend with Dave, so relax, she'll be back tomorrow night." "One vodka and lemonade!" shouts Freddy from behind the bar, it's on your slate Al." "I'll get it," says Little John, as he walks over to the bar, "and a packet of Smith's Crisps Freddy."

"So what have you been up to since Friday night?" says a cheerful Maggie. Merrill tilts his head as he looks at Maggie, "Oh, nothing much, did the club last night got in about 3 this morning." Jock throws Merrill a knowing look, "Oh we've just been talking about Bruges." Sensing something up going on Maggie looks at Jock and Merrill, "I said something wrong then?"

As Jock is about to reply, he just hears the sound of a car smashing into something outside. Rushing to the door he runs outside, a few moments latter, he walks back in as laughingly says. A Metro has just hit a lamppost outside the World's End." "Did he nearly did a John, and smash into the barrier," laughs Big Steve. "Oh for fuck sake," sighs Little John, "Ain't I ever going to live that down?" Big Steve, laughing his head off, looks at Little John, and says, "No!" Maggie who is now sitting at the next table, turns around, and looking at Little John, she says, "I didn't know you could drive?" "That's the point," sniggers Jock, "He can't." Waiting for the laughter to die down, Maggie looks at Big Steve and says, "So what happened then?" Big Steve, still smiling replies, "I think that would be better coming from John!" Maggie looks at Little John, frowns, and then says, "Well!"

Little John, now seeing the funny side, starts to laugh, and says, "Well, it was like this. We were all in the Weatherby, drunk out of our fucking skulls, when Ken Tanner gives me his car keys and says, 'As you can't drive you can have me car keys, so I won't drive home drunk.' So I takes them and puts then in me pocket, and forgets about them." "Ken, that's that Shed boy who hangs around with you lot in the Weatherby ain't it?" he?" inquires Maggie. "Yeah," says Jock, "With any luck he'll be joining us on the North Stand, but like Spider, he don't like leaving The Shed behind." "Fucking good fighter though," quips Lenny.

"So anyway," continues Little John, "I'm getting fucking plastered and I decide to get a bit of fresh air, so I goes outside. Thinking that I'll have a fag, I put me hands in me pockets looking for me them, when I pull out these fucking car keys. What the fuck are these I think? So as I'm leaning up against a car, I decide to see if they fit." "And did they? Says asks a fascinated Maggie. "'Course they did!" chuckles Big Steve, "It was Ken's car." "Do you mind," says Little John sarcastically, "I'm telling this fucking story. "You tell him Pal," laughs Jock.

Waiting for the laughter to die down, Little John continues, "So, fuck me, I thought as the key fitted and opened the door, result! Then as it was fucking freezing I decide to sit inside. Then I thought, fuck it, I'll turn the heater on. Then as the engine comes to life I decide to have a driving lesson." "But you were drunk!" says Maggie. "Yeah, I know that, I was totally fucking rat arsed! You think I would try driving when I was sober?" Little John shakes his head and smiles, "So I pull out onto the Kings Road, and just as luck would have it, right in front of a fucking filth van." "What a Black Maria?" says Maggie. Little John looks over to Merrill, a blank expression on his face, "She with you?" Merrill collapses with laughter as Maggie fails to sees the funny side. "So, I'm looking in the rear view mirror at the filth, when I feel this bump, and fuck me, I'd taken out the bollards by the World's End. Well 'cos of the impact, I lose control and try to get it back, when fuck me, I take out the next set of bollards."

"Oh my Gawd!" gasps Maggie, while everyone is rolling about with laughter. "So what happened then, the law nick yer?" queries Maggie. "Oh no, I'm still fighting for control, and think, 'fuck this for a game of soldiers' and fall asleep at the wheel. Well, the car goes smashing into the barriers that are in front of the shops, writing the car off. Anyway, I wake up and the filth are looking down at me in the gutter." "How the fuck did you get there?" asks Maggie. "I fucking fell out of the car when they opened the fucking car door, didn't I," Little John continues with a smile, "So they take me down to Fulham nick and throw me in a cell for a couple of hours to sober up. So,

I'm thinking, right, I'll cop up for stealing the car so Ken will be covered by insurance, sorted." "What did Ken say?" laughs Maggie. "Well would you believe it, old Ken's in the station admitting he gave me the keys, so they wouldn't charge me with theft, and shouting at the top of his voice that he's gonna kill me. Then the next day I'm in court charged with 21 counts, including stealing the car and assaulting the police."

"Assaulting the police?" queries Maggie, who is now standing leaning on the seat behind. "Yeah, apparently I hit the copper and they kicked the fuck out of me in the van. So let's see," Little John pauses a moment, remembers where he's up to, and then continues, "Criminal damage, failing to stop, driving without a licence and insurance. Well, the filth, thinking that this is payback time, come out with I'm the leader of the North Stand, and summons Big Steve as witness." Maggie's eyes open wide in surprise. "So, I get up in the witness box and they ask me, 'Is he the leader of the North Stand?'" cuts in Big Steve, pointing at Little John, "So I say, you gotta to be kidding! You seriously think I'd take orders from that little squirt." Maggie nearly falls over the seat laughing. "So!" Little John continues, "The beak asks me why I crashed the car? So I tells him I was drunk and fell asleep at the wheel. Well, the beck goes ape shit, asking the filth why I ain't charged with drunken driving? So the fucking copper says I was so drunk, they put me in a cell to sober up. Well, the beck shakes his head in disbelief and fines me one pound on each charge."

"Wow!" gasps Maggie, "That was a relief! So, what happened to Ken?" At this, everyone knowing what's coming, breaks out into more fits of laughter, as Maggie looks about wondering why.

"Well, Ken goes into the dock," Little John says, laughing his head off, "And the beck fines him a hundred and fifty quid for letting me drive drunk." "But Ken didn't even know you were in the car, let alone driving it," says a concerned Debbie. "Yeah!" shouts Big Steve, "Classic ain't it!" as everyone collapses with laughter.

"Ha ha, that reminds me of Merrill at Ipswich," laughs Jock. Maggie turns and looks across at Jock, who is sitting opposite her with Veronica, "Why, what happened there?" Merrill frowns and shakes his head, smiling. "Well," he says, "He gets nicked from hitting a group of Shed boys at the station." Maggie turns her head and looks at Merrill in surprise, What did you do that for?" Before Merrill can answer, Jock cuts in, "We were on the platform when this group of Shed boys charge in from the booking hall. Alan gets pushed up against the train that was standing in at the platform. Well, he turns around and has a go at them, 'cos there are ordinary passengers getting pushed all over the place.

Well one of The Shed boys tells him to fuck off, so Alan decks him." "You hit a Chelsea supporter?" gasps Maggie. "Yeah, fucking right he did," replies Jock, "And, the best bit was, that there's a plain-clothes copper on the platform. He grabs Alan, so he turns and punches the him in the face, but the copper ain't alone, and three of them cart him off to the nick." "And you let them do it?" queries Maggie. "Had no choice in the matter, at that point, a load of uniformed police stream the platform with truncheons swinging," continues Jock,

"So, I go to court with him as a witness, and tell the beak what happened, and that he didn't know the guy was a copper. But the beak was having none of it, and give him the option of three months or a hundred and fifty quid fine." "Oh my Gawd!" gasps Maggie, as she looks at Merrill. "Anyway, this idiot looks at the beak and says, 'Fucking result! I'll take the fine. Do you take cheques up here?'" says Jock, laughing his head off, "So the beak bangs his gavel and says, 'and that's an extra fifty pounds for contempt of court.'"

After the laughter dies down Little John says "OK, what's the plan for the Leeds game then?" "How about doing the coaches again," says Big Steve. "Yeah, we ain't done them for a while." points out Jock. "OK," says Merrill looking at Jock, "What time did you tell the others to get here?" "One o'clock," he replies looking around to the door; "they should be here by now." Then just on Que. Colin, Lenny, Spider, and 'Beck's' walk through the door. "Where's Ghost' and Parkhead?" asks Jock, as they walk over to the bar. "Ain't got a clue pal," says Big Steve. "Right, Spider says we ain't done the coaches for ages, so we all up for it?" A mass "Yes" fills the air as all agree. You know they've been parking in Imperial Road lately?" says

157

Little John. "Yeah, I head that, we got any confirmation of it though?"

Jock says looking around. Big Steve raises his hand and says, "Well I parked down there when the ManUre played, and they had a dozen coaches there. "OK, " says Jock getting the map out, and spreading in out across the table. "So if we go down Gleys Lane," says Merrill, "and wait on the corner of Stephendale Road, we can take them from behind cutting through Fulmead."

"Problem!" says Spider, "How we gonna take them in the rear, when they'll be walking towards us?" Jock taps the map in thought, and then says; "We get 'The General' and the Stockwell to take them from Harwood Terrace." "Then how the fuck we gonna know when it goes off?" asks Davis. Merrill pulls out a long black plastic box, and puts it on the table. All eyes pear at the object, "That some kind of radio?" Beck's asks. "Yeah, it's a CB radio," answers Merrill. "I picked up a couple in California, they have a one to two mile range for a hand held, and they also have eight channels." Spider smiles,

"I like it," he says "So while someone stands in Imperial Road, he talks into that thing and the rest of us hear it, and come running." "Too much." gasps Little John. "So who's going to be in Imperial Road then," asks Big Steve, "the filth know our faces, and will move us on or nick us." Merrill looks around the table, "Why do you think I've been nurturing Bo, and kept him out of trouble like in Nottingham, when those Fulham filth, were working with the locals." "You crafty old cunt." gasps 'Beck's'. "So we send him in and the old bill won't smell a rat, I like it.

CHAPTER THIRTEEN

"Yeah!" says Big Al, trying to turn the subject away from knocking America, "How did all that hooligan stuff start in the first place?" Mark Diamond hands round his packet of Rothmans, then answers, "It goes back to before the First World War, there were loads of riots." Mike Gilmartin looks shocked, "It goes back that far? My God! You Brits just love a fight don't y'all." Ian Kirkman laughs, "It's that subtle blend of Celtic, Saxon, and Viking blood. We're a fighting race, that's why we carved out the biggest and greatest Empire this planet has ever seen." Big Al nods, with a wry smile, "They say the sun never set on the British Empire."

Kevin Darcy is annoyed that the Chelsea supporters are enjoying themselves with the American, and cuts in again, "You're talking about history, but what about the post-war hooligans? You say you're nothing to do with them, but you seem to know a lot about them." Kev sits down and settles back with an arrogant smile. Big Al nods his head and, looking over, adds, "So do you know how all this violence at games started?" Alan decides to put Kev and the Americans out of their misery.

Alan glances at Mark and half smiles, "Well, as best as I can remember, it was 1962 or 63, before the Bank Holiday Mods & Rocker battles anyway, and before the West Stand was built. We all stood on the halfway line, where the West Stand is now." He sees Maureen clearing a nearby table and calls her over, "Can I have some fries please," then, looking around he asks, "Anyone else?"

"But what about Shed," asks Ian Kirkman, "I always thought they were the first mob at Chelsea?" Alan Chandler nods his head, "Yes, we were all on the side line until the West Stand was built, then we all moved over to the East Stand, but there wasn't much room so we moved behind the goal and under cover." Big Al glances at his watch, then looks over to the other Americans, and says, "Hey! We have to go guys," then, looking back to the Chelsea supporters, he says, "Well, it's been nice talking to you guys."

Kevin Darcy looking upset that part of his audience is about to depart, cuts in. "Hey! Don't go! I thought you wanted to know what makes a hooligan?" Big Al looks at the other Americans, then nods his head, and says. "OK, we'll make this a final, final." He looks over to Alan, and asks, "So you claim not to be a hooligan, but you seem to know a great deal about them." Alan puts a French Fry in his mouth, chews it a couple of times, then answers Big Al. "Well if you don't move with the times, you get left behind." "Ah! So you were one of them then!" Kev almost screams in his glee that he has at last exposed the truth.

Big Al looks over to Kev, "You know, I always have a distrust of someone that tries to make capitol out of someone else. What bothers me is what are they hiding?" he pauses a moment, then says, "I always wonder what their hidden agenda is?" Kev looks perturbed at this assault, clearly thinking it's the Chelsea supporters that should be under attack. "The arrogant never like it when they think they're losing the limelight," answered Mark Diamond.

"It's obvious to me that Chelsea and Liverpool don't get on," observed Jim Boyle, "Is it like that with every club?" "Yes, we're all basically tribal, with most people turning to their local club," observes Dave Hughes nodding. "Unless they support Manchester United, that is," Mark interrupts with a smile, "All the poser's, and no lifers, claim to support United, 'cos they think it makes them big and important." "Yeah," adds Alan, "That's why we call them Manure!"

Big Jim, recognising the name, and thinks out loud, "I've heard of them, they're like the Dallas Cowboys insofar as their supporters are concerned. People like to identify themselves with success." "Yes," chirps Ian Kirkman, "If you don't have the strength of character to support their home team."

Alan nods in approval, and leaning forward, he adds, "Even Chelsea are suffering from that effect these days. We've been invaded by Yuppies who think it's oh so terribly trendy to support Chelsea," he pauses to take another French fry, "I remember ten years ago when we were in the Second Division, we had around ten thousand at home and took around two thousand to away games. But The atmosphere that that small happy band created was far greater than anything you get today with the bloody Yuppies."

FC BRUGES AWAY

Wednesday March 24th. 1971

Two thousand years ago Bruges was a Gallic-Roman settlement, which became the most important fortified town on the Flemish coast. The name is derived from the Old Norse 'Bryggia', meaning 'Landing Stage', but in the eleventh century, the coast line silted up, leaving Bruges land locked. In the middles ages, Bruges became an important trade centre, with Flemish cloth being exported to the whole of Europe. After a series of revolts, political unrest, war, and epidemics, cloth was replaced by luxury goods and banking. However, in the sixteenth century, Bruges lost its prestige to Antwerp, and a split from the Netherlands in 1584 led to further decline. By the mid-nineteenth century, Bruges was the poorest city in Belgium, but later found a rebirth as an arts and tourist centre. Bruges' picturesque architecture, which along with its network of canals, make it one of the most beautiful towns in Europe.

Getting bored with looking out of the coach window, Mandy looks over to Colin and Big Steve, "Where the fuck did you get those coats from?" she asks with a half smile. "You look like the bleeding James gang on the Northfield's bank job," cuts in Parkhead. Colin looks down at the white, full length coat he had bought in Ostend with pride, "This is fucking style Pal, something you have yet to learn about." Big Steve stands up, and walks into the aisle of the coach, and poses mockingly as though he was a catwalk model, "We're starting the latest Mod fashion Pal." "Hold on!" shouts Little John, "Didn't the Mods die out in the late '60's?"

"No!" storms Colin, "They evolved into the Skinheads, and we are the next step in evolution." Jock looks at Big Steve, with a frown, "Ain't they butchers' coats?" "Yeah, spot on!" replies Big Steve, "So what do yer think?" he quickly twirls again, but gives the game away by the smile on his face. "I think we're gonna set a new fashion," says Lenny, as he stands up and takes down a paper carrier bag from the overhead luggage rack, and pulls out a brand new white butchers coat. "Oh what the fuck!" sighs Jim, as he too reaches for a carrier bag, "I knew we should of bought a pair of sparkling spurs too," he says mockingly. "I like them, where 'bouts in Ostend did you get them?" inquires Mandy.

Oh fuck me!" gasps Dave. "Later dear, you want this lot watching yer," replies Sandy with a sarcastic smile. "Say Yeah! Say Yeah!!" laughs Little John. Mandy flashes him a look that could kill, and grabs Jim's coat before he has the chance to put it on, "So where did you lot get the money to splash out on these then?" Colin smiles, and looks at Jim, "Didn't you know, they have ghosts in Ostend?" Ghost, looking innocent, puts his hands up, "Hey! Is it my fault some dick-head felt his wages in his coat pocket?" "You're gonna get well busted one of these days" says Mandy, shaking her head. "No, he's far to good for that," replies Lenny, "Cunt goes into a shop and straight through the 'Staff Only' door, thirty seconds later he strolls out, cool as a cucumber."

"Well at lest I didn't show myself up on a push-bike in Ostend, pal," replies Ghost, with a smiling. Jock looks at Merrill and laughs, "I don't know what was more funny, you driving on the wrong side of the road, waving your arms at that Mercedes to get over, or getting stuck in the tram lines and falling off in front of it." "Fucking foreigners should drive on the proper side of the road," replies Merrill, grinning broadly. "You're the foreigner here pal," says Jock, "Typical fucking English, think everyone should do it your way." "I'm German and I'm surprised you didn't wear yer skirt to the game, you sweaty Wanker!" retorts Merrill, an even broader grin spreading across his face.

"He's scared it would blow up and show the world he has nothing up there," screams Big Steve. Maggie looks at Merrill and starts laughing. "That's nothing," says Merrill, "You should have seen him last night, in the bar while you girls were eating in the hotel. "Veronica looks at Jock and frowns, "Oh yeah, I didn't hear about this?" "Ah, didn't he tell yer?" laughs Big Steve. A broad smile snakes across Jock's face as he looks at Veronica. "Well," says Merrill, "We're in this bar, and as always with sweaty socks, they can't hold their drink and he gets into an argument. So this fucking huge bouncer comes over and grabs him." "And was he fucking huge, or what?" laughs Colin. "So, Jock looks at him, and says 'OK Pal,'" continues Merrill, "Well, the bouncer lets him go, and he walks to the bar and picks up an empty Coke bottle. Then he walks back to the bouncer, who is now walking towards the door, and smashes the Coke bottle down on the back of his head."

"Oh my God!" screams Veronica, as her hands fly up to her cheeks in horror. What happened then?" "This fucking bouncer just stands there and slowly turns around, puts his hand up to his head, and then looks at the blood on it," laughs Merrill. "Yeah, it was like a bird had shit on his head instead a fucking Coke bottle," shouts Little John who is cracking up with laughter. Jock looks at Veronica and shrugs his shoulders in mock innocence. "Well! So what happened?" exclaims Mandy. "He did a fucking runner," shouts Parkhead. Jock looks back and throws Parkhead a look, "So what would you do? The cunt was seven foot tall and four foot wide, for fucks sake. Anyway you can't talk! What about that brothel last night?"

"Brothel?" screams Maggie and Mandy in two-part harmony. Parkhead throws them both a blank expression, shrugs his shoulders, and says. "So?" Then after thinking for a moment, he continues, "You want a good meal, made by professionals, you go to a restaurant and pay for it. And, by the same token, if you want a good shag, you go to a fucking brothel, don't yer?" The girls look over to Veronica and shake their head. "Yeah, but if they won't let you in,' defends Parkhead, "You go outside, grab the nearest dustbin, and chuck in through the bleeding window, do yer?" The girls' jaws drop open in disbelief as everyone else roars with laughter. "Fuck em," laughs Parkhead, "Bastards fucking deserved it." As the laughter dies down, Lenny glances out of the coach window and shouts, "Fuck me! Look!" All eyes turn to the front and see that four more coaches are sitting in the fast approaching side road. "How many is that now?" says asks Jim. "I've lost count," replies Jock, "Got to be over twenty by now. "Merrill smiles, turns to look at Jock and says, "Someone somewhere has just organised us into a fucking army."

The coach pulls in and stops at a large roundabout as over twenty other double-deck coaches slowly manoeuvre and park. The free space at the roundabout quickly fills up as other coaches park at the side of the road. Hundreds of Chelsea supports slowly disembark and move onto the large grass area in the middle of the roundabout. Chants of 'Chelsea! Chelsea!' start to echo off the picturesque buildings on the edge of the town. The North Stand gather together at the side of the roundabout by their coach, their numbers swelled by the 'Foreign Legion,' to over a hundred. They stand and watch as police start moving the front members of The Shed towards the main street that leads to the ground. Shoppers stop in their tracks and watch in wonder as over a thousand members of The Shed start to move towards the ground. Sirens shriek as police cars drive after a small group that starts to run down the main street.

Big Steve looks around at the mass of Chelsea supporters, then looks back to the North Stand, "Fuck me!" he gasps, "This is going to fucking ace." "Be careful, and stick together," shouts Jock, holding up both hands. Merrill walks over to Tommy and Dave, "Keep your lot together, I don't like this." Tommy frowns and looks at Merrill, "You're fucking joking pal! This is brilliant! Look at them all!" He points to the last group of Shed boys as they move away from the roundabout and walk towards the main street. "We're in a strange country," says Merrill, "We don't know the streets, we don't know the filth, we don't know the ground, and far more important, we don't know the supporters." "Don't worry about them," says a beaming Dave, "We've got a fucking army here."

Tommy, looking around and soaking up the electric atmosphere, thinks for a moment, then turns to Dave, "He's got a point,' then looking at Merrill, continues, "So what we gonna do, form the rear guard and play it by ear?' "Yeah, and watch for the sides streets!" warns Merrill, as he walks of to join Jock and Little John who are still watching the last of The Shed move into the main street. "So what d'you reckon?" says Little John, as Merrill joins them. "Move in behind The Shed and play it by ear," says Jock. Merrill nods as he walks over to Big Steve and Colin, "Right lets go, and stay together."

The North Stand move in behind the last remnants of The Shed, and as they move into the main street, they can feel the change in the locals, for the initial sense of wonderment is fast turning into fear as they see the vase number of supporters singing their way towards the ground." "These shops look like they fell of a Christmas card," says Maggie, as she catches up with Merrill. He looks at the shops then back at Maggie, then smiling, he says, "Yeah, they do, but don't get sucked up by the atmosphere, we can be attacked at any moment." "You worry far to much," replies a Maggie with a smile. Merrill shakes his head, "Remember what it said in the papers, these are the hardest supporters in Europe, and they kicked the shit out of Sheffield when they were here."

As they approach the ground, Veronica pulls her ticket out of her bag and says to Jock, "I'd better make my way to the stand." "How d' yer know which one it is?" queries Jock. "Some of us can read and speak French you know," she replies in an indignant tone. Merrill sniggers as he over hears her. Veronica snaps a look of hatred towards Merrill, "Of cause some people haven't even learnt their own language yet, "How d' you put up with that fucking arrogant bitch?" thinks Merrill out loud. Jock laughs as he gives Merrill a friendly slap on the back, "'Cos she shags me, stupid!" "Hey! We're in this end," says Big Steve, as he walking back from talking to a policeman. Jock looks at his ticket and then at Big Steve, "This is the hundred and ten franc end?" "Yeah and wanna know something?" Big Steve says with a knowing smile. "What's that?" query Jim and Lenny in unison. Big Steve's face turns into a carbon copy of a Cheshire cat, as he says. "This is their end."

As the North stand are herded towards the gate at the side of the stand, Bruges supporters stop and watch. Several of them shout what appear to be insults. Several police move forward, stopping the lead elements and checking their tickets. An officer, who is called over, talks to several other policemen, who then move aside and let the North Stand march through the gate. The atmosphere is getting tense with more abuse shouted at them from the local supporters. "Fuck hell!" says Mandy, "This is getting dodgy." "You sure we're going?" Maggie says in reply.

Mandy motions to Maggie and points to a group of Bruges supporters standing just inside the gate and who are pointing at Merrill, "I don't think that SS Eagle on his jacket sleeve is going down too well." "Fuck 'em!" snaps Merrill, overhearing the remark, "Just keep walking." "I don't like this," says Maggie, moving closer to Merrill. "What's up with you," he says, as he looks at her, "Not nervous are we?" "Too bloody right I am!" she snaps, then as they turn the corner they see the pitch for the first time.

Bruges is a small ground not unlike many second and third division grounds in England. The far terrace is uncovered and already filling up with The Shed; small, narrow stands run along the side. The home-end is a steep covered terrace, now full of chanting Bruges supporters, with a narrow walkway along the front; a small wall separates it from the pitch. As the North Stand move down the side of the Home Stand, they turn the corner and stop as they look up at the packed and hostile terrace.

"Fucking Hell!" exclaims Jim, who is the first to turn the corner. He stops and looks up at the terrace as those Bruges supporters near him, surge forward. The nearest one kicks out, but Jim sidesteps it. Before he can retaliate, Colin rushes forward and stops at the metal crush barrier at the bottom of the terrace, "Come on you cunt!" he screams at the supporter who lashed out with the kick. Jock grabs Colin's arm and pulls him back, "Not yet!" he warns. "What's up pal, lost your bottle?" Colin snaps back. Jock, shaking his head, replies, "Calm down and let's suss this thing out." "This is what I like," shouts Big Steve, "Soak up the fear and get the adrenaline flowing." Yes!" Merrill shouts, "This is better than any fucking drug! Look at them and soak it up."

Little John walks over to Merrill and points at the rear of the terrace, "Look over there; at the end. There's a gap at the back." Merrill looks over to Jock, who nods back in agreement, "Right, along the front and then up to the back." "And ignore these cunts at the front!" screams Jock. Big Steve turns to the rest of the North Stand, waves his right arm forward and shouts, "Right! Come on you lot! Let's go," then, seeing Tommy and Dave, walks over to them and continues, "This is fucking intimidating, make sure your lads stick together." Tommy nods and turns to his boys, "Come on you lot, and don't start anything down here."

The Bruges supporters surge forward down the terrace once again, but are stopped by crush barriers. Coins are thrown as the North Stand move along the front of the terrace. The chanting is so loud that you can't hear yourself think. The lead elements of the North Stand turn and start to walk up the gangway that leads to the top of the terrace. Drums start to beat out a rhythm as heads turn and watch the group of Chelsea supporters move up the terrace. Bottles are thrown, arcing their way over the heads of the Bruges supporters, and fall around the gangway. A chant in English of "WE HATE CHELSEA! WE HATE CHELSEA!" rolls across the terrace, echoing off the low roof.

Trumpets then start a fanfare in time to the drumbeat, and a chant of "KILL THE ENGLISH, KILL THE ENGLISH." is sung to the rhythm. Lenny looks around him in apprehension as he climbs the stairs. Ducking a bottle, he sees the ashen face of Jim, "Scared?" he asks with a half smile. "Fucking right," answers Jim, "This is a bloody war zone." "Yeah, wicked ain't it!" laughs Colin, as he walks past them, "This is going to be something else!" "Look!" says Big Steve, "There ain't one of these fuckers under twenty five, and there's no women or kids!" Soaking up the tension, Colin smiles back and says, "This is going to be better than the Park Lane Massacre!" Merrill hears the talking and looks back, "Come on, kept moving. All the way up to the back." "And don't let any of these fuckers get behind yer either!" shouts Jock, who dodging out of the way of a punch thrown by a Bruges supporter at the side of the gangway. Spinning around he lashes out at the supporter who falls onto the gangway.

Little John, who is behind Jock, sees the supporter fall to the steps, "Cunt!" he screams as he kicks him in the head whilst he tries to get up. "Dave, take your lot to the right when we get to the top," orders Merrill, then looking down to Tommy, he says, "Take yours the left. Make sure none of these cunts get behind us, or we're all dead." Dave looks back to his group, "Come on move it." He looks around at the hostile crowd, then points to the right, "Up there, and don't let anyway of these cunts get behind us." Merrill reaches the wall at the back of the terrace and watches as the North Stand fan out along the wall. The Bruges supporters are jumping up and down in waves, as they surge forward and back, resembling the surf as it laps onto a beach. As the last of the North Stand move into the tightly packed group, Jock stands lapping up the tension, then looking left and right, happy that everyone is in place, he screams,

"WE'RE THE NORTH STAND!" And over one hundred English voices roar in unison... "WE'RE THE NORTH STAND! STAMFORD BRIDGE!" As they sing, a group of Bruges supporters charge up the gangway into the middle of the North Stand. Jock is the first to respond, kicking a supporter who falls back into the on rushing crowd. Parkhead, runs forward and punching left and right, doesn't see the hand wielding an iron bar that crashes into his right shoulder. Stumbling to his knee he hits the concrete terrace. Big Steve grabs him and pulls him up; they smile briefly then turn and punch out at the advancing hordes.

Lenny and Colin fight their way forward down the terrace and are surrounded, hitting out at anything that moves, punches reigning down on them. Jock sees their plight and moves towards them; Sandy joins him as they punch and kick their way to Lenny and Colin. "You cunts," she screams. "Jock told you to stand as a group." "But I'm enjoying myself!" laughs Colin, as he hits another supporter. "Come on, let's get back to the top! We're getting cut off here," warns Lenny. As they fight their way back up the terrace, Dave shouts across to Mandy to join him.

Jock turns to make sure she makes it and feels a punch in the back, the impact sending a shiver down his spine. He knows instinctively that this is no ordinary punch, and he spins around to see a Bruges supporter holding a Stanley knife. He grabs the bottom of his sheepskin jacket, and pulls him around. A second shiver blasts down his back as he sees it is cut open from collar to bottom. Looking back to the supporter, Jock sees the blade of the knife reigning down on him again, but before he can react, Merrill's left elbow slams into the right temple of the supporter, who instantly falls to the concrete. Merrill's face contorts with anger as his Cuban heeled right boot crashes into the supporter's cheek; a shallow crack echoes above the turmoil. The body rolls forward, turning over to reveal a cheekbone sticking out at an angle from his face; a flap of skin waves grotesquely in the wind from cheek to lip, blood suddenly gushing from the hole.

A grimace spreads across Jock's face at the sight, "Jesus Christ!" he gasps, as he looks again at the remains of his sheepskin jacket, "You just save my fucking life!" he gasps. "No time for all that shit now!" shouts Merrill, in reply, turning to look again at Jock, a grin beaming from his face, "Don't yer just love this?" Jock looks in astonishment as Merrill moves down the terrace hitting out at anything that moves. Colin runs over and grabs Jock's arm, "You alright pal?" he gasps as he looks at the slashed sheepskin jacket. Jock nods and looks down at the unconscious Bruges supporter. "Fuck him! He was tying to kill yer!" snaps Colin, then turning to the North Stand, he shouts. "This is war," and pulls a switchblade from his pocket. Raising his arm high he presses the steel button and the blade flashes open with a click, "Draw Sabres," he cries, and follows Merrill into the crowd of Bruges supporters trying to move up the terrace.

"Look! Here come the police," shouts Jim, blood streaming from nose and mouth. Big Steve runs over to join him and, seeing Jock looking at the sheepskin jacket, says, "Time we were out of here." Jock looks around the terrace and sees people being trampled under foot, then he notices Maggie standing petrified against the back wall; fear has over taken her ability to move. He looks back at

Big Steve, and says, "Get everyone down the other end." Little John grabs a Bruges supporter by the arm and swings him around smashing him into the back wall of the terrace; the supporter falls to the concrete unconscious.

"Get Maggie! We're going down the other end!" Big Steve screams at him. Little John looks down the terrace; he sees that a large gap has opened up around the North Stand, but as the Bruges supporters rally and press home another attack, he can see that they are out-numbered twenty to one. Turning to Maggie, he grabs her arm and screams, "Come on, we're getting out of here!"

Big Steve, Merrill and Colin lead the charge down the terrace, hitting, punching and stabbing Bruges supporters out of the way to clear a path. At the bottom, Merrill stops at the small wall and, turning to see the North Stand streaming down the terrace, and doesn't notice a Bruges supporter as he lunges forward and body checks him, the unexpected momentum pushing him backwards over the wall. Mandy reaches the wall, and as she helps Maggie over, a Bruges supporter grabs the shoulder strap of her bag; instantly her knee comes up and connects with his groin.

He falls and is bent double to his knees, when Lenny comes up behind him and kicks him in the rear, sending his head crashing into the wall. Tommy, reaching the wall and carrying a trumpet, turns, then in a flash swings it around with both hands and smashes it into the face of another Bruges supporter. Making sure that the 'Foreign Legion' are over the wall, he leaps over just as a policeman goes to grab him. Laughing like a hyena, he runs after the North Stand as they march around the side of the pitch to the other end.

"Jesus H Christ! That was as good as the Park Lane Massacre in sixty-seven," says Little John, standing behind the goal at the opposite end. "Those bastards all had fucking knives!" exclaims Big Steve. "Yeah! But we sure showed them what were made of Pal," beams Little John. "Ha! You can say that again, look up there," replies Big Steve, pointing to the Bruges end. They watch in silence as stretcher after stretcher are carried down the terrace and along the front behind the low wall. "I make that twenty-one of the cunts!" beams Big Steve, as he nudges Little John's arm. "Perfect timing as well!" Little John replies, pointing towards the pitch, "Look! Here comes the team!"

The roar is deafening as the final whistle is blown; the Bruges supporters around the ground, start jumping up and down in unison. Coins and bottles arc their way through the air and land amongst the large group of Chelsea supporters standing in the shocked silence of defeat behind the goal. The General is the first to respond. Looking around at the dejected faces, he shouts, "Show these bastards we are Chelsea." He moves through the crowd shaking

Chelsea supporters out of their silence. "Sing!" he screams. A faint echo of 'CHELSEA' starts to rise above the roar of the Bruges supporters.

The Bruges supporters answer with a chant of, "WE HATE THE ENGLISH." "Let's have these cunts by the fence!" cries Colin, pointing to the high iron fence that runs from the pitch to the rear of the narrow terrace, which separates the Chelsea supporters from the locals. "No!" shouts Merrill, "I think The General's going to take The Shed onto the pitch." Colin looks over to the massed ranks of The Shed as the General stands on the low wall by the pitch, "Come on then! Let's beat him to it." Shouts Ghost. Merrill looks around the terrace and shakes his head, "No! there's far to many to go solo." "He's right," agrees Jock, "If we all run as one, we can take this place." Colin shrugs he shoulders, and says, "Fair enough." "But dump the knives," shouts Jock, "Anyone gets caught with one, he'll end up doing years over here."

As The General leads the singing, he sees a Shed boy waving a large Union Flag He jumps down from the wall and moves through the crowd; taking the flag, he moves back to the wall. Standing once again on it, he waves the flag and shouts, "On the pitch! Everyone on the pitch!" Jumping down onto the pitch he takes a few steps forward and turns to The Shed boys and orders, "Come on! Get on the pitch!" Jock smiles as he watches the General, then turning to Merrill, he says, "Today we join The Shed." Merrill nods in reply, then turns to the North Stand boys, and shouts, "Follow The General! All on the pitch!" The North Stand move to the front of the terrace and climb over the small wall, then run onto the pitch.

The General marches at the front of The Shed, holding the flagpole and watching the Union Flag as it waves in the wind. He then looks over to the side of the pitch and taunts the Bruges crowd as over three thousand Chelsea supporters stream onto the pitch. "Look at that!" exclaims Dave, as he points to the Bruges end, "They're just standing there waiting for us. "Looking around at the massed ranks of The Shed slowly marching towards the centre circle, Mandy nods in reply. The Bruges supporters, lining along the side of the pitch, are also standing their ground; some of them jump the low wall and run onto the pitch, stopping only to throw bottles, before returning to the wall. The General sees them and starts to run towards them, followed by the Stockwell and Southfields boys, but come to a halt as they see police run along the side of the pitch and start to herd the Bruges supporters, back over the wall.

Returning to the centre circle, The General gathers the massed ranks of The Shed into a tightly packed group. He then looks over to Mickey Greenaway and shouts to him; Mickey immediately starts to scream out at the top of his voice, "ZIGGER ZAGGER!

ZIGGER ZAGGER!" The shed reply as one voice, "OI! OI! OI!" "Christ! This is something else," says Jim, who is standing at the back of The Shed, taking in the atmosphere. "So what'd we do," asks Colin. "We stay at the rear and look for weak points when they charge their end," replies Merrill. "Fuck that!" replies Big Steve, "Lets charge their end ourselves." Jock runs over and stands in front of Big Steve, "No! We're the fire brigade! We plug the gaps, so you stand and wait." "Bollocks! You're always spoiling my fun!" he laughs. Jock throws him an angry look, but Big Steve just laughs out loud, and says, "Relax you Sweaty Sock! I'm winding you up."

Hold up!" shouts Little John, "The General's charging their end." The North Stand watch as The Shed stream towards the far end with the General at their front, holding the Union Flag aloft as he runs. As he nears the low wall in front of the terraced home end, bottles start to rain down again. Some Chelsea supporters fall to the grass as the bottles start to find their target. Bruges supporters at the left side of the terrace, start to jump the wall, running onto the pitch and rushing towards the rear of The Shed. "Look!" Merrill shouts in warning, "They're trying to encircle The Shed!" "Well, let's have 'em then!" screams Parkhead, whose his face is still covered in blood. "Look!" shouts Little John, "Here comes their filth! Anyone still got a knife better get rid of it them." "Like fuck!" replies an indignant Ghost.

"You get caught with a knife, they'll throw away the key after what we did before the game," warns Big Steve. Ghost thinks for a moment, and reluctantly takes his switchblade out and throws it on the grass.   Merrill turns to the North Stand, "Stay together whatever happens." He looks at Jock and nods, then Jock raises his right arm and throws it forward, screaming, "Charge!"

The North Stand stream towards the Bruges supporters who are now nearing the side of The Shed. Heads turn as they hear the cries of the North Stand. Taken by surprise some turn and run back to the side terrace; those that stand their ground are engulfed in the speed of the charge. Big Steve runs past the first of the Bruges supporters and picks up a bottle from the grass, then turning, he brings it down on the nearest head. Tommy ducks another bottle as it flies past him. Stopping, he picks it up, turns to his Bolton boys, and shouts, "Use their bottles against them." The sound of breaking glass punctuates the turmoil and soon the Bruges supporters stream back to the safety of the side terrace.

The Shed are stopped short of the low wall by the hail of bottles, and the Bruges supporters start to sense this is their moment. They leap the low wall in one's and two's and run towards The Shed, but are turned back by the superior numbers. Small numbers of police reach the rear of The Shed boys, but are quickly set upon and

170

beat a hasty retreat. It is at this point that one of the West Hampstead boys proudly walks around the back of The Shed with a police dog on a lead. "Look at that crazy bastard," laughs Maggie. Jim looks over and smiles, "He's taking the fucking thing for a walk."

"There's a copper!" shouts Jock, pointing to a policeman kneeling on the grass clearly dazed after being beaten up. Jock races towards him and kicks him in the head. Turning back, he looks down policeman who is writhing in agony; bending over, Jock pulls a gun from the officer's belt and stands looking at it. He runs back over to Merrill, showing off his trophy. and shows off his trophy. "Don't be a cunt, they'll fucking shoot you, then give you fucking life over here, for using that," Merrill warns. "Oh well! Fuck it! Easy come, easy go," he says, as he unloads the pistol and throws the bullets away. He looks at the gun one last time, then throws it back towards the centre circle.

"Hey look! The Shed are over the wall," shouts Little John. "And here comes the charge!" warns Big Steve, pointing to the large group of Bruges supporters running across the terrace, towards the Chelsea supporters already on the terrace. "Now's the moment, let's take them in the rear," cries Little John, then raising his arm, he shouts, "Charge!" The North Stand stream towards the right side of the terrace, but as they near the low wall, they run into a hail of bottles. "Pick them up and throw them at the roof,' commands Merrill, pointing to the low roof that covers the terrace.

Mandy runs over to him and opens the bag she has been carrying since they left Ostend, "This is the moment I've been waiting for!' she gasps, as she takes out a number of small bottles. "What the fuck are those?" Merrill asks in amazement. "These mate, are sulphuric acid!' she replies with a smile, bringing her right arm back and throwing the first bottle at the roof. They stand and watch as the small bottle smashes against the roof, sending its contents pouring down onto the Bruges supporters. "Fucking Ace!" shouts a jubilant Big Steve as he watches the Bruges supporters screaming as the acid falls on them.

Jock moves over to them and points to the centre of the terrace, "Look The Shed are on the terrace!" Heads turn and watch as The Shed fight it's way up centre of the terrace. Jumping the wall, Merrill and Jock attack the Bruges supporters trying to work their way around from the side terrace; as they are joined by the rest of the North Stand, the Bruges supporters are beaten back and start to run down the outside of the terrace and retreat through the main gate. "Come on!" screams a jubilant Big Steve, "We've got them on the run." "No!" shouts Merrill, "Back to their end, or we'll get sandwiched between the two."

Big Steve stops in his tracks, looking at the departing Bruges supporters, "Fuck it! Just when we had them on the run." "We still have to do their main mob yet pal," Colin reminds him. Big Steve turns and runs back towards the terrace. Looking back he shouts, "Well, don't just stand there! Let's do the fuckers!"

Colin shakes his head and smiles as he runs after Big Steve; turning the corner and looking up at the terrace, he sees The Shed have nearly cleared it, but one pocket of resistance remains. A group of around twenty Bruges supporters are standing their ground. Tommy and his boys are attacking the rear of the group, while Dave and his boys are fighting the left side; neither is giving ground.

As Merrill and Jock run towards the fighting, they see a Bruges supporter standing apart from the main group, swinging a hollow metal pole rescued from a broken crush barrier. "Fuck me!" cries Jock, "Look at that cunt in the white! No-one can put him down! I'm not surprised, "retorts Lenny; "the cunt's got to be six foot six, and I've already been hit by the bloody pole, and believe me it fucking hurts." Merrill looks towards the man in white, just in time to see Jim run up from behind and jump on his back. The man in white brings his left arm up and grabs Jim's shirt and sharply leans forward throwing Jim over his body in an arc.

He lands on the concrete terrace in a motionless heap. "Right you lot!" commands Merrill, "Take him from the front, and keep his attention." Jock and Lenny look at each other with raised eyebrows, "It's always fucking us!" sighs Lenny. Eight of the North Stand charge the man in white in a frontal attack, but fail to get near, as they duck and dive out of the way of the metal pole.

Merrill stands and watches the man in white as he takes on all comers, then walking up a dozen steps he moves behind him, then running down the terrace, he jumps in the air swinging both feet out in front of him. The drop kick lands on the left side of the head of the man in white, who falls forward to the concrete. The pole goes crashing down the terrace, and is caught by Mandy, who picks it up and runs towards the man in white, just as he starts to pick himself up. "No, you fucking don't, cunt!" she screams as she brings the pole down on his head. "Fuck you!" shouts Merrill, as he just rolls out of the way of the pole.

The General comes running over, chasing a group of Bruges supporters down the terrace. "Nice of you lot to have turned up;" he shouts, mockingly. Jock throws a glance at The General, "And that's the thanks we get for watching your back." "Well, don't just lay there, Merrill," The General taunts, "We've got them on the run." "Ignore it," laughs Spider, as he runs over, "He's winding you up." "I should fucking hope so,' Merrill replies, holding his hand out to be pulled up. Spider pulls him up, and smiling, says, "Well you can't blame the guy. He comes over here and sees you laying having lay down on the job." Merrill sees the funny side, and replies, "Once a Shed boy, always a Shed boy?" Spider throws his head back in laughter, "You learn."

With the Bruges supporters now in full flight, The Shed march across the near empty terrace picking off the stragglers. "WE ARE THE SHED, WE ARE THE SHED, WE ARE, WE ARE, WE ARE THE SHED!" The chant echoes across the home end as The Shed disappear around the corner towards the main gate. Lenny, holding his ribs, looks around and suddenly shouts, "Look out!" Too late! A lone Bruges supporter runs across to Parkhead, and bringing a knife down, plunges it into his back. "Fucking hell!" screams Parkhead, as his left hand grabs his side. The supporter runs down the terrace and disappears into The Shed boys. Maggie runs over and lifts up Parkhead's jeans jacket, then pulls his Fred Perry tennis shirt up to reveal a short cut above his kidneys. "You're lucky," she says, "It's only a scratch. Your jacket took most of the impact." A relieved Parkhead lets go of his jacket, to reveal a blood stained Celtic scarf, "Fucking Cunt's ruined my scarf!" he yells in anger.

As The Shed charge for the open streets, police force the main gates shut, trapping them in the stadium. The General and Spider organise the Stockwell and Southfield's boys into human battering rams as they repeatedly charge the gate. The Pimlico & Battersea join them. Spider sees that one of the gates is giving way at the top hinge, and spurs on The Shed. Then suddenly, with an eerie sound of breaking wood, the gate gives way and slowly falls into the street. The police panic and run as The Shed charge out of the ground and onto the main street. The North Stand round the corner of the home end as the gate falls, and Big Steve starts jumping up and down, "Fucking Ace! They've smashed the gates down." "Well, let's join the fucking party then!" screams Colin. The two of them run wildly through the gates, followed by Lenny, Jim and Parkhead. Little John turns to Merrill, "Well? Let's join them then!" Merrill looks at Jock who nods in excitement, "OK it's party time!" he yells, as they run through the gate.

Frightened shoppers run for cover as the Chelsea supporters now run riot. Shop windows are smashed and cars are over-turned. Sirens scream as police reinforcements race to the main street. At the rear of the ground, those Chelsea supporters that didn't join the attack, are confronted by two police water cannons. Then as the bulk of The Shed move up the street, the North Stand stream out of the ground. "Hey! There's a bar over there!" shouts Little John, who runs over and disappears inside. The North Stand walk over and stand outside the pub, then look up the main street at the damage. "Shit! This is a fucking war zone," says Big Steve. "Time for a

173

drink," replies Mandy. "Well, just don't go throwing any more fucking acid," says Jock, as he walks inside. "Used it all in the ground," Mandy replies with a smile. As they walk inside, Little John is in a heated argument with the owner who, seeing more Chelsea supporters, shouts in English, "No English in here! Get out!"

Jock picks up a chair and smashes it over his head, "I ain't fucking English you bastard!" "Bet he didn't say that when we fucking liberated these sorry cunts from the Krauts!" says Big Steve. "He saw your SS jacket," laughs Little John, as he leaps the bar and helps himself to a bottle of whisky. After a few quick swigs, he throws it at the mirror at the back of the bar. "Hey look!' says Merrill, "They've got a pool table." He walks over and picks up a red ball; looking at it, he tightens his grip and then punches a local who is about to hit him with a pool cue. Mandy picks up a small round table and throws it through the front window, shouting, "That'll teach these bastards to beat us two nil."

Little John, on seeing the pool table, runs across the bar, and leaps onto it, and standing in the middle, he jumps up and down, singing, "We all come from London, do da do ad.!" When there is a loud crack, Little John stops in his tracks as the sound of breaking wood echoes across the bar. Then with a louder bang the slate cracks in two, and the pool table splits across the middle and collapses. Little John lands in a heap in the middle of what remains of the pool table. Everyone starts to laughs at him as he lays on the floor, but they are interrupted by Maggie shouting form the front door, "Watch out here comes the filth!" Tommy and his boys, who never made it inside, pick up the tables and chairs outside the bar and start to throw them at the advancing police.

Lenny and Ghost run out with a hand full of beer bottles and start to throw them at the police. Big Steve gives Little John a helping hand to his feet and they run outside, followed by the rest of the North Stand and throw more bottles at the police. "Come on," shouts Little John, "Let's make a run for the coaches." As they run off, the police enter the pub and see Merrill and Jock sitting on the bar drinking bottles of Stella. "Time we weren't here Pal," says Jock, who looking around, sees a door at the back of the bar, "Come on, this way."
I'm trying but this fucking thing has stopped in it's tracks!" shouts Colin. "What the fuck are you doing exclaims Jock. "I've always wanted a Juke Box!" laughs Colin. "Well it would help if you unplugged the fucking thing first" laughs Jock. "Hold on!" shouts Merrill, as he picks up bottles of Scotch and throws them on the floor in front of the police. Jock looks back from the back door, and shouts, "Come on, it's clear out here." Merrill pulls a small book of matches out of his pocket, tears one off and lights it, then holds it over the

other match heads, that burst into flame. Looking up at the police, who have stopped in their tracks and are staring at him with expectant eyes, he smiles and then throws the book of burning matches across to the large pool of spirits on the floor. The police turn as one and run for the front door, as the flaming book of matches hit the large pool of spirits, there is a soft whoosh, followed by a dull bang, as the spirits ignites. As flames dance into the air, Merrill runs for the back door and with Jock they disappear into a back ally.

The damage after the 'Battle of Bruges' was so bad that the tour company that organised the trip, were banned from operating in Belgium for a year. And there was even questions asked about the riot in the House of Commons.

CHAPTER FOURTEEN

Kev, raising his arm in excitement shouts, "You had low crowds because people like you created an atmosphere of violence and the normal supporter was scared to go." He sits back with a confident smirk. "Oh bollocks!" exclaims Dave, "The crowds dropped because we were shit and got relegated. Only the really committed supporters continued to go during the hard times." "Yes," says Dave, "All the flakes fluttered away. It was only the ones with passion in their heart that stayed, and when people slagged the team, the commitment and passion came out."

Kev looks at the Americans and proudly announces, "Yes, and did you know it's a well-known fact that Chelsea is full of Right Wing Racists. It's a breeding ground for the National Front!" he screams, knowing he was on the defensive.

"Oh please the National Front are just a bunch of frightened little boys, whose fears are fuelled and used by control freaks;" says Alan Chandler, as he reaches over to take another French fry, only to discover that they are all gone. "Their average age is 18 to 20, but when they grow up a bit they realise what Pratt's they've been. I mean how many 30 or 40 year olds do you see on rallies? Not many, 'cause they've grown up, and have different priorities, like raising a family."

Kevin Darcy sensing that this is his moment, Stands up and starts to wave his right hand, in a manner that if you were to put a square moustache on his upper lip, he would be the parody of the man he professes to hate. "Tell that to the people that are intimidated by the Union Flag," he screams, "the flag that is the symbol of the subjection of their homelands; the flag that is the sign of imperialistic capitalism." Everybody sits back and looks in horror at Kev; they can't believe what they are seeing. Then after a few moments Ian Kirkman says, "Yes just because they misuse the flag, is no reason to be ashamed of it." Kev will not be put off, and continues to raise his voice, "There are many immigrants in Britain who are not British Nationals, and who feel under-valued and excluded. We should be striving for a multinational country. The flag is offensive to many people of ethnic origins; it symbolises the National Front." He stops in mid flight, sensing that even people inside the Brit, are turning round in an effort to see just what is going on outside.

"But the Union Flag is a flag of a multinational people;" Points out Dave Hughes, "it represents England Ireland Scotland and Wales." "To say that the National Front has hi-jacked our flag, is just a left wing excuse to de-value our county;" says Alan, looking for something to do with his hands, so he pulls out a packet of JPS.

"The left wing will stop at nothing, to do all they can to discredit anything British, so they can then install their own brand of totalitarianism. I mean you can't talk openly and freely at the moment, because you people scream your heads off, and throw pathetic labels about, like racist, sexist, and anything else they can dream up, just to appease the weak, and advance you're own mad lust for power."

"We will not tolerate free speak, when it is offensive to immigrants." replies Kev, throwing caution to the wind. But Mark stands up and shouts, "No, you and your elk are the real racists, for you are climbing over the backs of immigrants, using them as your pawns, your hidden agenda." He looks round at those at the table, realising that the best way to get your point across is to stay calm. He sits down again, and then continues. "When we all know that you are only interested in power. You're already dictating just what we must say and do, according to your dictate. Can you imagine what the hell it will be like if the likes of you ever got into power?"

Kev is starting to go red in the face, in the wake of this attack on his integrity. "They would install a Stalinist regime with secret police," says Ian; still shaken from the theatrical outbursts of Kev, he lights a cigarette, looks up and continues in his normal soft voice. "Directing people to grass on each other, in order to gain brownie points; it will be a witch hunt with the innocent the victims as always. "See!" screams Kev pointing at the Chelsea supporters, "They are all right wing fascists."

MANCHESTER CITY AWAY

Wednesday April 28th, 1971, Manchester City 0 - 1 Chelsea

Many people describe Manchester as the arse hole of England, a description that the North Stand would entirely agree with. An industrial centre from the eighteenth century, its many factories and ex-work houses are now nothing but dirty brick canyons in run-down areas. The terrace houses, originally built for the workers, have now turned into slums, which are rapidly becoming no-go areas. Main Road, the home of Manchester City, is in just such an area. Also built of red brick, it is surrounded by scruffy terrace houses.

At one end of the ground, by the turn-styles, a supporters' club has been built as part of the main structure. Walking inside, you are greeted with a poorly lit hall, the centrepiece of which, is a number of snooker tables. There is a bar over on the far wall. The dirty fitted carpet and unwashed walls, shout out the fact that you are now in the North of England. The main rule of the house is that no away supporters are allowed inside these hallowed portals, but the North Stand, are the exception to the rule and every year they drink in the club. As with the other main 'Firm' pubs across the country, the Man City Supporters Club is 'Holy Ground'. There is an unwritten law amongst fighting firms, that you don't break the truce of 'Holy Ground'. Man. City is unusual in that the local end is not an end, but takes up the standing terrace that runs along one side of the ground, known as the Kippax. Man. City supporters, unlike their United neighbours, where it is a miracle if you hear a Manchester accent, are respected for not joining the bandwagon and supporting United.

Today is a special occasion; Dave from Salford is out of jail and this is his first match back with his North Stand 'family'. As this is a Cup game, a larger number of Midland Chelsea have turned up than normal, and Dave has brought thirty of the local Salford firm with him. Standing outside the Supporters Club, they wait for the main North Stand to turn up; already attracting attention, from the local supporters, they are ready for action at a moment's notice. The sun is setting fast through the overcast sky, earlier showers, giving a gloss finish to roads and pavements, adding to the evening's already tense atmosphere. A Manchester accent shouts, "Dave!" and heads turn. Dave looks over towards the rapidly approaching youth who is wearing a Man City scarf. Dave turns back to his Salford crew and warns, "It's all right, I know him."

He walks over to Brian Stone, leader of the main Kippax firm, the Mainline, "Good to see you, I heard you were inside," he says as they shake hands. "Yeah, I was. Got out last week. You see any of the others hanging around?" Brian shakes his head, "No mate, I saw The General leading The Shed towards the Kippax, but the police were holding them up." Dave raises his eyebrows in surprise, "How many of them then?" "Hard to say really. looked over a thousand though, took up the whole fucking street," replies Brian. "Dave!" shouts one of the Salford boys, "Here's Tommy!" Heads turn, and Dave looks over to see Tommy leading around forty Chelsea from Wigan. "Hey! Great to see yer, you old bastard! So what was it like being banged up in Brixton?" Tommy says, slapping Dave on the back. "Fucking shit mate! Too many bloody Cockneys," laughs Dave. "Come on, I'll buy you a drink in the club," says Brian, as he starts to walk to the club entrance.

"No, it's alright there's far too many of us, besides I'm waiting for Merrill and Jock, then we're going into the Kippax. I've got a lot of time to make up." Dave says in a menacing tone. "Dave! Dave!" shouts a female voice. as she runs with open arms towards him. "Fuck me, I think Mandy's discovered she has female hormones," laughs Spider, watching her run towards Dave with open arms. "Bet he's on a good thing tonight," jokes Jock, as they walk towards the Supporters Club. "You know, I somehow just can't visualise Mandy making love," says a puzzled Little John. "I bet she'll be one of those that likes in on top," observes Jock. "Yeah, with fucking spurs on and a whip in her hand," Spider chuckles. "And don't forget he sprained his wrist in his cell," continued Spider. "How'd he do that then?" queries Ghost. "He was thinking about Mandy," laughs Spider.

The main North Stand firm, walk over to Dave and Tommy, watched by nervous local supporters waiting to go into the ground. "Right, I'm for a quick drink. Come on Dave," says Merrill, as they shake hands. "Thank for trying to raise the money for me trial," replies Dave,

"Think nothing of it pal," he pauses, looking at Jock, "Well, we don't have to bother about that now do we. "Hold on, we can't all go in, there's far too many of us," Colin says, observing as he looks at the growing numbers of the North Stand. "Shit!" says Jock, "Dave, Tommy, Steve, and Little John, you come with us, the rest of yer wait near the Kippax." "Oh cheers pal!" says an indignant Merrill. "Well, I took it for granted you'd be joining us," laughs Jock. As they approached the club entrance, Brian runs out to meet them, clearly agitated, at the site of so many Chelsea. "Can't stop," he yells, "The Shed are in the Kippax!" He runs off, closely followed by around one hundred City supporters.

Jock turns and looks at Merrill, "Shit! It must be bad if that lot are leaving already!" "Yeah, let's get round there then," he replies. Tommy walks over and, watching the departing City supporters, says,

"What's going on?" "Looks like The General and The Shed have taken the Kippax," Jock replies. "Right, Tommy, Dave, get your boys and follow us," Jock commands, looking around to the rest of the North Stand, "Line up along the back wall." He looks around, making sure everyone is listening, "No-one moves in 'till we suss out what's going on." Just over one hundred Chelsea North Stand, start to walk around the corner of the ground to the Kippax entrance, where they see a group of police moving through the turnstiles, "Shit! Looks like all hell as broken out!" gasps Little John, as he sees the police pushing people out of the way as they go towards the turnstiles.

"Hey! There's The General!" shouts Colin, pointing towards two policemen who have just released him, and are now going back through the turnstiles. Chants of 'Chelsea! Chelsea!' echo through the evening air from the Kippax. Ghost starts laughing, "Hey, look! He's paying to go back in." "Hello, what's going on?" says a raised voice from behind Merrill, who turns to see Bo running up to him. "Hello mate, I think World War Three has just broken out in there. Stay close, this is going to get brutal." Bo nods and looks around to see the increased numbers of the North Stand, "They all Chelsea?" he says in surprise. "Yes," answers Merrill, "That's the North Stand's Foreign Legion, all the Midland and Northern boys that can't make the games in London. "Shit!" exclaims Bo, "I had no idea there were so many." Merrill laughs as they reach the turnstiles. Bo looks at Merrill, and noticing the black shirt and Black trench coat, says, "So where's your trade mark camouflage jacket then?" Merrill shrugs his shoulders and says, "It was getting too well known. I was getting a tug from the filth, just for wearing it."

Merrill moves into the narrow corridor that houses one of the turnstiles; the noise of fighting greets him as he pushes past the turnstile gate and walks into the packed passageway. "Fucking Cockney Bastards," says a Manchester accent. Merrill, looking over, sees a youth leaning up against the wall, his face covered in blood. He casually walks over to him and says, "You alright pal?" The supporter freezes in terror as he hears the Cockney accent. "Talking like that can damage your health," says Ghost, softly to the youth, then swings his elbow round and lands a blow squarely on the youth's nose, who falls pole axed to the floor. It is then that Merrill notices the small United badge on his lapel. "Fuck me!" says Jock, can't yer wait 'till we get upstairs?" Ghost looks around and says, "No-one calls me a Cockney bastard."

"Hello Captain," says a man with close-cropped blonde hair and a German accent. Merrill spins around in surprise, "Stefan!" They embrace like long lost brothers. "Here," queries Jock, "He called you Captain?" "Yes," answers Merrill, with his arm around

Stefan's shoulders, "This is Sergeant Pottel, one of my men from the Congo." Jock looks at the German in amazement, "Fuck! You were in the Congo together?" "Yes," says Merrill, "But later, we have other fish to fry now."

"So that's where you were when you kept going missing." Says Jock. "That and a few other places, but not now, we have work to do," replies Merrill. "You know that there are a lot of people here with United badges on?" says Stefan, "Yes," says Spider, who has just walked through the turnstile, "They asked to come with us against City, but we told them to fuck off. We only run with Millwall." Little John walks through the turnstile and over to the others, "Hello, who's this then?" he says, pointing to Stefan, "He's with us," answers Merrill, "An old friend. Come on let's get up the stairs."

They start to walk up the stairs, and Ian moves over to be with Stefan, "So, got any dirt on Alan then?" he says with a smile. Stefan looks at him as they climb the stairs, and chuckles, "You are Jock then?" he asks. Ian frowns as he looks at Stefan, "Yes why? "Stefan laughs out loud, "Relax, I've heard all about you. So did Alan ever tell you about zee Cuban slags, in Anglo?" Ian shakes his head, but smiles in anticipation of a juicy tit bit, "No, so what happened?" "Well," Stefan continues, as they climb the stairs, "We found a patrol of our Afrikaans, with their private parts cut off and shoved in their mouths." He pauses as they reach the terrace and move along the back wall, "We find one of them that has been shot, and vas left for dead. He tells us that they'd been ambushed by a patrol of Cuban bitches, so Alan shoots him and we go looking for them." Jock, with a horrified look says, "Alan shot one of your own men?"

Stefan looks back, surprised at the remark, "Yes of course, we travel light on horse back, and have no provision for caring for non-walking wounded, and everyone knows that rule before they start." Ian stands there, unable to comprehend what he is hearing. "Anyway we find them, ambush them, and take six prisoners." "But you just told me that you don't take prisoners," says a puzzled Jock. "Yeah," Pottel continues, "But Alan hands them over to our Afrikaans so they could have some fun with them. Then after they've raped them, and brutalised them," Stefan is cut short as Merrill shouts over to them, "Enough of the Chin wagging, we've got work to do."

Spider, enjoying the view from the back of the Kippax, starts to sing, "BELL BUMS LEE," Then everyone joins in, "LEE BUMS BELL, BELL AND LEE, BUM SUMERBEE, WITH A NICK KNACK, PADDY WHACK, GIVE A DOG A BONE, WHY DON'T CITY, FUCK OFF HOME."

"Look there's The General," Colin interrupts, pointing over to the right. Everyone turns to look at the right hand side of the covered terrace where The General is in full flow with his Stockwell and Southfield's boys. "Come on, let's get stuck in," shouts Lenny Brown. "No!" wait!" commands Merrill, observing the whole of the Kippax, "Look!" he points over to the left at Brian and five hundred of his Kippax firm that are charging towards The Shed, "Take them from behind as they go past." The North Stand wait and watch as the Mainline charge across the terrace and past them lower down the Kippax, and race towards The Shed in the thick of battle As the last ones run by, Merrill shouts, "NOW!"

Over one hundred and fifty of the North Stand charges down the terrace, taking the Mainline firm from behind. Bo swings an arm around a City supporter's neck sending him crashing down the terrace. Parkhead grabbing another, he swings him around with his left hand and lands a right hook on the chin. The youth falls back losing his balance and rolls down the terrace. Colin jumps on the back of another City supporter, but lands on his feet as they both fall; lashing out with his right foot, he sends him flying. The Kippax mobs, now realising that they are surrounded, start to move down the terrace and back across to the left-hand side. Merrill feels a hand grab him from behind and turns, but seeing it is a just one of a dozen policemen, freezes, and lets him grab his arm and lead him up the terrace to the exit.

Stefan seeing him go, shouts, "Hold on Captain." "No," shouts Jock, grabbing his arm to stop him, "He's just being led out. There's too much fighting for them to nick anybody right now. Besides we've learnt that when you get nicked, and you can't get away, you stay calm, 'cos a lot of times they'll let you go when they get you outside the ground. It's only the idiots that fight back, and then when they get you in court they fucking invent the evidence as they go along. Plus the fact that if you give them a hard time, they kick the fuck out of you in the van and then say you fell over, when questioned about the bruises. No mate, its common sense. Go quietly, and you get away with murder."

Stefan looks up the terrace and shrugs his shoulders, "OK then, but I don't like it," he says, as he grabs a Kippax youth by the collar of his bomber jacket with both hands and head butts him. The youth is knocked clean out. Tommy, seeing Maggie surrounded by City supporters, runs over and grabs one by the hair. He swings him around, and smashing his head into one of the metal crash barriers. Steve grabs another City supporter by the neck and punches him in the face. He then drags him over to a crash barrier forcing him over the top of it and pummels punches onto his head.

Another City supporter runs up behind Big Steve and punches him in the back, Bo, turning around, sees him and sends a rabbit punch crashing into the back of his neck, dropping him like a brick to the ground. One of the newly arrived police, seeing Dave, runs over and grabs him by the arm and starts to lead him out. Mandy walks over to the policeman and, with an angelic expression, and says, "Excuse me Sir,"

He stops in his tracks, looking confused, and asks, "Yes what do you want?" Mandy's expression changes to one of the possessed, and shouts; "Your balls!" With this she brings up her knee, sharply into his groin. Both Mandy and Dave run, and vanish into the mass of Chelsea.

As more police swarm onto the Kippax, they slowly form a line down the terrace and start to expel the Chelsea supporters, who are released as soon as they are marched out of the ground. They then run around the corner and pay to get back in. "Looks like the filth are gaining control," says Spider, as he looks around, at the milling crowd. "Shit man, this is fucking wicked! There are thousands of Chelsea in here," gasps Tommy. "But we can't get at City now!" sighs an annoyed Ghost, seeing the four deep police line stopping them from getting at the City supporters. "OK, everyone over by the wall! shouts Jock, pointing to the low wall that marks the start of the empty terrace still under construction behind the goal,

"Let The Shed do their thing." "Bollocks!" exclaims Colin, "We can have the filth from behind." "And then get taken from behind ourselves?" says Merrill, pointing to the police running around the side of the pitch to get into the Kippax.

One hundred minutes later, the despondent Mainline and other City firms, are lusting for revenge; not only for losing A European Cup Winners Cup Semi Final, but for the humiliation of having the Kippax taken. Pouring out of the ground like a pack of hungry Wolfs, they try and get past the police lines, but The General outsmarts them and leads The Shed into Main Road itself, and takes them on a D-tour around the block, in order to come back to the ground, taking City in the rear. Five thousand jubilant Chelsea supporters start singing. "WE'RE GONNA WIN THE CUP, WE GONNA WIN THE CUP, AND NOW YOU'RE GONNA BELIEVE US; WE'RE GONNA WIN THE CUP," as they disappear into the damp evening, their feet splashing in the rainwater.

As the crowds stream out of the stadium, the North Stand leave the ground, but are stopped from joining the massing ranks of The Shed by a police cordon. Looking back, Jock sizes up the situation, "I don't like the look of this." "Too fucking right pal!" says a nervous Parkhead, "We get cut off here, we've had it." Jock looks over to

Merrill, and shouts, "Well, which way?" Merrill points to a side street, "Up here, and make it quick."

"OK, everybody. Make your own way to Piccadilly, either by bus or taxi," shouts Jock. "What's going on then," asks Stefan, as he moves over to Merrill. "Well, we were going to ambush the Mainline mob in Piccadilly, but all the City firms are together in one group," answers Merrill, pointing to a police cordon by the corner of the ground, with thousands of City supporters behind it, "And we're split up into small groups, so if they come across us walking back to the station, even we wouldn't stand a fucking chance." Spider is the first to turn the corner and sees two buses, pulling up at a bus stop fifty Yards down the road.

"Quick," he yells, looking back, "There's two buses." As Over a hundred Chelsea supporters run down the dimly lit street, giving off ghost like reflections from the puddles of rainwater. The conductor seeing their headlong rush towards him panics and rings the bell to start the bus, "Quick!" shouts Little John, the fucking things going." He reaches the rear open platform and jumps on; stretching up he rings the bell twice. The bus skids to a stop, sending the conductor, flying forward.

"Oi! What the hell do you think you're doing?" he yells at Little John, as he rings the bus off again. "Shit! How many got on?" says Jock as he climbs the stairs to the upper deck. "About a dozen, by the looks of those left behind," says Ghost, looking into the darkness out of the upstairs back window and seeing the group of North Stand trying to get on the other bus. "OK, let's have a head count," says Merrill, as he stands at the front of the bus, "Right, Jock, Ghost, Little John, Colin, Lenny, Tommy," he pauses a moment and smiles, "Might of known Dave and Mandy would be together." "Don't forget me!" shouts Big Steve, from the back; "And me!" shouts Parkhead. "OK, don't have a baby," he says grinning. "There's Maggie downstairs, Bo, and your German geezer," continues, Ghost.

"I'm here," says Jim Crow, as he leads the others up the stairs. "Shit! Only fifteen!" exclaims Jock. "No problem," says Ghost, "We all bit through our own umbilical cords, and the mainline are still sucking their mummy's tits." The others laugh, but know that if they get caught on their own, they'll be in trouble.

"Hey! Jim shouts from the back of the bus, "The other bus has turned off!" Fourteen heads turn as one to see the rear of the other bus disappear from view. "Fuck that, do they know where to meet?" says Lenny, "Yes," answers Colin, "But if we don't all meet up together it could get dodgy." Maggie walks up to Merrill and sits on his lap, "Did all of Tommy and Dave's boys catch the other bus?" "Fuck knows," replies Colin, he looks back to Tommy, "Did you see them?" Tommy shrugs his shoulders, and says, "I saw a few get on the other bus, but most of them were left behind." "No problem," cuts in Dave, "They'll join up with The Shed." "I don't like all this confusion!" snarls Parkhead, "This ain't like us."

The conductor climbs the stairs, and stands at the back looking nervously looking at the North Stand, "You want us to pay then?" says Colin. "Where are you lot going, or is that a silly question?" says the conductor, looking nervously around the upper deck. "Relax pal," says Jock, "We ain't here to cause trouble, just call us when we get to Piccadilly." The conductor, looking relieved, now finds his voice, "Well, as long as you don't cause any trouble, you can ride for free," then as an after thought, he says, "Least I can do for you lot beating City?" Spider looks back to him, and says, "Oh no, not fucking Manure?" The conductor stops smiling as Stefan asks, what the fuck is Manure?"

"Ha!" says Merrill, "Man United, Man U., Manure, get it?" Stefan laughs, turning to Spider, "One of yours I suppose?" Spider smiles back then looks to the conductor, "Well, at least you're the first fucker I've met that supports them and actually lives in this dump." "Where the fuck did you come from?" exclaims Colin. "Getting me breath back down stairs after running for this fucking bus," replies Spider.

The conductor looks out of the window, and says with relief, "Hey this is your stop!" Merrill looks out of the window into the dark and damp night, and then turns to the conductor, "Where the fuck are we?" The conductor, pointing to the front of the bus says, "Piccadilly is three blocks that way." "OK! Let's go!" shouts Spider, as he gets up from his seat. Stepping onto the damp pavement, Colin huddles over and to stands under the bus shelter, then putting his hand out, he watches the rain splash on his hand.

"What do you expect, it's fucking Manchester!" mutters Spider, as he too ducks under the shelter. "Right, let's get down to Piccadilly," says Merrill, as he starts to walk along the pavement. "Hadn't we better wait for the others?" queries Colin. "How do we know they'll get off here," answers Jock, still under the bus shelter. "Aren't we going to wait for the others?" asks Bo, quickly walking after Merrill. "No, they'll follow. We need to get to Piccadilly before the City do," replies Merrill.

At this moment the silence is broken by a deafening roar coming from around the corner; everyone stops and looks back. At that moment a mob of around one hundred supporters comes running into view. "They're fucking Cockneys!" shouts one of them. "Get the bastards!" shouts another. They run towards the bus shelter, where a dozen of the North Stand are still sheltering. "Oh shit!" cries Jock, as he turning to face the mob, "Come on then!" he screams at the top of his voice at the mob.

185

Spider breaks shelter and runs towards them, followed by the others from the shelter. Those at the front of the mob stop dead in their tracks surprised that so few have the bottle to charge so many. Little John runs over and throws a punch at one of those standing at the front, then turns and runs, "Wanker!" shouts Little John. Jock runs up and kicks another as the front-runners of the mob start to move back.

Merrill, seeing the mob surrounding the bus stop, shouts, "Come on, help them out," and starts to run back to the bus shelter. Bo and Stefan run after him, followed by Tommy, Dave, Jim Crow, Mandy, and Maggie. . On seeing this second group of Chelsea supporters running towards them, those at the rear of the mob panic and start to run. Merrill raises his elbow and, on the run, smashes it into the first face that runs past him. Stefan grabs another and holds him from behind in a bear hug. Mandy runs up and kicks him in the crutch. Dave follows her and punches the youth in the face with a right upper cut. "They're on the run!" shouts Spider,

"Quick after them," shouts Little John, but Jock turns and grabs his arm. "No stay here," Steve shouts, "Look! Alan's going after them!" Jock looks up and shouts "Alan!" but at that moment his heart stops as over a hundred City supporters stream around the corner. "Fucking hell!" yells Steve, backing as he backs up to the bus shelter. "Get back to the wall!" shouts Jock. Spider, Little John, Colin, Lenny, Tommy from Bradford and Parkhead, back up to the wall of the office building at the bus stop.

"This lot didn't put up much of a fight," says Stefan to Merrill, as they run after the first mob. "Watch out for them stopping and turning," says Merrill, "Just run straight into them if they do." Bo looks around as he runs and sees, Bo, Jim, Mandy and Maggie, running with him. "They're going into that pub," says Stefan. "Right! After them, we've got 'em," shouts Merrill. The first of the mob charge through the door of the pub, but those following start to pile up behind them, fighting amongst themselves as they try to push their way into the pub. Stefan and Merrill charge into those still trying to get through the door, closely followed by the rest. Bo hits one of them, but is knocked off balance as they turn to run down the road. Mandy sticks her foot out and trips one over as he runs past.

Jim runs into those nearer the door, hitting anyone who that gets in his way. "Leave those that run, get those in the pub," shouts Merrill, as he grabs one of the mob and runs him into the pub wall headfirst. Most of those outside now start to run towards Piccadilly. "Look!" shouts Maggie as she pulling a scarf from one of the mob, "They're fucking Manure!"

Little John kicks out at the first City supporter that runs over to the wall; Spider grabs another, swinging him around into the wall, then letting him go, he turns, but is kicked in the leg. Jock jumps on the back of the one that throw the kick and they both fall to the floor. As Jock rolls over and gets up, as Lenny kicks the City supporter full in the face. as he is getting up. Now having them completely surrounded, the City mob press home their attack. Parkhead is the first one to go down, attacked by three supporters, one of which grabs him from behind and holds him while the other two start kicking and punching him. Spider sees them and moves over, bringing his elbow down on the nearest head, with a crack,

"Shit!" he shouts as hits his funny bone. Jock, seeing Parkhead on the pavement, pushes over to him. As he bends down to pick him up, a kick lands on his right thigh; he turns and punches his assailant in the face. Then turning back, he picks up Parkhead, and pulls him over to the wall. Spider grabs another City supporter, by the neck, and starts to rain punches onto his nose; letting him go he falls to the pavement. Little John grabs another around the neck and runs him into the bus stop, letting him drop; he turns and receives a punch on his left cheek. He staggers back a step, before racing forward to the City supporter who then turns and runs.

Merrill is the first one to make it to the pub door. Kicking it open, he runs in, and seeing a flowerpot on a wall stand, he picks it up and throws it into the mass of people in the bar. Stefan and Jim follow him in. The people sitting near the door, panic and get up, rushing further inside. Stefan, picking up one of the vacant stools, moves in, using it as a club. Jim picks up another two, and looking over to Merrill, he shouts, "Alan! Here!" Merrill turns to see a stool flying towards him and, putting his right arm up, he catches it and brings it down on the nearest head. "Leave them and get in the pub," shouts Mandy to Bo, as those of the mob still outside, start to run towards Piccadilly. "What about them!" he shouts, as he points over to the people pouring out of the other door. "Leave 'em! They don't want to know." She runs inside and joins in the mayhem.

Most of the people in the pub have now run out and the fighting is centred on those pushing their way to the other door. Merrill brings his stool down on the back of one of the Manure, sending him goes crashing to the floor. Bo and Stefan are standing over three bodies by the bar, "Hey! This is nearly as good as Afrika," he chuckles to Bo. "Oh, I see! You mean it makes a change from killing Blacks?" Stefan throws Bo a curious look, "Hey I get paid to fight, and I don't give a fuck, if they're black or white, as long as their money's green." "Hey! You two!" admonishes, says Maggie, as she walks over to them, "You're supposed to be on the same side! You want to start that shit, don't do it with us!" They both at, Maggie then look back to each other and raise their eyebrows.

Little John is quickly surrounded by City supporters, who punch and kick him to the ground. Jock runs forward to help Little John and comes face to face with Brian Stone, then without hesitation he grabs him by both ears and rams his head into his up thrusting knee. Stone collapses like a brick, knocked clean out. The other members of the Mainline, seeing their leader motionless on the ground, start to run. Jock then grabs Little John and they both back away to the bus shelter where the others are still fighting. At this moment police sirens cut through the damp night air; those City supporters around the bus shelter start to join those already running. Spider and Colin charge forward, shouting, "Chelsea!" Colin catches one fleeing Mainliner around the neck and kicks his feet from under him. Spider knees him in the face as he goes down. Steve, covered in blood, runs forward, followed by Tommy and Parkhead, but the Mainline have joined the rest of the fleeing mob.   "Hold   on!" shouts Jock, grabbing Steve, as he grabs Steve, "Stay here, or we'll get split up again!"

The others turn around and start to take stock. Big Steve, Lenny, and Parkhead, are cut and bruised. Jock is standing looking at his blood-covered clothes as Spider walks over and says, "You cut?" Jock starts laughing, "Hey! Look! None of this is mine," he says with relief, then looking around and taking stock, he says, "Where's Merrill and the others?" Parkhead staggers over holding his right side, and pointing, says, "I don't know. Last time I saw them, they were running in that direction." "WHAT!" Jock shouts in disgust, "He fucking ran?"

"Oi! You lot stay here!" shouts the pub landlord, "I've called the police!" Merrill looks around from the door to the landlord who is standing behind the bar, then looks over to Stefan and nods. Stefan grabs the landlord's shirt with his left hand and picks up an empty Watney's Brown Ale bottle with the other, bringing it down on the landlord's head. "Oi!" shouts Bo, "That's going too far!" "No it ain't, he's fucking Manure! Look around you!" Merrill retorts, throwing him a menacing look. Bo looks across to the wall next to the bar, and seeing the Manchester United Team photo's, replies, says, "There's no need for that though."

Stefan picks up another empty bottle of Brown Ale, then turning to Bo, he says, "You don't like it kaffa, what you going to do about it?" Bo backs off, his face contorted in anger. Turning, he looks over to Merrill and sees that he has also grabbed a bottle. Bo looks around at Jim and Mandy; they too have bottles in their hands and are looking directly into Bo's eyes. Merrill walks over to Bo, and as they stand face-to-face, he calmly says, "No-one questions what we do. If you don't like it, leave." Bo stares back at Merrill, and slowly shaking his head, knowing he's on his own, turns and walks out of the pub in disgust. Maggie walks over to Stefan, "You bastard!" she shouts. Stefan looks over to Merrill, who shakes his head,

"Let's hope you don't have weaklings with you next time we meet Captain," he says as he walks over and shakes Merrill's hand. They embrace, slapping each other on the back, "I don't know if there will be a next time, I'm thinking of staying in London," says Merrill. Stefan gives a shocked look, and says, "I'm off to Mozambique next week. Auf Wiedersehen, Captain." "Stefan!" Merrill calls after him, as he walks to the door, "Don't touch Bo, he's OK really, just not used to the things we do. Besides his old man's a big knob in Africa and we may work for him one day." Stefan looks back, smiles and says, "No problems Captain."

"Hey there's the station!" says Spider, more in relief than surprise. "Good! Let's get up there and have a drink," answers Jock, as they turn the corner, and see the ramp that leads up to Piccadilly Station. "I could do with a drink after that," says Little John. "Fuck the drink," replies Tommy, "I could do with a kip! I fucking hope the train's in." The eight of them walk up the ramp that is now lined with police; they smile and make jokes at the sight of eight Chelsea supporters covered in blood and bruises. Walking into the packed station, they push their way into the bar; no-one says a word as they look at the blood covered North Stand.

The General walks over to Jock, and says, "What the fuck happened to you lot?" Jock looks up, replying, "We just took on the whole of the Kippax mob, on our own." The General shakes his head in disbelief, "You're fucking mad you lot," then looking around, adds, "So where's Merrill then?"   Jock looks around at all the silently staring faces, and replies, "Last time we saw him he was running away." The look on The General's face turns to one of shock, "You're fucking kidding! I thought you two were joined at the hip.

"What the fuck happened to you?" says Merrill, walking into the bar, smiling when he sees Jock. "You cunt!" screams Jock, "You fucking ran and left us." The smile on Merrill's face quickly fades, and his expression too, turns to one of shock. Jock looks up in disbelief, "When that mob came round the corner you fucking ran, look at me!" he wails, says handing out his blood stained arms, "You fucking left us!" Merrill turns around to Jim, Mandy, and Maggie, frowns in disbelief, and then turns back to Jock, "We chased that mob of United into a pub and smashed the fucking thing up. I never knew you weren't with us, 'til we emptied it." He pauses and looks around at all the staring faces, "There were two fucking mobs?" he pauses and thinks then continues,

"Manure must have been running from the Mainline." On hearing this news, Jock's mouth drops open, "Shit! I had no idea!

When that second mob came around the corner, we stood and fought." Spider walks over to Merrill and Jock and, putting his arms around both, he says "Easy mistake in the heat of battle." Jock looks Merrill in the eye, "But you owe me a drink for this," pointing to a cut above his eye. "Shit man! I had no idea there was a second mob," replies a shocked Merrill. Jock shakes his head and smiles at Merrill, and says, "Forget it,"

CHAPTER FIFTEEN

Alan sees Maureen through the window of the Brit and motions for her to bring another drink for Kev. "The National Front is a political system that is unworkable," continued Alan, "As is any one-policy party. Can you imagine all the immigrants lined up waiting to collect their £1,000, and go on the ship? What happens the first time someone says, "No I won't go". What are they going to do then?" he pauses to emphasise his point,

"I'll tell you, there is only one thing they can do! Start the Death Camps, 'cos without them, their policy of compulsory repatriation won't work. There is only one system that works, and that's the one we have got now, where you are free to vote anyone out of office, because believe me, if the far right or left ever got in power, they would cut out elections." Mark nods his head and smiles,

"And it's gullible and weak people like you, who give them the excuse for existence." "NO! That's total and complete rubbish," screams Kev, starting another pint of Miller Ice, "I'm not gullible. I'm politically aware." "You're gullible because you can't stand up and think for yourself," says Alan, "You're nothing but a sheep, and you follow what ever you think is trendy. It's not the National Front that's a danger. It's the Anti Nazi League who attract people like you, 'cos you will gladly let these people gain control, then you'll turn around to the people you now put down and plead for help."

"Oh that's right! Do twist everything I've said," Kev says hesitatingly, realising that he's getting drunk, "That just proves that you're nothing but Nazis." Alan looks at Kev, laughs and says, "But there is no difference between National Socialism and communism who are in fact International

Socialists. They are both totalitarian control freak systems, They both sustain their power through fear, which seeks to suppress the will of the population until there are just puppets on their string." Dave nods, and adds, "And you'll be one of the puppets." Big Al stands up, and looks at the other Americans, "I think it's time we got going." He then walks around the table to shake hands, and while doing so, says, "Mean trick that." pointing to Kev,

"I'm only now starting to appreciate your English dry humour." Ian laughs as he shakes Big Al's hand, "Did you notice that the more he drinks, the more the real him rises to the top?" Jim Boyle shakes Alan Chandlers hand, and says with a smirk, "I think that was a cruel trick. How's he going to get home in that state?" Looking

over at Kev, Alan answers, "Well, that'll just teach him to take the piss out of Chelsea when they lose."

"Sorry about yanking your chain earlier." Alan says as he stands up to shake Big Al's hand. "No problem," he replies, "I knew what you were up to, and that's why we didn't bite." There are a lot of you Brit's around here," says Mike Gilmartin, who moves over to shake hands, "And we get it in the neck every time we go to a Brit bar." Ian Kirkman shakes hands with Big Al and smiles, "Well it was worth a try." Jim Doyle smiles and says, "You should try it on with some 'Red Necks'."

Big Al laughs and chips in, "You know the type you get on the Jerry Springer Show." Ian Kirkman smiles and answers, "No, it would go right over their heads." "Yeah they've never heard of logic." chuckles Mark Hughes. "Whatever!" says Jim Doyle with a frown.

"Talk about the truth hurting," Alan says as he picks up his glass of Pepsi, watching the Yanks walk towards a giant sized Chevrolet Suburban; he then turns and walks towards the front door of the Britannia. Ian turns to Mark and shakes his head; "It would appear that their cars are as big as their mouths." Mark laughs, but then notices Kev is falling asleep in his chair, and is now in the full glare of the sun.

"What do we do about this idiot?" Ian looks back and smiles, turns to Mark and says, "Nothing!" They then both follow Alan back into the Brit, and the refreshing coolness of air-conditioning.

Sitting at a table near the bar, Alan is talking to Maureen, when Ian and Mark join him. "Hi guys, what'll you be having?" she asks with a smile. "I'll think I'll just have the usual, love" Maureen, being used to the English takes the 'love' as a compliment; when most Californian women, being as shallow as they are, would take the politically correct route, and make such a remark a case of sexual harassment.

"She's alright, she is," observes Mark. "Yeah, she's been around the English so much she's become normal," laughs Alan

INCIDENT AT TRAFALGAR SQUARE

Saturday May 18th. 1971

Putney High Street is just over the river Thames, from the bottom of the Kings, and Fulham Roads. As you drive south across the bridge, you'll see a church on the right hand side; that is one of those things that you know you've seen before, but can never remember when. Until you see the 'Omen' movie, and then it all comes flooding back, for this is the church where the flagpole falls, and impales the priest, who was in fact the second Dr, Who. Putney High Street itself, is a Mecca for those shopaholic's that live near the river, A working class shopping centre, where every well know working class shop has a branch. It's only down side is the fact that the road itself, in typical English fashion; is a hang over from the horse drawn carriage days gone bye, and is only two lanes wide.

"Hmm, see what I see?" says Ghost as he thinks out loud. Spider turns his head and looks at him, in puzzlement; "What you on about now?" Ghost drives the Ford Thames Trader van half onto the pavement, so as not to halt the bumper-to-bumper traffic, on the High Street. "Just take a look at that," he points to a Bedford TK truck, also parked on the pavement. The driver of which has just unloaded six boxes each containing a brand new 21-inch colour television set; onto the pavement. "See that," he continues, "the driver has just gone in to find someone to take those TV's in." Spider looks over to the branch of Rumbalow's electrical shop and the six boxes, now sitting invitingly on the pavement.

"Open the side door!" Ghost says as he gets out of the van, and walks the thirty feet to the boxes. He pauses and looks into the shop; just as any normal shopper would; then casually turns and picks up one of the boxes. Walking back to his van he places it inside, "Move this out of sight, I'll be back in a mo," he says to Spider; who looks on with amazement, but doesn't move out of the passenger seat. "Right," exclaims Ghost as he puts the second box, in the side doorway of his van; "Pull that one in, and shut the door." "Put them in yourself, I'm no fucking thief Pal!" answers Spider. "For Fuck sake, what's your problem?" Then as calm as you like he pushes the two boxes into the middle of the vans rear compartment, then walks around the front of the van, climbs aboard, starts up the engine, and pulls into the traffic. "Are you out of you're fucking mind!" Spider says. "Has anyone come out of Rumbalow's yet?" replies a beaming Ghost. "No, not yet, but fuck me, that's taking the piss!" gasps Spider as he looks into the rear view mirror. "Spider, me old mucker; if someone is cunt enough to present an opportunity, then I for one, ain't going to let it pass by. Those fucking colour TV's are worth a hundred and fifty quid a piece, and only fifteen percent of the population has got one, what we have in those boxes, is a status symbol old son, a status symbol that I can unload for a oner piece."

"If you'd have got caught, they'd have nicked me as an accomplice you cunt!" Says an angry Spider, as he turns to Ghost, content that no one has even noticed what they have just done. "Well let's see, how does fifty quid strike yeah?" says Ghost as he stops at the traffic lights at the bottom of the road. Spider still angry, starts to smile, "Hmm, OK that'll do nicely." They both start laughing as the lights change, and the Ford Thames Transit van drives North over Putney Bridge towards the church.

Thursday evening at around six thirty a Black Shelby Mustang, crosses Regent Street, from Vigo Street, and drives into Brewer Street. Slowing down it parks outside the Kilt and Celt pub. Alan Merrill gets out of the Mustang, locking the door; he looks around, and then walks into the pub. Situated on the corner of Glasshouse Street, and Brewer Street, the Kilt and Celt has a triangular ground floor, an oversized long wooden table, surrounded by wooden chairs, sits in the middle of the sawdust covered floor. The bar almost spans the length of one wall, of this working class public bar, and tourist trap. In total contrast the wine bar upstairs is small and intimate, and very posh.

"Hello Alan," says Roy Bell, the landlord of the Kilt and Celt; "You and Jock thought about doing the bouncing in here again?" Merrill smiles and says, "No mate, not now I've got the club up in Hampstead, thanks all the same. But you could always ask Jock; he should be here soon. "Right," answers Roy, "Grolsch?" "Cheers pal," says Merrill, as he looks around at the twenty odd punters in the pub. "Here Ya go," say Roy putting a bottle of Grolsch, and a glass on the counter; "it's on the house." Merrill lifts the bottle in a salute, "So how's business then?" Roy looks over as he puts empty glasses into the washer; "Still get the idiots, and the two plonkers, I've got at the moment, are bottle droppers." Merrill bites his bottom lip as he thinks, "Err, I may have a couple of boys for yeah, give me a day."

Roy looks up, and his eyes follow two girls, as they go up the stairs to the wine bar. The first one is five foot one inch, with mousy long hair; wearing a brown suede mini, the size of a belt, and a white top, with printed strawberries. The other has short dark hair, five foot three, and is wearing skin-tight shrunk jeans and a low cut top, with bulging cleavage. "Here look at the arse on that one with the suede mini," says Roy with just a tinge of lust. "You dirty old man!" chuckles Jock, as he walks into the bar, "I'll tell them two, just what you were looking at and it weren't their faces, was it?" he jokes. "Oh yeah, like you know them, I don't think," says Merrill; raising his eyebrows. Jock smiles and replies, "Shows you just how much you know. They both work for me, I brought them with me for a drink." Merrill looks long and hard at Jock, "Wonderful, and

just how the fuck we going to talk business, with those two around?" "No problem, that's why I sent them upstairs," replies Jock, "besides, I phoned Roy earlier, and he's going to lend us his office for ten minutes. Merrill turns his head to look at Roy in an unbelieving fashion, Roy nods, and then Merrill looks back to Jock. "Good thinking Batman."

"So!" exclaims Jock with a beaming smile, "Wait till I tell Maggie about your lecherous thoughts." "Oh bollocks," retorts Merrill, "She's just a friend." The smile on Jock's face vanishes, "Oh really? I wonder if she knows that?" Merrill frowns as he looks at Jock, "Err; what you on about?" "Oh come on pal, you telling me you don't know?" Merrill's face turns to one of shook, "Know what, she ain't fucking pregnant is she?" Jock shakes his head and slowly says, "And you'd give her the elbow if she was, wouldn't yeah? No pal, she ain't; but she is besotted with you, and you couldn't give a fuck about her could Yeah," he pauses and looks at Merrill's expressionless face. "You can't go treating women like shit just because of some stupid notion of revenge on your ex-wife, Maggie's a human being, she has feelings, and your heading to smash them."

Merrill sits thinking, then looks up and says, "You think I'm using her just to get back at Linda?" "Yeah, of cause you are, and then you know what will happen don't Yeah?" says Jock, who is starting to get angry. "What?" snaps Merrill. "She'll turn out the same as you, fucking bitter, looking for revenge, on the next bloke, and never finding true happiness. You really want to do that to her?" "This is all bollocks, She's just a friend, so we sleep together, big deal!" says an indignant Merrill. "Look at you, you fight in other peoples wars, you treat women like shit," says Jock, "Where do you think your heading?" Merrill looks around the pub, to make sure no one is eves dropping, and then says; "So what makes you Dr. Fraud already?

Jock shakes his head, looks at Merrill, and then says "You're heading for a fall, You've been getting more violent at games. You got so carried away at Manchester that you ran off after that mob, without thinking of us. You nearly murder a copper, now you treat Maggie like shit." Jock pauses, to take a drink, then continues; "I think the best thing you can do is sit down with one of those Goddess of yours and have a very careful look at yourself, and where you're heading." Merrill attempts to answer, but Jock cuts in, "Don't have a go at me, I'm telling you as a friend, the same as you once told me, I'm trying to help pal, we're all we've got, we need each other." "Oh fuck off; you'll be giving me a kiss next!" Merrill replies with a laugh, to deflate the situation. "Bollocks I'm no queer and nor are you, so don't try and deflect the truth." Merrill runs his fingers through his hair in thought, then nods, "OK I can see where you're coming from, let's talk business." Jock looks at Merrill, then smiles.

Merrill turns to Roy who hands him the key, and they walk over to the back wall by the stairs, as Merrill is unlocking the door, Jock says; "Oh by the way, I had a chat with Maggie, on the train, while you were having a kip." Merrill opens the door, and they both walk in, turning to shut the door Merrill says, "Oh, and I thought you'd finished preaching to me, so what were you talking about?" Jock looks over and says, "Yeah sorry about doubting that you took that pub, but we got a right good kicking, and I lost me rag at the station." Merrill sits down at the office table, and looks over to Jock as he sits on the sofa, by the door. "It's not a problem; now let's get down to business." Jock takes out a packet of Dunhill King Size, and lights one up. "So what's happening then?"

"Well I was sitting at home last night after getting in from Manchester, and found myself starring at Mafdet." Jock nearly choking on his cigarette smoke, stutters, "Excuse me, Mafdet? What the fuck is Mafdet?" Merrill looks over with an annoyed expression, "You know that Shepherds Crook, with the cat climbing up it, in my sitting room?" Jock nodding his head says, "Oh Yeah, the one with the axe blade on it; that's something to do with your Pagan mumbo jumbo, ain't it?" Merrill ignores the insult and continues, "That's Mafdet, the Ancient Egyptian Goddess of Revenge, and before you take the piss, ever heard of the Pharaohs curse?" He pauses a moment for the question to sink in, "Well that's Mafdet, and she gave me a vision last night."

Jock nods and says, "Oh Yeah, of cause she did, how silly of me not to have realised." Merrill grimaces and says with menace, "I don't take the piss out of your Jesus, cause that's your belief, so don't belittle mine." Jock raises his hands, "Yeah OK, sorry, I believe Yeah, so just what did she say to Yeah?" Merrill shakes his head with a half smile, and then continues; "She told me to buy the club." "I thought you already owned it?" "No I just rent it two nights a week" Merrill replies. "It' a big risk if you ask me, what if you get nicked at football and get sent down; you'd lose all your money" Says Jock. "Mmm you've got a point there," Merrill replies, he chuckles and adds, "With all that money you make from diamonds, you should be so worried! But I'll think it over, now down to business, the Yids are playing at Southampton on Saturday, I fancy ambushing them at Charing Cross when they come back."

Ten minutes latter Jock smiles as he gets up from the sofa, and looks up at the ceiling, then says, "Let's go upstairs and meet the girls then," he pauses a moment, then continues; "So were you ever happy being married to Linda?" Merrill thinks for a moment, smiles then says; "I never knew what happiness was, till I got divorced." They walk out of the office and over to the bar, hand Roy the keys, then turn and head for the stairs. "Oh by the way I'd better fill you in about the girls," says Jock, as they start to climb the narrow staircase. "The one in the jeans is Brenda, she's so easy you only have to cough and she'll drop 'em." Merrill laughs, as they turn to climb the second flight, "So what about the one with the arse?" Jock stops and looks back, "That's Nina; forget about her, she's an iron petticoat pal. You've got no fucking chance." They reach the door, and Merrill looking through the glass says, "Well we'll see about that."

They walk into the small but snug wine bar; Brenda sees them and smiles, while Nina is talking to a youth of about twenty, by the bar. Brenda walks over to Jock with a smile, and says, "So this is Alan then?" "Yes but take it easy on him," says Jock, looking at her bulging cleavage says with a smile. Merrill meanwhile ignores Brenda, and walks over to Nina, "Hi, I'm Alan," he says to brake the ice. Nina turns to look him in the face, and he notices for the first time, her sparkling big blue eyes. After a moments hesitation looks at him and then says, "Yes I know exactly who you are, Ian has told me all about you at games."

Picking up her spirit glass from the counter, she continues; "I don't talk to animals." With that she turns and moves over to the youth sitting on a barstool. Lifting herself up on to his lap, her mini-skirt slides up the length of her ample thighs. Merrill eyes slowly travel from her small feet, and slowly work their way up her nylon-covered flesh. Nina takes a sip from her cocktail glass; then turning her head to look Merrill in the eye, she raises her glass in a mocking salute of rejection. "I remember you at the Park Lane Massacre in '67, hitting those Yids with that mallet"; Colin says laughing at "Parkhead"; who is sitting at the table in the corner of the Weatherby. "Excuse me pal," says "Parkhead", "That bastard hit me with it first, I managed to get it of him. What the fuck do you expect me to do, hand it back to him?"

Dave sitting at the next table, with Mandy sitting on he's lap shouts over, "Yes but the best thing about it was, that photo of you in the Evening Standard, getting thrown out of the ground." Mandy then shouts in a mocking voice, "My hero." "Parkhead" getting wound up shouts back, "Bollocks if it weren't for that fucking photo, I won't have got three fucking mouths, would I?" Mandy looks at Dave with a puzzled look. "Some old Yid bag saw the picture in the paper," Dave explains; "So she writes in and tells then that he was hitting people with a wooden mallet, so the filth nick him at the next match, and he gets three months."

Everyone laughs, and "Parkhead" shouts, "It ain't that fucking funny, and then starts to laugh himself. Mandy looks at Dave, and gives him a long slow kiss; in the clinch Dave brings his hand slowly up, and starts to caress her left breast. "Oi," shouts over Russell from behind the bar. "That's enough of that; this is a pub, not a brothel!" "Shut the fuck up, you cunt!" shouts Colin; "You're a shagging barman, not the defender of our fucking morals." Russell throws him an angry look, but is wise enough not to say anything.

"If you don't like it pal," says Little John, "We can always take it outside." Russell turns and walks through to the Saloon bar. "Pick on one, pick on all of us Wanker," Big Steve calls after him. "Hello, having fun?" asks Jock, as he walks through the door, followed by Merrill. "Just winding up Russell," answers Spider. "Paul about?" asks Merrill. "I think he's upstairs," says Maggie as she walks over to Merrill putting his arm around him. Merrill takes her hand from his waist, and looks at Jock, "Good keep Russell busy." He turns and walks out. Maggie watches him go, then turns and walks towards the ladies crying, Mandy seeing her cry, gets up and runs after her.

Mandy comes out of the ladies, followed by Maggie, and they walk over to Dave's table. Tommy gets up and walks over to Maggie, "You alright?" he asks. "Yeah," she replies, "I'll be alright." Tommy looks at Mandy as she sits down, and asks, "What's the matter with her?" "Nothing she's just feeling down at the moment." Tommy looks across to Dave and frowns in disbelief. At this moment Merrill walks back into the Weatherby, and walks over to the bar, and shouts; "Russell!" Tommy gets up and walks over to Merrill, and says, "What's up with Maggie?

Have you two broken up or something?" Merrill looks at him with a blank expression, puts his left hand on Tommy's right shoulder, and says, "Err what?" he pauses, as if he has just gathered his thoughts, and is back in the land of the living. "Oh that, err; well yes I suppose we have, sorry I was miles away." Tommy looks at him, pauses as if to gather the courage, and then asks, "Well if you ain't going with her anymore, is it OK for me to ask her out?"

Merrill takes his hand down as he sees Russell walk back into the Public Bar. "Yes go ahead, fell free," then as an after thought he says, "Tell her we're still friends, but Yeah go for it." Tommy smiles, turns and walks back to the table, taking the seat next to Maggie. Jock walks over to the bar and stands next to Merrill; "I thought you were going to take it easy on Maggie?" Merrill looks at

Jock, then Maggie; "Am I." he replies standing by the juke Box, putting on Neil Sedaka's 'Breaking Up is Hard To Do?"

He pauses, raises his eyebrows, and tilts his head, then says; "I am taking it easy on her, look; Tommy's going to ask her out." Jock turns his head, looks over to the table, and then turns back, "So what was she crying for?" Merrill shrugs his shoulders, and says, "Don't worry I'll have a word, it'll be OK." Jock shakes his head, and walks over to Spider's table, Merrill watches him go, then turns to Russell, and says with a beaming smile;

"Hello mate, got me usual?" Russell turns and takes out a bottle of Pepsi from the Chilled cabinet, and puts it on the bar, "Well you're in a good mood tonight," "Yes," Merrill replies, "I feel like a new man." He smiles, and walks over to Maggie's table; looking down to where she's sitting and says, "Can I have a word?" He turns and walks over to the door; Maggie looks at Mandy, raises her eyebrows in surprise, and follows him out.

Merrill walks over to the Mustang, turns and says, "Sorry for doing that, I was wrong." Maggie swallows and says, "So it's over then?" "You were getting to serious, I can't handle that," he pauses, "It's not you, it's me, I just can't get close to anyone right now." She nervously smiles, and says; "You could have told me first, before showing me up like that." Merrill looks into her eyes and sees the hurt, putting his arm around her, he says, "Don't take it personal, you're OK, I just." "It's just that you want your freedom?" She interrupts him. "Yes," he says with a guilty look, "We're still friends, and I'll always be there for you, besides I think Tommy has got the hot's for Yeah, he's a good bloke,"

Merrill seeing a tear appear in the corner of her eye, raises his right arm, and touches her on the chin, "Hey I ain't worth it love. So stay away from the bitterness and anger, that I felt towards Linda, it only destroys you. I found that out the hard way. And you're too good for that shit." Maggie puts her arms around him, and they kiss. "Hey," he says, "let's go for a drive around the bloke, you can't go back in like that." "No," she replies, "I'm OK." Wiping her eyes, she looks up and smiles, "But you're still a bastard," then pausing she continues; "but we're still friends."

Saturday evening in Trafalgar Square was wet, the rain had been spitting all afternoon, and continued into the night. Built as a tribute to Lord Nelson's naval victory against the French and Spanish in 1805. The square is a favourite tourist spot, and is famous for it's pigeons; it's also the main London venue for rallies and riots. Designed by John Nash, and built during the 1830's, the centre piece is the 165 foot Nelson's column, dating from 1842, and enhanced in 1867, by the addition of Edwin Landseer's four impassive lions, guarding it's base.

It is also unique in that it has nine roads leading off it. Running off the north face is Pall Mall East, which houses the National Gallery, also dating from 1842. On the west side sits Canada House, while on the east side, is South Africa House. Running off the south-west side is Cockspur Street, and Spring Gardens; then the Mall, guarded by the 1910 Admiralty Arch. Along the south side is a traffic island that is the site of Charing Cross; running off it is Whitehall, and Northumberland Avenue. The Strand runs off the south-west side, with it Charing Cross station. While on the north-west corner, is Duncannon Street, and Charring Cross Road, on the corner of which stands, St. Martin-in-the-Fields. Built by James Gibb in 1726, this is the masterpiece that set the 'Colonial' style; there has been a church on this site since the 13th. century.

Spider walks up the stairs from the tube station exit, on the south-east side of the square. "Wow, it's still bloody raining," he says, holding out his right hand. "Right look for any Manure out for a night on the town, after the Yids game," says Little John. "Or better still a bunch of Yids out looking for Manure," adds Jock. "OK split up into fours, and spread out, we'll find a few, but leave any civvies," says Merrill as he walks into the light rain, that thankfully is keeping most of the pigeons, grounded. The North Stand are head hunting, and split into three groups of four, with Alan Merrill, Jock, Big Steve, and Little John, crossing the road and walking past the South African Embassy towards St. Martins-in-the-Fields. Colin, Lenny, Tommy and Maggie, cross the road, and stand near the south corner of South Africa House, looking up towards Charing Cross Station. Spider, Carlos, Dave and Mandy, walk over to the Charing Cross traffic island at the top of Whitehall.

"Fuck me," gasps Colin, as he looks over to Tommy, and Maggie, "They'll be shagging each other in a minute!" Lenny turns from looking up towards Charing Cross station, to see Maggie leaning with her back up against the waist high railings, by the Tourist souvenir booth, at the southern corner of South Africa House. Dave is standing in front of her, their arms are entwined, and they're tongues are tangling, like mad. "Ha," laughs Lenny; "you're just jealous," Colin smiles at Lenny, and shaking his head he answers, "No I don't think so somehow."

"What are you two looking so happy about?" says Spider, looking over to Dave, and Mandy laughing and giggling on the corner of the traffic island. "Ah, leave 'em alone," laughs Carlos; "they're in love; besides Alan's booked then a room in some hotel tonight, surprised they come here first." "Wow, I'll have to ask him to get me one for my bird," jokes Spider. "Oh Yeah I'm sure," replies Big Steve; "Cathy's dad's got more money than Alan and Ian put together, that's the only reason you go out with her." Spider laughs out loud, then looks at Carlos; "I'm like that old Contours record, 'First I Look At The Purse." Carlos smiles, "The Contours," he queries, 'Ain't they the ones that did "Do You Love Me?" "Yup that's the ones, best roar R&B group on Tamla Motown," replies Spider.

Spider looks over to Mandy and Dave and says, "Why don't you two skedaddle to that hotel, you look like your going fuck each others brains out any second." Mandy blushes, as she looks over to Spider, "What's up love, not getting any tonight?" "Hey Dave! I didn't know you were big enough to satisfy Mandy." Carlos jokes. Mandy looks over to him and shouts, "Oh dear is that all you blokes think of is the size of your dicks?" she starts to laugh, then continues; "I'll let you into a little secret shall I? We girls don't go for size, we go for staying power, and a ten second wonder like you ain't no good for me," she pauses a second to see Spider's mouth drop open; "Oh by the way, we also put thickness before length too."

"Well he qualifies there then," laughs Dave. "Hmm, it don't look like we're gonna get a bite tonight," says Angus looking around from the Square, along Duncannon Street, towards Charing Cross Station. "Well give it another fifteen minutes, and then we'll call it a day," says Merrill, standing on the steps of St. Martins-in-the-Fields. Standing next to him Jock says "You always get a couple coming down to see the square, before heading home," he pauses and looks up to Big Steve, standing by the railings on the corner; "They'll turn up."

"By the way!" says Jock as he turns and looks at Merrill, "How'd Yeah get on with Nina then?" Merrill turns to him with an annoyed frown. "Oh Yeah," says Big Steve; "So what we missing out on then?"

"He's going out with Nina, had to ask her about twenty times before she'd take a lift home with him," Jock starts to laugh, "I'd already told her about him, and she wasn't very interested was she Alan?" Merrill walks onto the pavement, still clearly annoyed, he says nothing. "You don't mean that little 'Iron Petticoat; from your office, is the one?" queries Big Steve. "What the one with the eighteen inch waist and wicked arse?" says Little John, "Oh, you naughty boy you," he continues in his teasing. Merrill turns and snaps, "Well for your knowledge we're going horse ridding tomorrow." Realising he's just given them more bait; he turns towards Charing Cross Station. "Horse ridding," laughs Big Steve, Oh, giddy up there."

Merrill throws Big Steve a dirty look, "Well for your information, I often go horse ridding, know a wicked stable up in a village called Nash, about six miles outside Bletchley." Jock seeing Merrill getting wound up, says, "He knows she's 'Iron Petticoat', and knows he's wasting his time." Merrill turns and shouts, "Heads up,

Yid alert!"   Three heads turn as one, following Merrill's finger towards Charing Cross Station.

"Fucking great," says Big Steve; there's about twenty of them." Merrill looks down towards the south end of South Africa House, putting his fingers to his mouth; he gives one short sharp whistle. Seeing Colin and Brown looking up, he points towards the station. "Right let's go," says Jock. "Steve, John on the other side of the road," orders Merrill. The four walk down Duncannon Street, towards the Tottenham supporters, who cross the Strand, and start to walk along the side of South Africa House towards Trafalgar Square. Once out of sight the four run to the corner, then walk over to the Strand, and shadow them.

Colin, Lenny, Tommy, and Maggie, walk slowly towards the Tottenham supporters, Colin is the first to reach the unsuspecting group, and he walks past the first four, and then throws a punch into the face of the biggest one, who reels back, caught totally by surprise. Lenny kicks out at another, while Tommy and Maggie charge in to help. Taken completely by surprise, the back four start to run back across the Strand, straight into Merrill and Jock. While Big Steve and Little John charge into the middle where, the Tottenham supporters are recovering from the shock of the initial attack. Traffic comes to a screeching halt in an effort to avoid running over anyone. A bus that has come to a halt, starts to honk its horn at the melee spreading across the road.

Hearing the horn, Spider looks over towards the corner of the Strand, seeing the fight he shouts, "Come on let's go!" Running into the wide road, followed by Carlos, then Dave, and Mandy, they charge head long towards the fight. "Chelsea!" screams Spider, dodging in and out of traffic coming across the south part of the square from Whitehall. Mandy runs past Dave looking only towards the fight. Suddenly there is a screech of tyres, as they try to find some grip on the rain soaked surface of the road.

The driver freezes with shook; his foot slams down on the brake, as the car aquaplanes out of control. Dave seeing the car glide across the road; shouts "MANDY!" But too late as the front of the Black Humber Super Snipe, catches her before she has time to react. It throws her body ten feet into the air. Dave screams "NO!" as he slides to a halt, watching helplessly Mandy falls like a rag doll, head first onto the road. He stands like a statue watching her motionless body, unable to take in the horror of what he has just seen. Spider, runs past him and falls to the floor like a stone, "Mandy," he yells in panic; "Mandy you OK?" Carlos runs over and stops dead in his tracks, he looks down at the blood flowing out from Mandy's hair, and mixing into grotesques patterns with the rainwater.

Merrill hearing the shouts of panic, and turns to see the traffic coming to a stop, and people running into the middle of the road. Instinct telling him something is wrong, he turns to Jock, and if by instinct screams "Mandy's been hit!" Forgetting their fight he starts to run towards the growing crowd. The fighting slowly stops as everyone starts to realise what has happened. The North Stand run across the road, pushing people out of the way till they come to the front of the silent crowd. Merrill and Jock stand there speechless as they see Dave, bending over Mandy's motionless body. He starts punching the road, as tears stream down his rain soaked face. Then looking up he starts screaming uncontrollably at the moon "She's DEAD, she's FUCKING DEAD!"

EPILOGUE

Alan Chandler walks over to the bar, the stranger smiles as he sees him approaching. Alan watches the stranger as he nears him and frowns in curiosity; why is he smiling? Does he know me? Anxious to obtain answers, he stops next to him and leans his left elbow against the bar, with his left elbow, and, then looking into the stranger's eyes, he says, "You got a problem!" The stranger's eyes light up as smiles, then answers, "You're Merrill, ain't yer?"

Alan, taken totally by surprise, stands there with his mouth falling open; no-one has called him by that name since the seventies. "Yeah, thought you were," the stranger continues. Alan stops smiling, stands erect and snaps, "So who the fuck are you then?" The stranger puts his hands up and steps back, "Hey hold on! I remember you from the seventies, only I wasn't sure it was you." Alan relaxes and looks at the stranger, searching his memory for any sign of recognition, "Sorry, I don't remember you." "Oh you wouldn't," says the stranger, "I was just a kid when you and the North Stand were doing your thing." He pauses, putting out his hand, "I'm Mark Turner, I live up by Fisherman's Wharf, in San Francisco."

Alan relaxes and shakes hands, "So you remember me from all those years ago," he queries in astonishment. "Yeah, but when you're a kid on the sidelines you don't tend to forget things like that. I remember you and Jock were like brothers." He pauses as he momentarily thinks back, "Do you still see any of the North Stand?" "Oh yeah, me and Jock still go to games together when I'm in London, and we met up with a bunch of the others last time I went back," Alan thinks for a moment, then continues, "You know it's funny, 'The General' still avoids talking to me and Jock." "Well, I suppose he saw the North Stand as competition," says Mark Alan chuckles, "I don't see it myself, but what the fuck!"

"You should write a book about those days," says Mark, "I mean, I remember that night game at Charlton when you took on West Ham, Tottenham, and Millwall, then what about you lot at Millwall. God, I'll never forget that one, there were only about half a dozen of you left in their end by the end of the game. Then there was that great street battle at Nottingham and when you pushed the police bus into the Trent River" Alan cocks his head to one side as he stands and thinks back, "That was the first game with Millwall after the Charlton game. Shit!" he gasps, "That was some battle! Three hundred of us went in the Cold Blow Lane at the start of the game

and after a non-stop fight throughout the game, there was around a dozen of us left in the corner at the final whistle. Millwall were good. We were the first crew to stay in the CBL at Millwall. That was some battle! A shame really, 'cos until the Charlton game, we used to run with Millwall. I had a lot of friends there, and they're still my second favourite team."

"That was a classic, but what about the battle of Bruges! I remember you lot steamed their end when you charged the length of the pitch at the end of the game." "Yeah," continued Alan, "But to give 'The General' his due, he led that charge. A good example of The Shed, and North Stand working together." "What about Man City and Wolves! I remember you got knocked out up there once." Alan laughs out loud, "Shit! Yeah! I got concussion and a fractured cheek bone." He looks over and his eyes follow Maureen as she walks past, "You been back lately?" "Oh yeah! I go to all the continental games and all the England away games," Mark pauses as he thinks back, and then continues, "So you still see a lot of the old crowd! So what happened to them all?"

"Well you know that Mandy was killed?" says Alan. "Yeah that was shocking, she was far too young to die," Mark pauses for a moment, then continues. "But what's everyone else doing these days?" Mark queries. "Well, Maggie, got some disease and went blind, and died a few years ago." "Shit!" gasps Mark, "I remember her! You used to go out her didn't yer?" "Yeah," replies Alan, "She was a good kid, but I lost touch, when I went inside." "Oh yeah, that was at Plymouth, wasn't it?" says Mark. "Yeah, I got fitted up for attempted murder, got ten years, and did just over four, when I won my appeal, and the conviction was overturned." He thinks to himself a moment, and continues, "I'll have to put that in a book as well, trouble is there is so much, I doubt it would all fit into one book." Alan pulls a packet of John Player Special out his pocket, and offers one to Mark, who declines.

"Well let's see," he continues, as he lights up a cigarette, "Jock is still the same, and still deals in diamonds. Spider has hardly changed and is doing well. He's got his own building firm now and his two brothers are with him. Little John is doing well too, and coaches a football team in Sutton, along with Steve. Colin has got what he always wanted. He owns his own pub in the Wembley area. Lenny started his own cleaning firm and is doing very nicely thank you. Sue married but he divorced her for adultery, and she disappeared of the scene." "oh did you know that Ghost got finally caught and got 20 years for taking part in an armed Bank raid at Victoria?" asks Alan. "No Way!" replies a shocked Mark, "He should have stuck with the small stuff, they never learn do they." Parkhead got married, and as far as I know returned to Glasgow."

205

"Let me see," says Alan thinking aloud, and pauses a moment. "Dave returned up North, so did Tommy, Not seen either since the Seventies, but I heard that Tommy still comes down to the occasional game.

Mark stands there fascinated, and asks, "So what happened to Mickey Greenaway?" Alan's happy demeanour changes to one of sadness as he continues, "Well Mickey got really ill a while back. He lived near Hither Green station and Spider used to see him often, but then Mickey stopped answering the door so no-one knew what was happening until a neighbour came out and said that Mickey had died." "Shit!" gasps Mark shaking his head, "No-one knew he was dead? That's rough!" Then trying to lighten up the mood Mark asks, "So what are you doing over here?"

"Well like most people here, I'm into computers and I'm just about to go up to Foster City, where I live, as I coach a football team up there," answers Alan as he starts to walk to the door of the Brit, followed by Mark. "Really!" says Mark in surprise, what team?" Alan walks through the door and stands in the warm sunshine of the California morning, glancing over to the sleeping body of Kev slouched in his chair. He chuckles to himself, then turns to Mark, "Well, strange as it may seem it's a girl's team." Mark looks back in surprise and says "Blimey! How the hell did you get into that?" "Pure fluke really," answers Alan, "I was in O.D.'s my local bar in Foster City, when a local comes up and hears my accent, so asks me about soccer.

So we get talking, turns out his daughter is in a team, but they're not that good as they don't know much about the tactics of the game." So he asks me if I would like to go to one of their practice sessions, and I get there, they are playing bunch ball, the whole team is crowded around the ball." "What are they called?" queries Mark. "The Foster City Blue Devils," replied Alan, "And their strip is identical to Chelsea's."

Alan laughs as he leans against the wall of the Brit and lights yet another fag. "So we get them into a 4-4-2 system. They had a girl whose dad comes from Liverpool, she was a great winger. So I spread them out to use the whole pitch and steam down the wings and cross to the centre, where we had a couple of hot shots. We went on to win the San Francisco League, and Cup." "Wow! So you showed them the English way and they did OK then?" says Mark "Basically yes, they'd only won two games the year before," says Alan. "Then we were invited to enter the California State Cup, which is basically a 1st Div. Affair, so being a Div 3 outfit.

We were quite honoured we got through to the quarter final, and lost by only one goal." Alan thinks to himself a moment then continues. "This Septic comes up to me after the game and says he'd never heard of us, so I told him I wasn't surprised as we were a 3rd Div. Outfit, and he couldn't believe it, then he starts saying we cheated." "No," Mark interrupts, "How'd he reckon that then?" "Well," continues Alan, "He reckons that we cheated because I'm English, and that gave us an unfair advantage." "So what did you say?" queried Mark. "I told him to fuck off and get a life. He just stood there so shocked he couldn't move, bloody Wanker!"

Mark takes a business card from his pocket, handing it to Alan, he says, "Here give me a bell, and we'll go for a drink in the week." "Sounds good," says Alan, as he puts out his cigarette and walks over to his La Baron. The white convertible drives slowly out of the Brit's parking lot, and turns onto the 260 Freeway, and heads to a place he now calls home. As he drives down the seemingly endless highway, he glances up to the cloudless sky. Thinking back to the time when every day was a 'Boy's Own' adventure and his mates were his family. When the lust for battle, mixed with the pain of a metal toe capped boot against his temple was for him a way of life; when people lived and died for their tribe called Chelsea.

He thought too of the fickle new supporter, who thinks more of success and glory, than the passion of the game. The yuppiefied masses that now sit in luxury corporate boxes, sipping champagne and eating Prawn Sandwiches; mingling with those that are only there too be seen; those whose loyalties lay with the opposition, or even worse, with no-one. He thought of all the young dudes, who sacrificed everything to follow Chelsea across England, win or lose; week in and week out. These were the real supporters, those that were willing to give their last penny and their lives for Chelsea.

As the undulating hills of the San Andreas Fault glide past, he thinks back to those 'Golden Days' of the early '70's. Football is the greatest game in the world. Chelsea is my tribe, it's total commitment, its electric excitement, it's raw passion, it's every muscle and sinew in your body tingling; it's euphoria. He glances up to the sky again, and there for the briefest of moments he thought he saw Sandy running across the North Stand terrace with Debbie not far behind, and he could just hear the cry of Mickey Greenaway's 'Zigger Zagger', echoing in the distance.

He starts to sing loudly and passionately to no one in particular,
"WE'RE THE NORTH STAND,
WE'RE THE NORTH STAND;
WE'RE THE NORTH STAND,
STAMFORD BRIDGE!"

ABOUT THE AUTHOR

Every Kid is old enough to be aware of their up coming fifth Birthday, and I was no exception; filled with anticipation the night before my Birthday, I remember I could hardly sleep, wondering what my present would be. Back in 1951 the best present any Kid could get was a Tin Plate, Clockwork Train Set, and that's exactly what I wanted.

Come the morning I excitedly went downstairs to have my Breakfast, and receive my present. Imagine my disappointment when there wasn't one, depressed I remember I went to my bedroom, and played with a wooden Battleship. Then came Lunch, and once again I rushed down the stairs, expecting this time I'd get my Train Set. Well once again I was disappointed, as no present was forthcoming. Then after Lunch, my Dad said get your shoes on we're going out. "Yes!" I said to myself, we're going to the model shop. Now full of excitement once again, I put my shoes on, and walked down Britannia Road hand in hand with my Dad.

Turning right we walked along the Fulham Road towards the Rising Sun Pub, but pasted the bus stop on the other side of the road. Starting to wonder just what the Hell was going on, we finally crossed the Fulham Road, and walked into the forecourt of Chelsea Football Club, confused I looked back at the Fulham Road, and wondering why we weren't still walking to the bus stop. Then going through the Turnstile, I saw what to a five year old, was a giant flight of steps. Totally gutted I still remember climbing what seemed like a never ending series of steps, totally disappointed and near to tears.

Then on reaching the top I stopped in awe at the sight that presented itself, the South Terrace upon which we were now standing in, had more people than I'd ever seen in one place before, following the South Terrace along till it became the West Terrace, and along still until I saw the for the first time The North Stand. At this moment the crowd erupted into a cacophony of noise, as everyone started cheering the two lines of men walking onto the pitch., that excitement was starting to transfer itself to me, and seeing that that one line were dressed in red, and the other in blue, I asked my Dad, who were the ones in Blue; (Blue was already my favourite colour).

"That's Chelsea!" he replied, I remember immediately jumping up and down shouting "Chelsea!" "How do you like your Birthday present?" asked my Dad, as the fever had already grabbed me I remember replying "Wonderful Thanks". I don't remember much of the game, except when one of the Chelsea players, scored his second goal, I remember asking who he was, and my Dad replied "That Roy Bentley", well Mr, Bentley immediately became my first Idol. Then the biggest roar of the game was reserved for the final whistle, and Chelsea had beaten Manchester United, Four, Two.

I remember on the short walk back home, I thanked my Dad for the best present ever, and he replied that it wasn't over yet, as we were going back to Stamford Bridge in the evening for the Greyhound racing. That day the tenth of November 1951, will live with me till the day I die, as it gave me two things that have become a fundament part of my life, Greyhounds, and Chelsea Football Club.

I also remember two other games from my first season, the first was my first away game, but it was only a long walk to Craven Cottage, home of local rivals Fulham, and we won 2-1. The other game I remember was my first real away game, involving a long ride on the underground, to Liverpool Street Station, I'd never seen a train station so big, and was filled with excitement, as we boarded the first steam train I ever remember seeing. After a short ride we got off and walked to White Heart Lane the home of Tottenham Hotspur. But this was the FA Cup and we played Arsenal, and drew, I also remember going back for the replay, where we lost, and were out of the Cup, I was upset, but not downhearted.

We went back to White Heart Lane near the end of the season, to play Tottenham this time. Imagine my disappointment when we again lost, starting a deep seated hatred for Tottenham; that has lasted to this day. But my Dad trying to cheer me up took me home by way of the first Tram ride I remember, and sitting on the front seat of the top deck; I will never forget going down a slope at Aldwich, and going under ground, and stopping at a station with square columns holding the roof up.

The next few years were uneventful, apart from getting a new manager, but coming from Arsenal, I took an instant dislike to him. But he gave us a badge that I loved, and we started to play better football, and finishing in the Top Ten of the League; I was starting to like him.

Then in 1955 came my most memorable game as a child, Sheffield Wednesday at the Bridge. I was standing near the corner flag, where the South Terrace meets the West Terrace We won 3-0, and at the final whistle a few people started to leap the small wall and run onto the pitch. Thinking we had won the league I took one look at my old man, who was soaking up the atmosphere, and climbed over the wall and followed the crowd. The next thing I heard was "Come Here", I looked round and saw the 6 foot 3 inch "Giant running after me, and took to my heels. Pushing my way through the crowd I got to the front, and saw the old wooden East Stand, just as the crowd fell into a deadly silence.

Then after a short wait, that seemed like hours at the time. A man said something on a big old-fashioned microphone, I never heard what because everyone went berserk jumping up and down, and shouting there heads off. I felt a hand on my shoulder and looked around, it was my Dad, who now had a beaming smile on his face, "Manchester United have lost," he said, then he shouted at the top of his voice…"We've Won The League!"

I retold this story on the Chelsea Chat site back in the early 1990's and no one believed it, but then someone (I can't remember who), posted a film clip from Pathe Newsreel, and said "There's a small boy running across the pitch, in the same place you said you ran, have a look" And to my amazement there I was! Then in the Match Day programme for the Fulham game in 2005, there was a full page photo, from that day. And to my surprise there I was right in the front.

Well after 1955, life at Chelsea returned to normal, finishing in the bottom half of the League for the next few years until 1961/62 we were relegated. But it didn't dampen my spirit, for 1957 saw the arrival of one Jimmy Greaves; and scoring 22 goals in his first season, he became my new favourite player. He scored 32 in 58/59, 29 in 59/60; and then in 1960/61 he scored an amazing 41 goals, and to this day he is still my favourite all time Chelsea player.

When in 1957 we moved up to Swain's Lane at Parliament Hills Fields in North West London. This didn't stop me going to games though as I was old enough to go by the Tube at Kentish Town, to Fulham Broadway. But the move did bring something new into my life; Bullying! And Music. At night I'd listen to Radio Luxembourg and fell in love with R&B, I also found out fast I was the only Chelsea supporter in my new School, the Acland in Tuffnel Park. I learnt very fast that the only way to combat bulling is to stand up and fight back. Bullies are in fact cowards, they only operate with a pack behind them, and they always go for the easy targets. They pick on those that they see as weak, or different. I learnt the lesson fast, and also learnt how to fight. The main bullies were Tottenham supporters, and it only intensified my hatred for them. But after a couple of weeks I was left alone, as they found easier targets that didn't fight back. Mind you in 1961 when they won the League, I'd steam into them when ever they started boasting how good they were, and got into trouble with the teachers, because of the fighting.

At the end of 1961, a couple of friends at Chelsea told me about a Club in the West End that played records, so I went there, and loved it, only fifteen years old at the time I was 6 foot tall, and looked 18 and soon got asked to be a stand in DJ. The La Discotheque was a Socialite Club with stars such as Diana Doors & Frankie Vaughan as regular visitors. Mandy Rice Davis, and

Christine Keeler were also regulars, and then when the Profumo scandal hit the papers, things changed at "La Disc", the stars stopped going, and because we were now playing more R&B than the Pop records we started to get a new breed of punter coming coming to "La Disc", the Modernists. The Twist and Mashed Potato were the dance of the day, and I soon found out that a number of the new punters were Chelsea supporters.

Then in 1963 The Modernists had evolved into the "Mods". And Chelsea was the first club to feature Mods as a core group of supporters. I'd bought a Scooter, and along with the other Mods, would park it outside the Rising Sun on match days. The core support on the terraces were Mods; and the main group gathered on the West Terrace, and were all local lads, mainly from the North End Road area. I made friends back then that I still drink with at matches to this day. We called ourselves the Half Way Liners, as that was where we stood, on the half way line.

Then in September 1963, the first fight I remember took place, we were playing Burnley at the Bridge. We were all lower and middle teens, and soon found out that a large group of Burnley supporters all in their thirties or older, starting slagging off Chelsea. This was too much, and we turned left and charged them, but being older they gave us a right kicking. But it moulded a bond amongst us, we had been blooded, and now instead of being just supporters, we became comrades!

The very next home game was Liverpool, and walking over the Fulham Road from parking our scooters, we heard a number of bangs. Turning around we saw that some Liverpool supporters had kicked over one of the scooters, and that had started a domino effect, and all the scooters had fallen over. We charged back across the Fulham Road, and into the Liverpool supporters standing laughing at the fallen scooters. This time we won, and were Cock-A-Hoot at our "Victory", Soon we were patrolling the North End Road and would attack any opo supporters that were wearing scarves on their wrists, or from their belts; as that was a sign they were firm.

In 1964 we had to vacate the West Terrace as Chelsea were going to build the West Stand on it; this meant we had to move, first to the North Terrace, but as that was the area for away supporters the police always moved us on, so we ended up in the front of the East Stand. But as there wasn't enough room, one of our number suggested moving to the South Terrace, under the cover used by the Greyhound crowd. He said it was like a Shed, and wrote to the match day programme officially naming the Greyhound cover, "The Shed". The funny thing about that time being Mods, we set the fashion, and were laughed at way games up North, but the next season we laughed at them as they were wearing the fashion we had last year, and that's the way that Mod fashion spread across the country before TV jumped on the bandwagon.

Then in 1966 we played away to Leicester in the Final of the League Cup, and won our second past War trophy. Coming out of Filbert Street stadium, we were attack by Leicester supporters. The battle soon turned into a running battle, as we had to make the Main Line station in time to catch the only train back to London. I got separated from the main group on the High Street by a Wimpy Bar, and found myself with a Scots guy; the two of us were cornered, by around fifty Leicester supporters. But a crate of milk bottles by the door of the Wimpy Bar came in handy, and the two of us charged and made it to the station, leaving one of the Leicester in the Wimpy Bar via way of the window. To this day that guy is my best mate, and was best man at my wedding.

So too 1967, and the Cup Final at Wembley, losing that was the biggest hurt to me and all the other Chelsea supporters that went to Wembley. And we vowed there and then to take our revenge. We left our part of the terrace, and ran along the main inner concourse to the other end, and steamed into one to the sections. That was the first time there had ever been fighting inside Wembley for a football match.

Then the first away game to Tottenham, about 50 of the North End Road Boys met up at Liverpool Street Station, from there we went by BR and arrived just before 11 O'clock, walking round the corner onto the High Street, we found it deserted so we crossed the road, and went into what is now Valentino's. A lot of us were wearing Tottenham scarves, so we didn't get stopped by the police. In the pub the landlord took us as Spurs fans and served us, then around 11:30, the real Spurs turned up, and we took the scarves off and chanted "Chelsea", and steamed in; they never knew what hit them. Over the bar, grabbing the optics, they went flying through the windows, tables and chairs were smashed, then the sound of Police cars, so we scampered up the High Street toward Edmonton. Those of us that made it around 20, went into a café, and had dinner.

Then around 1:30 we strolled down the High Street, now packed with people, we met up with some of those that were in the pub with us, and went in the ground. Once inside we straight away realised we'd got in before the main Yid firm, so we kicked off with those standing on the terrace near the entrance gate behind the goal. Clearing it we waited for the inevitable and it came from behind as the Yids came onto the terrace from an entrance gate further down. They charged, we stood, and it went toe to toe. More Chelsea arrived to swell our numbers, and we forced the Yids back towards the other entrance gate. A few of our number were attacking those that tried to come through the gate we were at. One of our number had a wooden mallet, and was knocking Yid's out right left and centre.

Then the police arrived, and formed a line between the us and the Yid's and started throwing people out, but moments latter they'd reappeared after paying to get back in again. DA reappeared Five times, I myself three times. The fighting continued as more of the Shed arrived to swell our numbers. But the Yid's were also increasing their numbers, and the fighting continued as the teams came out. Then a breakthrough. The Yid's, who were down by the pitch wall, were getting battered, and started to climb over the low wall, and onto the pitch. Some of us followed them and the fight continued on the grass behind the goal. Then a few of the Yid's ran, and it lead to a Sheep like stampede. We stood there cheering, but were charged by a group of Filth, so jumped back over the wall, and took a large group of Yid's from the rear, who were fighting the Shed.

Taken by surprise they started to run. I then noticed that we had cleared the Park Lane End, and it was totally under Chelsea control. We then saw that the ref had taken the players off the pitch, and it was 3:20, when things stared to calm down. But small pockets of Yids kept being found and dealt with.

It was the first time in Post War football history that a kick off was delayed for so long. And when Yid's were seen to be massing on the Shelf we charged them, and the fighting carried on till half time. By now the Filth had grown in number as reserves must have been called up. And they formed a number of human barriers; although fighting erupted a few times more as the Shed cleared the Shelf. The Park Lane Terrace and Shelf were firmly in Chelsea hands and stayed that way for the rest of the game.

With the game over, we left the ground en mass, and saw a huge mass of Yid's waiting on the High Street. Holding everyone back, till we were all in the street, DA shouted charge. There must have been around 5,000 of us, and we went through the police lines like a knife through butter. Steaming into the waiting Yid's our momentum forced them back across the road, then they started to run.

As a footnote, the Evening Standard ran a back page story about the riot, and had a photo taken of the fighting from the pitch. And there in the middle was one of the North End Road Boys, in a Stripped T-Shirt, and some old biddy wrote in saying he was the one with the mallet. A few days latter he was arrested and got 6 months.

WE'RE THE NORTH STAND

ALAN GARRISON

Made in the USA
San Bernardino, CA
28 December 2017